FARUNDELL

FARUNDELL

L.R. Fredericks

WINDSOR
PARAGON

First published 2010
by John Murray (Publishers)
This Large Print edition published 2011
by AudioGO Ltd
by arrangement with
John Murray (Publishers)

Hardcover ISBN: 978 1 445 85429 8
Softcover   ISBN: 978 1 445 85430 4

British Library Cataloguing in Publication Data available

X000 000 039 2752

Printed and bound in Great Britain by
CPI Antony Rowe, Chippenham and Eastbourne

To Isis Myrionymos
and to Ruth, who Knows

Temple of
Hermes

Chapel

Arcadia

To the River
Isis and
Exley

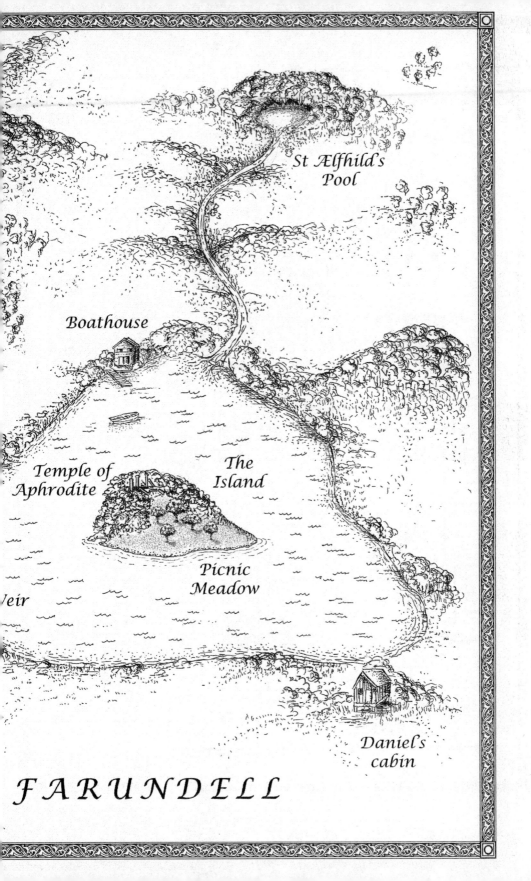

St Ælfhild's Pool

Boathouse

Temple of Aphrodite

The Island

Picnic Meadow

Weir

Daniel's cabin

FARUNDELL

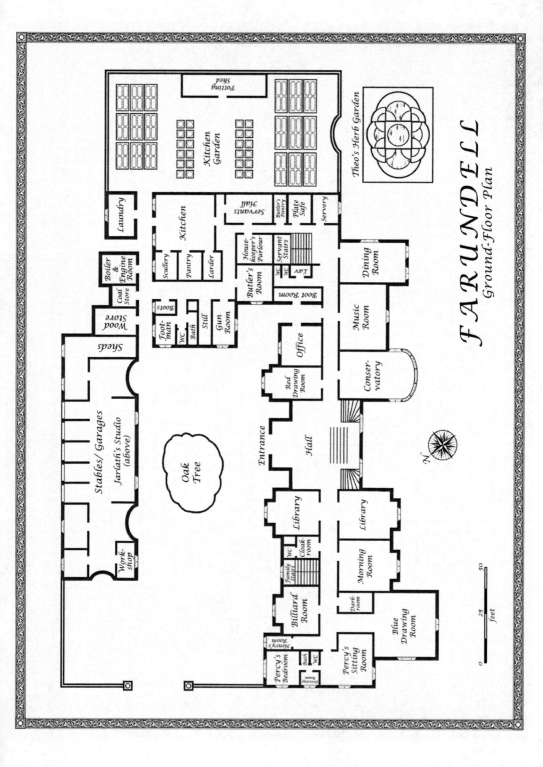

FARUNDELL
Ground-Floor Plan

Potting Shed

Kitchen Garden

Theo's Herb Garden

Laundry

Kitchen

Servants' Hall

Butler's Pantry

Plate Safe

Servery

Scullery

Pantry

Larder

House-keeper's Parlour

Servant Stairs

Boiler & Engine Room

Coal Store

Wood Store

Sheds

Butler's Room

WC

WC

Lav.

Dining Room

Boots

Foot-man

WC

Bath

Still

Gun Room

Boot Room

Music Room

Office

Red Drawing Room

Conservatory

Stables / Garages

Jarlath's Studio (above)

Oak Tree

Entrance

Hall

Library

Work-shop

Library

Morning Room

Dark-room

Blue Drawing Room

Billiard Room

WC

Cloak-room

Family Suite

Henry's Room

Percy's Bedroom

Bath

WC

Dressing Room

Percy's Sitting Room

N

0   25   50
feet

FARUNDELL
1st-Floor Plan

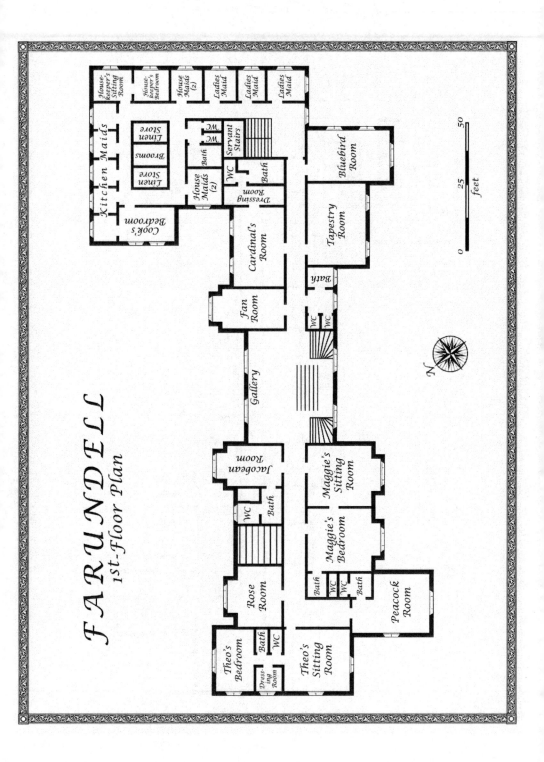

N

0   25   50
feet

Housekeeper's Sitting Room

Housekeeper's Bedroom

House Maids (2)

Ladies Maid

Ladies Maid

Ladies Maid

Kitchen Maids

Linen Store

Brooms

Linen Store

WC

WC

Servant Stairs

Bath

House Maids (2)

Bath

WC

Dressing Room

Bath

Cook's Bedroom

Cardinal's Room

Bluebird Room

Tapestry Room

Fan Room

Bath

WC

WC

Gallery

Jacobean Room

Maggie's Sitting Room

WC

Bath

Rose Room

Maggie's Bedroom

Bath

WC

WC

Bath

Peacock Room

Theo's Bedroom

Bath

WC

Dressing Room

Theo's Sitting Room

FARUNDELL
1st-Floor Plan

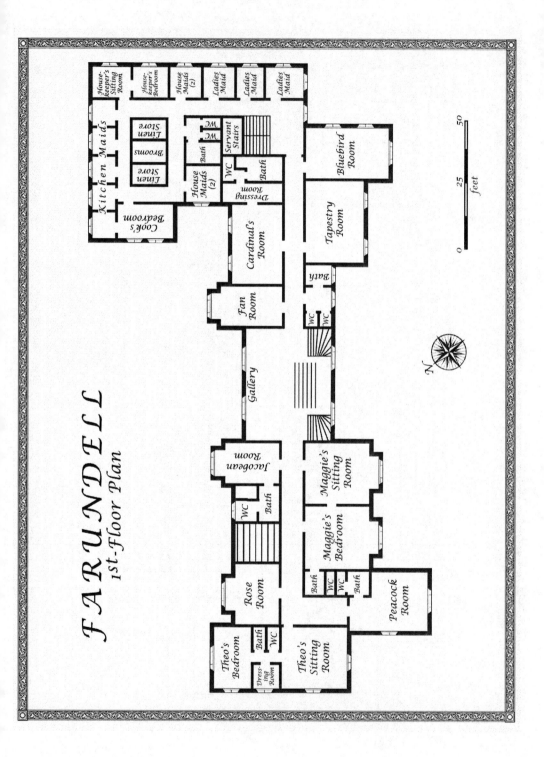

Housekeeper's Sitting Room

Housekeeper's Bedroom

House Maids (2)

Ladies Maid

Ladies Maid

Ladies Maid

Kitchen Maids

Linen Store

Brooms

Linen Store

WC

WC

Bath

Servant Stairs

Cook's Bedroom

House Maids (2)

Bath

WC

Dressing Room

Bath

Bluebird Room

Cardinal's Room

Tapestry Room

Fan Room

Bath

WC

WC

Gallery

WC

WC

Jacobean Room

Maggie's Sitting Room

Bath

WC

Rose Room

Maggie's Bedroom

Bath

WC

WC

Bath

Theo's Bedroom

Bath

Dressing Room

WC

Theo's Sitting Room

Peacock Room

N

0   25   50
feet

So spare me not upon this day
Machinery and cartonnages.
The great and little light of heaven employ,
The stars you may as freely squander;
Cliff-drops and water, fire and thunder,
Birds, animals are in supply.
So in this narrow house of boarded space
Creation's fullest circle go to pace,
And walk with leisured speed your spell
From Heaven through the World to Hell.

Goethe, *Faust*

Autumn 1918

Prologue

The force of the explosion flung him to the ground. Searing flash, black nothing, then he floated high over the ruined earth. Smoke roiled from the mouths of the cannon and shells ripped the air but Paul heard only silence, a sweet, singing silence. His body was an abandoned house, far below. He turned, reached for the gilded clouds but something pulled him back; the light slipped through his fingers and he slid down the spiral of pain, and darkness, and dreams.

His father stands above him, sabre drawn, a distant and deadly smile on his face. 'Not yet,' he says.

The sky closes over with a deafening clang; the earth shakes and tosses him down like a rag. Someone moves and whimpers in the mud. 'I'm thirsty,' he says, but his abdomen has been blown away.

'It doesn't matter, carry on,' Paul says.

The girl looked up. 'I can't understand what he's saying, but he won't let go of my hand.'

'You can sit with him, if you like.'

'Thank you, Doctor. What's his name?'

'Asher. Paul Asher. Medical Corps. He was at the clearing station where Captain St John Vere crashed.'

'Oh, is he the one who . . .'

'Yes, that's right.'

She pulled her chair closer. 'Paul, can you hear me?'

1

'I can't.'

She takes his hand. 'Yes, you can.'

The water rises and he floats. 'You can swim,' she says, and without knowing how, he swims, gliding through the water at her side. Desire burns like thirst; he reaches for her and she wraps her legs around him, draws him deeper. He discovers that he can breathe underwater—it's easy, natural; he's always known how.

'Who are you?' he says, but his words float away.

She presses her mouth to his; her tongue speaks to his mind. You know who I am.

He was still holding her hand when he opened his eyes at first light. She'd fallen asleep with her head on her arm, leaning against his bed. She sat up and rubbed her shoulder. 'Good morning,' she said.

Paul tried to speak but his tongue was thick and dry.

'Would you like some water?' She raised his head and held the cup to his mouth; the soft curve of her cheek came near. He was stunned by the clean, smooth perfection of her skin; he couldn't remember when he'd last seen skin that was not filthy, bloody, torn.

'Who are you?' he said.

'My name is Rosalind. You're in the field hospital at Abbeville.'

'What happened?'

'Don't you remember? You pulled him,' she pointed to the next bed, 'out of his aeroplane, which he conveniently managed to crash on top of you, then a shell landed and nearly blew you both up. He's my brother Val. They told me you saved his life.'

2

Paul searched through the cotton wool that filled his brain. He'd been watching a dogfight; the Camel was hit, the pilot tried to land in the road, clipped a tree, somersaulted. He'd been running towards it . . . and that was all he could remember.

'Don't worry, you'll live.' She reached for the chart. 'Abrasions and contusions, a broken arm, clavicle and several ribs. There were a few bits of metal in your body but we got them out last night.'

Paul explored his sensations: dull aches, a ferocious headache and a heavy weight on his feet. He raised his head and tried to look.

She pushed him down. 'Lie still.'

'What's on my feet?'

'It's a cat. A rather large cat. He came in on the stretcher with you and we haven't been able to shift him.'

'Madagascar,' Paul said. 'It's Madagascar.'

The cat opened his eyes, yawned and walked up the bed to the pillow where he settled, purring. The girl smiled and stood. 'You should try to sleep some more now, but I'll come back later.' She touched his hand. 'I'll come back.'

The scent of rosewater lingered like a dream; Madagascar's purr droned in his ear. Had she been real?

She swims away and he can't follow, he can't swim any further, exhaustion drags at his limbs. There is a roaring in his ears and blackness all around, mud in his mouth and eyes. The bodies at his feet whimper and moan. Someone is crying for his mother.

'It doesn't matter,' Paul says. 'Carry on.' He tries to stand but an immense, invisible hand slams him down and he's swimming again, oh, the relief,

3

swimming deeper and deeper through the cool, sweet water, towards her face as it wavers and changes in the changing light.

Spring 1924

1

Paul gazed down at a tableau of wheels, levers, ropes and chains. It looked as though a giant clock had undergone the tidiest of explosions, or unfoldings, and only just come to rest. Mist curled around its base; a light, gradually brightening, shone from behind the wheels. Thunder rumbled and a trumpet sounded. A troop of animal-faced demons appeared, casting long shadows before them as they swarmed over the structure, pulled ropes, pushed levers, the wheels engaged, began to move. And stopped.

'Oh, damn.' The light went out and an angry man strode on to the stage.

At the back of the theatre, Paul took off his dripping hat and waited for his eyes to adjust. He spotted Val in the middle of the stalls, reclining across several seats like an elegant spider. 'Hello, Val.'

Val turned, disentangled his legs and leapt up. 'Paul, you came! But you're soaked, how on earth did you get so wet? Did you swim the Channel?'

'This is England, it's raining; what a surprise.'

'Come and sit. Where's Madagascar?'

'I left him at your house with his nose in a kipper. Your cook spoils him.' Paul dropped into a seat. 'You look well, Val. Success suits you.'

'Whereas you look like something Mad dragged in. Even so, it's marvellous you've come. I never imagined you'd be able to tear yourself away from

5

Paris, from Justine, or was it Claudette, or Simone?'

'Marie, lately. I have torn myself away, altogether away.'

'Altogether?'

'I gave it up, Val. My love affair with language has come to an end. I'm tired of her or she's tired of me; it doesn't matter which. The result is the same. The more I look at words, the more vacant they become.'

'The little buggers. I know what you mean. So now what? Are you going back to Boston?'

'Boston? In a coffin. I'd sooner die than give my father the pleasure of seeing me crawl. I'll find a job here, some ordinary job.'

'But what of art, the queen of your heart? And truth, beauty, passion, her handmaidens? Have you forsaken them all?'

'Hah. They forsook me first. If they want me again, they can find me. I have a cousin in an insurance firm in Fetter Lane; maybe he'll give me a job, or recommend me to someone. Oh, don't look so aghast.'

'Fetter Lane? It sounds positively Dickensian. Will you have to wear a stiff collar and scrape a scrupulous copperplate on to parchment with a quill?'

'No doubt. Can we not talk about it any more? Tell me about the play—have you changed much? Who's that angry man down there and what are those wheels all about?'

'The angry man is Desmond Fanshawe, our esteemed director, and the wheels are his way of adding useless bits of business that can only go wrong. Of course I've dulled things down to

6

navigate the antediluvian obscenity laws but our dear little *Nino the Golden Catamite* should still offend a great many people.' He lit another cigarette from the end of the last. 'Maggie Damory is playing the women; she's our big star. Her family and mine go way back—that may explain why she agreed to do this. The rehearsal was meant to begin an hour ago but we're stuck in an eternal purgatory of technical run-throughs. We're opening next week and the damned demons can't get the wheels to turn. Come along, I'll show you our wonders.'

Stagehands were at work among the wheels, whose pulleys had become entangled. They were supposed to rotate a series of gateways, Val explained, through which Nino had to pass; in the final scene they operated the trapdoor as the goddess emerged from the sea.

'It looks very . . . ah . . . complicated,' Paul said.

'Oh, it is, it is. We are in the hands of a true master of the art of complication. It's darling Desmond's very own Deus Ex, God help us. Now look, you must see this—it's my favourite.' A long piece of sheet metal hung in the wings. Val gave it a push and thunder rolled through the theatre. 'It can make the most almighty crash if you give it a good whack, but I've been requested to refrain.'

'Val loves the thunder sheet.' A very pretty dark-haired girl joined them.

'Ah, Sara,' Val said, 'meet my friend Paul Asher. Paul, this is Sara Paragon, the violinist who leads the Chorus. And here is Arlen Winter, our psychopomp.' A tall Negro strolled over. 'Arlen is a countryman of yours, and he's a genius with a trumpet.'

7

From the orchestra pit came an ironic drumroll as the demons returned to their stations and took up the ropes. Cogs engaged, great wheels with lesser ones; a cheer broke out, the demons pulled and pushed, the wheels acquired momentum.

'Hurrah,' said Val. 'Maybe now we can start.'

*   *   *

Paul is in his room on rue Rosinard. It's raining; grey light falls through the uncurtained window with its view of the wall of the alley. Sara Paragon raises her violin. 'Listen,' she says, and plays a few bars, then steps through a door Paul hadn't known was there. He follows, but she's disappeared. The room is white and bare, windows open to the sky. Oh yes, he thinks, I remember this room. Scraps of paper cover the floor, each with a word. When he tries to read they blur and fade and change. A door opens on to another room, empty and full of light; beyond there's a hall, with doors in all directions. His footsteps echo on the floorboards and the sound of the violin drifts through the air.

He woke to the soft patter of rain, turned and stretched, unable for a moment to remember where he was. A house with empty rooms, the sound of a violin, words that slipped away. The dream faded and he opened his eyes: Val's house, London.

He put on his dressing gown, rang the bell, lit a cigarette and contemplated the day ahead. He'd made light of it with Val, because Val was incapable of Taking Things Seriously, but in fact the thought of working in a place like Fetter Lane did not fill him with joyous expectation. Wasn't it

8

only common sense to avoid a place with a name like that? He tried to imagine himself as a clerk, in a stiff collar and tie, reporting every day to his post in Fetter Lane, fettered to his post, a long chain leading to an iron collar around his neck. Day after day scraping away with his quill, his spine deformed, his eyes rheumy and dimmed. He would die there, at his post, only discovered when someone noticed that his quill hadn't moved for a week. When they touched him he would turn to powder on the spot, thus saving the cost of a funeral.

A housemaid appeared with his tray, twitched back the curtains, bent to light the fire, vanished. Rain seeped from the sky, a milk cart clanked below and from the streets beyond the square came the ceaseless mutter and hum of motor cars and omnibuses. A pigeon flew by. Paul remembered the first time he'd stayed in this room—Rosalind had brought him home for his convalescence. He'd lain here for days watching pigeons crossing the window, inventing meanings. One bird, the war would end. Two birds, it would last forever. Three, Rosalind loved him. Four, she didn't.

He pulled his mind back. That was another life. Afterwards, Val had taken him to Paris, and Paris—Paris had changed everything. It was a world like a breaking of worlds, and one night, when perhaps he'd broken enough, he had come upon the notion that he could reinvent himself, remake himself, somehow, in his own image. But it was turning out to be a more ambiguous proposition than he'd imagined, full of subpropositions, preconditions, detours, false

9

clues, red herrings, loops and diversions. He reached for another cigarette. Egyptian Deities, his last extravagance. The picture on the box showed a lady on a throne, a deity he supposed, a child on her knee.

And how the hell was one supposed to know at the time what was a genuine clue, and what an irrelevance or a trap? Which the diversion and which the straight path? All of which anyway assumed there was such a thing as a straight path and where one wanted to go—should one be fortunate enough to have a definite goal in mind— was somewhere that could be approached in a straight line, just by setting off in the correct direction and continuing until one arrived. He'd begun to wonder if there were not, perhaps, some destinations one could only approach sideways, observe in peripheral vision, stalk while seemingly headed elsewhere.

You are a fool, his father's voice sneered. You are wasting your life.

At least the idea of Boston—he could not call it home—made Fetter Lane a somewhat less unappealing prospect. If the refusal to go in one particular direction could be considered a direction, he thought, then let that be my direction in life.

He bathed, shaved, studied his reflection. Could this man be a clerk? His hair was too long, and wouldn't lay flat. He could get a haircut, but it was the look in the eyes that gave him pause. An appraising, cautious look, and under the caution? The look of an animal about to bolt. 'Come on, animal,' he said, 'it'll be all right. You're the one who wants to be warm and fed, remember?'

10

*   *   *

Fetter Lane was as narrow as its name; Bonnerby, Pinchon & Pritchett occupied a tall building halfway up the road. Paul opened the shiny black door, approached a clerk at a desk, asked for Mr Horace Pritchett, gave his name, sat down to wait. Posts and fetters were nowhere to be seen, but that did not stop him from imagining them in rows, out of sight in back rooms.

Young men marched in and out, up and down the polished stairs, bearing papers and boxes and files. What were they thinking about, with their compressed lips, their airs of importance, or urgency, or determination? Credits and debits, losses and gains, valuations and documentations, qualifications and accreditations, certifications and authorisations. They began to look like a flock of automated penguins and he made an effort to remember that they were men like him. There might even be some among them whose great goal in life was not Clerk in Insurance; away from Fetter Lane they might be poets or artists, philosophers or mystics, and perhaps other, stranger notions than facts and figures percolated beneath their smooth exteriors. He looked closely as they hurried by, but any wild thoughts going on in there made no outward sign.

After a time someone came to escort him up two flights of stairs and along a corridor lined with frock-coated, gilt-framed Partners, each more august and dispiriting than the last. The master penguins.

'Paul, what a surprise.' Cousin Horace, corpulent

11

and pink, stood behind an enormous desk. 'Sit down, my boy, sit down. Haven't seen you for years.' He shuffled papers, looked at his watch. 'How are you feeling?'

'Very well, thank you. And you?'

'Yes, quite well, thank you. Terribly busy, you know. What brings you here, if I may ask?'

'Of course. I won't take up much of your time. I just stopped by to ask about a job.'

'A job? For you? So, you are better?'

'Better than what?'

'I mean, you have recovered?'

'Recovered? From what?'

'From your ... er ... problem.'

'Which problem?' Paul asked. 'There have been several.'

'Now, young man, we all know you have been through terrible things, and of course they take their toll. One must not try to deny it, everyone understands.'

'Understands what? I'm very sorry, but I have no idea what you're talking about.'

'What have you been doing lately?' Horace's tone was patient, careful.

'Well, I've been living in Paris—you remember, I went there with Val St John Vere after the influenza ... after his sister died. I've been writing, or I should say trying to write. I had a few poems published in *Littérature*, and a short story in *New Writers of 1920*, and I wrote a novel which made a lovely fire, although it didn't last very long.'

'So you deny you have suffered a ... how should I put it ... mental collapse?'

'Mental what? No, I mean yes, I do deny it. At least I think I do. Where did you hear that?'

'Your father told us about your . . . difficulties.'

'Ah yes.' Paul stroked his jaw. 'Those pesky little difficulties of mine.' Val would love this, he thought. It's just like his plays. 'And when did these difficulties . . . occur?'

'Three years ago, more or less, I believe. Don't you . . . don't you even remember?'

'No, I don't. Tragic, isn't it?' Three years ago he'd written his father a last letter telling him precisely what to do with his advice and destroyed all his subsequent letters unread.

'Your father did say, my boy, if you ever came to us we should urge you to return to America where you could receive the best possible care.' Horace nodded his chins and smiled, though his small eyes were wary.

Paul was tempted to jump on to the desk and bark. But that would be childish. He stood. 'Thank you for your time; this has been vastly more entertaining than I had dared hope. Good day.'

He strode past the smirking Partners, down the stairs and into the street. He didn't know whether to laugh, cry or kick something. He walked, lit a cigarette, walked on. When he looked around, he was in the Strand. Stranded he was—but not fettered, a little voice said, though he ignored it.

He found his way down to the Embankment. The skies had lightened and watery sunlight played over the river. It was on the surge; its slick dark skin swirled with cross-currents and whirlpools, merging and parting, twining and plaiting. He felt a twist of vertigo, lifted his eyes and looked back across the road. The mass of buildings towered like giant anthills.

How amusing, he thought—I'd hated the idea of

13

being a clerk in Fetter Lane and now I'm very annoyed I shan't be. No, of course, it's not that. It's my father, reaching all this way to fuck with my life. The bastard. What a malicious lie. Did he believe it himself? Would that make it better or worse? Paul spat into the river and turned away. Lucky escape, he heard the small voice say, and this time he nodded. He lit a cigarette and walked west under the sharpening shadows of the plane trees, following the curve of the Thames upstream. He'd begun to enjoy the day.

*   *   *

The next morning he perused the classified advertisements. A room, he discovered, would cost him at least ten shillings a week practically anywhere in London. With money for food, cigarettes, and so on, he needed to earn eight pounds a month at the very minimum, but the jobs paying that amount all required skills he lacked. There was a great demand for mechanics of every sort, but he could hardly tell a nut from a bolt. Also, of course, clerks, but everyone wanted experience and references. It occurred to him, not for the first time, that he lacked any qualifications for anything whatsoever. He made a mental list of his more notable achievements. West Point Military Academy: sent down. Harvard Medical School: quit. The Great War: survived, more or less. That did not qualify him for any of the jobs listed here. Outside, birds were singing and sunshine spilled across the table. He tucked the paper under his arm and went to the park.

Young mothers and nannies with babies in prams

promenaded by the lake. Everyone looked content; everyone looked like they were where they belonged. Paul sat on a bench in the sun. Children were playing a game in which a stone was a castle, a shrub a forest, a stick a sword, a muddy bit of lawn the field of chivalry, a hapless dog a caparisoned charger. How easily they made it all mean something. Did I ever see the world so? Sad world. He kicked it gently with his heel. Sad old world, that used to mean something and doesn't any more. Still shone on by the sun, though, and that, at least, is still free. He raised his face and closed his eyes. I wish I could sit in the sun forever, he thought, that life could be as simple as sitting in the sun. Why shouldn't it be? After all, I'm doing no harm, and who could say, whatever their profession, they'd done no harm? If only one could eat sunlight one could live very simply, though probably not in England.

*   *   *

'. . . roof leaked, and rats . . . couldn't find any . . . bit the bailiff's . . . baby was dead . . . never heard from him again . . . sister stole my boots . . . wasn't no use . . . don't care if they ever . . . tried and tried, then . . . lost the damn key, didn't he?'

The rough, sour voices crowded the steamy air of the teashop in Waterloo. Paul ordered a ha'penny bun and a cup of tea, pushed the overflowing ashtray to one side and rested his elbows on the two worn places indicated on the oilcloth. The bun and the tea arrived with a bang and a slop; the bun was stale and the tea scalded his tongue.

The past week had taught him that most items in

the Positions Offered columns referred to positions no longer being offered, that had perhaps never really been offered at all. He'd fallen into a drifting shoal of men, swept into the anterooms of hundreds of offices and back out to the street. Some fellows' faces were becoming as familiar as old friends'. He finished his bun and lit a cigarette; a man at the next table stopped talking to his companions, glanced at Paul and made a little cough. Paul offered the box.

The man lifted a cigarette, sniffed it. 'Ah, Turkish. Haven't had one for years. No, no light yet, thank you, I'll save it for later if you don't mind.' Three other faces leaned closer; three hands reached out with delicate, purposeful greed and when Paul withdrew the box it was empty.

He emerged into pelting rain and a chill wind nearly tore the hat from his head. He trudged through traffic-clogged streets down to the river, stuffed his hat in his pocket and set out across the bridge.

*   *   *

'. . . resurrection . . . bedtime story . . . never fall in love with a client . . . gossip is deadlier . . . give him love, or cash . . . what language was that? . . . oldest family . . . blood and a bone . . . his sister found . . . monkeys under the table . . . not the words, only the definitions . . .'

Paul sat on the stairs with a glass of champagne. Val's opening-night party filled the house. The first performance of *Nino the Golden Catamite* had been a sell-out, though half the audience were Val's friends and the other half obviously hadn't

16

known what they were attending. Perhaps, Val had said, they thought a catamite was a small feline. The event had been punctuated by angry protests and fistfights; a small riot spilled into the street. Val was so delighted that Paul wondered if he'd stirred it up himself from the back of the stalls where he'd lurked.

There was a flurry at the door as Maggie Damory arrived with the movie producer Albert Laski, who to Val's extreme consternation kissed his hand and declared the play a 'vork uff cheenius'; he refused to relinquish the hand until Val consented to an immediate film adaptation, and promised to write the screenplay himself. On Maggie's other arm Paul recognised her husband, the painter and occultist Jarlath Quinn, in his famous cloak and broad-brimmed Borsalino. His omnivorous sexuality was a legend in Paris, where he'd been a crony of Aleister Crowley. Someone had said he was a black magician, whatever that meant.

'You look lonely.' Sara Paragon sat down on the step beside him.

'In this mob? No chance. Sara, you were splendid tonight. You play wonderfully.'

'Did you think so? Desmond didn't allow us to rehearse. He wanted us to seize the inspiration of the moment, as he put it, but I was terrified there wouldn't be any inspiration, or I wouldn't be able to seize it. Do you have any idea what I mean?'

'Yes, in fact I do. So what happened? Did you prepare something, just in case?'

'I did, a few bars, to get me started in case I froze. I wouldn't have dared go on otherwise. But I didn't need it. I touched the bow to the strings and

17

. . . I don't know how to describe it. It felt like the music was coming from somewhere else; it already existed, and all I could do was let it happen. I don't understand it myself. Probably I need some more champagne.' She grabbed a glass from a passing footman and danced away.

At three, the first editions of the papers arrived and they gathered in the drawing room with the reviews.

' "Valentine St John Vere, Viscount Hetheringham," ' Maggie read, ' "DFC, MC, DSO, VC, has turned upon the hand that fed him and sunk his teeth to the bone. The decay of Western Civilisation is further advanced than we thought." '

'Oh, they have no idea,' Val said. 'Say, rather, the rot at the very core.'

' "He has sullied the London stage with this vicious, vituperative, blasphemous, disgusting . . ." '

'Mind, you're spitting.'

'Can't help it, *he* must have been. ". . . assault not only on our morals but on our very language . . ." '

'How can you assault morals without assaulting language? I promise you, it can't be done.'

'Wait,' Paul said. 'They're not all so upset with you. Listen to this: "Avant the Avant-Garde. Valentine St John Vere's surrealist mystery play passed right over the heads of most of its audience at the New Alexandra Theatre last night. Few will have recognised its source in *The Golden Ass* of Apuleius, a great moral tale of magic gone wrong and the quest for redemption. The eponymous hero has to pass through a series of gateways that themselves became hurdles for the audience to overcome. Regrettably, though not surprisingly, most fell at the first, and few remained to see the

18

play's powerful and indeed moralistic climax. I would like to compliment St. John Vere, who I understand has resided in Paris of late, on writing a play that is sure to be one of the most misunderstood works of our time. It is commonly said that London is twelve years behind Paris in matters of culture and art; if this is so, *Nino the Golden Catamite* may have to wait many years to receive the recognition it deserves." '

'What a remarkably perceptive fellow,' Val said over his shoulder as he was called to the telephone.

'The reviews,' he said when he returned, 'are now mere curiosities. We have received the ultimate accolade: it's been cancelled. That was the theatre. They've been told if they permit another performance they'll be prosecuted, as will I. So will you, Maggie, and Fanshawe, and a list of other people. I'd love the chance to defend it, but one can't expect them to carry on for our sakes. They'd be forced out of business.'

'Ach, one must be philosophical, is it not so?' said Laski. 'And so we start the film immediately, yes, tomorrow.'

Val put another record on the gramophone, turned it up loud, and induced Laski to attempt a Charleston. Maggie sat on the long sofa beside Paul and Madagascar, kicked off her shoes and tucked up her legs. 'What a magnificent cat,' she said.

'His name is Madagascar. Mad, this is Maggie Damory.'

Madagascar looked steadily at Maggie, then blinked.

'Blink back,' Paul said. 'It shows you're friendly.'

19

Maggie blinked her green eyes, and Madagascar blinked his. After a time he permitted her to scratch briefly behind his ears.

'You're Val's friend Paul, aren't you?' she said. 'You live in Paris, I'd heard—what on earth brings you to dreary, backward old London? Or did you come just for our one-night stand?'

'I did come for Val's opening, but also to look for a job.'

'Oh? What sort?'

'Anything. I'm not qualified for much.'

'Well, as it so happens my father—he lives at Farundell, our house in Oxfordshire—has decided he wants to write his memoirs. He's blind, you see, and not terribly well, and he needs someone to help. He asked if I knew anyone, and I didn't, but now . . . here you are. You can read and write, can't you? That's all that's required. Oh, can you operate a typewriting machine?'

'Yes . . .'

'Splendid. So, what do you think?'

'I think it's an extremely kind offer, but Maggie, he doesn't know me—what if he doesn't like me? And then there's Madagascar.'

'Oh don't worry. He'll like you, he's not in the least a county sort, you know—they'll all like you, and Madagascar too, of course, if the two of you can bear to be country cats for a while? Or perhaps you're thinking it'll be deadly dull. Compared to Paris it is, although not as bad as one might suppose—lots of interesting people come to Farundell all the time. Do say you'll do it, please.'

'Well, I . . .'

'Can you go right away? He's awfully urgent about it, now he's got a bee in his bonnet. All you

20

have to do is take the train—the nearest town is Exley. Val can explain.'

'Er . . .'

'Wonderful. I'll telephone to let them know. Father will be so pleased.'

Paul admired how neatly he'd been handled. Did he fancy being an old man's secretary? Did it matter whether he fancied it or not? It was a job, and Madagascar seemed to have given his approval. 'All right,' he said. 'We'll give it a try.'

A jazz band arrived, friends of Arlen; Maggie got up to sing. A cocktail virtuoso practised his lethal art in the corner; the noise level increased, the smoke, the incoherence of conversations. A walk was what he needed. He found his coat and hat and, when he turned to leave, Sara was at his side.

'Are you going out?' she said. 'Would you like to walk down to the river? The thing is I need to go home that way . . .'

'Let's go,' Paul said. He helped her on with her coat and offered to carry the violin, but she said she'd feel unbalanced without it.

They walked in thickening fog along St James's Park, where the willows loomed like giant haystacks and an owl hooted. Sara raised her face for a kiss. The owl hooted again and he whispered, 'Who, who are you, Miss Sara Paragon?'

She laughed and, taking his hand, drew him on. Passing the bulk of Parliament, felt rather than seen, they walked on to Westminster Bridge and paused under a streetlight. The deep tolls of Big Ben moved through the air in slow waves. Sara took out her violin and tightened the bow. 'It won't like all this damp, but maybe a minute or two.' She tested the tuning, took a deep breath, closed her

21

eyes and began to play.

The music rose and swirled in the mist; it flowed into Paul and blossomed like a memory, like a dream. He tried to defend himself but it was too late; tears burned in his eyes. He turned, pressed his face into his hands. The music pierced him, flayed him, sliced through him. He reached for words but none were right; it was love and loss, beauty and sorrow, and some nameless, elusive light at the heart of it all, that he'd longed for, searched for, wanted for so long . . . It doesn't matter, carry on, it doesn't matter, carry on; by the time the music ended on a long, wavering note he was able to turn to Sara with a smile.

She put the violin away and kissed him once, hard. 'Thank you for being here,' she said, 'for listening.'

They walked on in silence, footsteps muted. He kissed her goodnight at her door and returned to the bridge. He stared into the fog, listening for echoes of the music, of that feeling. The night was thick all around him—was he where he thought? For a terrifying moment the bridge and the city dissolved and he was back in the Flanders mud. No! He stamped his foot. This was real, solid, not a dream that could slip out of his control. 'This is real,' he said aloud. 'I am awake.' He forced himself to picture the road ahead: the end of the bridge at the Embankment, Parliament on the left, Whitehall on the right, St James's Park, Birdcage Walk, the Palace, the Royal Mews. He sent himself forth on the imagined route, and made his way safely to Val's.

Paul and Nino leave the city and come, at first light, to the shore. Sea and sky merge at the horizon; seagulls call high in the lucent air. Nino, naked and mute, prays to the pale disc of the setting moon. A boat approaches, a white-haired old woman in the prow. Her sad eyes study Paul with disinterested compassion. He understands that the boat can come no closer because the water is too shallow, so he wades out.

There is no solid ground beneath him, only mud. The sky screams and howls. He crawls towards a body, but it's just a torso. It doesn't matter, carry on. He searches desperately for the rest. Legs and arms, hands and feet and heads are churned like chunks of meat in a grey-brown stew. He pulls out an arm, wipes off the mud. Sick horror washes through him—it's his own. He tries to drop it but the hand seizes him and will not let go. A feral dog approaches, teeth bared, starving, snarling; it grabs the bloody stump and pulls.

Paul awakened with a jolt and sat upright, heart pounding; his hands clenched the bedclothes so tightly they ached. He prised open his fingers, stumbled to the bathroom, splashed cold water over his head. He caught a glimpse of his face in the mirror; the nightmare lingered in his eyes and he looked away.

He rang for coffee, lit a cigarette and willed his hand to stop shaking. The soothing smoke rushed into his lungs; he eased himself into a chair, leaned back and exhaled the dregs of panic. Madagascar came to lie across his lap. He'd not had the nightmare for a week or so; it was becoming, thank God, less frequent. He remembered how it had begun—the scene at the shore, the low moon, the approaching boat. He'd been with Nino from Val's play; there had been that same feeling of longing, of loss, that had swept over him on Westminster Bridge as Sara played. No words seemed right for it. How could such a powerful feeling have no name? Language took him further from understanding; could one step out of it, he wondered, as from a boat that has landed on some desired shore?

*   *   *

They set out for Paddington under mild and cloudy skies. Madagascar, wearing his collar and lead, rode atop the rucksack. Paul bought a ticket to Exley and with a couple of minutes to spare settled in an empty compartment and lit a cigarette.

He'd learned from Val that Maggie's father, Lord Perceval Damory, had spent several years in the Amazon collecting moths and conducting anthropological research. His very wealthy American wife had died some time ago and now he never left Farundell, which according to Val was in 'the absolute precise middle of nowhere'. But then, Val thought anywhere beyond Hyde Park extremely remote.

There was a hoot and a whistle and the sound of doors slamming up and down the train; it jerked and began to move. Beyond the gritty glass roof of the station a stone-walled ravine cut through the

24

gardens of once genteel homes, now stranded high above the clank and rattle. The embankments gave way to freight depots, hostlers' yards, factories, caverns of machinery serviced by acolytes clad in black oil from head to toe like their charges.

He'd always loved trains: the sense of going somewhere while sitting still and doing nothing, the strong rhythm of the wheels and the scratchy upholstery, the smell of hot metal and tobacco smoke, newspapers left behind and something indefinable that as a child he thought was the odour of travel itself. He spent his pocket money not on sweets or games like the other boys but on random journeys. He'd go to the end of the line and return, often without leaving his seat. A round-trip ticket was a balanced equation; there was no danger of hurtling off into nowhere, continuing forever as he'd imagined one might on foot or in a motor car, forgetting to turn back, forgetting the way, or somehow losing the power to return.

They clacked across a bridge; below the open girders a river ran brown and foamy. Weedy, rubbish-strewn lots, then rows upon rows of brick houses, garlands of laundry across their thin backs. Paul stared, hoping for an uncurtained glimpse, fascinated and repulsed by the lives he imagined behind those windows. Children skipping; a barking dog; a baby strapped in a chair, its mouth a bawling, toothless hole; a woman in a doorway, her mouth slack, a silent, toothless hole. Another river-crossing, another skeletal bridge, yet more ordered suburbs, then villages set among fields. Patches of blue showed between the clouds; Paul opened the window and moist, fragrant air flooded

25

in. He allowed himself to be mesmerised by the passing images, like a movie, but private, exclusive, just for him, as the little compartment of his senses was borne unresistingly along. He imagined that he was sitting still while the world moved, now slowly, now fast, pouring into him through his eyes and spooling into some grand, minute repository; or through him altogether and out the other side, as though he was no more than the eye of a needle through which a fragile thread of reality was steadily being drawn.

By the time the train arrived in Exley the day was sunny and hot, a premonition of summer. They were the only passengers to disembark. An elderly stationmaster waved to the engine driver from his chair in the shade.

'Hello,' Paul said. 'I'm going to a house called Farundell—do you know the way?'

'You another one of them treasure hunters?'

'Treasure hunters? No, I've come to work for Lord Damory. Can you give me directions? Is it far?'

'No, not far at all. Mile or two. Go by the Green Man,' he pointed up the road, 'turn right at the Gilded Tree, cross the river and on into town past the Dog and Bone, to the end of the high street, right at the Black Beetle, along the Oxford road to the Midnight Sun, left up into the hills and after a bit you come to a few houses by a bridge, that's Farundell hamlet, then over the brow of the hill, and on the left there's the old gate, you can't miss it.'

Paul thanked him and set off; Madagascar trotted alongside, head high. The sign of the Green Man showed a wide green face; a mass of leaves and vines surged from his grinning mouth. 'Green,' he seemed to say, 'greeen and greeeeen and greeeeeener.'

The Gilded Tree stood on the riverbank by a bridge. The water was running high, a dark, bright greeny-brown, blue where it reflected the sky. A plaque at the centre of the span told him: *This bridge over the River Isis, or Thames, first built in 1167, was restored in 1823.* Could this peaceful little river be the mighty Thames? And why did it have another name here? Paul leaned on the parapet and unfolded the map Val had given him. At the centre of all the converging lines was Westminster, where he'd stood with Sara Paragon. His memory drew him away in search of that music and that strange, unnameable feeling, but it slipped through his mind like water. He moved his finger over the paper. The river meandered about a lot but yes, it was the same one in whose upper reaches, for some reason, it was known as the Isis. He remembered several bridges on the journey— all, he now saw, had crossed the same river.

The road, lined with shops and offices, climbed the opposite bank. In a deserted market square stood a bronze memorial inscribed with the names of *The Glorious Dead, 1914–1918*; Paul always had to remind himself that the phrase was not intended ironically. Outside the Black Beetle two old men, cigarettes clamped between their teeth, watched a dog trying to mount a bitch. Madagascar indicated that he would like to resume his position on the rucksack, so Paul lifted him up.

The Oxford road had received a new coat of tarmacadam, black and acrid in the sun. Paul walked on the dusty verge past flat fields and tidy market gardens, each with its old man or woman, bent and brown. At the edge of town, opposite the Midnight Sun and a new motor garage, a faded sign pointed to Farundell.

The road wound between ridges and vales, rising and falling in a leisurely, deferential way as though yielding to the terrain. Tilled fields gave way to pastures with clumps of sheep like dirty clouds. The hamlet of Farundell was a dozen houses by a steeply arched bridge; a trio of small children stared from an open doorway. Paul waved; they giggled and fled within. A black dog with strange pale eyes watched from the shade.

The hilltop was crowned by a stand of tall trees. On the left, an old stone wall and pillars flanked a narrow drive; ornate iron gates stood open, wedged knee-deep in vegetation and entwined by some climbing plant. A man wearing sunglasses and an old-fashioned frock coat sat on the wall, a book open on his knee.

Madagascar jumped down, arched his back and hissed, then crouched, growling low in his throat. Paul looked at him in astonishment. 'What's got into you, Mad?'

'Cats don't like me,' the man said.

'My apologies, sir. Do you happen to know, is this Farundell?'

The man removed his sunglasses and looked Paul up and down. 'It certainly is,' he said, a glint of amusement in his eyes.

Paul straightened his tie, resumed his hat, dragged Madagascar away and stepped through the gate. The new-leafed branches of great trees, meeting overhead, made a long green tunnel. Weedy edges and centre strip were a reassuring

28

sign—he'd feared an immaculate grandeur. On the right, fields and meadows sloped to a lake at whose centre an island rose to a wooded summit. Paul glimpsed tall white columns among the trees.

Pink and white flowers crowded the road; drifts of blue patched the forest floor on his left. He could identify a few trees because of childhood visits to an arboretum, but here were dozens of different plants, not to mention insects and birds, few of which he recognised or could name. Well, that would be something to learn.

The house appeared through a grove of birches, a long sprawl of golden-grey stone. A low wall bounded a gravelled courtyard with an ancient, lichen-mottled oak in the middle, stables and outbuildings opposite. The façade of the house was in shadow, its mullioned bays framed by roses. A white-haired old woman dug among their roots, distributing manure from a wheelbarrow, while a skinny girl of perhaps thirteen read to her from a book.

They turned as Paul approached. 'Hello,' the woman said. 'You must be Paul Asher. Welcome to Farundell. I'm Percy's sister Theo, and this is Maggie and Jarlath's daughter Alice.'

'How do you do?' Paul said.

'How do you do?' said Alice. She tilted her head to look down her nose at him.

'Very well, thank you. It's a pleasure to meet you.' Paul suppressed the urge to click his heels.

'Maggie telephoned to say you were coming, but she didn't give us much notice,' Alice said. 'You really do have a cat.'

'Yes, this is Madagascar.' Paul unbuckled the collar and lead to let Mad know they had arrived.

'It's very kind of you to let me bring him.'

Theo looked down at the cat, who looked up at her; they blinked at each other.

'I see you speak Cat,' Paul said.

'I've observed that to stare at a cat is considered rude.'

Madagascar walked around her legs, leaning in and rubbing his face. Theo held out her hand, allowed him to sniff, stroked him once. He sat at her feet and wrapped his tail formally around his paws. 'How did he come by his name?' she asked. 'And have you always had him?'

'No, only since the war. He belonged to my colonel, who'd found him abandoned as a tiny kitten in Madagascar, trained him to wear a collar and lead and ride on his shoulder. When Colonel Woods was killed, Mad for some reason attached himself to me.'

'I have a cat, too,' said Alice. 'Her name is Artemis. Do you know who that is?'

Paul nodded.

'She's my favourite character in Greek mythology, or at any rate she was my favourite when I named her, but that was long ago when I was little.'

'Who's your favourite now?'

'Hermes, I think. At the moment. I'm reading a hymn to Hermes in Greek.' She held up her book.

'You read Greek?'

'Oh yes, and Latin. And this year I've started Hebrew. But I like Greek best. Listen.' Alice opened the book and began to recite.

'Alice dear, perhaps you can translate for us?' Theo said.

'I was going to. "In Arcadia the son of Time lay

30

with the . . . rich-tressed nymph in dark . . . sylvan glades, unseen by immortal gods and mortal men, at dead of night. And when his . . . will was fixed in heaven, she bore a child of many . . . forms, Hermes: cunning in word, a bringer of dreams, a watcher at the gateway to sleep and death."'

'Thank you, Alice,' Theo said. 'That's lovely. And now I must go and water the peas. Perhaps you can take Paul to his room.' Madagascar followed her across the courtyard and through a wide archway.

'I think I've lost my cat,' said Paul.

'They're just going to the kitchen garden,' Alice said. 'Would you like to see your room?'

Under the rose-hung portico a wide door with elaborate iron hinges opened on to a stone-floored hall. 'Tustian!' Alice called. A bald, stocky man in plimsolls appeared. 'Mr Asher has arrived and he really does have a cat, but it's gone off with Theo. Tustian is our major-domo,' she said to Paul. 'He has bunions.'

'Good afternoon, Mr Asher,' Tustian said. 'Welcome to Farundell. May we show you to your room?'

'Follow me,' said Alice. She led the way up an ornate staircase, across a gallery, along wainscoted passages, up another flight of stairs and down a narrow corridor.

'We thought you would like this room,' Alice said. 'It's under the eaves but you do have a view of the lake.' She opened the window. 'Oh look, a feather's caught in the ivy. Red kite, I think. It's lucky to find a feather before it touches the ground. You can have it, though, as it's your room.' She put it on the sill.

31

'Thank you,' said Paul.

'Now along there is the bathroom and the WC,' said Tustian, 'which you share with Mr Aubrey, and here is the bell. Do ring if you need anything. Morning tray at eight? Just coffee, or . . .? Just coffee, then. Very good. Tea will be on the terrace today, in about half an hour. Come along, Miss Alice.'

When their footsteps faded it was so quiet Paul could hear his own heartbeat. God knows what he'd expected—he'd tried not to have any expectations at all—but it could have been awful and it was beautiful—clean and simple, airy and bright. On one wall a fireplace with a plain stone mantel, a fire ready laid, a fat-bellied brass bucket full of coal. Opposite, the bed: chastely single, pristine white cover, white iron curlicues of leaves and vines at head and foot. A washstand and dresser, a desk, an armchair in old leather, a bookcase, shelves half filled with books.

Paul crossed to the window. From this height he could see that the lake flowed over a weir into a stream which wandered through fields and joined what must be the River Isis near the cluster of roofs and steeple that was Exley. Hills rose on either side, patterned in a thousand shades of green. Below, broad terraces descended to the ha-ha; sheep grazed the meadow. Two muddy children were trudging up towards the house.

Paul unpacked, washed his face and found his way downstairs, following the sound of voices to a room whose French doors opened on to the terrace. The muddy children looked as if they'd been hosed off; they jostled for sandwiches and cakes. Alice sat at a distance from them with a wispy young man in a floppy tie and ink-stained velvet jacket. He noticed Paul and a smile lit his homely face.

'You must be Paul, hello, do come and have some tea. Our cook, Mrs Beal, makes the most wonderful walnut scones. I'm Stephen Aubrey, by the way, tutor I suppose you'd say, for my sins. Of course you've met Alice; these wild animals are also, inexplicably, Maggie and Jarlath's. Roger and Sophie, grunt to Mr Asher.' The children looked up from their food.

'I told Percy you were here,' Alice said. 'He has a cold and has to stay in bed today, but he wants to meet you tomorrow. The archaeologists wore him out.'

'Archaeologists?' Paul said. 'That must be why the stationmaster asked if I was a treasure hunter.'

'We had a bunch last week,' Alice said. 'Percy lets them dig. I think it amuses him, especially if it rains a great deal and they don't find anything.'

'Various little things turn up,' Stephen said. 'Lots of Roman bits. People have been searching for the legendary Farundell treasure for centuries; now they call themselves archaeologists.'

'You mean there really is a treasure?' Paul said.

'Oh, it's just a myth,' Stephen said. 'I'm sure if there was one, it would have been found and spent long ago. Every old house is supposed to have its treasure, its secret passage, its ghost.'

'We do have a ghost,' Alice said. 'My great-great-great-great-grandfather Francis Damory.'

'I've never seen him,' Stephen said. 'Have you?'

'Well, no,' Alice said. 'Not actually seen. But other people have. And there's a secret passage, too.'

33

'Really? You never told me. Where is it?'

'If I told you it wouldn't be secret, would it?'

'I believe I may have mentioned from time to time, Alice, that no one likes a smart aleck. And see? It's time for your bath.' A maid was waiting to take the children inside.

Stephen lit a cigarette and offered one to Paul. 'I think you're quite brave,' he said, 'to come all the way out here to work for someone you've never met, who might be an absolute monster, or, worse, an awful old bore. He isn't, of course, but how were you to know?'

'I thought Lord Damory was the brave one,' Paul said, 'taking on an unknown person who could be utterly incompetent, or who'd make off with the silver in the night. I'm lucky to have any sort of job at all.'

'So am I,' said Stephen, 'so am I. Never thought I'd be a tutor, but there you are. These things happen.'

'Have you been here long?'

'About two years. I came to recuperate from some . . . problems. Alice used to read to me, when I couldn't do much but sit and listen. When she found out I'd read Classics she insisted I teach her Latin. So now I teach them all—a bit of everything. Maths, a scattering of botany, geography, history, literature, French and German, and for Alice, the ancient languages, for which she seems to have a gift. Being with the children helped, in its way, and Theo, well, Theo is the most sane person, you know—sane from *sanare*, to heal, as Alice would tell you.' He glanced at Paul. 'I was in a very strange state—untethered, lost. I don't know if you can understand that one can lose

34

oneself, just not have one's self any more. One can give it away, not realising what it is, or that it's valuable. Or misplace it, through carelessness. Or sell it, for something one thinks is love. Or it can be stolen. Or all of those at once.'

Or one can hide it, the thought came to Paul, hide it so well one forgets where it is, or that it even exists.

'I'd fallen into a hole,' Stephen was saying, 'a hole with no bottom and no sides—no meaning, no reason, no path. And Jarlath climbed in, and got me out, and brought me to Theo, who'd been his teacher long ago.'

'What do you mean, climbed in and got you out?'

'Ah, what do I mean? Do you know anything about magic?'

'Magic? I don't suppose you mean conjuring tricks? No, thought not. In Paris, I heard Jarlath described as a black magician.'

Stephen laughed. 'A black magician, eh? People are ignorant, that's all. I believe Jarlath would say that white magic has as its sole aim one's own enlightenment, and everything else is black. Though he is quite strict in his definitions.'

'But I don't understand what magic is in the first place.'

Stephen sighed. 'Well, I'll try to explain, but I expect you'll think I'm deluded, or very stupid, or both. What if I said there was another world, other worlds, as real or realer than the material one?'

'Other worlds—you mean out there, in space?' Paul gestured to the sky.

'No, inside—inner worlds. Have you ever had one of those dreams—I'm told they're not uncommon—where you're in a large, beautiful

35

house and you realise it's your house, but somehow you'd forgotten all about it . . . or maybe you're in your own, familiar little flat and you discover a room that you hadn't known was there?'

Paul's memory flashed a brief glimpse of a white room beyond a door . . . then it was gone, but a feeling of familiarity remained. 'Yes, I think maybe I have.'

'Well, that's an image, or a metaphor, but there really are other rooms, other planes of existence.'

'Look, don't be offended, but I don't believe in any of that.'

'Tell me, have you been to Kathmandu?'

'No . . .'

'So how do you know it exists?'

'Other people have been, and they . . . I see what you mean. But one doesn't have to take their word for it—one can go there. It may not be the most accessible place in the world, but it's real. There are travellers' reports, maps, guidebooks.'

'Just so,' said Stephen. 'Travellers' reports, maps, guidebooks, even guides. One can go there. If one wants to. And sometimes if one doesn't. I was lost in there, and Jarlath, who knows his way around Kathmandu, as it were, found me and brought me here. I hope I never have to leave.'

The sun slipped behind the hill; the air grew cooler. They smoked for a time in silence, watching the changing light. High above, almost invisible, dark specks poised on the wind, songs threading the sky. 'What birds are those?' Paul asked.

'Skylarks,' Stephen said. 'They're guarding their nests in the meadow—there, look, that one is diving down against the other, to drive him away.

36

They sound so lovely, don't they? But those are war cries we hear.'

As the sky turned from blue to gold-hazed green, Paul went upstairs and ran himself a bath. The tub was ancient, claw-footed, long enough to stretch out in. A round window showed a disc of darkening light, one faint star, then another.

A simple family dinner was followed by coffee in the music room where the children put on an impromptu performance in Paul's honour: Alice on flute, Roger on a small cello and Sophie on the piano. As soon as he could, he excused himself and went up to his room. He lit a candle, sat in the armchair, smoked a cigarette, listened to the sounds of the household: doors opening and closing, steps on the stairs, faint laughter. Someone was playing the piano, far better than Sophie; a Chopin Nocturne, plangent and diffuse, drifted up the stairs and along the corridors.

Eventually all the sounds ceased; the house slept. Paul blew out his candle and opened the window. The land below shimmered in all shades of grey; moonlight spread over it like water. A small form meandered down to the lake, blurred as though swimming: Madagascar, or another cat, or some other animal altogether. The night was huge and silent: no motor cars, no voices; just the sibylline hoot of an owl, stretched long like the whistle of a distant train. After a time he undressed and climbed into his new white bed.

*   *   *

When the moonlight crept across her floor Alice stirred in her sleep and with a turning, twisting

37

motion she knew well, left her earth-body behind and went out into the night. The air was shiny and silky; her body a pale glimmer swathed in a gossamer nightgown. My moon-body, she thought. She held up her hand and observed the light. Each of the tiny motes was spinning and vibrating; when she listened she heard their silvery hum.

Drifting like a bit of mist she followed the zigs and zags of a fox, all tooth and hunger, as he trotted and sniffed across the meadow. She stopped beside a young willow tree on the bank of the lake, tasting the sharp acid-green of its new leaves. In the shallows overhung by its branches somnolent fish floated among the moon shadows. The island glowed on the dark water; its crown of trees sparkled emerald at their tips.

The new cat, Madagascar, prowled the shore. Artemis was coming—surely she wouldn't permit a stranger to walk in and take over where she ruled? Alice held her breath as the cats approached, but they touched noses, sniffed and circled each other in a very friendly way.

There, behind that window on the top floor, was the cat's owner. Her curiosity drew her near. He was in his bed—was he dreaming? He turned on to his back. Afraid she'd somehow awakened him, she retreated to her favourite tree, an enormous beech at the edge of the woods, and perched beside the tawny owl. He stretched his wings, released the branch and glided over the meadow. Alice followed his intent and saw the mouse pulsing far below, heard its tiny squeak, felt its fear and death, watched its wisp of life float away, at first clinging close to the ground then rising like a feather on an updraught, spiralling towards the stars. She set off to follow, but before long—she knew this would happen—her limbs grew watery, a heaviness pulled her down to her room, to her bed. She re-entered her earth-body with a brief steep slide and a click at the back of her head and fell deeper through the dark gateway of sleep.

3

A path of gleaming moonlight crossed the lake and the meadow, splashed on the sill and silvered his skin. Paul was standing by the open window, though he couldn't remember getting out of bed. The air was resonant with some music just beyond the edge of hearing, a hum, a buzz in his ears and eyes and all over his body. He turned to gaze around the room, but couldn't focus. Everything he looked at dissolved into millions of particles of effervescent light. There was someone asleep in the bed; he recognised his own face. Am I dead? he wondered, as a dark wave of fear flooded his senses. He fought against it but it sucked him under and pulled him helplessly down, and down, and down.

Paul awoke and sat up fast, eyes wide, breathing deeply until the room steadied. He'd been having one of those awful falling dreams—the endless spiral of vertigo, the terrifying wait for the impact that never comes. He unclenched his fists from the sheet and shivered. The air was cold and damp. He pulled on his dressing gown and crossed to close the window. It was morning; there was no moonlight, but the house was deep in a thick white mist. The ground was invisible; he might have been floating in a cloud.

Promptly at eight, a maid appeared with his tray and introduced herself as Mavis, Mr Tustian's niece; one of four. 'There's Tilly, the eldest, head house parlourmaid, and Beryl, next, then me, then Abby in the kitchen. You'll never keep us straight, no one does, we don't mind. Would you like the fire, sir? I think so, what a cold morning it is.'

*　　　*　　　*

After breakfast, Alice and Theo escorted Paul to Percy's rooms. Alice, tour guide, led the way past dining room, music room, boot room, office, red drawing room, conservatory and across the hall to a long room that spanned the house from front to back, with windows at both ends and thousands of books in shelves from floor to ceiling. 'This is the library,' she said. 'My favourite room. It's in the oldest part of the house, built in 1539 on the site of a Carmelite nunnery.'

Chairs and tables stood in groups, inclined towards each other like old scholars in the midst of profound discourse. Over the mantel hung a painting of a golden-haired woman beside a woodland pool. A man's severed head and limbs lay at her feet; blood flowed among black stones and tiny white flowers. Paul felt his stomach rise, shook his head, pushed it down. It's just a painting, he told himself; it has nothing to do with me.

'That's St Ælfhild,' Theo said, and Paul caught a glimpse of understanding in her eyes. 'Alice, tell the story.'

'St Ælfhild lived in the seventh century,' Alice

said. 'Her father was a Saxon king; he had a palace here. One day she was bathing with her maids at the pool below the spring on the hill, and she had a vision of the Virgin Mary.'

'Well,' Theo said, 'she thought it was the Virgin Mary, or, more likely, someone told her it was. I beg your pardon. Do go on, Alice.'

'She forswore all worldly ties,' Alice said, 'and lived alone in a hut by the pool. She'd been engaged to Prince . . . Somebody and when she refused to marry him, he tried to abduct her. But the instant he touched her his hand fell off, so he grabbed her with the other, and it fell off too, and his arms and his legs. Afterwards, she felt sorry for him so she poured water on to his limbs and healed him. To *heal* is from the same root as *whole*, an Anglo-Saxon word in fact, did you know that?'

'No, I didn't,' Paul said. 'The painting's a Jarlath Quinn, isn't it?'

Theo nodded. 'He did a series of paintings from the history of Farundell—there's another one.'

They crossed to a canvas showing a man in a fur-trimmed robe, standing by the lake. 'That's Tobias Damory,' Theo said. 'He was a scholar and a famous alchemist during Elizabeth's reign. We know quite a lot about him because many of his journals and letters have been preserved; they're in the Ashmolean now. He had one of the largest libraries in England, hundreds of volumes. That was a time when it was possible for one man's scholarship to encompass pretty much the totality of human knowledge, and when there was not such a wide gulf as there now seems to be between such subjects as philosophy, the natural sciences and . . .

41

what we would today perhaps call mysticism.'

Tobias was gazing out at the island; he held a small green book open in his hands. 'What's that book?' Paul asked.

'It's called *Pymander*—Tobias's English translation of a famous collection of Greek texts, mostly dialogues between Hermes Trismegistos, an ancient Egyptian sage, and his disciples; they recount the teachings of Pymander, the mind of god, about the nature of reality and the journeys of the soul. See, Jarlath has written Tobias's favourite passage around the frame: "It is possible for the Soul to become a God while yet it abideth in the Body of a Man, if it Contemplate the Beauty of the Good."'

'Hm,' Paul said. Theo had read it off with an air of great familiarity. 'What does it mean?'

'That's a good question.' Theo studied him. 'Or several good questions, since you'd have to start by asking what he means by each of his terms: soul, become, god, and so on. And of course, it's of limited use to consider only what these words might mean to you today—you'd have to understand what they meant to whoever wrote them. That sort of enquiry inevitably turns into a Hydra.'

'Yes, I suppose it does.' Paul waited, hoping she'd make a start on the monster, but that was apparently not her intention.

'There are many interesting books here, including, of course,' she gestured to an adjacent shelf, 'the *Pymander*. Feel free to explore the library yourself.'

'Thank you. I could get lost in here.'

'Well, as they say, the further in you go, the

bigger it gets. I suppose that could just as well apply to libraries.'

What? Paul thought. He'd never heard anyone say that.

Alice led them past—she pointed and named—the morning room and the family stairs, the blue drawing room, the billiard room. At the end of the hall Theo knocked on a final door, which was promptly opened by a short, dapper, bow-legged man.

'Hello, Henry,' said Theo. 'We've brought Mr Asher. Paul, we'll leave you here.'

From the doorway to a bedroom emerged a gaunt old man, leaning heavily on a cane, eyes shielded by tinted spectacles. His face was deeply lined but lively and intelligent; he was impeccably dressed in an elegant herringbone suit. 'How do you do, Mr Asher? Welcome to Farundell.' He extended his hand and Paul returned the strong, bony grip.

'How do you do, Lord Damory? It's a pleasure to meet you.'

'Oh, drop the title; it's a truly useless appendage. I've always found it a trifle embarrassing, to tell you the truth. We don't go in for a lot of formality here, as you may have noticed. Call me Percy. Please, come and sit down.' He made his way unerringly to a chair by the fire and gestured Paul to the chair opposite. Henry dropped a blanket over Percy's knees. 'Stop fussing, Old Hen. Go away.'

'Yes, sir,' Henry said. He tucked the blanket in before he left.

Paul surveyed the room. Windows and a French door overlooked a lawn, still cloaked in mist;

43

dozens of glass-fronted display cases containing moths of every size and colour covered most of the walls. Percy filled a pipe from a jar at his elbow. 'If you smoke, Paul, would you be so good as to do so now? It will save me some trouble with Henry if he thinks the smoke is yours.'

'Of course,' Paul said, and lit a cigarette. 'Though I don't think he'll be deceived; he gave you a very suspicious look before he left.'

'Ha, the Old Hen. He likes to fuss; it gives him something to do and I'm sure he thinks that without his steadfast influence towards the good I would never have survived so long. He may be right. Never mind, we have twenty minutes of peace before he comes to check on me.' He pushed aside the blanket, lit his pipe, coughed, and puffed more carefully. 'Maggie said you were a friend of my great-nephew Val St John Vere, and you'd lived in Paris.'

'Yes, that's right. I went there after the war—I thought I could write. I had a small inheritance from an aunt, and I made it last, but now . . . well, I'm very grateful for this job.'

'I'm grateful you've come,' Percy said. 'I think we'll get on well. You're American, aren't you? You don't sound as American as some.'

'My family's English, I had a Scottish nanny, and I haven't been to America for years.'

'I like the accent. My wife Odelia was from Virginia.' Percy gestured to a portrait over the mantel. 'That's her. Jarlath painted that, oh, twenty-odd years ago.'

A pale, sweet-faced woman sat in a chair, gazing down at a smoky, translucent crystal sphere in her hands. The man who stood behind her seemed to

44

be from another time—an array of extravagant curls tumbled over his shoulders and frilly cravat. He was sketchily painted, blurry and vague, though the face was clear: long nose, lips compressed, an air of sadness and hauteur. Whoever he was, he wasn't Percy, though he looked vaguely familiar.

'Who's that with her in the painting?' Paul said.

'Ah, that's my great-great-grandfather Francis.'

'The ghost? I've heard about him. Does he really exist, then?'

'Really exist? I couldn't begin to speculate. Theo's the one to talk to if you have a metaphysical hair you want split. I'm told he dislikes the term ghost—finds it demeaning and inaccurate. I've never seen him myself, you understand. Some people do, some don't. Jarlath does, obviously, and Theo, of course. I can . . . sort of feel him, if you know what I mean, when he comes around. Which is not that often, I don't think, now Odelia's gone. I expect he meets her elsewhere.'

Paul studied the portrait. Behind the sombre, unsmiling expression, Jarlath had caught a hint of amusement in the man's eyes and Paul realised why he looked familiar. That fellow by the gate had been the very image of him—he supposed the surrounding area must be full of Damory by-blows.

'Francis and Odelia had an extremely close friendship,' Percy said; 'indeed she knew him before she met me or came to Farundell. He brought her here, in fact. I used to be quite jealous of him. Now, I find that extremely amusing.'

'But if he was your great-great-grandfather,' Paul said, 'he must have lived at least a hundred years ago, so how did she know him?'

45

'She saw him, in that stone of hers.' Percy relit his pipe. 'Do have another cigarette, Paul. Henry will be back soon. Now, about the work. Knowing my daughter, I have no idea what she may have told you about my plans.'

'She said you want to write your memoirs.'

'Yes, and I seem to have left it too late to do myself. Please understand—my blindness is not something I regret. I can see,' he tapped his forehead, 'right here. I'm beginning to believe nothing is ever lost, it's all . . . somewhere, waiting to be remembered.'

He paused for a long time and Paul wondered if he'd fallen asleep; then he spoke again. 'There is a story I have to tell, about things that happened far away from here and long ago, things I still don't fully understand but that are closer and more present to me now than any of this.' He gestured at walls, floor, furniture. 'I came to a certain moment and I made a choice, though only lately have I recognised that it was a choice, and because of it my life is not a vague line that began nowhere and trails off into nothing. No, there's been a point to it, after all—a point around which it always has revolved, though I didn't know it. The choice, the moment, the memory of it, has been burning in me like a dark sun whose gravity pulled me and set my path long before it happened, and ever since. And I cannot move on until I find my way back to that moment, remember it, tell it and get it out of me. It's not something I want to do; it's something I have to do.'

Henry returned to a room clouded by thick smoke. 'It's very foggy out this morning, sir,' he said. 'Shall I open a window for a moment?'

Percy chortled. 'By all means, Henry, if you think it advisable.' His laughter turned into a coughing fit and he made no resistance as Henry replaced the discarded blanket. 'I think that is enough for today, Paul. Tustian will arrange a desk and a typewriting machine for you in the library and you can order whatever supplies you need from the stationers' in Exley. Thank you for coming. Perhaps we can begin tomorrow.'

*   *   *

Paul stood in the middle of the library and turned slowly around. It was, without question, the most wonderful room he'd ever seen. All his life, books had been his companions, his solace and his luxury. His father bought antique volumes by the yard to furnish the library in the Beacon Hill house and never opened a single one. Paul had prowled the neglected shelves whose contents were arranged by colour and size rather than subject: astronomy and palaeontology next to long, complex eighteenth-century novels, travellers' tales around the corner from architectural histories, an illustrated zoological encyclopaedia rubbing worn shoulders with schematics of locomotives. Here at Farundell, while there was evidence of an underlying order, it was disappearing under more recent accretions. The shelves were stuffed with books, books piled horizontally into every gap, stacked on tables and the floor. He inhaled the seductive scent of paper and ink, vellum, buckram, linen, leather—the scent, to him, of words themselves, and the thoughts of writers long dead or far away—a bit musty, overlaid with beeswax, lamp oil and wood smoke. He imagined wandering from book to book, mind to mind, world to world, following a random trail of gold-lettered, multi-hued volumes: the weight of a book in his hand, the smooth binding, the soft cr-cr-crackle as he opened it, the coloured endpapers, the first glimpse of the old-fashioned typeface, with its elaborate serifs and decorative chapter headings; the red silk marker holding the last reader's place. Where to start?

Postponing the pleasure, he crossed the room to look out over the meadow and misty lake. Near the window stood a glass-fronted cabinet filled with curious statues and artefacts: Egyptian animal-headed deities and inscribed coffin-like figures, a chalcedony sphinx, a narwhal tusk. A pale ray of sun broke through and fell on a sphere of smoky crystal—it must be the one Odelia had been holding in the painting. The key was in the cabinet's delicate brass lock; Paul had reached out and turned it without thinking, then stopped himself. Would anyone mind? But no, surely if they didn't want one to open it for a closer look they wouldn't leave the key.

The ball was far heavier than he'd expected, but it seemed to grow lighter as he held it up to the window. He could see himself and the room reflected in its surface, and below the surface a landscape of ephemeral cliffs and ravines, meandering veins like cloudy rivers in the rock. He turned it slowly in his hands and was drawn deeper into the interior until a sudden wave of vertigo nearly buckled his knees and he tore his eyes away.

What the hell was that? It felt like a falling dream, or that weird swimmy sensation that sometimes came over him as he lay in bed waiting to fall asleep. It had been common when he was a child, he recalled, haunting those times between waking and sleep. He'd feared it, and learned that he could avoid it by never sleeping on his back.

He replaced the crystal carefully in the cabinet, locked the door and returned to his tour of the bookshelves.

Tustian appeared with a typewriter. They moved a table to the window overlooking the courtyard; lamps and a chair were brought into place. Paul made sure that his back would be to the painting of St Ælfhild, facing instead a little portrait— another Jarlath Quinn—of a girl with a rabbit in her lap. Her features were too strong to be pretty, but combined to make a face of idiosyncratic beauty. Her dark eyes gazed out with a disconcerting directness.

'Who's that?' Paul asked.

'That's Miss Sylvie,' Tustian said. 'Mr and Mrs Quinn's eldest daughter. She's in Italy now, studying fresco painting, I believe, but we expect her home next month.'

Paul made her a small bow, as he'd be seeing her every day.

*　　　*　　　*

After lunch the sky cleared and Stephen invited Paul to join the children on a bird-watching expedition. They set off up a track that curved around the hill behind the house, crowded by oak and beech and dotted with puddles like small lakes. Roger and Sophie raced ahead, with points for maximum splashing. Alice walked sedately with

49

Stephen; they conversed in Latin and paused from time to time to peer through binoculars and consult their *Pocket Guide to the Birds of Britain*.

When they came to small stone bridge across a brook Roger and Sophie clambered down the bank. 'Alice, come and see!' Roger called. 'There's been an awful disaster.'

Paul looked down. Miniature houses in a variety of architectural styles perched on the edge of the stream, joined by winding lanes and steps cut into the rock. Carved wooden dolls sat in gardens, stood on the streets, gathered on the wharves where boats and barges moored. Further downstream a medieval castle loomed over a lake with a rocky island. Little cows and sheep and horses grazed mossy pastures; isolated farmsteads dotted the hills.

Paul climbed carefully down the bank and bent to examine the fine detail on a villa near his left foot. There was a figure at work in the garden, posed with a tiny wheelbarrow. The buildings and dolls had clearly been made by various hands, but all to the same scale, about an inch to a foot.

'Welcome to Arcadia,' said Stephen.

'Stay on the Path of the Gods so you don't hurt anything.' Alice pointed out a series of stepping stones.

'Arcadia?' Paul said.

'The mythical kingdom of Hermes,' Stephen said. 'Francis Damory built a temple of Hermes at the top of the hill, so this became Arcadia. He also built a temple of Aphrodite on the island in the lake—looted, I've heard, from Cyprus, as was the done thing in those days.'

'Who made it? I've never seen anything like it.'

'It was started by Percy and Theo's father and his sisters and brothers,' Stephen said, 'then expanded by each generation.'

Paul picked his way through the town to the lake. Its island was topped with little columns and a hugely out-of-scale Venus de Milo on a plinth inscribed 'Souvenir du Louvre'.

Roger and Sophie were clearing detritus from a flood that had overturned some boats and dumped mounds of mud in front gardens. They uncovered three of the dolls and summoned Alice to examine them. One, she said, was dead, and this she put in her pocket. The others were tucked into their houses.

They continued up the hill; the children wandered off in search of rare birds. A clearing opened out on the left; a path led to a stone building overgrown with ivy.

'The family chapel,' Stephen said. 'Not much used, as you can see.'

'It looks like something out of a story,' Paul said. Tall windows of plain glass arced between stone mullions, one on either side of the door. 'Can one go in?'

'Of course. That's the key. It was awfully creaky last time I tried.'

Paul took a large iron key from its hook by the door, inserted it into the lock. It rasped, turned a few degrees and refused to move further. He extracted it with difficulty and replaced it. 'Not today, apparently.'

He peered through a window. The walls were plain white plaster; there were no pews, but a congregation of unmatched wooden chairs ranged about the single open space and an enormous old sofa sagged beneath a high, round window at the far end.

Behind the chapel generations of Damorys reposed under modest headstones, with an occasional obelisk or angel. Stephen pointed to a corner of the graveyard where a slab tilted among the thick roots of an ancient oak. 'That's the oldest—Tobias Damory. He built the chapel.'

Paul bent to read the inscription, still legible though weathered and mottled with lichens:

Tobias Geoffrey Herbert Damory
1538–1620.
God made Eternity, Eternity the World,
the World Time, and Time Generation.

'And that's the newest.' Stephen indicated a plain headstone near the path. 'James Arthur Damory, 1883–1915. Percy's oldest son. I don't think he's ever got over it.' They turned away from the graves and back to the track. 'You were in the war, weren't you?'

Paul nodded. 'Medical Corps.'

'Do you mind my asking? No one wants to talk about it. I know it was awful, and everyone wants to forget. I was too young to do anything more than roll bandages and read the names in the Killed and Missing columns.'

'Did you lose anyone in your family?'

'A brother, and two of my uncles.'

'Oh. I'm sorry.'

'No, it's all right, past now. What about you?'

'My two half-brothers.'

'I'm sorry too. Do you miss them?'

'Not especially. We were never close.'

'Were you in the same regiment?'

'No, I'd come to England to join up, in '14. They were both officers in the US Army, so they had to wait until the States came in.'

'You came all the way over here to join up? Gosh, how awfully brave.'

'Hardly. At the time, it was the easy option.'

'What do you mean?'

'Oh God, long story.'

'That's fine, it's still a long walk to the top.'

Paul laughed. 'All right. I'd been sent down from West Point—that's the American Sandhurst, you know—my brothers had gone there and done very well . . .'

'And you didn't.'

'No. My career there was a disaster.' He grinned, remembering. 'It's funny now, but then, well, it was a disaster. In all kinds of ways. The one thing I learned was that I don't have the right temperament for an officer. It was all pretty pointless, and to give absurd orders seemed even more stupid than merely obeying them.'

'I can understand that,' Stephen said. 'I used to wonder why everybody didn't just stop, just simply refuse to do such patently idiotic things. I was told a child couldn't understand. But you joined the Army anyway—why? That is, unless it's nosy of me to ask. Tell me to shut up if you like.'

'I don't mind,' Paul said. 'Anything before the war feels like it happened to another person. After the West Point debacle my father sent me to medical school. It is his view that no profession is really suitable for a gentleman but war, and if, through age or infirmity—or, worst of all, the

53

misfortune to live in peaceful times—war is not available, politics. But I was too young for politics, so he settled on medicine as the least ignoble alternative. Lawyers were beneath contempt, churchmen ridiculous, business for peasants— what else was there? It never occurred to him, or even to me, that I might have something to say about what to do with my life. At first it was all right; I enjoyed chemistry and biology and the elegant anatomical engravings we had to copy. But then I made the rather awkward discovery that I could not abide the sight of blood, and the very idea of cutting open a body was enough to make me ill. At my first glimpse of the cadaver laid out for dissection I dropped into a dead faint, and I repeated this performance regularly until I gave up. It was because I didn't dare tell my father I'd quit that I caught a boat for England. Everyone thought the war would be over very fast—mostly, we worried it'd be over before we had a chance to see any action. Now that's really a laugh, because if ever there was a war of inaction, that was it. And if any action occurred in one's vicinity, one was unlikely to see it before one was blown up or shot to pieces.' He glanced at Stephen. 'Sorry.'

'No, don't apologise. Go on. How on earth did you end up in the Medical Corps?'

'Oh, that's the most amusing part. When they found out I'd been in med school, they assumed I had to be nearly a doctor and reassigned me. The Army is a literal-minded beast.'

'Good grief. So how did you manage?'

'Well, they don't take no for an answer. They don't ask in the first place. An enlisted man is their property. One does what one is ordered to do, or one is shot. Quite simple. I was attempting to resign myself to a ridiculous fate when our colonel took me in hand and taught me a few little tricks. He was a strange man, Colonel Woods. Not the sort you'd expect to find in the Army at all. He taught me that one can control what one thinks, what one allows into one's mind. He taught me a way of looking at things,' Paul made his hands into a telescope and raised it to his eye, 'a way of cutting out what one doesn't need to see and focusing very hard on the job one has to do. A way of concentrating, I guess, and not getting distracted. He taught me to keep saying, over and over, "It doesn't matter, carry on, it doesn't matter, carry on." And it helped, and I managed. By the end nothing bothered me at all, not blood or bodies or piles of amputated limbs or . . . oh God, sorry.'

'No, don't be sorry. It's no good if we all try to pretend it never happened.'

'Isn't it? I don't know. It was so . . .' Paul groped for words and failed, '. . . that I sometimes find it easier to believe it was just a long, horrible dream, best forgotten.'

He stopped, turned away, lit a cigarette and stared into the trees. He'd noticed that just looking at trees calmed his mind, and the colour green, in all its variations, nourished him as though he could absorb it through his eyes. Stephen walked ahead and disappeared from sight; after a minute Paul followed slowly. The track curved around the hillside; water trickled from crevices in the rock on one side and on the other, beyond the waving treetops, cloud shadows marched across the valley.

A wide arc of steep, stone-cut steps led upwards.

At their foot, a chipped teacup sat beneath a dripping spring, overflowing into a shallow basin. Paul, suddenly thirsty, drank eagerly. The water was icy and delicious.

The temple of Hermes stood on a narrow sward of tufty grass with trees crowding close behind. It was round and domed, and quite a bit larger than Paul had expected. A deep colonnade surrounded it, with a mosaic floor and stone pillars. Stephen was lounging on a sunny bench beside an open door.

Paul stepped inside. The air was cool and hushed; the high, curved ceiling glowed with golden stars on a deep blue ground. The floor of green marble was inlaid with red stone in a pattern of interlocking circles, angles and lines that disappeared into the dimness of the interior. There were eight doors alternating with murals showing Hermes in various forms, surrounded by quotations and epithets in *trompe l'œil* chiselled marble letters.

Here was Hermes Psychopompos, guide of souls, sitting on a rock with his foot in the River Styx. *He led them*, read the inscription, *through the mire of war, past the streams of Okeanos, the White Rock, the Gates of the Moon and the Land of Dreams, and soon they came to the field of Asphodel, where the phantoms of the dead have their habitation.*

In the next panel Hermes Logios, god of language, was shown strolling with a tall, elegant woman identified as Mnemosyne, goddess of memory. Flowers sprang up in their footsteps and each, Paul saw, was a word.

There was Hermes of the Crossroads, Hermes of Guard Dogs, Hermes of Rustic Divination, casting pebbles on the ground. In his role as Bringer of Dreams, he had a little vial of something blue and silvery that he poured, smiling, into a sleeping woman's ear.

Marble statues stood around the room—Hermes with caduceus, Hermes with crescent-moon-topped staff, Hermes with lyre and adoring nymph. Paul circled the tableau, caressed the nymph's cool, silky calf.

'You appreciate my beauties,' said a voice from the shadows. A man's voice, too deep to be Stephen's.

'Hello?' Paul turned round. 'Who's that?'

'Who were you expecting, the great god Hermes himself? On your first visit?'

A man in a pale green velvet coat—Paul saw the nap of the velvet with extraordinary clarity—sauntered from behind a statue.

'What?' said Paul. 'Who?' It was that strange fellow at the gate . . . or no, could it be? 'Oh my God, you're Francis Damory.' He felt a rush of light-headedness, as though he'd inhaled ether.

The man inclined his head and made a small genuflection.

Not taking his eyes off the figure, Paul called out, 'Stephen, would you come here for a moment, please?'

Francis twirled his silver-headed walking stick. The handle was a crystal egg, with a serpent twined around. It sent off little slivers of light.

Stephen appeared at the door. 'What is it?'

Paul pointed at Francis. 'Don't you see him?'

'See who?'

'Well, I'm pretty sure it's Francis Damory.'

'The ghost? Really? Where?'

'Right there, about ten feet in front of me. I'm pointing at him.'

'It's rude to point,' said Francis.

'There, didn't you hear that? He said it's rude to point. You really don't see him, do you? Or hear him?'

'No, I don't. Are you sure it's Francis?'

'You could always ask, you know,' Francis said. 'I am standing right here, after all. And just because you suppose me to be some sort of ghost,' he held up his hand, 'no, don't try to deny it—there is no excuse for discourtesy.'

'I beg your pardon,' said Paul.

'What for?' asked Stephen.

'Not you,' said Paul. 'Are you Francis Damory?'

'Of course I am, you numskull.' Francis rapped Paul smartly on the head with his stick and strode out of the door.

'Ouch!' Paul hurried after him, but when he reached the portico there was no one in sight.

'I take it he left,' Stephen said. 'Gosh. You really saw him. And talked to him. What did he look like?'

'Exactly like the portrait in Percy's room, and completely real—not pale or grey or transparent at all.' Paul reached for a cigarette, lit it without paying attention to what he was doing, failed to shake out the match, burned his fingers. 'Ouch. Damn.'

'Do you often see ghosts?' Stephen asked.

'No, never. At least I don't think so.' He remembered the man at the gate, and Madagascar's strange reaction. That must have been him as well. But surely ghosts should appear more . . . ghostly? He reached for a cigarette, then realised he was already smoking one.

Had that really happened? From above came a hoarse, mewing cry; he craned his neck to watch a large, reddish bird circle. Already Francis was fading from memory, becoming vague as a dream. The event was so unlikely, so singular and fundamentally incompatible with his mundane life, the sunny day and all the normal things it contained that it was easiest to place it in the category of dream and let it slip away—as if ordinary reality itself wanted to seal over the strange rupture as fast as possible. He rubbed his head, fingers finding an incipient lump. How on earth did a ghost leave him with a lump on his head?

*   *   *

That night Paul sat up late trying to remember every detail of his encounter with Francis. He'd been besieged with questions that he'd answered as best he could, embarrassed by all the attention and feeling that his own understanding was driven further away every time he opened his mouth. By evening the story had spread throughout the household. Tustian ventured to offer his congratulations, and proudly informed Paul that he himself had once seen Francis in the old days when Lady Odelia was alive, though only as a vague, shadowy figure. Alice had asked a highly detailed series of questions about Francis's speech, appearance and manner, and made notes of Paul's answers. Percy seemed pleased, and asked after his great-great-grandfather as though he were any old friend. Theo merely smiled, and Paul had the impression, rather disconcerting now he thought

59

about it, that she wasn't surprised.

He'd been speaking about his colonel to Stephen, which was an odd coincidence. Colonel Woods was always seeing ghosts hanging about the battlefields and the wards. Sometimes, he'd said, the air was so thick with them it shimmered. But Francis didn't shimmer; he'd appeared as solid as a living man. Paul fingered the bump on his head. That was certainly real, and perplexing. For some reason a curious reticence had come over him at that point in the telling and he'd not mentioned it to anyone. Why the hell did Francis hit him? To prove he could have an effect in the physical world? All right, point proved. So what? He'd called him a numskull. Just a random insult, or did he really mean numb skull? Was that a reason to cause it pain? He prodded the bump. Not numb there, anyway. Not now.

*   *   *

In the graveyard behind the chapel a ceremony is under way. A hole in the earth gapes open; his father stands at the head. At his command soldiers seize Paul, bind him and lower him into a stone sarcophagus. Tobias steps forward and reads from a little green book. 'God made Eternity, Eternity the World, the World Time, and Time Generation.'

The soldiers slide the cover into place. The darkness is complete. Fear grips him for the first time, and he struggles against the bonds. 'Stop this dream!' he says out loud. 'I don't like it.'

To his relief he wakes instantly. He lies for a moment in the quiet darkness, his fear fading. Sitting up to reach for his cigarettes, he smacks his head

60

against . . . against what? Stone. He hasn't woken after all; or he has, and he really is in some sort of tomb. He extends his hands and feet, encounters stone in all directions, cool and smooth. 'Am I dreaming?' he whispers.

There is a faint echo but no answer.

'OK,' he says, refusing to whisper in his own dream. 'Let's apply reason. How likely is it that I've been taken unawares from my bed, because that's the last place I remember, and transported to a tomb? It is obviously far more likely that I'm dreaming, in which case I have only to wait and see what happens next.'

He folds his hands behind his head and begins to hum. The acoustics in here are marvellous, he thinks. He listens to the tune he's humming and can't place it at first, then realises, with a snort of laughter, that it's last year's hit, 'I'd Much Rather Be Dreaming'.

'Do be quiet,' Francis says, and Paul sits up with a start. To his surprise he doesn't crack his head on the stone. He's in the temple of Hermes, reclining on a blue silk chaise longue. 'Thanks for getting me out of there,' he says.

'You did it by yourself.'

'I did?'

'Your body is a stone box, as it were, and you got out by remembering that you're dreaming. You're in another dimension.'

'I'm sorry, but I don't believe in any of that,' says Paul.

'Nevertheless, here you are.'

Paul gets up, finds his cigarettes in his pocket and lights one, then offers one to Francis, who accepts. He sits back down, suddenly aware that he's been

61

having a conversation with a ghost.

'I am not,' says Francis, 'a ghost, if by ghost you mean a wafty, fugacious, pathetic remnant of a being whose disturbed soul compels it to linger on the material plane after it has died in the usual way. But you would not understand and anyway, you won't remember.'

'I won't?'

'No, because you are dreaming now.'

'I am? Oh yes, of course I am. I'm dreaming now.'

4

Alice summoned Roger and Sophie to her room, locked the door and turned out the lights. It was always good to make sure they understood the seriousness of the occasion, and they were afraid of the dark. She allowed their nervousness to build until she judged the time right, then declared in a sonorous voice, 'Let there be light,' as she struck a match and lit the candle. It cast ghoulish shadows up her face, and she'd spent a long time in front of the mirror assessing different angles to determine which was the worst.

She placed the candle on her nightstand, which, pulled to the centre of the room, served as the altar. The Arcadian who had died in the flood lay on a handkerchief. She directed Roger and Sophie to stand on either side and picked up the Book of Records. 'We are here to bury this citizen of Arcadia,' she read his name ribbon, 'Philemus Abacus Dexter. Let him be made ready.' She gestured to Roger. 'You, Priest Roger, remove his

62

worldly attire.'

'His what?'

'His clothes, stupid. Take off his clothes. And you, Priestess Sophia, fetch water for the laving.'

'For the what?'

'Oh Bleeding Jesus, Mary and Joseph.' It was her new favourite curse, learned from the butcher's boy. 'Why are you so ignorant? It means to be washed, stupid—lave, same root as lavatory, laundry, obviously to do with washing. Don't you know anything?' She gritted her teeth. 'So, Priest Roger, is he ready to be laved?'

'Yup.'

'Say, Yes, High Priestess.'

'Oh, Alice.'

'Say it, or I'll get you while you're sleeping.'

'Yes, High Priestess.'

Alice lowered Philemus Abacus Dexter into a silver tureen while Sophie brought the pitcher from the washstand and poured. She lifted him out and held him as Priest and Priestess wrapped him in strips torn from an old sheet. 'These are his cerements,' she said, '*cere* meaning wax.' She dripped a few drops from the candle on to the wrapping, to hold the end in place, then impressed her right forefinger. She thought that the strips of fabric should be somehow soaked in the wax, but she'd tried that and it hadn't worked. 'Philemus Abacus Dexter, we send you to your rest . . .'

'To sleep perchance to dream,' said Roger.

'To your eternal rest,' Sophie said.

'No,' said Alice, 'not eternal. Eternal means forever. This is not eternal, it's only until he gets reborn.' The bundle was tucked in a little coffin, and the coffin in the bottom drawer of her chest.

'And now that this one has died and been buried,' she made a tick in the Buried column in the Book of Records, 'it is time for someone else to be reborn.' She opened the top drawer of the chest and surveyed the Arcadians sleeping there, each in a plain white robe. She selected one and took up an old Roman coin with an Emperor's head on one side and a lady in flowing robes on the other. She spun it on the altar; it landed with the lady side uppermost. 'A woman,' she said. 'And now she shall receive her new name. You first, Priest.'

Roger screwed up his eyes. 'Pod . . . Pon . . . Pomeroy.'

Alice turned to Sophie.

'Pomeroy . . . Pomeroy . . . Pomeroy Butterfly.'

Alice sighed. 'All right. Pomeroy Butterfly.' She consulted the list of surnames. 'Pomeroy Butterfly Eichenhorn.' She turned the pages of the Book of Records, entered the name and date. Sophie cut a length of white silk ribbon and Roger wrote the name in indelible ink.

'And what shall be her occupation?'

'Cook,' said Roger.

'No, nurse,' said Sophie.

'What about a soldier?' Roger said.

'No,' Alice said. 'She shall be a gardener.'

She lifted the figure towards her lips and whispered in her ear, 'Pomeroy Butterfly Eichenhorn, you are reborn as a gardener in the Land of Arcadia.'

Sophie discarded the old water and brought fresh while Roger selected garments from a basket. Alice removed the white robe, dipped the figure in the water, passed her through the candle flame, tied the name-ribbon to her neck and

64

handed her over to be dressed. When she was ready, she went to sit atop the chest until morning, when she would begin her new life.

Alice dismissed Roger and Sophie. They were annoying beyond belief, but they were all she had to work with. Maybe she'd be better off with dogs, or horses, or cats. If they could be trained to obey. It was an unkind thought but what was the difference? She had to tell them everything. Come, go, pick up this, do that. They had no understanding at all.

She stared into the candle. The flame twisted and danced. Sometimes if she stared at it hard enough it grew and grew until it filled all her vision, and she could see little lizards squirming inside it.

Artemis leapt on to her lap and the flame shrank to its normal size. It was nearly midnight. She changed into her nightgown, blew out the candle, climbed into bed, then got up again. She checked whether she was awake, pulled on her dressing gown and went to see her Great-Aunt Theo.

*   *   *

Theo sat by the fire in her sitting room, Simon de Greer's classic *Alchymical Garden* open on her lap. The book had belonged to Tobias. The fine vellum was still supple after four hundred years, and lavishly illuminated with diagrams of planting arrangements suited to the various planetary influences. Circles and arcs and waves interlaced with triangles, stars and squares; leaves, flowers and roots surged beyond their borders, colonised the margins and the gaps between words.

She stroked a gilded capital, let her mind drift towards its source. The stone carrel by the cloister, slip-slap of passing feet, breath held, the strip of gold leaf catches the sun, is pressed into place, burnished.

No, further. Master de Greer, not a copyist.

The old man turns, beckons. Bundles of drying herbs crowd the low ceiling, strange scents hang in luminous, many-hued clouds. A brazier, banked down, glows red; a stone bowl steams. 'For Luna,' he says, 'poppy, gillyflower, orpine. For Venus, thyme, self-heal, dittany; for Sol, rosemary and angelica. But you must not,' and his eyes grow fierce, 'forget Lord Mercury, for he is Hermes, the shower of the way, and his herbs are lavender, fennel and dill.'

The image faded as she slid back into time. Someone was coming. Ah, Alice. She put the book aside as her great-niece appeared at the door, a tartan robe belted over her nightdress, feet bare.

'Theo,' Alice said, 'there's something I keep meaning to ask you but I only remember when I'm about to fall asleep, and I usually fall asleep and forget but this time I made myself get up.'

'Come and sit here, then.' Theo patted the spot beside her.

Alice sat and folded her legs under her. 'First I have to ask if I'm awake right now.'

'That depends what you mean by awake.'

'I mean not asleep.'

'That depends what you mean by asleep.'

'Oh Theo, please.'

'Yes, all right. You're awake right now, here with me, and not asleep in your bed.'

'Oh good. Because sometimes when I come to

see you I'm not, am I? Awake, I mean. Or is it that I'm dreaming and I haven't really been to see you at all?' Alice stopped, entangled in words. It was so clear in her mind, but the harder she tried to explain, the more confused it became. 'Sometimes at night I wake up, not all the way up but definitely not a dream, because I'm always here, I'm always me, and in dreams usually I'm in different places or I'm other people, and dreams feel different.' Was this taking her closer or further away from the simple thing she wanted to ask? 'So when I'm like that, awake but not really . . .'

'Let's call that something,' said Theo, 'since it's a distinct state of being. What do you think is a good name for it?'

'I call it my moon-body because it's silvery and light, and because when I'm in it I can see my other body, my earth-body, this one,' she patted her leg, 'still asleep in bed.'

'Those are good words,' Theo said. 'Let's use them. So what's the question?'

'Why do I hardly ever see anyone in their moon-body except you, and sometimes Sophie or Roger, or other children, and why, when people are in their earth-bodies, don't they see me?'

'Oh Alice, I hate those "why" questions. Where should I start? What thread should I follow? And any one thread is meaningless unless one understands the fabric.' She pointed to Alice's sleeve. 'Tell me what this is.'

'It's my dressing gown. An ordinary tartan dressing gown.'

'Those are all abstract ideas: my, ordinary, dressing, gown, tartan. I asked what it is.'

'But that is what it is.'

67

'No, that's what you think it is.'

Alice pressed her head between her hands. Sometimes talking to Theo made her brain feel like one big knot.

Theo smiled. 'I'm not being deliberately annoying, Alice. There really, really are no truths one can put into words. I learned, at various times, all sorts of definitions and labels for things like moon-bodies and tartan dressing gowns, and I also learned, eventually, that they were all wrong in one way or another.'

'Oh Theo, why can't you ever just answer?'

'Because an answer someone else gives you is a box.'

This was more confusing than ever. 'A box?'

'If you try to see your own experience through someone else's words, you put yourself in a box, and then you can't see anything at all. I would like you to have the freedom to think, and imagine, and understand the world for yourself. It's for you to decide, Alice. Do you want the pat answers we give to children and the unintelligent or are you ready to live with question after question?'

'All right, I'll live with the questions. But I've got so many—where do I start?'

'Start with your own experience.'

Alice looked at her sleeve again. 'I see colours: red, purple, yellow, blue, white and orange.'

'And?'

'It's a pattern made of threads in these different colours, that pass above and beneath each other.'

'And?'

'It's made of wool, of fibres from an animal, from the hair of an animal that hold together, but are floppy, not stiff . . .'

'And?'

Alice raised it to her face, sniffed. 'It smells like wool.' She stroked it with her fingertips. 'And it's a bit scratchy.'

'And?'

'Oh, Theo, and what? What more is there?'

'You tell me.'

'I can't think of anything else.'

'Then stop thinking.'

'How can I figure it out without thinking?'

'Don't figure, don't think. What is the experience of it?'

Alice set her jaw and glared.

'You are banging at it from the outside, Alice. Go *in* to it.' Theo tapped Alice's forehead.

Alice closed her eyes, remembering how it felt to put on her dressing gown, in the evening after a bath, or in the morning if she was cold. It was warm and comfortable, made her feel snug. It was more like being dressed than wearing her nightgown only, but not as dressed as clothes. A sort of in-between feeling, not for daytime, waking life, nor for sleep. Like her moon-body, in fact . . . ah, that was the experience Theo was trying to make her recognise—the experience of something slipped into and out of as she hovered between waking and sleep. She opened her eyes. 'It's the in-between-ness of it, isn't it?'

'Very good,' Theo said, and seemed prepared to leave it at that.

'So now will you answer my question?' said Alice.

'All right, Alice, as you've worked so very hard on experiencing your dressing gown, I will give you an answer, but you will find it only leads to more questions.' Theo ruminated for a long time; Alice's anticipation grew. 'I beg your pardon,' Theo said at last, 'but what was the question?'

'Oh Theo. You're teasing me, aren't you?'

'Yes, just a little. You are so very serious.'

'But will you answer? Please?'

'I will tell you something about one thread.' Theo drew her finger along a red line in the plaid. 'You can follow it,' she traced it up Alice's sleeve, 'to see how it connects with other threads.'

Alice studied the path of the red thread. Where it crossed yellow threads, they made orange; where it crossed blue, they made purple. She'd never really looked at her own dressing gown before. 'I think I understand,' she said.

'If you look at your experience,' Theo said, 'you will notice that there are four distinct states: ordinary waking state—what you call your earth-body, an in-between state—your moon-body, a dream state and, beyond that, a state of deep sleep, the contents of which very few are able to remember. When people get older they tend to forget everything but what happens when they're in their earth-bodies.'

'But you haven't forgotten.'

'I nearly did. I tried to, but then I remembered again. Most people never remember until they die.'

'How can that be? It's like forgetting how to read, or walk, or swim!'

'Do you remember everything you do in your moon-body?'

'Well, I can't know, can I? If I've forgotten, how can I know what I've forgotten?'

'Exactly.'

70

'But sometimes I remember pieces of things, that I know must be parts of something. It's the same way with dreams—sometimes I remember, and sometimes not. That's the next question I wanted to ask, Theo. What are dreams?'

Theo had refused to answer that, or any other questions; she'd told Alice to contemplate her own experience. And she laid a particular emphasis on the word 'contemplate', confirming that she did not mean merely to think about, saying only, 'You will learn it by trying to do it.'

On the way to her room Alice went into the schoolroom and pulled out the Skeat's *Etymological Dictionary*. Etymology was always the first step. Contemplate, from Latin *contemplari*, to observe, consider, used originally of the augurs who observed a *templum* in the sky; from *con-*, together; and *templum*, a space marked out in the sky for observation—the root of the English word temple. Of course, a temple. She turned the pages. Temple, *templum*, from the Greek *temenos*, a sacred enclosure, a piece of ground cut off and set apart for religious purposes, allied to *temeneis*, to cut. The same root as atom, which meant not-divisible; that was very useful. Her thirsty mind soaked up the information like water. Somehow the very shape and arrangement of the letters that made each word carried, in a mysterious and beautiful way, the meaning itself.

When she got into bed, she lay on her back and imagined a hole cut through the ceiling, a patch of night sky framed, a question to contemplate: Why do people forget? Did they forget suddenly, or just remember less and less often until one day they'd left it too long and realised they'd forgotten? Then

71

forgotten that they'd ever forgotten anything. She wouldn't let herself forget, she'd remind herself every day, every night. Forgetting to contemplate the question any further, she fell asleep.

*   *   *

First thing after breakfast Alice climbed to the schoolroom. It was Stephen's day off; Roger and Sophie had gone to the home farm with Mavis. It was wonderful to be alone. She walked down the familiar hallway of the children's wing: the dark gleaming floor, the green chair, the low chest, the curvy-legged table with the jug of flowers. A scent of wax and polish floated in the air. The corridor was lined with doors—Roger's room, Sophie's room, her room, the door to the servants' wing, the old nursery, guest rooms. She imagined that it was all hers; this was her flat. She was grown up, and this was her very own flat in London, where she lived alone. That would be the dining room, there the sitting room, here her study, her bedroom, her bathroom, a room for the occasional guest. And outside a street, a tree-lined street in the city, with omnibuses and motor cars passing. And her own key to her own door. She stopped and closed her eyes. The person inhabiting these rooms, her grown-up self, was a shadowy figure, tall and lithe, strong and certain. She was busy with something important. Alice struggled to see her face, but she turned away and faded.

When Alice opened her eyes she almost expected the world to have shifted into her imagined one, but it hadn't. She felt around for it again, sensing it was near. It hovered like a soap

72

bubble; she could see into it, dimly, but she couldn't get in. She let it go and went into the schoolroom. There was work to do. She was determined to make up for having fallen asleep without pursuing her questions as she'd intended.

She sat at her desk, reread the entry in the Skeat's and thought about the augurs who marked out the space in the sky. So what was augury? Back to etymology, gateway to the infinite webs of language. Augur, a soothsayer, a diviner by the flight and cries of birds, a priest at Rome who foretold events and interpreted the will of the gods from the flight and singing of birds. From *auis*, bird, and -*gur*, telling. Bird-telling. She listened to the birdsong flowing in the open window and gazed out at the sky.

Three sparrows flew across; immediately she understood why it was necessary to mark out a space to observe. You had to have some way of saying All right, I'm paying attention, show me here, show me now. Else how to know what was a sign, a message from the gods, and what was random chatter?

More birds crossed the window, but she still had no way of interpreting their appearance. One needed a dictionary or a grammar: a single bird meant yes; two meant no; three meant maybe. Flying left to right was good; right to left bad, et cetera. Did the augurs of Rome have such handbooks?

A mouse appeared from behind the cupboard, ran along the skirting and scaled a pile of books. Alice watched, very still. Fortunately Artemis and Madagascar were elsewhere. The mouse sat up to clean itself, preening its fur and combing its

73

whiskers with tiny hands. It had no idea it was sitting on a book, a book containing words, words about ideas, ideas about—she tilted her head to read the title—*The Renaissance View of Nature.* Sometimes the mice ate into books; they'd found holes gnawed. Stephen said they were after the glue in the bindings. What was it like to eat words?

She wrote *Contemplation* on a scrap of paper in her best handwriting, put it in her mouth, chewed, swallowed. It felt as if the world of knowledge, of understanding, the world she wanted to inhabit, was like a giant library and she was a little mouse nibbling at the corners of things. I learn new stuff all the time, she thought, but the amount I still don't know never seems any smaller.

She closed her eyes and imagined the *temenos*, an ancient place, white marble columns, peace and stillness. 'Why do people forget their moon-bodies?' Her enquiry slipped into the silent space and hung, unanswered, in the air.

Start with your own experience, Theo had said. What happens to the experiences I don't remember at all? And dreams—what are dreams? Why do I remember some of them and not others?

Oh, contemplation was turning out to be very difficult. The questions multiplied, no matter what she did. This, she thought, is exactly what a Hydra is, and her peaceful temple was suddenly filled with a writhing multi-headed beast. It was not an angry, snarling beast but a smiling, mocking one. Nevertheless it was expanding to fill the space.

'Stop,' she said aloud. To her surprise, it did. 'Shrink,' she said.

When it had absorbed all its heads but one, it

said, 'May I be permitted to retain one? In order to answer a question, perhaps?' It slithered across the floor to her feet and raised its head. It was only a common green garden snake.

She bent and offered her hand; it slid on to her palm. 'Why do people forget?' she said.

'They grow up; it happens.'

'To everyone?'

'Maybe.' It flickered its tongue.

What an annoying creature. 'Do I have to grow up?'

'Consider the alternative.'

'What alternative? Oh. Well then, how can I be sure to remember?'

'Just be sure never to forget.' And with that, it coiled around her wrist, squeezed gently and vanished.

Alice opened her eyes. Her wrist still tingled. To remember, don't forget. What unimpressive advice. Nevertheless, she could make use of it. She found some green ink and wrote REMEMBER REMEMBER REMEMBER in a spiral around her wrist. That would help—she'd renew it every day. Maybe she could get a tattoo; old Malcolm the head gardener had a faded rose on his arm, with the word 'Mother', but she suspected she wouldn't be allowed.

She stood up and stretched. It was hard to concentrate. She went to the window, leaned out and listened; the woods were full of trills and chirrups. Was it possible that, with proper attention, one could read ordinary things as signs from the gods? She doubted that the gods, whoever they were, would bury their messages in the ceaseless chatter of small birds. They would use a grander bird, a hawk, probably.

Just then, a red kite's hoarse, screaming call sounded from the top of the hill, and was repeated. A shiver ran down Alice's back. 'What are you telling me?' she whispered, and waited, holding her breath. If, she thought quickly, if you call again before I have to breathe, it is a message from the gods. The kite called, and Alice released her breath.

'Thank you,' she whispered. She didn't know what it meant, so she'd just take it as general encouragement.

The hall clock chimed eleven. Maggie had arrived very late last night, but would probably be up by now. Alice went downstairs and silently tried her mother's door; it wasn't locked.

She knocked and went in. 'Bonjour, Maman.'

'Hello, darling,' Maggie said. She was sitting up in bed with a tray of coffee and a pile of letters and magazines. 'How many languages can you say Hello, Mother in?'

'English, French, German, Italian, Latin, Greek, Hebrew. Seven.'

'You're too brilliant, sweetheart. But don't call me Mother; it makes me feel old. Come, let me look at you.'

Alice perched on the slippery peach coverlet. Maggie wore a matching bed-jacket, trimmed with marabou feathers. 'I don't see why you won't have a bob, darling,' Maggie said. 'It would suit your face. And I wish you'd come shopping with me. There is no need to dress like a sixty-year-old governess already.'

'You know I think all that is silly and trivial,' Alice said, in a high-pitched, governessy voice.

76

'Oh yes,' Maggie poked her in the stomach with a long red nail, 'you, are, a, very, serious, girl, who, never, ever . . .' she wiggled her finger, 'ever, ever, ever, laughs.'

Alice had trained herself to be untickleable, which was really very easy—all you had to do was keep breathing calmly, no matter what anyone did. She had triumphed over the best efforts of everyone else, but Maggie had a devastating technique. Alice retreated, nearly upsetting the coffee pot, and went to the dressing table. She rearranged Maggie's scent bottles, moving them around like chess pieces. There was the fat blue one: a Chinese gentleman, kind but cunning; the tall, aristocratic red one, pointed and supercilious like a cardinal; the low, oval white one, a spoiled, fat princess who never went outside; and the gold filigree one with the enormous tasselled bulb—a maharaja on an elephant. She positioned it carefully, sprayed, sneezed.

'Don't inhale while spraying, darling,' said Maggie.

Alice opened the powder box. The ostrich-feather puff was tucked inside, a little sleeping animal. She dusted her arms. 'Do you think I could possibly have a tattoo? You know, like Malcolm has . . .'

'Good heavens, what do you want a tattoo for?'

'Oh, just to help me remember something.'

'What an odd girl you are, sweetheart. No, you certainly may not have a tattoo.'

Alice went upstairs, scrubbed off the powder and perfume, which smelled a lot and was very hard to wash off. Was she really supposed to like things like that? She studied herself in the mirror

77

and tried out a smile; the face twisted into that of a stranger; she scowled and recognised herself again.

5

Paul woke early, before sunrise. The sky was clear and blue above, washed with gold in the east. He pulled on his clothes, went outside and walked down the meadow to the lake. Yellow and purple flowers spread over the muddy shore under the willows; frogs plopped out of sight as he approached. He passed a dock and a weathered boathouse; one path went on around the lake, another climbed beside a rill. He chose the ascending path and worked his way up over tussocks and rocks, sometimes crossing the bright, quick-rushing stream on stepping stones. The soughing of the wind in the trees and the calls of the birds made a densely woven mesh; he stopped to listen and gradually became aware that one of the strands could not be coming from a bird. It was a distinctly human whistle and there were snatches of what he was pretty sure was Handel. It came from the hillside above.

The woods thickened as he climbed and he followed the path to a glade where the water, falling from higher rocks, widened into a pool; he recognised the setting of Jarlath's painting of St Ælfhild. The whistler sat on the bank, eyes closed and body swaying. His hair, streaked with grey, hung halfway down his back; his beard covered his chest. His clothes were shabby, he was thin and barefoot. Near him, on a branch, sat a blackbird; it seemed to be learning the Handel. Paul tried to move quietly, but the bird flew up with a trill of alarm and the whistler leapt to his feet.

Paul opened his hands to show he meant no harm. 'Hello,' he said. 'I heard you whistling. Handel, wasn't it?'

'The G minor Sonata.'

'It was very beautiful.'

'Not as beautiful as him.' The man gestured to the tree where the blackbird perched, wary-eyed.

'I'm sorry I startled you,' Paul said. 'I was exploring. I've just come to Farundell, to work for Lord Damory. My name is Asher, by the way, Paul Asher.'

'Pleased to meet you,' the fellow whispered, and scurried into the woods.

Paul returned the way he had come. The seamless web of birdsong waved over the land, but he was listening for the one strand that had ceased.

In the kitchen garden he met Theo and Alice. 'Is there a resident hermit?' he asked. 'I came upon an odd person, long hair, whistling. I think I frightened him.'

'Daniel!' Alice ran off.

Paul looked from Alice, disappearing, to Theo. 'Who's Daniel?'

'Daniel is Percy's second son,' Theo said. 'James, the eldest, was killed early in the war; Richard, the youngest, is with the Foreign Office. He served safely in Whitehall; he's in Singapore now. But Daniel came home from Flanders with shell-shock, as they call it.' She gestured to the bench outside the potting shed. 'Shall we sit? Have you a cigarette?'

Paul lit their cigarettes, leaned back and stretched his legs. The sun-warmed wall of the shed gave off a faint odour of creosote that mingled with the pungent green scents of the garden.

'He stopped one day, like a watch,' Theo said, 'and couldn't be got going again. He wouldn't feed himself, but would swallow if soft food was put in his mouth, and would walk if one pulled him along. He didn't speak at all.'

Paul nodded. 'I knew men like that.'

'Nothing could be done for him in any hospital, so in the end they sent him home. The moment the ambulancemen left, he walked out of the house and down the meadow. We followed, but he ignored us. He walked all the way round the lake to the cabin we'd used as a summerhouse and fishing hut. He went in, closed the door in our faces, and that's where he's lived ever since. We bring him food, and now and then catch sight of him by the lake or in the woods. Alice visits him often, but he never comes near the house.'

'He was whistling wonderfully,' Paul said.

'He was quite an accomplished violinist, though he hasn't played since the war. He has his eccentricities—he's not cut his hair or beard, he can't bear to touch metal and he won't eat meat. We're just glad he's found some way to live that suits him. And who knows? Maybe he'll emerge one day. Maybe he'll have to.'

Paul realised that Daniel would sooner or later inherit the estate and title and suspected that the timid, feral creature he had seen would not consider it a blessing. 'The place where I saw him—it was a pool, up on the other side of that hill.' He pointed. 'I recognised it from the painting.'

'Yes, that's St Ælfhild's pool. It's still considered a special place—did you see the ribbons tied to the hazel?'

Paul shook his head.

'People come to say prayers, or make wishes, and it's the custom to leave something as an offering.'

'An offering to whom?'

'Ah well, I suppose that's up to you.'

'Oh, I didn't mean me, particularly.'

'No?'

'Well, no—that is, I hadn't thought.' But as he spoke he remembered that he'd had an impulse, dismissed almost before it was noticed, to leave something at the pool, as if in hope, or perhaps in thanks—though in hope or thanks for what he had no idea.

*   *   *

Alice burst into the cabin. The narrow wooden bed was made, Daniel's coat hung on its peg, his collection of stones and pebbles spread across the floor in a new pattern. He wasn't there. She ran back out and started up the slope, pausing every couple of minutes to call his name.

She found him among the trees near the top of the hill. His eyes were clouded, his shoulders hunched. His feet clenched the earth, bones and tendons taut beneath skin so fragile that a fierce protectiveness seized her heart. She turned and led the way down the path. 'Are you all right? Paul said he saw you. I was going to come this afternoon anyway, to tell you about him. He's come to work for Percy, to help him write his memoirs. He met Maggie in town and she sent him. He's a friend of Val's. I think he was in the war, too . . . He's all right. Probably. You might get along. Would you like to meet him? I could bring him one day. He came with a big tomcat named Madagascar. It's funny, but I think Artemis likes him—at any rate, she hasn't driven him off.' Stop chattering, she told herself, pressing her lips together.

In the cabin, Daniel knelt at the hearth, stirred the embers of the fire with a stick and placed a small log exactly in the centre.

'I'll make chocolate.' Alice poured milk into a saucepan and set it on the ring. While she waited for it to heat, she took down the violin and opened the case. 'Have you played at all?'

He shook his head.

She lifted the instrument from its bed of thick velvet. 'Is she in tune?'

He shrugged and rearranged a line of pebbles.

Alice picked up the bow, tightened it and stroked the E-string. 'How is this?'

He pointed upward. She tightened the peg, stroked it again. He cringed and put his hands over his ears.

'Well, you do it, then,' Alice said. 'You're the one with perfect pitch, and you're the one who can play this bloody thing.'

He mimed shock.

'Bloody is a very minor curse word, surely you know that.' She replaced the violin in its case. 'Maybe next time I come, I'll bring my flute and we can play something together.' His mouth tightened and she regretted her words. How often had she told herself she must never push him? 'Never

82

mind. We don't have to.'

They took their mugs to the edge of the lake and sat on logs. Rushes fringed the shore, rattling in the breeze; coots called to their chicks. Daniel whistled softly, a much more beautiful sound than she'd ever be able to make on her flute. She'd practised whistling for hours but never came anywhere close to his effortless, fluid slides and arpeggios.

Daniel stopped whistling and cleared his throat. 'I want . . .' his voice creaked at first. 'I want to build a coracle. A little round boat, like the Welsh use on the rivers.' He cleared his throat again. 'Would you help?'

'Of course I'll help.'

'I'll need lots of things. Wood and . . . maybe we can make one for you as well.'

'Oh yes, let's. We can explore the lake together, and get away from everyone, and have picnics on the island.'

His smile was like a shy deer, peering from behind his beard. 'We need green willow. Long pieces. We have to weave them together like a basket. And a canvas to wrap it, and tar to make it waterproof.'

'Where do we find the willow?'

'Come on, I'll show you.' He got up and started off along the shore.

Alice followed with a skip—because he wanted something. Because he had plans for a future. Because he needed her help.

*   *   *

'A Journey to the Interior,' Percy said, when Paul

83

had settled into a chair with pencils and a pad of paper for the first day's dictation. 'That will be the title of these memoirs.' He lit his pipe; Henry had been banished and forbidden to return until summoned.

'When I was a boy, I liked rainy days best. I would lie on the old leather chesterfield in the library, a stack of books at my side: tales of adventure, of heroes striding out into the world in search of treasure, or love, or glory. My favourite book was Jean de Léry's *History of a Voyage to the Land of Brazil*, first published in 1580, and the bible of explorers and anthropologists ever since. The full title remains, to me, an incantation, a gateway into that land. I can recite it still: "*History of a Voyage to the Land of Brazil, otherwise called America. Containing the Navigation and the Remarkable Things Seen on the Sea by the Author; the Customs and Strange Ways of Life of the American Savages; Together with the Description of Various Animals, Trees, Plants and Other Singular Things Completely Unknown over Here.*"

'I loved it so much I reread it every year and it planted in me, like a seed, an image of La Selva, as they call her: the forest herself, the great goddess Nature. It seemed an Eden to Jean de Léry and the engravings that accompanied the text showed Noble Savages, strong and beautiful . . . and naked. And this earthly Paradise became more real to me than the chilly English room in which I lay.

'When I left university I got a job with the Foreign Office and, because Brazil was one of the least favoured destinations, secured with no difficulty a posting there. I stuck it out for nearly a year before I found an excuse, and the courage, to resign. I had been collecting moths since I was a boy and I heard that in the deep jungle some species attained a wingspan of several inches, and drank blood. I was of course sceptical, but I was desperate to get away from the moribund São Paolo society with its mandarin manners, its tea dances, its frilled ranks of marriageable daughters. An expedition to the interior was a lark, a romantic adventure, and my hero Jean de Léry was leading me on.

'I equipped myself with all the paraphernalia available to the modern Scientist and Explorer: cameras and glass plates—that was in the days before film. Hundreds of specimen boxes, chloroform to kill the moths, pins to stick them to the board, labels to inscribe. I even sent to London for a microscope and slides. I'd heard that porters were easy to hire and cheap, so, troubling myself not at all about weight, I added duplicates of everything, just in case. Tins of coffee and tobacco, oatmeal, milk powder, tea and salt. Two pistols and two shotguns, with ammunition. Three linen suits, one light woollen tweed, eight shirts. A tough twill jacket with twelve pockets. Two pairs of spare boots and ten pairs of socks. A medicine chest, a book chest containing my Jean de Léry, of course, plus a complete Dickens and Shakespeare and a dozen blank notebooks for recording my Scientific Observations.

'All was packed into crates and accompanied me up the Amazon, broad as a sea, to Manaus, where I met the man who became my travelling companion. Frank Sinclair was a botanist and orchid hunter. He was a strange man, taciturn yet poetic, formidably strong and astonishingly impervious to physical discomfort of the most extreme varieties. Just the sort of man you'd want in that situation. He was on a quest for the legendary bleeding moon-flower, an orchid of unparalleled rarity, reputed to open only once every few years for one night only. Seeing it was his life's goal. He never touched spirits, but was drunk on the almost certain futility of his quest.

'We decided to leave most of the equipment in the care of the British trading outpost and head upriver to reconnoitre. We hired an old river boat, not too leaky, with a captain who claimed he knew where the flower could be found. That was, of course, a complete lie—our Captain Pedro had never even heard of it. We set off to the sound of the mission bell. Sinclair said it sounded like the death of civilisation. He was uneasy, but I felt altogether exultant and longed to be out of reach of that clanging, unnatural bell. Civilisation could bloody well die, as far as I was concerned; I had no use for it.

'Although we had planned a four-month expedition, Sinclair and I spent more than a year together in the jungle, and during that time I came to love him like a brother. He had a wild innocence, a child's belief that the pure act of clinging to his quest would, simply by its force and completeness, induce the universe to align itself in his favour. I don't think, in the end, the object of the quest mattered at all—it was the ferocity of his desire that drew him on, and me with him.

'I envied him his obsession. He had a sense of meaning and purpose that I believed was, in me, constitutionally and permanently disabled. It is like any other sense, that sense of meaning—like sight, for instance; without it one cannot see what is right in front of one.

'There's a photograph that I want for the book, Paul. It will be in the green album on the bottom shelf next to the fireplace. One of the last pages. I'm standing among a group of natives, the Caiyuna, among whom we lived for a time.'

Paul found the album and turned the pages. 'I think this is it.' Percy, thin and bearded—the resemblance to Daniel very noticeable—in shorts and a tattered panama hat, towered over a crowd of grinning brown faces.

'The Caiyuna do not like photographs,' Percy said, 'but not because the image steals their soul or any such nonsense. They know it's just a piece of paper but they thought it was ridiculous to try to capture a time that has passed. They thought that my love of these little scraps was very amusing, as though I treasured my excrement. They had a word for people who hold on to the worthless part of things and ignore the valuable: shit-keepers.'

Percy coughed and tugged the blanket over his legs. The sounds and the scents that flowed in at the window told him it was Farundell, but the memory of the dank jungle was just as real. He listened to the soft sounds as Paul turned the pages of the photograph album and imagined the images entering his young secretary's eyes, becoming his memories.

'Have you ever done any photography, Paul?' he said.

'No, I haven't—always thought I'd like to, though.'

'Why don't you use my cameras? I'll never use them again, and no one else is interested. Go on,

87

fetch them out, have a look. I believe they're in that cupboard.' He pointed to the corner. 'And I made a darkroom down the hall, so you can develop and print. It's kept locked, obviously, all those chemicals. Tustian will give you the key and Henry can teach you the basics in no time.'

Paul put the album aside and opened the cupboard. There was a massive teak Sanderson on a tripod, several box cameras of varying degrees of unwieldiness and a wonderfully compact Kodak that Percy suggested was a good one to start with. His blind fingers agile and quick, he demonstrated how to open it, extend the bellows and use the autographic feature with its hinged flap and metal stylus.

*   *   *

'Do you know what dreams are?' Alice asked. 'Is it something everyone knows and it's so ordinary it's nothing to talk about?'

'That sounds like a question for Theo,' Paul said. Alice had been atop the library ladder when he'd come to his desk to type up the day's dictation.

She climbed down and gave him a look. 'Naturally I tried Theo, but all she told me was to contemplate my own experience. My main experience of dreams is that I've forgotten them, so . . . well, I was wondering if there was some obvious thing I'd missed.'

'I'd never thought about it,' Paul said. 'I usually forget mine as soon as I wake up.' Thank God, he thought, for that mercy.

'Stephen says some famous old rabbi said, "A dream unremembered is like a letter unopened."'

Paul thought of the letters his father had sent to him in Paris as grasping grey tentacles reaching across the ocean from America to seize, bind, throttle. The memory of burning them unopened still gave him a sense of satisfaction. 'There's no law,' he said, 'that says you have to open every letter.'

'Oh, I could never leave a letter unopened, I'd be too curious. I hate it that I forget my dreams, that no matter how hard I try to remember, they slip away. It's hours and hours of my life, and I can't remember it.' Frustration made her want to kick something, but she didn't. 'I was hoping there might be a book about dreams, but so far no luck.'

Paul watched Alice searching the shelves; she'd stop, pull out a book and open it; she'd scan a few pages very intensely, then put it back, find another. She handled the books with affection, respectful yet familiar; she stroked their spines absent-mindedly as she turned the pages. It was so like his own way with books that he felt a rush of kinship; she could have been his little sister. For a moment he let himself imagine the life he'd have had, growing up at Farundell, with these books, these people . . . He pushed the thought aside and lit a cigarette.

He'd received a letter from his actual sister; it sat on his desk unopened and he regarded it with a twinge of guilt. Muriel had written to the Paris address and it had been forwarded to Val's house in London. There hadn't been room for another address on the envelope, so Val had sent it in a fresh one, with a note saying that Albert Laski had begun filming *Nino the Golden Catamite*—retitled, less controversially, *The Story of a Child*—using an experimental new method that recorded sound along with the picture. Val reported that he just might survive the experience, if Desmond Fanshawe could be persuaded to abandon the physical demons and wheels in favour of more manageable metaphorical ones.

'Aha!' Alice struck gold. *'The Art of Time: Dreams and Augury in Ancient Rome.* This might be good.' She brought it to the window, opened it and leafed through. The epigraph was from Spenser: 'In Dreams we live the immortal Masques of the Soul.'

'Do you know what augury is?' she asked Paul. 'It's bird-telling. That's what the word means. The augurs were priests in Rome who would mark out a space in the sky and watch to see if birds flew past, or if any particularly important birds happened to call at just that moment.'

'How would they know what it meant?' Paul said.

'That's the part I don't understand either,' Alice said. 'But it works. I've tried it. You think of a question, hold your breath, and if a bird calls before you have to breathe again, it's Yes; if not, it's No.'

'But the birds are calling constantly.'

'Well, you have to wait for an important bird, like a hawk, or you could do it at night, when only the owl might hoot. There's red kites living on top of the hill above the temple of Hermes and they have a really loud call, more like a scream. Surely you've heard it.'

'Yes, I suppose I have.' Paul remembered the large reddish bird that had circled over his head after he'd seen Francis.

'Do you want to try? We could try it right now.'

Alice opened the window. 'Think of a question. Mine is, Will I ever understand dreams?'

'Mine is, Will I ever understand anything?'

Alice wondered if she was being teased. 'Is that a joke?'

'Sadly, no,' Paul said, and laughed.

'All right,' Alice said. 'Ready? Now hold your breath.'

They held their breath and leaned towards the open window. Their eyes met and Alice nearly started giggling, so she quickly looked away.

Paul closed his eyes and listened. Soft air washed over his face: scent of roses, of sunlight, of green depths from the woods behind the house. He forgot about breathing; he forgot about birds, about questions; he had a glimpse of something that made all the questions irrelevant; then the red kite called and he opened his eyes, astonished.

'Wow,' Alice said. 'See? It really does work.' Her eyes gleamed and they grinned at each other.

When she'd left he picked up Muriel's letter. His sister's round handwriting looked still childish; he always had to remind himself she was no longer the little girl he'd protected and comforted, and whose devotion was the one thing he'd missed. She had been a shy and awkward sixteen and although she sent photographs from time to time, the last living image lingered. For a while he'd thought she would want to be rescued, and tried to persuade her to come to Paris, but apparently a life of destitution and dissolution lacked appeal. The old man kept her on a short lead. Paul opened the letter.

My dearest brother,

I hope this finds you well. I'm writing to say that Father has been quite ill; he suffered a stroke three weeks ago and although he is recovering, it is slow. Fear not! I do not suggest that you return! I asked him just now if he wanted to see you and he gave me one of his glares, set his teeth hard and made that brusque, dismissive gesture of his with the one hand he can move.

The situation is under control; I have hired round the clock nurses and ignore him when he tries to complain about the cost. It is enjoyable to be able to tell him he MUST rest!

Now that he is going, I'm becoming almost fond of him. He is the merest shadow of that grim giant of our childhood—he ceased to be that long ago, truth be told.

Please, write and tell me how you are, what are you writing about, are you in love again? I even like to hear about the weather in Paris. Here it's awful, still feels like February. How's your fascinating friend Val and that rogue cat of yours? Are you going to Provence again this summer? Maybe, maybe, maybe someday I'll join you.

Your loving sister,
Muriel

Paul sighed and took up pen and paper to reply. He recounted the bare bones of leaving Paris, finding this job in the country. He didn't describe Farundell, or say how much he liked it. It was unfair, somehow, when Muriel was stuck in Boston with that ghastly old man, even ghastlier now that

92

he was weak and powerless—Paul shuddered at the image of his tall, overbearing father shrunken and shrivelled and grey-faced, sour-breathed, unshaven, sunk into his bed, querulous and feeble, yet still hard and hateful. He was clenching his own teeth so hard they ached; he shook his head, looked around the beautiful room. He was far away and out of reach; he was safe.

He inserted a sheet of foolscap in the shiny black Underwood and started on Percy's dictation. It didn't take very long, although his typing was far from expert. He read through the pages and corrected his errors.

The library was dim and quiet; beyond the far windows the meadow and lake were blurred by the imperfections in the old glass. Jarlath's painting of Tobias Damory, in the same landscape, looked just as real. Paul walked over to read again the words on the frame: *It is possible for the Soul to become a God while yet it abideth in the Body of a Man, if it Contemplate the Beauty of the Good.* Was he to imagine that such a thing was possible, whatever it might mean? And then what was a soul, that it could change its nature through its own effort? Theo was right; each question spawned a dozen more. Possibly the book would explain. On the shelf Theo had indicated were several editions, several languages: *Pimander*, *Pymander*, *Poimandres*. He chose one whose title page informed him that it was an 1888 facsimile edition of Tobias's original, which had been published in 1593.

Tobias himself might well have stood here many times, he thought, perhaps with his own copy of this book in his hands. Paul had the odd notion

93

that if he could look hard enough, or in, somehow, the right way—sideways, perhaps—he could see through to another moment. It seemed just a blink away, but the very act of reaching for it pushed it further, like trying to pick something from the surface of water, and it receded at once to an uncrossable distance.

He opened the book and read:

Once, when deep in contemplation, I rose from my body and soared high above the Earth, where I beheld an infinite being.

'Who are you?' I asked.

'I am Pymander, the Mind of God. What seek you here? What do you want?'

'I want to learn what is real,' said I, 'and understand Nature, and know Truth.'

And what do I want? Paul thought. Images came to him of the children playing in St James's Park, their forests, swords, castles; of poor Nino the golden catamite praying on the shore; of Sara Paragon with her violin on Westminster Bridge. Something clawed at him. He was holding the book so tightly his thumbs were white. He eased them, took a breath. 'All right, yes,' he said, with sudden, unbidden solemnity, and quickly, before he could hesitate, 'yes, Pymander, whatever you are. That's what I want, too—to learn what is real, to understand, to know.'

6

In the cool bright morning, at the centre of the green, dew-drenched world, Theo began her new garden. She called to Malcolm; the old man brought the stake and string. She measured three times the span of her outstretched arms, set the stake at the centre of the first circle and watched while he paced the circumference trickling sand from a sack. He looked up. Yes, it was good. They outlined the other beds and the path that wound among them.

As Malcolm began digging, Theo climbed to the higher terrace and looked over her design. Was it too formal, too neat, too self-contained? Already she wanted to mess it up, break it open, disarrange the symmetries. But time would take care of that.

Maggie and Jarlath emerged from the dining room with their guests and Theo ducked into the kitchen garden. In the long potting shed her seeds and seedlings waited. She set to work thinning the chervil. A fly buzzed from pane to pane of glass until he found the open window and was caught in the waiting spider's web.

Theo sorted through her seeds. Time to sow French beans, kale, celery. By the bench rested a sack of the dark, fragrant potting soil she'd concocted during the winter: well-rotted manure, garden compost, leaf mould, kitchen compost, a bit of sand for drainage. She sank her hands into it, then her arms up to her elbows. It was beautiful. She scooped up handfuls, filled a tray and prepared drills.

Malcolm plodded by with wheelbarrows of turf, returning heaped high with manure. The digging unearthed artefacts: a few coins, a piece of clay pipe, an elaborate buckle. She cleaned them and arranged them on a windowsill among other such finds. Mrs Beal brought her a sandwich for lunch.

In the afternoon Theo walked in the woods above the house. The trees thrummed with sap; their leaves spread like sails, drank in the sun. She let her senses open. The blue sky smelled of artemisia, with sharp, pointy notes of orange like piccolos and a vein of scarlet running through like a trumpet. A crow winged by, cawing ochre streaks. A silky mistle thrush called from a branch: brilliant blue and gold, strawberries and champagne. The blackbirds' song twirled crimson and purple and white, vanilla-sweet; the turtle doves' purr was frilled lavender velvet.

High on the hillside, hidden among dense shrubs, was a little glade Theo had discovered as a child. All her brothers and sisters married or at school, old Nanny Hodges asleep in her chair, she had wandered the woods alone every day. This was the place she'd first met Francis.

She's nine again, in a daze of colour and sound and scent, following a bumblebee as it spirals up through the trees, vanishes in a thin bright line of melody. When she drifts back down, Francis is there and she can tell right away that he sees her. He's looking right at her, ignoring her body asleep under a tree. Hello Theodora, he says. She hears him clearly inside her head, though his lips don't move and he makes no sound.

She had loved him at once. That was more than fifty years ago and now, she thought, I'm old, and

96

he's still . . . whatever age he wants to be. She stepped into the clearing; it always felt untouched, as though she was the first human ever to set foot within. Bees buzzed over a sweet cloud of yellow archangel, stitching flower to flower with their golden hum. She stood for a long time, adrift among the trees, whispering with the breezes, singing with the nightingales and dancing with leaves.

Sun moved; light changed. She walked across the hill to St Ælfhild's pool, black-green and deep. Silence lurked beneath the birdsong; clouds of human fears and longings clung to the hazel. As she made her way down towards the lake she saw Paul sitting on a stone, a cigarette burning unheeded in his hand, staring at the island. Paul Asher, she thought, who are you? She unfurled another sense and collected an impression of abundant energy, tightly contained; a dynamism reluctantly grown careful. There was considerable sensitivity in him, though he was obviously unaware of it himself; like many, he would have his own good reasons to suppress it. The fact that he'd seen Francis was a clear indication that his inner senses were not entirely blocked. There was a layer of anger, a deeper layer of yearning, a nagging feeling that something had been lost, the sense of being a stranger everywhere. And like a tiny seed within him, a newly born determination to . . . what? she asked. To understand, to know, came the answer. She sought no further—closer than this she would not go uninvited. She walked on; he rose as she approached.

'Hello, Paul,' she said, and holding his eyes for the briefest moment, sent him a message of goodwill, saw it received, saw the hint of wariness fade. With relief, she thought. He was not naturally a cautious or reticent man. She seated herself companionably on a rock.

'Have you another cigarette?' she said. 'I seem always to be asking you that.'

'It's a pleasure to oblige.' How odd, Paul thought; he'd just been thinking of her. As she bent to the match her thick white hair, worn loose over her shoulders, brushed his hand and he felt a rush of desire that astonished him. Good God, Theo must be old enough to be his grandmother. He stared at her mouth as she sucked on the cigarette. Why had he never realised how beautiful lines were, how they echoed a woman's smiles, how they framed her mouth, her eyes . . . he met her eyes and in the instant before they turned opaque he got the distinct impression that she knew what he was thinking. The look in her eyes was patient, kind, and deeply, deeply amused. His cigarette had burned out and he busied himself lighting another.

'It's a side effect,' Theo said. 'It's not personal.'

'It's a . . . it's not . . . what?' The sensation was fading now, and he could begin to see that it had not been simply sexual; it was different, more subtle yet more pervasive—the cells of his body responded to her like iron filings to a magnet. Is that what she meant by not personal? He stared out at the island and tried to recover his composure.

'What do you see there?' she asked.

He found that he was able to meet her eyes again. 'Just before you came I had an odd experience. I was looking at the water, not

98

thinking of anything in particular; then suddenly I was in a boat, halfway to the island, but I knew I was sitting here on the shore the whole time. It was a very queer sensation.'

'Maybe you were remembering a dream.'

'A dream? I usually forget them right away.'

'That does not mean they cease to exist.'

'That's like what Percy said about his memories—that nothing was lost, it was all . . . somewhere inside. If that's so, why don't we drown in all our memories?'

'Because we make a boat, and separate ourselves from the sea. Or, we are a boat, until we realise we're not, and fall into the sea.'

'You've done it again,' said Paul.

'Done what?'

'Perplexed and intrigued me.'

Theo smiled and got to her feet. 'Must shift these old bones,' she said. 'Cheerio!'

Paul watched her walk away. A side effect, she'd said. Side effect of what? Every question leading to more questions. Naturally. Theo really was the most . . . what would the word be? Confusing, disconcerting, yet definitely fascinating. Enigmatic, that was it. Was she making fun of him? He didn't think so. Enigmatic, but not deliberately so, and not unkind. The difficulty was in his own perception; from her point of view, he suspected, she was being perfectly clear, or at least fairly clear. Or at any rate not intentionally obscure. Stephen had described her as sane. In this mad world that was quite a distinction, or an accomplishment.

* * *

99

As the sun dropped towards the west Theo returned to her garden. The neatly cut beds lay dark against the lawn, stalked by blackbirds listening for worms. She looked up as Jarlath approached. 'Yes, I know, I've been ignoring everyone.'

'Our loss,' he said.

'I find a little society goes a long way for me these days.'

'Do we bore you?'

'Well, maybe just a bit.' Theo squatted down, scooped up a handful of earth, crumbled it between her fingers. Malcolm had forked the manure in well; it was perfect. A fine tilth, what a lovely expression.

'I envy your silence,' Jarlath said. 'You're like an island, a peaceful island. It's a paradox. I can only reach your silence by breaking it.'

'That's a good one, I'll add it to my collection.'

'Collection?'

'Of paradoxes. See?' she gestured. 'Arranged on the mantel of my mind.'

Jarlath laughed. 'The mantel of your mind, dear Theo, has paradoxes stacked ten deep. Speaking of paradox, do you remember, you used to scold me for always trying to get somewhere? If it's real, you said, it's here right now.'

'Of course I remember.'

'I found that so hard to grasp. Still do, but I think I'm beginning to understand what you mean. All this seeking we do, this questing for the answer— all these methods and systems and disciplines turn out to be just ways to postpone enlightenment.'

Theo stood, smiling at the percussive symphony

of her joints. 'Tell me, have your knees begun to crack yet?'

'Yes, they started cracking a couple of years ago. Is it a sign of enlightenment?'

'Everything is a sign of enlightenment. Come walk with me.'

'Are you reading me?'

'No, of course not. It doesn't take special abilities to see you've got something on your mind.'

'Oh Theo, if you'd have had me, what an easy life it would have been.'

'There are no easy lives.'

They walked down the meadow, their long shadows alongside. Theo noted how reluctantly Jarlath checked his pace to match her leisurely amble.

'I was thinking about a fairy tale,' he said, 'I can't remember what it's called. It's about a child who has to travel through a wild forest and evade a wolf to get to Granny's house—but when she gets there, the wolf has arrived before her, eaten Granny, and is pretending to be Granny. The wolf is the world, I think, which a soul hopes to avoid and go directly to God, the Grandmother. But it's impossible—by the time she gets there—that is to say, by the time time passes—God is inside the world, which, pretending to be God, devours the child.'

'So it's something to do with Sylvie,' Theo said, 'the world and its wolves?'

'Hah. Yes. I know it's quite ludicrous, but I find myself playing the stern pater.' He lit a cigarette, and one for Theo. 'In her last letter she mentioned she'd fallen madly in love with some chap who calls himself Count Lando da Bari. I asked around;

he's a notorious fortune hunter. Not really a count, and he's forty if he's a day. And of course she's not in love; she only says it to shock, to show she's all grown up. When we decided to let her stay with my sister in Florence we assumed she'd be looked after. What is my sister doing? How could she allow someone like that near Sylvie?'

'How could she keep him away?'

Jarlath gave a short laugh. 'Oh God, listen to me. I'm turning into my father. But I can't bear the thought of some old roué mishandling her, or, perhaps worse, some callow pimply boy. She doesn't understand the world—how could she, living here? She's been sheltered—that's been good, but now—well, she won't be here forever, will she? She's starting at the Slade in September; that'll mean staying in London, meeting new people—men. She has no idea, no idea. She'll be nineteen in a few weeks—is that grown up? She obviously thinks it is. I don't want to clip her wings or anything of the sort; I just want to make sure she's ready to go out there. Maggie throws up her hands, says a father's influence is what's needed.'

'You'd have to be around, for that.'

'You know, I wouldn't mind. I'm tired of all that out there. I work better here.'

The sun dropped behind the hill and when they turned to walk back to the house the meadow was in its gloaming. A swan circled overhead and descended to the lake with a whirring of wings and a slow splash, trailing lengthening ripples that caught and curled the malleable light.

'Sometimes,' said Jarlath, 'I want to be one of those romantic landscape painters, obsessed with the ideal of Nature and then I think no, what an awful fate. It's impossible, nothing can even begin to compare with the least, effortless, unthought effect of Nature herself.'

*　　　*　　　*

After dinner, Alice and Theo retired to the music room for Alice's flute lesson. Theo settled at the piano and warmed up with some Bach. Alice took her flute from its case, lifted it to her lips and tried to follow, but soon gave up. 'Do you think it's possible,' she said, 'that I'm not as musical as everyone else in this family?'

Theo smiled. 'It's possible, but you can play very well when you choose. Shall we try the Vivaldi?'

Alice got out the sheet music and they worked their way twice through the piece. The best part of music lessons, she thought, was when they'd finished and she could get Theo to play or sometimes even sing. 'Would you sing something?' she asked.

'*Schafe können sicher weiden, wo ein guter Hirte wacht. Wo Regenten wohl regieren, kann man Ruh und Freide spüren und was Länder glücklich macht* . . .' Theo's pure contralto flowed like honey. It was one of Alice's favourites, from Bach's Hunt Cantata—the gentle melody, the stately rhythm, the idyllic image of sheep sleeping safely, a good king ruling a peaceful kingdom. The flute part was childlike and simple; she played along easily.

Theo finished the song and slid into a Schubert piano sonata. Alice watched her great-aunt's eyes. She was gazing into space as though listening and her fingers moved over the keys without effort. Alice had learned that if she asked Theo a

103

question while she was doing something else, like playing the piano or gardening, she was more likely to get an answer, though not always one she understood. 'Theo,' she said, 'why did you try to forget about your moon-body?'

Theo wished the music could answer for her. 'My moon-body was . . . became . . .' shimmering blue diminuendo . . . 'more real, stronger than my earth-body. When I was your age I lived more in that world than in this one until . . .' deep, solid chords like the loamy scent of the oaks . . . 'eventually someone noticed I wasn't eating and I seemed to sleep all the time. But I wasn't sleeping, I was travelling . . .' arpeggios up the scale, lemon-bright . . . 'about in my moon-body. I was declared ill, frail, of a nervous disposition—even, by one eminent doctor, congenitally feeble-minded. A life of bed-rest was imagined for me, enlivened by long sojourns at Baden-Baden.' *Andante ma non molto*, nutmeg brown.

Schubert gave way to Mozart. Theo let her hands find their own way; they led her to the twenty-first piano concerto. That had been Odelia's favourite. 'Until Odelia came, when I was twelve. She knew what was going on, that I'd wandered too far and become lost. She brought me back, and she used music to do it. Music became something I wanted, so I had to stay in my earth-body to train it, and when I went to the Conservatory a few years later, I decided—with youthful zeal—that my moon-body must be forgotten, put away; it was dangerous and I must not ever allow myself to use it.'

'But then you remembered again,' Alice said.

'I remembered again. The music that led me out

104

of the moon-body world led me back in. Nothing moves in a straight line.' She returned to Bach, another cantata: '*Ich habe genug,*' she sang.

Alice translated: I have enough. She caught a glint in her great-aunt's eye and took the hint. She picked up her flute and tried to accompany Theo, playing rather better than she'd expected.

*　　　*　　　*

Paul stands at the shore, praying to the disc of the setting moon. A boat approaches, a white-haired old woman at the prow. 'I know who you are,' Paul says.

Theo smiles and beckons, and he wades out into the water. When it comes to his waist he stops. 'I can't reach you,' he says. 'I don't know how to swim.'

'Yes, you do,' she says. 'It's easy. You've done it before. All you have to do is remember.'

As Paul wades further, the water thickens around his body and drags at him. The boat seems to recede with every step he takes. Fear grips his heart and numbs his limbs. The moans and whimpers begin again, the screaming in the sky. He's back in the crater, gritty earth in his mouth. He gropes in the mud, finds a foot; it comes away from its leg, flesh rotted. He gags and drops it; the black dog seizes it and runs off. It doesn't matter, carry on, it doesn't matter, it doesn't matter. Nearby lies a body, face down. He turns it over; his own eyes open in a dead man's face. A great, gasping chasm cracks the world and he's falling, falling . . .

A large hand reaches in and pulls him out. It's Jarlath, wearing a top hat, red satin cloak and an enormous false moustache. He drags Paul ashore on the island and leads him up the path to the top,

105

where Theo sits on a throne made of the roots and trunk of a great oak. 'I found him lost in Kathmandu,' he says.

Paul falls at her feet as a wave of longing rises from deep, forgotten places and he sobs with pain, with loss and sorrow until, exhausted, he looks up into her face.

'Sleep now,' she says, and as Daniel's whistling floats across the lake, he drops into sleep like a stone.

Paul woke to the sound of Daniel's whistling drifting through the pre-dawn stillness. Nearby another virtuoso woke and proclaimed his territory, and another; within a few minutes the individual songs had melted into an intricate sea of sound. He lay quietly, remembering a dream. Jarlath had been in it, and Theo, and a feeling of strange peace as though some part of him had come home and settled into his heart like a small bird in its nest.

*   *   *

Paul spent the morning with Percy, taking dictation and selecting photographs from the albums. After lunch he went to the library, transferred Madagascar to another chair without waking him and settled at his desk. He lit the oil lamp to augment the feeble electric and started on the typing.

Stephen appeared at the door. 'Hello, hope I'm not disturbing. I'm looking for a book for Alice. She's grown tired of Shakespeare, can you imagine, and wants Spenser's *Faerie Queene*, which she has heard is very difficult.' He squinted up at the shelves. 'Gosh it's dim in here. Can't see a

106

thing. I'm sure it must be somewhere near there.'

'Hang on, I'll hold up the lamp for you.' Paul rose to help.

'I think that's it at the top, Wait, I'll get the ladder.' Stephen rolled it over, climbed up and tugged at the book; it fell through his fingers and on to Paul's head. 'Oh God, I'm so sorry!'

'It's OK, don't worry.' Paul rubbed his head. It was the same spot that Francis had struck—the lump had never subsided. He bent to pick up the book, which had fallen open at the epigraph:

True, without error, certain and most true, that which is above is as that which is below, and that which is below is as that which is above, for the unfolding of the infinite permutations of the One.

The words were attributed to Hermes Trismegistos. Who was this Hermes fellow? The *Pymander* sat on Paul's desk; his attempts to read it resulted in a degree of perplexity second only to that induced by Theo, but something made him persist and he tried to dip into it every day. 'Do you know anything about the *Pymander*?'

'Ah, the *Pymander*,' Stephen said. 'Old Mr Pym. Here's a question for you: do you believe the golden age is past or yet to come?'

I believe the belief in a golden age was slaughtered and trampled in the mud, thought Paul. 'The golden age?' he said. 'Is there such a thing?'

'Oh, assuredly. It used to be in the past; now it's in the future. Until very recently, when people began to believe in Progress, everyone assumed that the older something was, the better, because it was closer to the source, to the gods or god. The Romans revered the Greeks, the Greeks revered the Egyptians. And the Corpus Hermeticum, which includes the *Pymander*, was believed to be very old indeed. Please forgive me if I wax academic.'

'Not at all. I asked.'

'In the fifteenth century it found its way to the library of Cosimo de Medici in Florence. He had it translated from Greek into Latin and it circulated throughout Europe. Although it was soon proved to date from only the second century, its influence continued to spread—the Renaissance was the rebirth of what they believed to have been the philosophy of the golden age, represented in its purest form by that book.'

'What's a Pymander, then? I couldn't find it in the dictionary.'

'Hah. That's one of those words—Alice loves them—whose meaning and etymology are uncertain. It might be from the Greek word for shepherd, which I suppose makes some sense, or from a Coptic phrase meaning the mind of god—a likelier derivation, in my view, but overlooked by academics because it suggests the text may be older than is commonly believed.'

'But what does it mean?' Paul said. 'When he says that a soul can become a god, for instance.' He gestured to the painting of Tobias.

'Oh Lord, that's another question. I don't know—I find it utterly inscrutable. You should ask Jarlath,' Stephen said as he left.

Paul returned to his desk, lit a cigarette and looked out of the window. A damp pigeon sat, shoulders hunched, among the dripping leaves of the oak. Jarlath spent most of his time in his studio over the stables, just across the courtyard. His gramophone played mainly opera; Mozart and Wagner were favourites, and the stream of music had come to mingle in Paul's mind with Percy's stories of the jungle. Jarlath was always perfectly charming, even if Paul sometimes had the feeling he was being . . . scrutinised. Paul hesitated to approach him, though he couldn't put his finger on why. Of course his reputation was colourful, but that wouldn't in itself have deterred him; and as to the black magic business, well, he could scarcely blame that, since he didn't believe in magic—whatever it was—in the first place.

The typing finished, Paul resumed his leisurely trawl of the library. It was a kind of heaven, as he'd known it would be, and he indulged his passion for random reading as never before. He selected a large illustrated volume entitled *A History of Country House Architecture* and settled in a chair by the far window where the light was best. There ought to be, he thought, a word for this sort of peripatetic reading; as snacking is to dining, as strolling is to marching. But the book failed to hold his interest; the bump on his head itched and seemed to have swollen. Damn Francis.

Breaks appeared in the clouds; the sky shook out a last brief shower that pebbled the surface of the lake. He opened the casement and a surge of flower-laden air rushed in; the sun was coming and he had to catch it.

He came upon Theo at work in her new herb garden. She was kneeling, pushing seeds one by one into the soft earth.

'It's a mystery to me,' Paul said, 'all this growing business. It always astounds me that those,' he pointed to the seeds, 'turn into—well, whatever they'll turn into.'

'It never fails to astonish me either, no matter how often it happens. Would you like to try? You could help me plant the fennel. Hold out your hand.' She unfolded a brown paper envelope and shook a few dry brownish specks into his palm.

He knelt beside her, picked one, placed it on the earth and pushed it in with his finger. He imagined it sending down roots, stretching up stalk and leaves, exploding into flowers, bursting with seeds, each a replica of the one he'd sown, yet each different, generating a unique plant that would produce more seeds, ad infinitum. It reminded him of what he'd just read, something about infinite permutations, above and below.

A sense of understanding brushed the edge of his mind, slipping by too fast to grasp. He glanced up and met Theo's eyes. Get it? she seemed to say, and smiled. 'Look,' she said as she returned to her planting, 'the sun is coming.'

The last of the clouds blew off to the east; the sun broke through. Paul stood up and lifted his face to the warmth. A golden dazzle permeated everything, rich and honey-thick; the scent of honey filled the air. He closed his eyes.

'Can you smell the sunlight?' Theo said.

'Yes,' he said without thinking.

She moved around him, humming softly. If I were a plant, he thought, I'd like to be a plant in Theo's garden. He imagined himself a seed, pressed into the earth by her hand. There was a tickling in the soles of his feet, as though he was

110

sending down a root. He wiggled his toes; the sensation increased. He had the urge to laugh out loud.

7

It had been more than two weeks since Francis had appeared to Paul, and Alice had been certain she would see him soon - in the next minute, the next hour, around the next corner, after counting to one hundred, after counting to one thousand. She pretended to everyone that it was a matter of utmost indifference that her great-great-great-great-grandfather had appeared, for the first time in ages as far as she knew, to someone who was not even a member of the family. No one, not even Theo, knew how much she'd always wanted to see him.

On the night of the full moon she packed her satchel with a pullover, a candle, candlestick and matches, a handkerchief and biscuits. She paced her room until the household was asleep, then roused Roger and Sophie. As instructed, they'd slept in their clothes. She led them down the stairs and into the red drawing room, climbed on to a chair and lifted the small, elaborately framed portrait of Francis from the wall. 'Take this,' she said to Roger. 'Be careful with it.'

She crossed to the liquor cabinet, studied the contents. What would he like? The nicest bottle was called Napoleon Cognac, VSOP. That would do. She wrapped it in the pullover, put it in her satchel and considered the glasses. Something not too fragile. She chose a chunky cut-crystal one, wrapped it in the handkerchief and tucked it next to the bottle, closed the cabinet and gestured to Roger and Sophie to follow her to the boot room.

Sophie reached for her boots. 'Oh Alice, why do we . . .'

'Be quiet. Don't put your boots on until we're away from the house.'

'But Alice . . .'

'Shhh. We mustn't make any noise.'

'But the ground's wet . . .'

'I brought some biscuits.' Alice had learned recently about carrot and stick. 'We can eat them on the way.'

They tiptoed along the edge of the courtyard, gravel on one side and thorny roses on the other. The window of Henry's room was open and his high-pitched snores broke the stillness. When they reached the track to the temple of Hermes they pulled on their boots and Alice distributed the biscuits. She tried to hurry them along but the uneven moonlight made the surface of the path difficult to read; they stumbled over roots and into puddles. Sophie stopped by the path to the chapel. 'Alice,' she whispered, 'I really think this is awfully bad of us.'

'No one will know.'

The owl hooted right above and Sophie whimpered. 'It's spooky up here at night.'

'It's the same as during the day, why should it be any different? It's not even that dark.'

'It is, and it's scary.'

'Roger, hold her hand.'

'I already am. Alice,' Roger said, 'what if he . . .'

'Shhh. Come on. Don't dawdle.'

112

'No, but wait, Alice, we . . .'

'All right,' Alice said. 'Enough of this muttering. Are you with me or not?'

'We don't understand . . .'

'You don't need to understand. You need to do what I say. He's our great-great-great-great-grandfather, isn't he?'

'Yes.'

'That means we have a right to see him.'

'Does it?'

'Of course it does, nitwit.' She grabbed the portrait. 'Look. I can do this on my own. You can go back alone through the woods or stay here alone by the graveyard, whatever you prefer. But if you come with me you are to keep quiet and do as I tell you.'

She walked up the track; they hesitated, then followed. She'd thought they might be useful, but they were more trouble than they were worth. She had planned this all very carefully and if they ruined it . . . Maybe she should send them back, but now they'd probably refuse to go. Never mind. She'd just have to be absolutely firm with them at all times.

The moon shone on the pillars of the temple. Alice strode forward, opened a door. The hinges creaked and she forced herself to breathe calmly as she circled the room and opened the others. The statues glowed like ghosts and despite what she'd said to Sophie it was different at night, very different. She leaned the portrait against a plinth in a bright panel of moonlight. Dark curls framed Francis's face; his hand with its many rings rested on a silver-headed walking stick. She knelt and beckoned Roger and Sophie to either side. For once they obeyed without argument. She lit the candle, unwrapped the bottle and the glass, poured out an inch of cognac and placed it before the portrait. She'd brought it as an offering because people always made offerings, and because she supposed he liked that sort of thing, and because she reasoned that spirits connected somehow with spirits. It looked, however, very unimpressive.

She had imagined this moment as full of power and significance; she'd thought she would feel something. Now that they were here and everything was ready, it all seemed pointless. She saw three children playing some juvenile game—meaningless, having no effect whatsoever. What on earth were they doing? They'd get into trouble and accomplish nothing. She wished Roger and Sophie had gone back, so she could go back herself after a bit and pretend that something wonderful had happened, something too wonderful to speak of. Never mind. She would do what she came to do and at the very least it would show that she was serious, was willing to act, not just wish and hope.

She stared into the feeble flame. It looked as if it might blow out any second; she should have brought a lantern instead. The floor was cold and very hard; she should have brought something to sit on. Her muddy boots were staining her dress and she'd left muddy footprints all over the floor. Her legs started to go numb, which was probably a good thing. She realised she was holding her breath and let it out with a hiss. She simply had to begin.

'Lord Francis . . .' There was a tickle in her throat; she couldn't help it, she had to cough. The sound bounced off the walls. She didn't dare look at Roger and Sophie. Taking a deep breath, she began again.

'Lord Francis Peter George St John Damory.'

She gestured, and Roger and Sophie repeated with her, 'Lord Francis Peter George St John Damory . . .'

'Great-great-great-great-grandfather.'

'Great-great-great-great-grandfather.'

Alice had no idea what to do next. She'd expected to be seized by inspiration. Maybe one was supposed to partake of one's offerings. She picked up the glass and sniffed. She'd been allowed an occasional sip of champagne but never anything like this. She tilted the glass and let a drop roll towards her mouth. It touched the tip of her tongue like fire and she nearly dropped the glass. Very cautiously she took a tiny sip. It seared her lips and tongue: bitter, sharp, impossibly complex. It was pure heat by the time she swallowed it; she followed its path down the centre of her body, where it expanded into a glow. Should she give some to Roger and Sophie? No, better not. Definitely better not. She looked her great-great-great-great-grandfather in the eye.

'Lord Francis, we bring you this offering, and we . . .' She hesitated. He didn't really look like the sort of person who came when called. 'We respectfully request the honour of your company.'

She turned to Roger. 'We, we . . .' his voice squeaked, '. . . respectfully would like to see you, sir, if it's not too much trouble.'

They both turned to Sophie. 'We, sir . . .' She lowered her head and wouldn't go on.

Alice sighed. Now what? Where would he

115

appear? Paul had said he just popped out from behind a statue. She wished she'd asked which one but hadn't wanted to appear too interested. She waited, held her breath, counted in time with her slowing heartbeat. She had to breathe again. Nothing happened. How much time had passed? She turned to the portrait. Please, she said silently. Please.

A soft sound came from the woods behind the temple and the candle flickered. Alice's scalp prickled. There was a rustle, then another, then another. Then barely discernible footfalls as he moved from the forest floor on to the stone of the portico, accompanied by a clicking sound—that must be the walking stick. The sounds stopped. She stared into the shadows. Why didn't he come out?

The cautious steps resumed at last and from behind a statue on the far side of the room a fox stepped into the moonlight. He looked straight at her with his smiling face, then lowered his head, trotted across the floor and disappeared into the night.

Alice released her breath. Her hands had gripped her thighs so hard they hurt. Had that been Francis? In the form of a fox? It could be, it must be. She bowed to the portrait. Roger and Sophie copied her. Should she say something? 'Thank you, sir, for coming . . .'

'Thank you,' echoed Roger faintly.

Alice stood up, then almost fell over as her legs gave way. She picked up the glass but it slipped from her stiff fingers and shattered on the floor. 'Oh damn.'

'Don't worry,' said Roger. 'There were dozens of

116

glasses; they'll never miss one.'

'No, I suppose not. You two close the doors.' Alice bent to collect the scattered shards. 'Ouch!' A quick slice of pain across her thumb and a few drops of blood fell, black in the silver light. Her blood. Damory blood. Francis looked out from his portrait—an amused, foxy look. That was you, wasn't it? She touched her thumb to the spilled liquid, knowing it would sting; she brought it to her mouth and sucked, salty blood mingling with the smoky, bittersweet cognac.

She gathered the glass into her handkerchief and packed it into her satchel. Roger and Sophie had shut all but the last door, and when she blew out the candle the temple was very dark. She picked up the portrait and hurried out.

Back in her room Alice was astonished to see that only two hours had passed. She hid her muddy dress and the broken glass at the bottom of the wardrobe; she'd think of an excuse for them tomorrow. She climbed into bed with her journal to record the night's experiences, but her eyes drifted closed.

Moon-body, she thought, rising through the hole in the ceiling. The land beneath pulsed with waves of life. The moon was setting; she drifted up the hill so that she could watch it set again. At the top the last rays touched the portico of the temple of Hermes. She went inside. It was filled with moonlight though she hadn't opened any of the doors. There was a pattern on the floor that she'd never noticed before: intersecting lines and circles, angles and arcs. She picked one line and followed it to a blank space in the centre.

Francis? Francis, are you here?

117

From the woods, a fox barked. Oh, not another fox. Please, I want my great-great-great-great-grandfather. Francis Peter George St John Damory, she thought hard, picturing his face and the letters of his name. It's me, it's Alice. I'm here.

*   *   *

'Good evening, Theodora.' Francis rose from his seat by the fire and bowed. 'I hope you appreciate that my obeisance, though elegant, is sincere.'

Theo repressed a smile. 'You don't know the meaning of the word.'

'I do, you know. I am pure as honey, through and through.' He looked around. 'I was wondering what you've done with my writing table.'

'Put it in another room. It's not your writing table any more.'

'No it's not, quite right.'

Would there ever come a day, Theo wondered, when she would cease to feel a guest in her own sitting room?

'I was admiring your new garden,' Francis said. 'Does it work?'

'We shall see. Gardens take time.'

'And who are you, dearest, to speak of time?'

'Does it weigh heavy, old friend?'

'It does not lighten.'

'You still hope.'

'Of course.'

'Paul?'

'An interesting man. Another great-great-great-great-grandson of mine, as it happens.'

'You know I will not act,' Theo said.

'But you will not interfere with my actions?'

118

'That would be to act.'

'Oh Theodora, you've become such a Buddha.'

'There is no Buddha.'

'That's what I mean.'

'Do I need to remind you that it must be left to . . . chance, shall we call it? Or fate?'

Francis sighed. 'I know. I may finally have learned—after a hundred and eighty years of regret—that when I try to make things happen before their time, it is a disaster—quite literally. So I wait, and watch. I like to keep an eye on all my descendants.'

'You think Alice . . .'

'Maybe.'

'You thought it was me.'

'You could have been,' Francis said. 'Could still be.'

Theo waved her hand. 'I choose not; therefore I am not. And Alice must be allowed to choose. You would be very . . . fascinating to someone like Alice. She's still a child in many ways.'

'Nearly as old as you were when you learned to shut me out. It's time I got to know her.'

'Yes, I know it is, but I set certain conditions.' She pointed her finger at him. 'Hear me.'

'Yes, Theodora, I hear.'

'You cannot take her out from Farundell, and you cannot invite anyone else in. You cannot mislead her or tell her an untruth of any sort. You cannot direct her or influence her for your own ends. You will respect her freedom to choose her own path. You will protect her from harm, and work only for her good.'

'I will, Theodora.' He held her gaze as she probed. He didn't flinch or fling up defences; he

119

yielded. She tested his weak points; she knew it hurt but he suffered her scrutiny.

'You see, Theodora? Becoming pure as honey.'

'But not yet so sweet, my dear. You may meet her tomorrow.'

'Why not tonight? She's back at the temple of Hermes.'

'She won't remember; already she forgets more than she remembers.'

'All the more reason, then, to make an impression.'

'No. Tomorrow, in daylight, in the physical. Be as ordinary as you can, please. Now goodnight.'

He vanished with a wave of a lacy handkerchief.

Theo tossed another log on the fire to keep her body warm and went up to the temple. Alice stood entranced in the centre of the floor, its colours flashing and shifting.

'Come on,' Theo said. 'It's time for bed. You'll meet Francis tomorrow.'

'Do you promise?'

'I promise.'

'All right then, I'll come.' Alice took her great-aunt's golden hand and slid sleepily down to earth.

*   *   *

'Stephen, could I borrow Alice for a while?'

'Of course, Theo.' He looked at the schoolroom clock. 'We can finish after lunch, Alice. Off you go.'

Alice closed the door behind her. 'What is it?'

'There's someone who wants to meet you.'

'To meet me? It's not . . . is it . . . Francis?' Was it possible Theo knew what she'd been doing last night?

'It is.'

'Oh!' Her heart jumped. 'Where is he?'

'In my sitting room.'

Alice looked at her ink-stained hands, her grimy cuffs. Why had he come now, in the middle of the day, when she wasn't ready? She wiped her fingers on her skirt and tried to arrange her jumper so the moth holes didn't show. 'Wait,' she said, before Theo opened the door. 'Wait, am I dreaming now?'

'No. You're awake and in your earth-body.'

Her great-great-great-great-grandfather sat in a chair reading yesterday's *Times*. He laid it aside when she entered. 'Hello, Alice,' he said.

His voice was rich, melodic, his accent somehow . . . different. It reminded her of the strange and complex flavour of the cognac. She stared at him, drinking him in. He looked utterly real. She'd heard that he did, of course, to some people, but had expected a bit of blurriness or perhaps transparency. He was handsomer than his portraits, his eyes a sharper green; his long wavy hair looked soft as a girl's. Her mind fixed on details: his rings—cabochon ruby, sapphire, emerald, the white lace at his cuff.

She felt light-headed and for a panicked moment forgot how to breathe, remembered with a gasp, blushed. She had an urge to curtsy. She wasn't sure how it went so found herself adding a clumsy wobble to a little bow. 'Hello, sir.' Her voice cracked. She wished she could disappear. She was acting like a baby. Like Sophie. He'd be sorry he came and he'd never come back.

'You wanted to meet me,' he said.

121

'Yes, sir. I've always wanted to meet you.' Oh, what a stupid thing to say.

'You've been frequenting my temple of Hermes.'

'Yes, sir. I didn't think you'd noticed.'

'I noticed.'

She took heart. 'That fox, sir, was that you?'

'Not exactly.'

'Then you were there?'

'In a way.'

'But then why didn't you come yourself?'

He glanced at Theo. 'I was not permitted.'

'An analogy,' said Theo. 'Children are not permitted to drink spirits because they are not able to understand or handle their influence.'

'Oh,' said Alice. Her great-aunt seemed to know in detail about last night's adventure. 'But now I'm old enough?'

'Are you?'

Alice remembered her decision not to give Roger and Sophie any cognac. 'Yes,' she said. 'I am.'

'Well then.' Francis crossed his legs, arranged his long hands one atop the other on his knee and smiled, Alice thought, exactly like the fox. 'Here we are at last. I am at your disposal.'

Alice had, over the years, prepared a list of questions she would have for Francis when she met him: careful, reasoned questions, which were all now forgotten. She knew she was still staring at him wide-eyed as a child, but she couldn't help it. She wanted to touch him, to know if he felt as real as he looked.

He extended his hand. 'Touch me, if you like.'

'Can you read my mind?'

'In a way,' Francis said, 'but your impulse was

predictable.'

Alice cursed herself. How awful to be so predictable, but she did want to. His hand was warm and firm and exactly as one would expect of a living man, the skin smooth and pale. The rings were hard, and cooler. His sleeve was soft green velvet. She let her hand close over his arm, sensed muscles and bones beneath the fabric. Greatly daring, she moved her fingers to his wrist, pressed. She felt a pulse and pulled back; somehow, she'd not expected that.

'A veritable simulacrum,' said Francis.

'Oh,' said Alice. 'I mean, what?' Her mind raced to guess the meaning. *Similate*, to copy. A veritable simulacrum—a truthful copy. 'So you're not a real—that is, I mean . . . what are you, sir?'

Francis raised his eyebrows. 'My,' he said to Theo, 'she does ask the questions, doesn't she?'

'Yes, she does,' Theo said. 'She certainly does.'

Alice didn't know whether to be embarrassed or pleased. She looked from Theo to Francis. Would he answer? She returned his gaze as steadily as she could. He was amused, she thought, not angry.

'What I am, my dear,' he said, 'is the story of my life, and it is too long a story for today.'

Alice wanted to protest that she had plenty of time but something in his face stopped her. It occurred to her that his existence might not be altogether to his liking, and the thought was so disconcerting that she looked to her great-aunt for guidance.

Theo shook her head. 'Francis cannot lie to you, Alice, but he doesn't have to answer every question. And there are some things that even you, grown up as you are, may not be able to understand right now.'

Already, it seemed, she had gone too far. Damn, damn, damn, why couldn't she have asked something else? 'Can Roger and Sophie see you?' She ought to ask something for them—they had, after all, obeyed as well as they could last night.

'Neither are able,' Theo said.

'Oh.' Alice tried not to be pleased. 'They'll be so jealous.'

'Will you tell them you've met me?' asked Francis.

'Well, I thought . . .'

'Do you have any secrets?'

Alice nodded.

'Suppose I become one of your secrets. Not, obviously, from Theodora. But I assure you I know from experience there are some things which are better not bruited about.' He winked at her. '*Scire, Velle, Audere, Tacere*, as they say.'

Know, will, dare, keep silent, Alice translated. 'Yes, sir, I think I understand. I won't tell anyone.'

*   *   *

Alice climbed into bed, tucked her feet under Artemis and opened *The Faerie Queene*. She understood what Stephen meant about it being difficult. Sometimes it was like chewing on felt, so dense and thick were the classical allusions, so heavy the moral tone. But she liked the story, and strewn about the text were some interesting ideas.

> Who all this while, with charms and hidden arts,
> Had made a lady of that other sprite,

124

And framed of liquid air her tender parts,
So lively and so like in all men's sight . . .

Alice reread the last few lines. A spirit is made to appear as a living woman, her body made out of liquid air. Liquid air? What was that? Her moon-body felt like liquid air, now she thought about it. She had never come any closer to understanding moon-bodies, or dreams, or why, no matter how hard she tried to remember, she forgot more and more. She'd become so frustrated she'd given up and gone to Theo, who had told her to look closely at everything and clues would begin to appear in unlikely places. Was this just such a clue ? Spenser seemed to be saying that this liquid air could be shaped into any form, and made to appear lifelike. If so, that could also explain Francis.

Francis. All thoughts led to him. She'd never imagined it would be so hard to keep a secret, but she was determined to show that she was grown up enough to be trusted. She combed over everything he'd said, recalled the feel of his hand, his sleeve, his pulse. There was something so uncanny about that pulse. Touching him had been the oddest experience of her life; the memory of it still caused her breath to catch. She supposed she would get used to it eventually, and seeing him would become routine, as apparently it was for Theo.

That was another odd thing—Francis had needed her great-aunt's permission to appear, which opened up questions Alice had never considered. Questions led to more questions, a thicket of questions, dense and growing denser. The weight of everything she didn't know pressed all around her. She'd expected that as she got older and learned more, she'd have more answers, fewer questions. But it was turning out just the opposite. Even things she thought she'd known were breaking up into uncertainties. Her head throbbed with questions, growing like brambles. She turned to *The Faerie Queene* and tried to concentrate on the text, but a few pages later she was again reminded of Francis:

> He then devised himself how to disguise;
> For by his mighty science he could take
> As many forms and shapes in seeming wise,
> As ever Proteus to himself could make:
> Sometime a fowl, sometime a fish in lake,
> Now like a fox, now like a dragon fell . . .

A fox? Was Francis like Spenser's magician Archimago, able to assume whatever form he wished? Archimago, meaning—she worked out the etymology—chief image or more likely chief mage. Mage, from *magos*, one of the Magi, the famous Persian enchanters. And *imago* is a likeness. The magician makes images—the magician imagines? 'By his mighty science'—science, from *scire*, to know. Science of liquid air, that could make any form.

The words swam about in her mind; their derivatives and cognates in all languages swarmed like a cloud of leaves, branched into infinity, met and married other words, begot new words that doubled back and linked with their ancestors. The book slid from her fingers and her moon-body slipped free, rose through the hole in the ceiling and straight up the hill to the temple of Hermes. Francis was waiting, reclining on a blue silk chaise

126

longue. Music filled the air, though she couldn't see any musicians.

He rose, smiled and bowed. 'May I have this dance?'

'I don't know how to dance very well.' Alice glanced down at her nightgown and bare feet. 'And I'm not dressed for dancing.'

'No, you're not,' Francis said. 'What would you rather be wearing?'

'Oh, anything.'

'Imagine what you want, and you will make it out of liquid air.'

Alice recalled a portrait of Francis's second wife in a magnificent gown, red and gold.

'Oh, no!' Francis leapt back as her skirts spread. 'God, I loathe that frock.'

Alice plucked at the stiffly embroidered fabric. 'Sorry.'

'What about . . .' He tapped her shoulder, and the dress turned aquamarine, with a draped neckline and long strings of beads. 'No, perhaps blue isn't your colour.' He tapped her shoulder again; it was saffron yellow with a bow at the waist.

'I don't like this style,' said Alice. 'It would be better longer, and coming in, here.' She moved her hands over the dress, pictured the changes as they occurred. The silk felt slippery and cool on her skin. 'Is this how you make your veritable simulacrum?'

He laughed. 'Dear Alice, laden with questions.'

Alice stamped her foot, noticing that it was clad in an elegant satin shoe. 'Don't laugh at me. And why not simply answer a question?'

'Has it really not occurred to you, dear child,' and Alice knew he said it to annoy her, 'that there

127

are no simple answers?' He clicked his fingers, and the music changed to a waltz. 'Now, shall we dance?'

Alice, about to say that she didn't know how to waltz, found herself waltzing effortlessly. Francis guided her across the floor; once again its pattern came to life and she grew dizzy watching the wheels spin. The dizziness pulled her down; she tumbled into her earth-body and dropped slowly through dreams to sleep and forgetting.

8

Paul reclined against a headstone and pointed the camera at the sky. He'd chosen this spot because the graveyard behind the old chapel made an almost perfectly circular clearing in the forest, into which the perfect triangle of the chapel's roof pointed. Three birds flew from left to right. Click. He turned the camera and opened the autographic door. With eyes averted, he slipped his finger into the book on his lap—the *Pymander*—moved it down the page, stopped, then looked. It rested on the phrase 'The Soul drawing near her Maker is the Cause of Time and Light.' This he recorded with the stylus on to the film before winding it on and returning to his observation of the patch of sky.

When he printed the film the words would appear within the picture as though they, like trees and birds and sky, were real things caught in his lens. He'd resorted to this rather Dadaist approach to the *Pymander* since, after all, it could hardly become more perplexing than it already was. He had a notion that when all the photographs were assembled, the random marriage of words and images would illuminate or elucidate or somehow shake loose a meaning.

He carried the Kodak with him everywhere; it added an enjoyable sense of purpose to his walks. It was easy to use and he was discovering an instinctive understanding of how to balance the demands of aperture and exposure—of, he realised—time and light. He loved the whispery click of the shutter, the paper-thin leaves of the steel iris, the precision with which they opened and closed. The autographic feature enchanted him; it was meant for such commonplaces as date and subject, but he'd seen other possibilities for the little oblong, hidden behind its own close-fitting door.

Looking for things to photograph, he had started to notice patterns everywhere in nature: in the surface of the lake, in stones and grasses and trees, in the intricate lace of leaves and branches, the play of foreground and background. Then by accident he'd caught birds in flight, making dark marks against the sky like words, or letters of a word. It had reminded him of Alice's augury—wherever he pointed it, the camera was the space marked out in the sky, and he the watcher for signs.

Two birds, left to right. Click. 'Sow in yourself the Seed of Regeneration,' said *Pymander*.

That reminded him of Theo, and what he'd come to think of as the Lesson of the Seed—a lesson he hadn't yet understood, though it had, definitely, taken root and was growing in his mind.

Who was this Pymander, more enigmatic even than Theo? Old Mr Pym, Stephen had called him, as though he was a dotty neighbour.

One bird, from the top of the frame to the bottom. Click. Paul's finger landed on the words: 'I am the One who makes the World by the Seeds of himself.' He stared at the book, reread the words, wrote them on the film, closed the book and the camera and stood up. He lit a cigarette and shrugged his shoulders vehemently to shake off the feeling that a very strange old chap named Mr Pym was standing just behind him, laughing silently. He tucked the camera and book into his pockets and headed down the hill.

When he reached the house he hesitated, then turned and crossed the courtyard. This was as good a time as any to call on Jarlath. His questions were, after all, perfectly reasonable; there was no need to be so bashful. The sound of an aria drifted down from the studio; it ended as he climbed the stairs.

Just inside the open door Jarlath stood in a makeshift kitchen. 'Coffee,' he said, pouring a second cup.

The second cup, Paul saw, had already been set out. 'Yes, thank you.'

'Have a seat, have a seat.' Jarlath waved expansively.

A pair of settees faced each other halfway down the long room, covered, like the rough planks of the floor, with Persian carpets. At the far end, under roof-lights cut between the high beams, stood easels and tables with brushes, tubes of paint, jars of pencils. The smell was an intriguing melange of coffee, tobacco, incense, hashish and turpentine that reminded Paul of Paris. He sank into one of the settees; Jarlath placed a small cup of very black coffee on a low brass table, sat opposite and studied Paul closely.

'Turn your head.'

'What? Oh.'

'Stand up.'

Paul complied.

'Take off your jacket.'

He shrugged it off, the pockets weighted by camera and book. He remembered why he had come. 'I wanted to ask . . .'

'And your shirt.'

'And my . . . ?'

'Shirt. If you please.'

'Er . . .'

'I won't bite,' Jarlath said. 'At least not so early in our acquaintance. Come and stand here, in the light.' He stared at Paul for a long minute, then extended one finger, pushed Paul's chin to a new position. 'Do not move.'

He propped a pad on an easel and began sketching. Paul had never seen such intense concentration, not even in the army surgeons. He tried to shift his weight, but Jarlath barked, 'Don't move!' without interrupting the swift motion of his hand, the constant flicker of his eyes from Paul to paper to Paul. Sticks of charcoal were reduced to slivers and discarded, pages filled and turned. Paul's body began to ache and he looked longingly at his coffee, abandoned and cold. He wanted a cigarette.

'Just one more minute,' Jarlath said, but Paul could tell he didn't mean it.

He tried to breathe steadily. The sun was warm;

131

the constant twitterings of the birds fell through the light like drops of rain and tingled on his skin. The smell of honey mingled with the other aromas and he remembered a dream in which he'd been swimming in thick golden air . . .

'Paul,' Jarlath's voice came from far away. 'You can move now.'

Paul rubbed his eyes. The air was hot and hazy, swimming with light. He had no idea how long he'd been standing there.

'Coffee's cold,' Jarlath said. 'Hope you don't mind. I saw something, had to get it, know what I mean?'

Paul stretched and yawned. 'I think so. I used to try to write.'

'Used to?'

'I gave it up.'

'Why?'

'It gave me up, I should say.' He pulled on his shirt. 'My lover, language, was not true.'

'Ah, the bitch-mother of us all. You must not expect truth from her; she gives us everything else. I resort to images. Would you come again a few times to pose?'

'All right, but why me?'

'Let's just say you have an interesting face.'

Paul reached into his jacket pocket for his cigarettes and found the *Pymander*. 'I was going to ask you about this book,' he said. 'And the quotation around that painting in the library—I don't understand that at all.'

'And you've seen Francis.'

Oh hell, Jarlath was turning out to be as confusing as Theo. 'So who was Hermes Trismegistos? Any relation to the Greek god

132

of the same name?'

'Lucky Paul. At the start of all these lines of enquiry.'

Paul pictured himself surrounded on all sides by floating threads receding to infinity in an ever-expanding sphere. He chose one. 'What does his name mean?'

Jarlath steepled his fingers and regarded Paul in silence. His hands were large and pale; the fingertips had a feminine taper and smooth, rounded nails. On the index finger of his right hand was a moonstone in a coiled silver setting. 'Hermes the Thrice-Great—three times great because great on the three planes of manifestation, or because the third and highest incarnation of one who had been Thoth in Egypt and Hermes in Greece. Or for other reasons. Then again, he may never have lived on Earth. People assume one can converse only with another incarnate being, but that is of course nonsense, a fallacy of these sadly ignorant times.'

'Oh,' said Paul. 'Of course.' Jarlath's answers, by their seeming reasonableness, drew him deeper, and then before he knew it he was lost in a fog. He was sure this was deliberate, but also sure there was a path if he could find it, and Jarlath was laying a trail. He pictured stepping stones vanishing into the mist.

'The way of Hermes,' Jarlath said, 'is an ancient path that leads through many mysteries.' His subtle emphasis of the words 'path' and 'mysteries' convinced Paul that Jarlath had either put the image of path and mist into his mind or read it there.

'It's a universal image,' said Jarlath, and smiled

133

to confirm and deny. He stood and walked Paul to the door.

'Thanks for the coffee,' Paul said. 'You're right about all those lines of enquiry, but I don't know how lucky I feel.'

'Oh, you are—not that there is such a thing,' said Jarlath.

* * *

After dinner Paul went to the darkroom. Henry had, as promised, taught him the basics—not nearly as complicated as he'd thought, and there was a shelf full of equipment manuals and books with titles like *The Complete Photographer* and *Advanced Darkroom Techniques.*

He unlocked the door and pushed through the two sets of velvet curtains into complete blackness. He reached for the switch and the electric filament began to glow in its cylinder of red liquid. He turned on the tap; the water burbled peacefully.

The darkroom was functional but also, somehow, romantic; the chemicals simple and predictable in their action and reaction yet the resulting transformations, the invisible made visible, mysterious and fascinating. He liked the measuring, the mixing and stirring, the waiting and watching as the pictures he'd imagined floated into existence. He enjoyed the simple act of entering the room, like penetrating a sanctuary through the three barriers of door, curtain, curtain; the sense of being cut off from the rest of the house; the absolute privacy. It was also, of course, like a woman: the layers part one by one and at the end,

134

or the beginning, the warm, wet, red, all-creative womb.

*   *   *

Alice leaned out of her window. The stillness of the early-morning air promised heat; it was going to be a beautiful day—too beautiful for lessons. She'd take a picnic to Daniel; maybe they could go to the island. They'd built their coracles and practised paddling about, but had stayed near the shore. The boat was proving much harder to control than she'd imagined, and seemed to have a mind of its own.

Tustian was at the kitchen table with his house books open before him, chewing on the end of a pencil. 'Good morning, Miss Alice. You're up very early today.'

'You're up even earlier.'

'Oh yes.' He sighed. 'I was informed last night that your mother will bring a number of guests this evening.'

'A number?' Alice loved the way Tustian avoided saying things. 'A large number?'

'Oh yes.' He sighed again, though they both knew he did it for effect. 'A very large number.'

'Oh my, Tustian! Have we room?'

'That is just what I was trying to work out. I'm afraid some will have to double up, or stay in Exley. I must remember to ring the inn.' He added an item to a list.

Alice leaned over his shoulder. She liked the smell of his shaving soap. 'How often do you shave your head, Tustian?' she said. It was part of their routine.

135

'Every day, Miss Alice, else I start picking up the wireless.'

'But then we could get the concerts.'

'Ah, but it itches so, especially the tuba.'

Mrs Beal appeared, tying on her apron. 'Morning, Miss Alice. Can I make you some breakfast?'

'May I have some coffee?'

'A little very milky coffee, if you don't tell.'

'Thanks, Mrs B. Could you make sandwiches? I want to take a picnic to Daniel.'

'Don't you have lessons today?' Tustian said.

'It's too nice. Tell Stephen I'm sorry but I had to go.'

'Very well, Miss Alice,' he said, attempting to sound stern.

'Ham sandwiches for you, and cheese for Mr Daniel,' Mrs Beal said. 'And hard-boiled eggs, and pickles, and a flan? And you could have half a chicken.'

'Yes, please,' said Alice. She pulled up a chair next to Tustian and studied the guest list. There was only one person she knew, her third cousin Val St John Vere. 'Who are all these people?'

'A moving-picture company, or crew, as I believe it is called, though the nautical connection escapes me,' Tustian said.

'Oh, the film people.' She knew Maggie was in a movie and hadn't yet decided whether that was a step down or up from theatre. 'But why are they coming here?'

'I understand they intend to shoot—I believe that is the correct term, though the hunting connection, I'm afraid, escapes me as well—a certain scene here at the lake, because of the

136

disaster that occurred on a previous attempt, somewhere in the Thames Estuary.' He pronounced the words with distaste.

'A disaster? What sort of disaster?'

'I gather it involved a great deal of mud, and being stuck, and rained upon.'

'Ah, that sort of disaster. Maggie loathes mud more than anything else in the world. That is why she finds children so trying. Or one of the reasons.' Alice turned back to the lists and charts. 'We have to give Val a nice room—how about the Tapestry Room?'

'Very good, Miss Alice.'

He labelled the room on his master plan, and Alice crossed Val off the list. 'Now who's next? Desmond Fanshawe, what a name. Well, that one's obvious, at least. D. Fanshawe, Esq., in the Fan Room.'

'Oh, very good, Miss Alice.'

Mrs Beal brought her coffee and a thick slice of bread and jam.

'Thank you, Mrs B. Look, here is someone named Miss Sara Paragon. Do you suppose that can be her real name?'

'I suppose it might be. A foreign name perhaps.'

'And Mr Arlen Winter—what a romantic name.'

'Indeed, Miss Alice.'

'Let's put them in the Bluebird Room and the Peacock Room respectively.'

'Better the other way around,' said Tustian. 'The Peacock Room has its own bathroom, and that is more important to ladies than to most gentlemen.'

'Ah, of course.' Alice ticked off the names and turned to her bread and coffee. When she was grown up she would drink very strong black coffee with no sugar, smoke Turkish cigarettes and have Napoleon VSOP cognac after dinner every night.

The picnic basket was ready; she swallowed the last of her breakfast and hurried out. Daniel's whistling floated across the water—Vivaldi's Spring Concerto. It was such an auspicious melody that her heart gave a joyful leap and she ran down the meadow as fast as she could, holding the basket at arm's length, her feet flying over the ground, the sun in her eyes.

Daniel sat on the porch of the cabin, the concerto finished. Alice sat behind him, and started picking burrs from his hair. 'This is like a horse's tail,' she said. 'You could give half of it to Tustian and never miss it. Remember I said Maggie was in a movie? They've been making it in London, but Tustian told me they're coming here, to shoot a scene at the lake. Twenty people.' Suddenly it seemed less like a house party and more like an invasion. 'I suppose they'll stay on the other side.' She wished she could put up a fence of some sort to keep all those strangers away. 'Oh, and Sylvie's not coming until Monday. Apparently she bunked off the first boat she was meant to be on. Maggie said never to fall in love with an Italian.'

Daniel made a snorting sound. Was that a laugh?

'Let's take the coracles to the island,' she said. 'We can have our picnic there.'

They readied the boats, distributing picnic basket, blanket and tea things between them. Alice left her shoes on the porch and when they waded into the water, climbed in and pushed off, she felt like a real adventurer on her way to some unexplored land like those Percy had visited, to an island inhabited by an unknown tribe who might be hostile.

They paddled across the placid surface, Alice rotating a quarter-turn with every stroke. Daniel, who'd mastered the art of forward motion, paused now and then to let her catch up, though he pretended to be resting. Alice's arms began to ache. She focused on their destination, the wide meadow that was the traditional picnic site. She tried to estimate how many strokes it would take to get there. A lot. She paced herself, counted slowly and tried to make her strokes even. The sun glinted on the water, sweat ran into her eyes. She was sticky all over. When she got there she would have a swim right away. The thought made her realise how hot she was. She stopped to rest, cupped a handful of water and splashed her face.

Daniel pulled up deftly. 'Try it,' he said, 'like this.' He leaned forward and moved the paddle in figures of eight without lifting it above the surface; the coracle slid along the furrow it made. Alice realised she'd been trying to paddle it like a canoe, pulling it through the water by force, but this was completely different. One had to shape the water into a path; the boat inevitably followed. It was easier than she thought, far easier than paddling, and by the time they reached the island she had begun to get the hang of it.

Daniel carried their things up the meadow as Alice tore off her clothes and plunged into the lake. She lay against the bank, the water lapping her chin. Tiny fish approached her feet; she wiggled her toes; they fled, then returned. She looked up at the clear blue sky. What's up there? Space, and stars, and nothing. Does it go on and

139

on forever, or stop somewhere? Her stomach twisted as part of her lifted, then a sharp stone dug into her back and she was suddenly cold. She climbed out, rolled herself dry on the grass and pulled on her clothes.

Daniel had set out the picnic. She fell upon the ham sandwiches and devoured them, then turned to the chicken. Her uncle was a slow eater. He approached his sandwiches systematically: the bread, crust first, then maybe, or maybe not, the slice of cheese. He would examine it closely, turning it over and over before he decided. Often he'd discard it, and then he didn't let Alice have it, either. If he did eat it, it was with tiny nibbles and a lot of mastication. Today he subjected the cheese to greater than usual scrutiny before putting it aside. 'Alice,' he said, 'would you please tell Mrs Kendall that I do not wish to eat cheese any more.'

'It's Mrs Beal now,' Alice said. 'Mrs Kendall died before I was born. I've told you.'

'Oh? Well, would you tell Mrs Beal, then.'

'She'll ask what you want instead.'

'Just bread is fine. Or tomato. Or cucumber.'

'I'll tell her, but she'll tut. She's convinced you're starving.'

Daniel lit a fire and, holding the kettle carefully by its wooden handle, put it on to boil while Alice rinsed their plates in the lake. They made tea. How civilised we are, Alice thought, with our teapot, our blanket and basket. What would it be like if this really was the middle of nowhere, if all around, in all directions, was an unmapped jungle? She stared at the opposite shore and tried to imagine that it was unfamiliar. She could just make out the corner of Daniel's cabin. Without that—

she held up her thumb to block it—there was nothing to see but the water and a strip of reeds, then trees, and a further wooded hill beyond. It could be anywhere. What if she was stranded on this tiny island—how would she survive? She caught a whiff of a state of uncertainty, tinged with fear but also with excitement.

Daniel had curled up and fallen asleep. His breathing was uneven, his eyelids twitched, his hands clenched and he was grinding his teeth. She couldn't bear to watch.

She walked up the path to the temple of Aphrodite, so silent in her bare feet that she was almost upon the fawn before it sprang from its hiding place and bounded away on gawky, fragile legs. A pregnant doe must have swum over and now couldn't swim back until the baby was grown; it happened almost every year. A squirrel chattered on a branch. 'Sorry to have disturbed you,' Alice said.

The columns that Francis had brought from Cyprus stood among the trees on the flattened top of the island. Several had fallen and were slowly drowning in ivy. She touched their pale, pitted surfaces. Were they really from an ancient temple or was that just a story? She could ask Francis when she saw him again. If she saw him again. She had a sudden feeling that he was behind her; she whirled around. 'Francis?' There was a rustling in the bushes—a fox? No, only a squirrel.

An ancient oak clung to the steep western edge of the plateau; beyond the tree the ground dropped away. She climbed among the gnarled roots; there had been a stair once, but now it was so overgrown you could hardly tell. As far as she knew, no one else even remembered it was here; overhanging trees hid the small, deep pool at the bottom. Perhaps long ago it had been open to the sky, but now only in the middle of summer did the sun reach the water. The spring that fed the pool emerged from a grotto whose entrance was so choked with shrubs and shrouded by thick curtains of ivy that Alice had come here for years before she'd noticed it. The walls and ceiling were covered with shells: scallop and cockle and clam, conch, mussel, periwinkle, oyster, cowrie and abalone arranged in swirls and wavy lines, the pattern obscured by ferns and roots and moss.

She knelt on a flat rock by the pool, gazed down at the reflection of her face, and beyond, into the clear depths. It was strangely quiet; the birdsong seemed distant and there was a droning of bees just at the edge of hearing. The still surface of the water showed a perfect image of the sky. A small cloud drifted by; then a bird crossed. *Temenos*, she thought, and the word opened like a door into that hushed and waiting space. She'd been trying to follow Theo's advice to contemplate her own experience and had begun to notice more and more little flickers of memory among and between her ordinary thoughts. Usually they slipped by too fast to catch, and she was left with only the certainty that she'd forgotten something, but if she was very careful, didn't try too hard, she could grasp it like the end of a thread and follow it to its source. Often it was something she'd done in her earth-body but forgotten because it was unimportant, but sometimes it was a bit of a dream, and very occasionally she remembered a brief flash of something she'd done in her moon-body. She didn't know how she knew which was which, but she did. It was as though each type of experience had its own flavour.

The sky clouded over and drops of rain began to fall as she walked back down the hill. Daniel had packed up the picnic things and was waiting by the coracles. As they paddled across the lake the rain fell harder, bouncing off the surface. Daniel whistled Handel's Water Music; Alice tried to whistle along. She moved her paddle in a steady, rhythmic figure of eight and flowed over the water with ease, almost as fast as Daniel.

9

'Nino is limping down to the lake; he looks very tired and dirty.' Paul described the scene to Percy, who had insisted on conducting their session on the terrace. 'It's that part of the story when he's escaped from the city and found his way to the shore. Now he's waiting for the goddess to appear.'

Henry approached with a blanket and tucked it over Percy's knees. 'It is warmer here than indoors,' Percy said, 'the sun is quite hot; there is not the slightest breeze. Go away. I am going to dictate now.'

Henry retreated and Percy reached for his pipe. 'Has he gone?'

Paul glanced around. Henry lurked inside the morning room. 'He's not gone far.'

'Oh the hell with him.' Percy lit his pipe. From the open doors came the sound of urgent

143

coughing.

'Go away, Old Hen!' Percy pushed the blanket to the ground. 'I must learn to ignore him. But he won't let me.'

'He's very devoted.'

'Rubbish. He's just likes to keep me under his thumb.' Percy sighed. He really didn't have the time to tussle with Henry any more, enjoyable as it was. 'What are they doing now?'

'Fanshawe's sending Nino back to do it again.'

The director, on a ladder with a megaphone, presided over a chaos of men and equipment. Chairs and tables, tents and a small marquee had sprung up; Val, in an immaculate white linen suit, sat under the willows with Maggie and Albert Laski. The company had arrived the previous evening, filling the house. Percy had enjoyed every minute and made Paul describe everyone in detail. Henry fretted so much he'd become ill.

Percy puffed on his pipe and listened to the sounds rising from the lakeside, the commands of the director, the shouts of the crew, laughter. 'I want to have a really big picnic and regatta this year,' he said. It may be my last, he thought. 'Like when I was a child. There were hundreds of people, or so it seemed.' The trumpet limbered up with runs and scales; he recalled Paul's description and remembered the man's handshake, large and gentle, his soft American voice. But names failed to stick. 'What was his name?'

'The trumpeter? Arlen Winter,' Paul said.

'Oh, yes. Lovely name. Sounds like a poem—"The Ballad of Arlen Winter".' Sara Paragon began tuning her violin. 'And the young lady violinist. Now I really should remember that one.'

'Sa . . .' Paul hinted.

'Ah, Miss Sara Paragon. Is that her real name?'

'I don't know. I asked her when we met in London but I don't believe she ever answered me.' She had greeted him last night with a very friendly kiss.

'And what are they wearing?'

'She's in a red ball gown, old-fashioned, tight at the waist, with a full skirt. Arlen's in tails. They look beautiful and a bit mad standing in a meadow, trying to keep their shoes clean. Tustian is leading a procession of housemaids with trays. They've stopped at Sara and Arlen and are serving coffee.' Paul thought Fanshawe really should be shooting that scene: the butler, accompanied by aproned housemaids, approaches the glamorous couple in the field; the silver coffee pot is flourished and china cups are filled; the procession moves on.

The scene shone vivid as though projected on to a screen behind Percy's eyes; the figures moved, bright and clear, full of life and colour yet transparent, transient, lantern slides shifting, present to past; images falling into place, remembered, rearranged.

Maggie's bright laughter dances up the meadow and a hundred Maggies whirl through his mind. She's a dignified eleven in a wimple made from a napkin, declaiming Shakespeare for the guests; she's newborn, red curls covering her tiny head, propped on Odelia's lap. She's running, laughing, ringlets flying, Jamie leaping and skipping after. Daniel tries to follow, trips and falls, gets up, runs, falls.

'I was not meant to inherit,' Percy began to

145

dictate. 'I thought I could get away from all this—property, land, ownership, position. I was the third son, entirely dispensable. Arthur was the first, everybody's favourite. Then Tristan, then three girls, then me, then the twins and Theodora, late and last.'

He sees them assemble on the terrace; it's Arthur's birthday and there's to be a party, and a treasure hunt later—is it a memory of life, of a photograph, or of a dream? Hard to tell; he's simultaneously within his own five-year-old body and somewhere just above, watching as Nanny gives his jacket a final tweak and takes her place behind. Father and Mother move up the line, with a smile here, a frown there.

Paul watched Nino walk down to the shore again, and again. He staggered forward, utterly exhausted, then returned with spry steps to his starting point. Eventually he got it right, and Fanshawe climbed down from his ladder. Sara finished tuning her violin and took her place opposite Arlen for the next shot. Fanshawe had chairs brought for them to sit on, then the chairs were sent away and they climbed on to stacks of equipment boxes draped with tablecloths. Paul took out the Kodak and framed the shot: the two pedestals faced each other like a gate; the strangely hieratic figures raised their instruments as the camera moved along a curving track between them. Click. He released the shutter and reached into his pocket for the *Pymander*: 'Death is not destruction but dissolving.'

'Paul?' Percy said.

'I'm here.'

'Ah, good. For a moment I forgot where I was, or

rather, maybe, when I was.' He gestured to Paul to continue writing.

'The Farundell treasure was a legend long before I was born, but no one had seriously believed in it, or sought it, for ages. It had something to do, we knew, with Tobias Damory, whose father built the original part of the house—Tobias the Alchemist, as he was known. Odelia told me that Francis had found it and for some reason hidden it again, but when I was a child the whole thing was assumed to be just a myth. The only treasure we cared about was the one contrived for our entertainment in grand, elaborate treasure hunts that spread over the entire house and grounds. My mother was expert at putting cryptic clues into very funny rhymes, and all the servants had roles to play as demons and animals and storybook characters. Some of them were instructed to tell us misleading things while others had genuine clues, and we had to ask the right questions. We formed teams—my brothers and I against various cousins and friends.'

Percy runs down the meadow, following Arthur and Tris. 'Come on, Percy, hurry!' Arthur takes his hand, pulls him along, then hauls him up and tucks him under his arm. He giggles and squirms, jolted breathless.

'Come on!' Tris calls. 'Before they see us. Oh, why did you have to bring him?'

Arthur tosses Percy into the boat; they push off and row towards the island.

Oh no, Percy thought. I see where this is going. I don't want to remember this . . . but that bright summer day seventy years ago had snared him and sucked him in.

'They're gaining on us,' Tris says.

147

'Pull harder,' Arthur says.

'Let's throw the baby overboard. He's weighing us down.'

Percy looks over the side. What would happen if I drop off the boat, like this? He lowers himself with a small splash and falls, and falls, and falls like a stone through the cool green water, laughing at the bubbles that trail so gaily away. The fluid shadow of the boat recedes, the golden glimmer of the fading sun. He turns lazily; far below him the waving water weeds part and another sun is revealed, kind and beautiful and terribly bright.

He's jolted from his reverie as someone grabs him across his throat. He struggles wildly, reaching for that bright sun; he twists, kicks out, strikes something solid. It's Arthur, his face contorted, then suddenly peaceful and they're swimming together now, down and down. 'See?' Arthur says. 'It's easy. Don't be afraid. You can breathe underwater. Just follow me.'

Another body slams into his; Tris thrusts him roughly towards the surface and surges past him after Arthur. Other hands grab him; the water is full of people now. He's pulled into a boat, thumped until he chokes and spews water from his mouth and nose. It's the worst day of his life.

I'd forgotten, Percy thought. I'd forgotten everything except that Arthur drowned in an accident on his fourteenth birthday. He reached for his handkerchief. His hand was shaking. Had that memory been waiting all this time? Arthur, fourteen forever, preserved like a flower in glass. He pictured his brother, his hero, the best person in the world—and suddenly he's real, right here, in striped jersey and shorts and ancient plimsolls, sun

148

gilding the golden hair on his shins. He leans close, peers into Percy's face; their eyes meet and in an instant Percy knows two things: Arthur is not dead, and he is forgiven.

*   *   *

After lunch Percy napped in his room and Paul wandered down to the lake. Sara sat on a box, gazing across the water. 'May I take your picture?' he said.

'Oh, hello. I was thinking of you.'

'Good thoughts, I hope.'

'Rather good.'

'May I?' Paul held up the camera.

'How did you know?'

'Know what?'

'I adore being photographed.'

'Do you?' He studied her image in the viewfinder, adjusted the aperture. 'Why?' He wished he could capture the red of her dress, the green of the island floating over her shoulder.

'Not sure . . . I think I like the attention. I didn't know you were a photographer.'

'Oh, I'm not. I'm only learning. Could you please hold still?'

She leaned towards him, pouted. Click.

'Thank you. Would you help me find some words?' He passed her the *Pymander*, extracted the stylus and opened the flap at the back of the camera. 'See? Space for a few words.'

'And you haven't any of your own?'

'My own seem a bit tired sometimes, and I'm not so sure what they mean any more, so I look to chance. Just close your eyes, that's it, then open

149

the book anywhere and put your finger on the page. Now open your eyes and read out whatever line you've landed on.'

'"At the Abyss you must surrender your Heart."'

Paul wrote the words, advanced the film and framed her again; she read out another phrase: '"The Moon, forerunner of Form and Instrument of Nature." What is this book?'

'That's a better question than you realise, and I don't know the answer.'

She handed it back with a smile. 'What's it like working here?'

'It's hardly like work at all.'

'It's awfully quiet, isn't it? I woke in the middle of the night and I couldn't hear a thing, and then some animal howled or yelped or something and nearly scared me out of my skin. It took me ages to get back to sleep. I miss the traffic.'

'I seem to have grown accustomed to it, somewhat to my surprise.'

'So which is your room?'

Paul pointed. 'Top floor, far end.'

'Is it a nice room?'

'It suits me.'

'Has it got a bed in it?'

'Indeed it does.'

'Is it a nice bed?'

'It's rather a small bed.'

'Oh, that's fine.' She hopped from her perch. 'Desmond summons. See you,' she placed a quick kiss on his lips, 'later.'

Paul grinned to himself; Val, sitting under a tree, raised his boater in salute. Paul walked over and framed the shot: white suit, striped tie, speckled light and shade.

'That's new,' Val said.

'From Percy.' Paul dropped into a chair and passed Val the *Pymander*. 'Look, it's got this box for words. Would you choose me some at random?'

'Delighted.' Val took the book, closed his eyes, spun it expertly while turning it several times, opened it and stabbed his finger to the page; it was upside down. He righted it without lifting his finger and read, ' "All men are subject to Fate and Change." '

'Thanks,' said Paul.

'I was remembering summer visits here,' Val said. 'All the cousins. Sons and daughters of cousins of cousins. Nasty brats, most of them. Liked nothing better than getting muddy. Ugh.' He gave a brief shudder.

'Clearly a hellish childhood.' Paul pictured the banks of the lake crowded with muddy children, squabbling and splashing. As far as he could recall, there hadn't been any mud available when he was a child. If I ever have children, he thought, I'll try to ensure they have as much as they want.

Val lifted a bottle of champagne from a bucket, refilled his glass and poured one for Paul. 'Maggie's little essentials. Hardly had a chance to talk last night, in the midst of this circus I travel with these days, but I'm dying to know—are you a country mouse yet?'

'Quite possibly.'

'Don't you miss Paris? Or London?'

'No. Not one bit. I could go up to town on my days off, I suppose, but I've not had any desire to. An occasional stroll into Exley is as far as I've been.'

151

'Maggie told me her father likes you very much.'

'I'm glad to hear it. I like him, too. The way he remembers things is so interesting. He swims about in his memories and surfaces now and then to dictate something. I sit, and wait, and write it down. Not terribly strenuous.'

'Writing anything yourself?'

'Just these words in the photographs. I'm trying to understand this book. You know that painting in the library with words around the frame?'

Val nodded.

'They're from the book, too. Something about contemplating Beauty.'

'So what will you do with these pictures?'

'When I have enough I'll arrange them in rows, and then I'll read them.'

'How will you decide in what order?'

'Chance will decide; I'll shuffle them.'

'Ah, but how will you read it? Left to right or right to left? Top to bottom or vice versa?'

'It might have different meanings depending on which way I read it,' Paul said, 'a vertical meaning and a horizontal one, a left–right reading and a right–left one . . .'

'Two brace of diagonals,' said Val, 'and of course the spirals.'

'Of course,' said Paul. 'We mustn't forget the spirals.' He lit a cigarette, gestured towards the scene at the lakeside. 'So how's this movie thing going?'

'Too collaborative for my taste. Next time I shall direct.'

'Have you a next time planned?'

Val nodded. 'I'm writing a screenplay about a group of people involved in making a movie. Laski wants to produce it in America. He lives in California; this is a quaint English frolic for him. He's in love with Maggie, of course.'

'I've noticed a lot of people are.'

'Not you?'

'She's gorgeous and great fun; I enjoy her. But in love, no.'

'You used to fall in love with everyone.'

'Or so I thought. It's like dreaming. While it's happening, you can never know for sure if it's real.'

'I wouldn't know. I've never been in love.'

'How do you manage this exemption? I've always wondered.'

'No idea,' Val said. 'Natural immunity? Or perhaps something missing in my character? Or just lucky.'

An ongoing argument between Fanshawe and the cameraman grew louder; Val got up and drained his glass. 'Must have a word with dear Desmond,' he said, and ambled off.

When Paul was halfway up the meadow, the violin began to play and he turned to watch. Sara was in a boat, being rowed away; Arlen stood at the end of the jetty and raised his trumpet to respond.

*   *   *

The meadow is silver with moonlight. Arlen stands on the shore; his trumpet sends long, slow waves across the water. Paul rises on his toes and lifts into the air. Oh yes, he remembers. I know how to do this. The music fills his body with bright ribbons of colour.

'Paul, wake up.'

'Mmmm?'

153

'Listen.'

Paul opened his eyes, but the music continued.

Sara struck a match, lit a candle. 'It's Arlen, he's down at the lake.'

The music pressed at the window; he got up to let it in. The night was warm, the sky clouded, pale with an unseen moon. Arlen was invisible in the darkness below but the music floated up in waves. Am I dreaming? Paul wondered. He touched the wood of the window frame, the glass, the curtain. All felt perfectly real. He turned to look at Sara.

She pushed the covers aside and reclined, a smiling odalisque. 'Come back to bed.'

'In a minute. I want to take a picture.' Paul balanced the camera on a chair. 'Can you hold very still for two minutes?'

'I can try.'

'Ready?'

She folded her arm behind her head. 'Ready.'

'Ah, wait. I meant to ask. Am I dreaming?'

'Is that a very sweet compliment or a philosophical dilemma?'

'It's just something I wonder sometimes. How to know.'

'Does it matter?'

'Hold still,' he said, and released the shutter.

One one thousand, two one thousand, three one thousand. The music blossomed into the silence, the candle flickered. Sixteen thousand, seventeen . . . Sara's pale body seemed to be dissolving, but it was only the play of shadows. Twenty-three thousand, twenty-four thousand . . . If this picture comes out at all, it'll be very blurry. The shadows danced along with Arlen as the trumpet took on a plaintive tone. Thirty-four, thirty-five . . . Light

154

and shadow, shadow and light.

'Paul. Paul.'

'What?'

'I'm sure it's been more than two minutes.'

'Oh Christ, I forgot to count.' He tripped the shutter. 'Well, there's no telling how that'll turn out.' He passed her the *Pymander*. 'Would you be so good as to find me a few words?'

She opened the book, stabbed her finger on to the page. ' "All bodies dissolve into eternal spirit," ' she read.

The music twined around Sara's body and he followed it with his fingers: her ankle, her knee, her soft inner thighs. She murmured something about the effect of having her picture taken, laughed low, and was making room for him on the bed when suddenly she sat upright. 'Listen.' The trumpet paused, and in the distance came the sound of an answering violin. 'Arlen will know right away that's not me.'

'It must be Daniel.'

'Who's Daniel?'

'Percy's son. He lives in a cabin on the other side of the lake. He was shell-shocked.'

The violin repeated a phrase and added a variation, found and sustained a sweet, sad note; the trumpet responded with a gentle query. Soon the voice of the trumpet receded; Arlen was making his way around the lake.

*   *   *

Percy stood by the open French doors of his sitting room. The music had fluttered at the edge of his dreams and drawn him from his bed. Theo stood at his side; he turned his blind eyes towards her. 'It's Daniel,' he said. 'I can hear him playing. I thought I was dreaming, but I'm not. Am I?'

Theo smiled and shook her head.

'But how is it,' he said, 'that I can see you?'

'You see with other eyes.'

'I don't understand.'

'You will.'

10

'Did you hear Daniel last night?' Percy said.

'Oh, yes,' Paul said.

Arlen had appeared at the lake in the same clothes as the previous evening, with his trumpet in his hand. He was napping in the shade as Fanshawe prepared the next shot.

'What are they doing?' Percy adjusted his old panama hat and lit his pipe. It was so hot on the terrace that Henry had at last been persuaded to dispense with the blanket.

'Maggie's in a boat, being rowed out on to the lake,' Paul said. 'She's wearing a long, very tight sequinned frock. Nino's waiting at the shore, flanked by Arlen and Sara on pedestals draped in black.'

Paul looked through the camera. Click. He reached for the *Pymander*. 'Seek one that may lead you to the Gate of Truth.'

Percy slips into memory; the story is calling. He watches the village disappear as they round a bend of the river. The sky is a hot and heavy lid, echoing with the cries of monkeys. They row against the

156

sluggish current; the rhythmic clunk and creak of the oars and the voices of the men melt into a muted stream. The brown expanse of water stretches before and behind; the impenetrable green of La Selva, the jungle, presses in on either side.

'We travelled for many days with no sign of humans, until one afternoon, when everyone was sleepy with the heat, I was gazing half-hypnotised at the jungle when it suddenly struck me that I had seen a face among the leaves. I looked again but it had vanished. About five minutes later I saw another; this time I pointed it out to Sinclair and he saw it too. Captain Pedro told us it was probably a Caiyuna. "Not good tribe." He grinned his black-toothed grin. "Eat people."'

One day blends into the next, yet over it all hangs the inexplicable feeling that something is about to happen. The storm has been brewing all day; towering cumulonimbus crowd the horizon, trailing sheets of blue rain. White birds with long tails circle against the darkening sky.

A loud peal of thunder rolled up the meadow.

'What on earth was that?' Percy said.

'They've got a thunder sheet,' Paul said. 'A long piece of sheet metal that makes the sound of thunder when it's struck.'

'How odd, how very odd . . . I was just remembering a storm in the jungle.' The thunder rumbled, more softly now. 'And you are telling me,' Percy said, 'that noise is coming from a . . . a device?'

Paul laughed. 'Yes.' He shaded his eyes. Nino was walking into the lake; the water reached to his waist, his chest, his shoulders, his chin. It closed

157

over his head and he disappeared as the thunder sounded again.

'Sometimes the rainy season comes slowly,' Percy resumed dictation, 'and the river rises gradually over days or weeks, but every so often comes a year when weeks' worth of rain fall at once. We were miles from the nearest landing, at a place where the river narrowed between steep muddy banks. The clouds boiled over; everything went black except for a vivid red slash in the west. The chatter of the jungle ceased, the thunder approached; the rowers redoubled their efforts. Moving ramparts of rain closed in from every direction. Captain Pedro's imperturbable face showed signs of concern; he urged the rowers on and took the tiller himself, angling for the bank. The thunder sounded from overhead, lightning cracked the gloom. The river grew choppy; waves slapped the sides, sloshed into the boat. Sinclair shouted to the captain to turn the bow into the waves, but Captain Pedro shook his head and gestured upstream. "Big wave maybe soon," he shouted back. "Best hold tree."

'Then the rain hit. I'd never imagined that rain could fall so hard; it was like being under a waterfall—solid and so heavy one could hardly stand. It fell down, it fell sideways, it even fell up, bouncing off the deck of the boat and the surface of the river. We were instantly blinded—it hurt to keep one's eyes open, and if one managed, there was nothing to see but water. The prow of the boat was invisible, the rowers had abandoned their oars and were bailing for dear life. I had to cup my hand over my nose to breathe.

'No one saw the wave coming. It lifted the boat,

spun it around and tipped it over; I scrabbled to hold on but was tossed into the air and flung into the water. I tried to shout, but something smashed into me and knocked the breath out of me. The next thing I remembered was being dragged up the bank by Sinclair and Captain Pedro. We shivered all night among the tree roots as the rain fell and the river rushed by a few feet away, unseen but very loud. In the morning there was no sign of the boat or the rest of the crew.

'Captain Pedro had received a gash to his foot; we bound it up as best we could and set off inland, towards higher ground. For two days we struggled through the jungle until at last we found a path. By then Pedro—to continue to call him Captain became an absurdity too far—was very weak, his wound badly infected. He was too heavy to carry. We waited with him for a day and a night but in the morning Sinclair said we had to leave him. Pedro knew. "Give me tobacco," he said; my pipe, tobacco pouch and waterproof matches had been in my pocket and survived. I gave them to him. I expect a jaguar had him by nightfall.'

*   *   *

When the drinks bell rang, Sara scrambled into Paul's dressing gown and darted down the hall to the bathroom. She must have encountered Stephen; Paul heard a giggle and a mumbled 'Excuse me'. He dressed, combed his hair, filled his cigarette case and buttoned Sara into her frock; she put on lipstick, powdered her nose and they went downstairs.

They met Val on the landing, leaning on the

159

banisters and observing the activity in the hall. The crew was bringing equipment up from the lake and stacking it in such a way as to create the maximum obstruction. Tustian, bearing a tray of glasses full of champagne, stopped to remonstrate with them; the front door burst open and Roger and Sophie ran in. Maggie, descending with Albert Laski, paused on the bottom step. Alice and Stephen, in the doorway, turned as an automobile horn sounded.

'It's Jarlath and Sylvie,' Alice called out.

As the car's headlights flared across the dusk of the courtyard, a crash of thunder exploded in the hall, followed by the sound of breaking glass.

'What the hell?'

'Christ almighty!'

'Oh bloody . . .'

'Sorry, sorry, sorry . . .' The men of the film crew retrieved the thunder sheet, loosing a further series of rumbles.

'Oh for Christ's sake,' Maggie said.

'Zowie,' said Sara.

'Simply smashing,' murmured Val.

Tustian glared from the offending piece of metal to the heap of shattered glass in its pool of bubbling liquid. He passed his hand over his face. 'I am very sorry, madam. Very, very sorry.'

'I didn't ask you to meet the damn boat in the first place!' A car door slammed. 'And I didn't ask to be dragged back here like some wayward child!' Another door slammed. 'And I bloody well didn't ask you to be my father!' A tall girl stalked in and stormed halfway across the hall before she noticed all the people.

'Welcome home, Miss Sylvie,' said Tustian.

160

'Sylvie!' Roger and Sophie hurled themselves at her and she staggered.

'Sylvie darling, what an entrance,' Maggie said.

'Aha,' said Jarlath, appearing at the door.

'It's a catastrophe,' Alice told him.

'Oh, very good,' Stephen said. 'An overturning indeed.'

Sylvie bolted for the stairs. Val and Sara leapt out of her way; she brushed past Paul, trod on his foot, stumbled up the last few steps and disappeared down the corridor. The silence that followed was punctuated by the sound of a final door slamming.

'Zowie,' Sara said again, with feeling.

Paul sat down hard. He felt very peculiar, something between having the wind knocked out of him and being about to float away. Everyone began speaking at once, but they sounded tinny and distant.

Val sat on the step beside him and offered a cigarette. Paul took it, smoked for a minute, then noticed it in his hand and was unable to remember how it got there.

Val looked at him closely. 'Ç'a été un joli coup à foudre, n'est-ce pas?'

'What?'

'Nothing.'

Percy, like the rest of the household, had of course heard The Catastrophe, as the event at once began to be called, but when Paul tried to describe it he couldn't recall how the incident had unfolded. Although he reminded himself many times that his light-headedness was no doubt due to hunger, the sight of the food on his plate turned his stomach. It was not until after dinner, when

161

everyone was gathering in the music room for an entertainment in honour of the film company's last evening, that Paul realised he'd forgotten all about Sylvie. She hadn't reappeared. He noticed at the same time that he was holding his breath in the fear or the hope that she would.

Oh damn. Oh damn, damn, damn. He stepped out to the terrace. The night was warm and still; the moon hovered over the lake. Conversation and laughter poured out of the open French doors; he stood in a shadow and lit a cigarette.

'Can I have one?' Sara appeared at his side.

For a moment he had no idea who she was. 'Ah, of course.' He fumbled in his pocket with unsteady hands.

'Are you all right?'

'No, maybe not.'

'Well, come back in. The music's about to start. They've made sweet little programmes for everyone, look. The children will perform, Maggie will sing, and of course I'll play, and Arlen too.'

'I'll come in a minute.'

'Paul . . .' Sara touched his arm. 'Oh, never mind. There's something I want to tell you, but it'll wait.'

Paul had forgotten to breathe; he inhaled abruptly, choked.

'Goodness, you really are ill!'

'Just something caught in my throat. Let's go in.'

She would have pulled him down beside her on a sofa, but he slid away. 'I'll get us a drink,' he said. 'What would you like?'

'A Sidecar, please.'

Tustian was serving from a trolley in the corner; his hands were a bit shaky too. 'A Sidecar please, Tustian. And a whisky. Dreadfully sorry about the glasses.'

'They were made in Vienna, those glasses, in 1825,' Tustian said sadly. 'I was, however, much cheered to discover that one had miraculously survived.'

He pointed to the mantel, where a glass of champagne bubbled under a glass dome. A neatly written card proclaimed it the Sole Survivor of The Catastrophe.

Val had taken the place beside Sara, the sofa and all the chairs were full. Paul found a dark corner, took a sip of whisky and leaned against the wall. The instant he released his mind from a tight focus on what had to be done, she was back. There was a wrenching in his gut and a sort of pain all over, as though he was being passed through a mangle. He noticed that he was watching the door to the hall while longing and dread, evenly matched, warred within him. He forbade himself to look in that direction again.

He studied the floor, the furniture, the people, building a wall to keep her out. Why did everything that was familiar suddenly seem so unreal, as though he'd wandered into another world, like his, but not quite? He looked down and for a moment didn't recognise his own clothes. Oh Christ, am I going mad? Is this what the first stage of insanity is like? Was my father right after all, merely premature? He fought the urge to laugh.

Roger was playing Beethoven, badly. He finished and Paul applauded along with everyone else, trying to get in step. He remembered to breathe, having forgotten again. I really have to get a grip, he told himself, but he didn't want to, oh, he didn't, he wanted to let his mind go and remember her, remember every detail . . . Stop, he said, almost aloud. Please stop. He forced his attention outward. There was Alice with her flute, accompanied by Theo on the piano. When the piece ended Paul joined in the applause, clinging to the ordinary activity, to its noise and sensations, as to a life preserver in a flood.

He concentrated fiercely on the performances that followed, but the sense of unreality persisted, as though all this was a stage show or a movie, in colour and complete with sound. He noticed a curious floating sensation, then with a click settled again. Oh Christ, oh sweet fucking Jesus Christ, what on earth is going on? He forced his attention back to the reality that appeared to exist in front of him, but there was only a blur of colours and shapes, abstract and unidentifiable, and a buzz of sound that mingled with the clear tattoo of his heart and the rush of blood through his veins.

With an effort he reimposed order: this was the music room at Farundell, there were the people he knew. It all looked perfectly normal and yet completely false, like a waxwork tableau. And, he realised, it has nothing at all to do with me; it's a bubble, floating just—there. Or perhaps I'm in the bubble, drifting through like a passenger on a very slow train. Something pressed at the edges and he glanced at the door. An image of Sylvie leapt through the gap in his defences, and he knew at once that she was the only real thing there was, and that was why all the rest had come to seem as it did.

Maggie began to sing, a slow sexy song. How like her daughter she looked. No! He slammed the door shut. This was completely impossible, entirely

164

out of the question. He made himself list the reasons. One, I'm an employee of her family—a servant, not to put too fine a point on it. Two, she's far too young. Three, she's not a girl to mess about with and I'm in no position to be serious. Four, we are living in the same house; I will see her every day. He pictured her at breakfast, a toast crumb on her lower lip.

Oh Christ. Just stop it. It doesn't matter, carry on, it doesn't matter, carry on. He tried to drop his mind into the familiar refrain, but it was like riding a tiny boat in a torrent. Why not let myself drown? Images arose that nearly made him groan aloud. This is ridiculous! he shouted at himself. I have seen her for approximately ten seconds, she ignored me, she trod on my foot, there is no reason to think she would ever do anything other than ignore me and tread on my feet and from the way she sounded, she'll probably have run away before morning in any case. Please God.

Maggie's song ended and Sara rose to play. Oh bloody hell, what to do about Sara? Pretend to be ill. Coward. But what's the alternative? Tell her? She won't believe me; she'll be offended, hurt. Or even if she does believe me, she'll still be hurt and offended. Better to be ill. And it's true, he decided. I do not feel at all myself.

Sara finished her piece with a flourish and grinned at Paul as she came back to her seat. She really was a wonderful girl but, like everyone else, tinged with unreality when compared to . . . He snatched his mind away just in time.

Arlen stood, smiling at the cheers that greeted him. He gazed out into the darkness; Paul followed his eyes and at the furthest, faintest edge of light caught a glimpse of Daniel.

As Arlen raised his trumpet and began to play, something happened inside Paul that broke down the wall he'd built. He gave up his futile, exhausting fight and let himself think of her. The music was about Sylvie, about loving her, and he couldn't help but let it in.

When Arlen finished, the room was silent. Percy buried his face in his hands, Maggie sighed, Sara blew her nose and Val lit a cigarette. Paul's cheeks were wet and for a moment he couldn't understand why. A wave of applause rose for Arlen, who was already halfway out of the door.

Paul followed, wanting silence and darkness, but the party spilled after him, the drinks trolley was rolled on to the terrace and the night filled with laughter. Arlen had vanished. Maggie and Laski strolled past carrying Chinese lanterns on bamboo stalks; other couples followed. A line of lights snaked down to the lake.

He lit a cigarette and tried to stop thinking about Sylvie. Where was she? Had she stayed upstairs in her room? Which room? Oh no, he warned himself. Don't try to figure out which is her room. It's not very far down the left-hand first-floor corridor, to judge by the slam, though he couldn't tell which side. There were several rooms along that stretch that he'd never entered—it was mainly family bedrooms. It had to be—he pictured the doors—one of four rooms. Probably.

Sara tapped him on the shoulder. 'Hello. You were miles away. Are you all right?'

'Yes,' Paul said, resolving never to lie in any matter concerning Sylvie. 'I'm fine.'

Tustian appeared with a bundle of lanterns; Sara chose a green one. 'Do you want to go down to the lake?' she said.

'All right.'

Someone put a record on the gramophone and turned it up very loud. '*I won't dance with anyone else, anyone else but you-ooo-ooo,*' Eddie Sturgis sang.

'Sara . . .' he said.

'Paul . . .' she said.

They laughed. 'You first,' Paul said.

'You remember I mentioned I wanted to tell you something.'

Paul didn't, but he nodded.

'Well, what I want to tell you is—but first I want say that I really, really like you a lot, and it's been wonderful. But the thing is, I've started seeing somebody in London and, well, he's not the accommodating type. So we can't carry on.' She stopped, held up the lantern and sought Paul's face. 'Do you understand?'

He smiled, a smile of sheer benevolence. 'Absolutely.'

'I mean, it's really all right?' She frowned.

Evidently she'd wanted a bit less understanding, or perhaps not such immediate understanding. She was a great girl; he really should protest. 'It's all right,' he repeated.

'Well,' Sara said. 'I suppose maybe tonight we won't.'

'No, we'd better not.'

A drunken trio tripped past, dropped their pink lantern, picked it up and stumbled on.

'I'll go back up to the house then,' said Sara. 'Do you want to keep the lantern?'

'No, you take it.'

'A last kiss,' she said, raising her face and closing her eyes. Impossibly churlish to refuse, thought Paul, but he kept his eyes open.

'Piccadilly bloody Circus around here,' said Sylvie, striding up the path. As she passed, her eyes briefly met Paul's.

After Sara left he stood for a long time without moving. The darkness closed in; no more party-makers wandered by, but their lights moved on the lake and their shouts drifted up the meadow. He sat down where he was and put his head in his hands, willing the earth to open and swallow him. Or maybe, he thought desperately, I'm dreaming, and when I wake there will be no Sylvie. Oh God, no. He reeled away from that thought as fast as he could and was left with a state of misery that occupied his mind like a cloud, grey and dank and heavy. Gradually he became aware that he was sitting on a thistle and got to his feet, cursing.

'Hello, old chap.' Val appeared on the path with a cheerful yellow lantern.

'Oh bloody Christ,' said Paul.

'Too true. Bed for you, dear boy.'

Val walked him up to his room and would have tucked him in but Paul waved him away. He took off his clothes and lay on the bed, smoked cigarette after cigarette as the candle flickered and the sounds of revelry faded. He didn't dare think about anything. The candle guttered and went out. She was somewhere in the house, or perhaps somewhere outside. She was awake, or asleep, or dreaming. Where are you, Sylvie? Not outside. Inside. That's why he couldn't shut her out. In one glance she'd leapt into him and expanded to fill all the hollow spaces. She pressed against the inside of his skin; when he looked within, he saw her face.

Sleep was impossible; he was thirsty and burning. He got up, downed half a ewer of water and leaned out of the window, aching for a breeze. The moon floated low in a misty sky; an owl hooted from the woods. He pulled on an old pair of shorts and slipped downstairs, let himself out and ran down the moonlit meadow, leaping as though he could fly. He had a fleeting thought that of course he could fly, all he had to do was leap higher, will himself upward, but the notion passed and he merely ran, his body strong and solid, the ground hard beneath his feet and coolness streaming by.

When he reached the lake he slowed, panting, to a walk. From across the water came the sound of the trumpet and the violin playing together, now, like old friends. He made his way along the shore and sat on a rock to listen, thinking not even of Sylvie, though she filled his mind, but of intimate colloquies such as the sky might have with the earth, or the sea with the land, or the stars and planets as they coursed the night airs.

When the music stopped and was replaced by the sound of harsh, rending sobs, Paul retreated fast. By the time he'd reached the jetty all was quiet, thank God. He was thirsty and very hot again. Perhaps he was ill, after all—but he felt perfectly well, only hot. He sat on the end and dangled his feet. How deep was it? He'd never learned to swim but there was a ladder . . . He climbed down; the cool water was an ecstasy. He felt for the ground but it was out of reach, so he held on under the dock, watching as dawn approached. The surface of the lake glimmered like mercury; one bird's

169

liquid trilling was soon joined by others'.

There was the sound of soft, fast footfalls as someone ran to the end of the jetty. Paul peered up between the planks. His breath caught in his throat; it was Sylvie. In one quick, fluid movement she pulled her dress over her head and dived naked into the lake. An unbearably long time passed before she surfaced a great distance away and swam for the island, sleek head carving the water like a seal.

Paul clung to the ladder. Her body arced into the water over and over, blazing like a comet, burned into his eyes and endlessly repeating. He climbed out, trembling. A pool of silk lay on the dock; he touched it with one finger.

He walked up to his room, stripped off his wet shorts and lay on the bed. She was imprinted on his retina; her glowing body crossed and recrossed the ceiling. Her face, her breasts, her legs. Her wild streaming hair, her belly, her thighs. When he closed his eyes it was worse. She turned, smiled, beckoned . . .

'But I can't swim.'

'Yes, you can. Don't you remember? You just . . . swim.' She swims away, then comes back. 'Swim,' she says, and, greatly daring, Paul lets go of the ladder. The water holds him; he moves his arms, his legs—he's floating, buoyant . . . he's swimming, swimming as though he's always known how, swimming like a dolphin, diving and turning.

'Let's swim to the moon,' she says.

Her naked body gleams in the dark water. Yes, he thinks, oh yes, I remember this. He reaches for her and she draws him into a kiss, presses her body against his. Her tongue flickers. Deeper, she says, and

170

tightens her grip. He closes his eyes and falls, deep and deeper. Down, down and down . . . how far have they come? He hadn't realised the lake was so deep. Panic rises, chokes him; he fights against the entwining arms and legs, pushes them away and flails for the surface.

He emerges gasping at the edge of the crater. Someone is holding his ankle; he kicks out sharply. He rubs his hands over his eyes but only rubs in more gritty mud. The shelling comes from all sides; he can't remember where his own lines are. The hand seizes his ankle, pulls him down. The crater is full of naked bodies, parts of bodies, chunks of grey and bleeding flesh. All the faces stare at him with dying eyes.

His own body is grey and naked, torn and rotting. Far below, an abyss opens and everyone is falling in. His legs fall off, and his arms; paralysed with fear he slides after them and falls, and falls, and falls.

Paul woke up with a jolt, heart pounding. Christ, that had been a bad one. He lit a cigarette with shaky hands. A patch of blinding sunlight lay on the floor and he forced himself to stare at it until his eyes ran with tears and the images washed away.

11

In the days that followed, the sense of unreality that had swept over Paul remained, though in a milder form; he was learning to live with it. Harder to live with were the few, brief encounters with reality. She came and went, glimpsed down corridors or vanishing round doorways, skulking about the house and grounds, snarling at everyone. Fortunately she seldom appeared at meals, and aside from a few difficult breakfasts Paul managed to keep his distance. She had a lot of friends and went out to dinner most nights. His initial hope that she'd take herself off somewhere had not materialised and he became adept at avoiding her. On the two occasions when they'd passed on the stairs, he managed a rather stiff Hello, and she'd responded with a cool nod.

His main problem was her portrait; it overlooked his table in the library and he had to draw an imaginary line in the air above which he must never allow his eyes to stray. He considered moving the table, but decided he simply had to endure it.

For the first time in his life he experienced insomnia. Unable to sit still, unable to read, he took long walks. There was a path he liked along the shore of the lake; it passed the cabin where Daniel, also always wakeful, brooded on his porch. Last night he'd shyly offered a cup of tea. They sat together, talking little, until Paul's burning drove him on and he followed the path across the hill to a huge old oak in the middle of a field, looking out over the River Isis, a moon-silvered serpent below.

His thoughts bounced between hopeful scenarios that ended in delicious seductions and painful enumerations of the reasons why they could never occur. Sometime around first light he would make his way back and fall face down on his bed to absorb a scrap of restless sleep. If he dreamed at all he did not remember; he woke with the same ache, the same hunger; the same images crowded

172

his eyes.

The only thing that helped was the photography. Looking at the world through the camera, oddly, made it seem more real, and as he quested for meaning among the images and the words of the *Pymander* he could, if not forget Sylvie, at least keep her at bay. He had the feeling that old Mr Pym was laughing at him even harder than before.

Jarlath had disappeared the day after he'd brought her home. 'No doubt fearing,' Maggie had said, 'he'll be asked to take her away again.' But he'd returned last night and invited Paul to come for a sitting the next day. It had seemed, at the time of that first visit, like a good idea. Paul had imagined interesting conversations, the chance to pursue all those lines of enquiry. Now—well, he'd rather be anywhere else. At four o'clock, unable to think of any excuse to back out, he climbed the stairs to the studio.

Jarlath had him recline on a chaise longue under the roof-light, and although he had to remove his shirt he was allowed, thank God, to keep his trousers on. He didn't know what he'd have done if Jarlath had wanted him nude.

Never, he thought, as Jarlath stepped behind his easel, had he been so closely observed, yet no gaze had ever been less intimate. He was seen and not seen, examined and ignored. He tried to relax and breathe, and gradually a lightness soaked into his limbs. There's that honey smell again. How curious. Perhaps there's bees in the eaves. Sweetness touched his tongue and a golden sea rose around him. Time passed, and when Jarlath's voice called him back he'd forgotten where he was.

He was lighting a cigarette, still shirtless, when

173

Sylvie entered without knocking. She looked from him to her father, emerging from the WC buttoning his flies, wheeled around and walked out.

'Oh dear, I do believe she's got the wrong idea about us,' Jarlath said.

Paul sank into a sofa. Something impossible had just had a further obstacle dropped in its path; so what?

Jarlath made coffee and brought it on a tray. 'Sylvie is a lot like me, apparently, as Maggie was at pains to point out last night. But I don't see it, do you?'

'Well, there is some resemblance . . .'

'She has a temper like mine, that's obvious. And she doesn't like being told what to do. Though the stubborn streak is pure Maggie Damory, and so, I suspect, is the deviousness.'

He pushed the sugar bowl towards Paul. 'But she has balls, that girl of mine. Do you know, she sneaked off the first boat she was meant to be on dressed as a maid?'

'Really.'

'She did, and went by herself all the way back to Florence, and God knows what would have happened if my sister hadn't in the meantime told Count Whatsit I'd turn him into an ass if he so much as thought about her.'

Paul choked.

'I beg your pardon?' Jarlath said.

'Would you have?'

'What do you think?'

Paul tried to look him in the eye. Of course such a thing was nonsense, absurd, impossible. A joke, surely? Or perhaps a metaphor. 'I wouldn't care to

174

speculate,' he said.

*   *   *

That night Paul wrote a letter to Val.

Dear Val,
Please forgive me if this letter is somewhat less
than coherent. I have been in a very strange
state this last week and remembering now your
remark about the joli coup à foudre I think you
may know why.
 I have to tell someone. I've fallen in love
with a girl who for about a thousand reasons is
entirely out of reach; she thinks I'm lovers with
another girl, which was true but isn't any more;
she thinks I'm her father's lover, which has
never been true, though I do see how she got
the impression. I have reason to believe that if
he knew what I've been imagining doing with
her, he'd turn me into an ass.
 Sincerely, Paul.
P.S. I have never felt anything remotely like
this before.
P.P.S. If it weren't so fucking painful it would
be funny.
He found it strangely helpful to write it out,
ridiculous as it was, and as he addressed and
stamped the envelope resolved to try much harder
to put Sylvie out of his mind.

*   *   *

A few days later he was having one of those
awkward breakfasts at which Sylvie was
unavoidable; the table was crowded and he'd

175

ended up next to her. He concentrated on keeping his elbows close and spent several minutes stirring his coffee.

'What did you dream last night?' Alice asked Roger.

'Don't remember,' Roger said.

'Oh, honestly, you're not even trying. What about you, Sylvie?'

'None of your business,' said Sylvie.

'Might a humble human enquire,' Alice said, 'why you are so beastly about everything all the time?'

'No, you may not,' Sylvie said.

'Why the interest in dreams, Alice?' Stephen asked.

'I'm reading a book about dreams and augury,' Alice said, 'and it says that at least thirty per cent of dreams are of things that haven't happened yet, so I'm conducting my own research. Or trying to, if anyone could be bothered to co-operate.'

'Oh look, here's the post,' said Stephen, taking a pile of letters from Tustian. 'Lots of post. Here's one for you, Alice, and pass this down to Paul.'

An envelope in Val's distinctive grey and blue stationery made its way around the table; Sylvie handed it to him without meeting his eyes.

'Another one for you, Alice, and quite a few for Sylvie,' Stephen said, and it took Paul a moment to realise that the letter on top of the stack approaching Sylvie was obviously also from Val. He stared at the envelope in his hand and with a feeling of foreboding tore it open.

My very dear friend,
Have received your latest missive and taken

176

the liberty of forwarding it to the correct recipient on your behalf. Bonne chance.

Sylvie had opened her letter. It held two sheets, one with just a couple of lines, and another . . . Paul considered snatching it out of her hand and running from the room. Too late; she was reading it. Oh Christ, what had he written? He tried to think of something to say, but before he could speak she'd slipped out to the terrace. No one else noticed her departure and by the time Paul got to the door she was halfway down the meadow, running fast.

'Damn you, Val,' he said. Nothing, nothing, nothing at all to be done about it now.

She ran well, whole-heartedly, not trippingly like most girls. She kicked off her shoes; they fell some distance apart, blue specks on the green field. Should he chase after her? Somehow that didn't seem like a good idea; she was heading away from him as fast as possible. He'd write her a note immediately, with an apology and pledge to desist, though how he would phrase that he had no idea, not to mention the impossibility of achieving it. The prospect of being turned into an ass began to look like a pretty decent option. He went to the library, sat at his desk and looked up at her portrait.

I'm sorry, he said to it. I can't help it; you've taken up residence inside me. Every time I see you it hurts. I ache with wanting you, and I don't want it ever to stop. What an ass I am, what a complete and utter ass. How could I have written all that to Val, what on earth did I think he'd do?

He took out pen and paper and gritted his teeth.

Dear Sylvie, he wrote. Dearest darling Sylvie, he thought. *I must apologise for my thoughts*, he wrote; I would gladly spend all my time thinking of you, he thought. *I'll stop at once*, he wrote; I'll never stop, he thought. *I feel for you only the greatest respect*, he wrote; I want to fuck you morning, noon and night, he thought.

He looked at what he'd written and pushed it away. How could he write such lies? He closed his eyes and pressed his head between his hands. An image of Sylvie arose, of Sylvie running down the meadow, except she wasn't running away, she was running towards him. Oh, what the hell, he thought, and for once made no effort to banish it, instead encouraged the image to live. Come here, he said. A soft honey-gold light filled the air; they floated, turning as in a dance. She came near, shed her dress like a silky skin.

'"I must apologise, I feel only respect." Is that how you really feel?'

He sat up and opened his eyes. Sylvie stood in front of his desk, pointing at the letter.

Paul willed himself to breathe. 'Hello,' he said.

'Oh. Hello. Well is it?'

'OK, no, it isn't.'

'In that case, would you like to go for a walk?'

Paul stared at her, blinked, stared again. Was this real or a dream? 'Yes,' he said, since that's what he'd undoubtedly want to say in either case. He followed her out of the house and down the meadow towards the lake. It most likely was a dream, and the best policy was to go as carefully as possible so as not to wake up.

'So you and my father,' she said, 'aren't . . .'

'No, I was just posing for him. We're not . . .

never were. I don't . . . that is, I only . . .'

'What you mean is you only fuck women, is that correct?'

'Blimey. Yes, that's correct.'

'Like that woman you were kissing.'

Oh Christ. Walked right into that one. 'Yes, like her.'

'But you're not fucking her any more?'

He winced. 'Do you have to put it like that?'

'How should I put it? How do you put it?'

'In polite company I would seek a euphemism.'

'Well you're not . . . whatevering her any more?'

'No, not any more.'

'Why not?'

'We each for our own reasons decided to stop.'

'What was her reason?'

'She'd been with someone else all along.'

'And what was yours?'

'You,' said Paul. 'I saw you.' And now will you please shut up? he thought at her, and let me try to grasp the fact that you are walking beside me and we are having a conversation. If you could call that a conversation. A sudden, enormous shyness filled him and for a moment his limbs felt so awkward he feared he would stumble. Placing his feet with exaggerated care, he tried to find something to say.

'Why did you write to my cousin Val?' She was on the hunt again.

'He's my friend and I thought, being a surrealist, he'd appreciate the situation.'

'Where did you meet him?'

'At an aeroplane crash in northern France.'

'Oh. Sorry. I guess that's the war, isn't it?' She gave a tussock a violent kick in passing. 'Ouch. Never mind. Sorry. I always put my bloody foot in

179

it.'

'It's all right,' Paul said, and for the first time it was, it really was.

'Why are you working for my grandfather?'

'Because he was good enough to offer me a job. Why do you get to ask all the questions?'

'You can ask a question. That's only fair. But just one.'

'Just one? How is that fair?'

She shrugged. 'All right, it's not.'

Was she trying not to smile? 'In that case,' he said, 'I'll save it for later, and try to make a slightly more informed choice. In the meantime, can we have a conversation that doesn't consist entirely of you interrogating me?'

'I'm not sure that's a good idea. You profess to love me, and I don't know anything about you. Don't you think I have a right to ask a few questions? You know lots and lots about me, you know my whole family, you're obviously very good friends with my father, and Percy, and Maggie— oh, that reminds me. Are you whatevering my mother?'

'Christ, no.'

'That's a relief. As I was saying, you've been living in my house for weeks and everybody but me seems to know you quite well.'

'First of all,' Paul said, 'I don't know lots about you, I hardly know anything.'

'You still know more about me than I know about you. Add up the facts you know about me and those I could possibly know about you, and you'll see for yourself.'

'How do I know what you could possibly know about me? You could have asked everybody who knows me quite well.'

'I'm not going to the children or the housemaids for gossip.'

'Oh, of course not. What on earth have the children and the housemaids been telling you?'

'Is that your one question?'

Damn. 'No.'

'So,' she resumed her inquisition, 'have you whatevered very many girls?'

Jesus! Was there any way to stop her? 'I don't believe that's any of your business,' he said.

'Oh, but I believe it is. You claim to love me, well, don't you think I have a right to know whether you have any experience of love? I mean, are you any good at it?'

Paul opened his mouth to speak, but a mixture of wonder and crazy hope seized his heart and no words came out. 'Is this,' he said at last, 'a job interview?'

'Is that your question?'

'OK, that's my question.'

'Yes,' she said. 'And no.'

'Oh hell. I should have expected that.'

She laughed, a low, musical sound, and a wave of pure joy passed through Paul. They made their way down to the shore in silence as he considered and rejected a dozen intelligent remarks. A small rowing boat was tied at the jetty.

'Do you know how to row a boat?' she said.

'Of course.'

'Row me to the island.'

Paul climbed in and took up the oars. Sylvie untied the rope and stepped down; he pushed off, praying that rowing was as easy as it looked.

She turned her knees sideways so as not to touch

his and watched him closely. 'You never answered my question,' she said.

'Which question?'

'Have you whatevered very many girls?'

Jarlath had mentioned something about a stubborn streak. 'What do you mean by very many?'

'Well, how many?'

'Oh, Christ, I don't know, I've never counted.'

'An estimate, then,' she said. 'More than a dozen?'

'Well, yes . . .'

'More than two dozen?'

'Well, yes . . .'

'More than a hundred?'

'No, for God's sake—what do you take me for, some Don Juan?'

'How would I know? We'll say somewhere between twenty-five and one hundred, then, shall we?'

'Fine.' This is excruciating, Paul thought, in an entirely novel way. 'I wonder whether I'm dreaming,' he said.

'You already had your question.'

'That was not a question. It was, if you recall, couched as a statement.'

She suppressed a smile. 'I won't be distracted,' she said. 'I think somewhere between twenty-five and one hundred is enough.'

'I'm glad to hear it.'

She reached into the pocket of her skirt and pulled out his letter to Val. 'Let's see. Oh yes, you say if my father knew what you'd been imagining doing with me, he'd turn you into an ass.'

'I wrote that?'

182

'It looks that way. So what sort of thing have you been imagining doing with me?'

'No,' Paul said, 'absolutely not.'

'Absolutely not what?'

'I am absolutely not answering that question.'

'Why not?'

Damn her. He couldn't very well say it didn't concern her. 'A man's thoughts are private, and he can't be held responsible for what he imagines.'

'Why not?'

'Well, because he's imagining things constantly; he imagines all kinds of things, things he thinks he hasn't a chance of doing.'

'Such as?'

Such as ravishing you, sweet girl, right here in this boat, in the middle of the lake. He shook his head. 'Please. Please don't ask me that. You have no idea how difficult it is to talk and row at the same time.' He checked over his shoulder to make sure he was headed in the right direction, not going round in circles. 'I've not been to the island before,' he said.

She took the bait. 'It's my favourite place. I used to think fairies lived there. I'd camp alone for days at a time and pretend it was my kingdom.'

Paul guided the boat to a narrow strip of pebbles and jumped out to pull it up the shore. 'You've soaked your shoes,' Sylvie said.

'So I have.' He removed them, and his socks, and tossed them into the boat. When he turned back she was climbing a steep path cut into the cliff. He hurried after her, then stopped, remembered to breathe, followed more slowly.

The path turned; she disappeared from view. Instantly he doubted her reality. He saw trees, rocks, sky, and for a moment had no idea where he was. Then a further turn revealed her once more and he climbed on, his bare feet surprisingly agile.

'Could I have a cigarette?' she said when he reached the top. She touched his hand as he lit it.

'Are you flirting with me?' he said.

'And that's another thing. No one seems able to tell me. What is flirting, actually?'

'I am fairly sure it is what you are doing.'

She strolled among the columns to the far end, climbed into the roots of an old oak and sat down. Her skirt rode up to her knees. 'This is a temple of Aphrodite, you know. The goddess of love.'

'I know.' I must stay, Paul told himself, at least ten feet away from her if at all possible. He wanted to touch her so much his hands hurt.

She opened his letter again. 'So we will continue with the . . . interview.'

Stubborn, he thought, isn't the word.

'Now that you don't have to row, and I do see how rowing and talking simultaneously must be frightfully difficult, we return to the matter of "what I've been imagining doing with her."' She tucked the letter into her pocket, selected a twig from the ground and began peeling the bark.

Paul shook his head. 'Sylvie, what you ask . . .'

'Don't tell me I've asked too much already! Well, it seems your love is a weak and flaccid sort of thing. If you can't even talk to me, how could you possibly actually do anything?'

Christ, he thought, she has a firm, if perverse, grasp of logic.

'You said a man imagines things constantly, imagines all kinds of things.'

And a very good memory.

184

'So if you were to imagine something now, what would it be?' She finished peeling her stick and pointed it at him.

The thought crossed Paul's mind that he had one last chance to resist her and this was it; it was passing, right now. Without a second thought he let it go. 'All right,' he said, 'all right.' He closed his eyes.

The wood doves called, bees droned. There was a fragrance in the air of flowers and honey. He remembered the sound of the trumpet, how it spoke without words, and he could almost hear Arlen playing as he had the night Sylvie first appeared. He took a deep breath, opened his eyes, caught and held hers. Sunlight fell through the trees and a breeze rustled the leaves.

'Sylvie,' he said. La Selva, he thought. 'You're so beautiful it hurts.' Honey-gold light touched her face. She watched him, wide-eyed. 'I imagine,' he said, surprised to find his voice steady, 'I imagine you're smiling at me, your eyes are shining. I trace the bones of your face with my fingers,' he raised his hand, 'your brow, your cheek . . .' Had she blinked? 'I touch the corner of your mouth. Kiss me, you say, and you part your lips,' and she did, as a blush rose from her throat, 'and raise your face to me, and I kiss you, darling Sylvie, I kiss you gently and I kiss you hard and I'm drowning in you.' His words came from far away, flowing through him, curling around her in bright ribbons. 'And I try to tell you all the reasons we can't, but you laugh, and now you're unbuttoning your blouse, Sylvie, and the sun touches your skin where my hands want to go . . .'

At last she looked aside and Paul drew a shaky

185

breath. He walked away, sat on a fallen column, lit a cigarette and gazed across the lake towards the house. Alice, carrying a basket, on her way to Daniel's cabin; Theo at work in her herb garden; Malcolm mowing the lawns. It looked remote and very peaceful. If that had been a battle, and it certainly felt that way, who had won? He'd been, he decided, lucky to scrape a draw. Now, in his own stubborn way, he wasn't going to say another word.

She sat beside him. 'Can I have a cigarette?'

Again, she touched his hand as he held the match; there was a jolt like the discharge of static electricity. He could tell she noticed it too.

'Don't tell me I smoke too much,' she said.

'I wasn't going to.'

'My great-great-great-great-grandfather Francis built this place.'

'So I've heard.'

'You've seen him.'

'Is that something you learned from the children and housemaids?'

She shrugged.

'Yes, I've seen him,' he said. 'Have you?'

'Not exactly, but sometimes I sort of feel him around.'

Francis lurking about unseen—what an extremely disconcerting idea. 'You don't feel him around now, do you?'

'No.'

Paul studied her profile. Had he really touched her only in his mind? He knew the texture of her skin, her lips, the taste of her mouth. It felt as though it would be the most natural thing in the world to put his arm around her, share a cigarette, talk quietly as though they'd been lovers for years. Yet she was a girl he hardly knew. From which position should he address her? He stood. 'Would you show me the rest of your kingdom?'

She led him across the temple and down through the wooded slope on the other side of the island. They walked in sun and shade, side by side, not touching. Thorny shrubs narrowed the path and Paul stood back to let her brush past.

'That's where I had my fort.' She pointed to a ledge. 'Look, there's still some stones piled.'

Paul pictured Sylvie in armour, with sword and spear and shield, guarding the pass. He grinned.

'What are you smiling at?' she said.

'Your warlike nature. I'm a peace-loving man.'

'Are you?'

'Well, usually. Unless irresistibly provoked.'

'Are you flirting with me?' she said.

'Aha, see? You do know what flirting is.'

They emerged from the dim, cool woods to a broad meadow dotted with enormous old trees. 'This is where we have the picnic every summer. Ash, elm, oak, beech, chestnut.' She pointed and named. 'My great-grandfather planted them.'

They walked down to the lake through a sea of long grasses and wild flowers, still dew-damp underneath. Sharp scents rose from the crushed plants; tall lacy flower heads nodded as Sylvie swept by. At the shore she lifted her skirt and waded out; Paul rolled up his trouser legs and stood in the balmy shallows.

'Let's swim,' Sylvie said. 'It's nice and deep over there—one can dive from that rock.'

'I can't swim,' Paul said.

'You can't swim?'

187

'No, never learned.'

'Poor you. Never mind. I want to swim. Turn around, please?'

'What?'

'I want to swim,' she explained with exaggerated patience, 'and as I don't want to soak my clothes, I shall have to remove them. Therefore . . .' She made a twirling motion with her hand.

'Ah, oh, of course.' He turned, stared at a tree. It doesn't matter, carry on. It doesn't matter . . .

With a whisper of cloth her blouse landed on a shrub, followed by her skirt and a couple of small silky items in a surprising shade of pink. There was a splash, and he imagined her naked body slicing through the water. He was very glad he couldn't swim; to have had to join her in the water would have been . . .

'You can look round now,' she called.

I'd rather not, Paul thought.

Sylvie was treading water, chin deep. 'Don't you want to learn to swim?' she said. 'I could teach you.'

'Oh? That would be . . . er . . .' He saw Sylvie, a stern but naked swimming instructress, holding him afloat and commanding him to kick, stroke, kick. 'That would be too kind, it would take far too much of your time, and anyway, I don't think one can learn so late in life, can one? Isn't it the sort of thing you either learn as a child or not at all?'

'Nonsense. Anyone can learn, any time. I think everyone naturally does know how to swim. You just need to be reminded.'

She submerged. A trail of bubbles floated to the surface and Paul pictured her swimming through underwater palaces, clothed only in her flowing hair, liquid-limbed, smiling.

'Would you turn again, please?' She'd surfaced silently, so close he could see the water beading her eyelashes. He turned quickly, lit a cigarette and, although soon invited, didn't turn back until he was ready. As he'd feared, she'd pulled her clothes on over wet skin; they clung damply, and her hair dripped down her shoulders. She was fresh-washed and shining as a child, though that knowing smile . . . 'What do you want, Sylvie?' He hadn't meant to speak out loud.

'I want a cigarette,' she said.

In the boat she was still careful to keep her knees from touching his, though her long bare calves were only inches away. She gazed at the water, at the sky, lifted her arms to push her hair out of her face. She didn't meet his eyes, except for an occasional flicker, as if to check that he was still there.

And where else would I be, he thought, except here in this boat with you? While they were on the lake, not yet landed, they could just exist. He didn't want to think about later. The steady cadence of the oars marked out the moments. He rowed in time with his breath, and tried to breathe as slowly as possible. Breathe, dip, creak, splash, pull, breathe, lift, creak, splash, breathe.

At last, despite his minimal efforts, they reached the dock; Sylvie climbed the ladder, glanced down at him, then turned and ran up the meadow towards the house. Paul watched until she vanished. He wished he could imagine where she went, but he hadn't yet discovered which was her room. He followed, still in a strange state, still wishing to prolong it. How slowly can I walk? he

189

wondered; how slowly can I make time flow?

Sylvie's shoes lay where she'd flung them, one off to the right of the path, the other some distance to the left. He picked them up, feeling like the fellow in the fairy tale. Had that really happened? That venture into a fairy kingdom, led by a warrior princess . . . yes, of course. It was real, more real than any dream—the problem was that it also seemed more real than this thing he was now so reluctant to re-enter: daily life, other people, ordinary conversations, the person he had to be. He gave himself a mental shake, but couldn't shake off the feeling of fragile dreaminess that permeated everything.

If I could photograph this, he thought, it would all be a blur, with near things seeming far, and far things near, the island reflected in the lake, the clouds sailing the water, the ground floating . . . With a rush of vertigo the world twisted and fell away, then with a wrench righted itself. He sucked a shaky breath, felt for his feet, moved his toes, gripped the earth. The sun was strong on the top of his head—between them, sun and earth held him upright, and he was grateful. He stood there for a long time, and gradually the realities of the situation settled into him like stones.

First was Sylvie herself, whose reality superseded all others'. She was . . . she was . . . he sought for words to put her in, but she leapt out of them effortlessly, disdainfully, flirtatiously. She was like fire, agile and untouchable. But she was a real girl, with a will of her own. No, she was a tornado, and she had torn up the meagre roots of his life.

He sat down, checking for thistles first, lit a cigarette and tried to turn his attention to certain other pertinent realities. If it now seemed possible that Sylvie herself might want . . . might want . . . he pushed the delightful speculation to one side— the facts of the situation had not changed. They could hardly sneak around the house—everyone would know within a day. And in any case, he couldn't deceive his employers. So could he court her openly? Ask her to marry him? Her grandfather's penniless secretary? Ridiculous. Flirt with him she might, but marry him? Never. And yet a wild thought seized him of running off with her to some distant land, living on sunshine and love, dwelling in a nest of flowers and leaves somewhere in a deep green jungle.

12

Mrs Beal had stuffed Daniel's daily basket with every treat she could think of. Alice shifted it to her other hand, stepped on a thistle and cursed. Ever since the film people had come and gone Daniel was eating even less than before, and Mrs B had threatened to call on him herself to find out what he really wanted. As far as Alice could tell, he'd stopped whistling. Nor did he play, though the violin wasn't put back on its shelf, either. The last time she visited he'd been holding it in his arms, eyes closed, rocking back and forth. She'd asked, later, what it had been like to play again, but he turned away and didn't answer.

Today he was sitting, as usual, on his porch. When he saw her coming he went inside. She was afraid it was because he didn't want to see her, but he reappeared a moment later with a folded piece of paper. 'Would you post this for me?' he said. 'I don't know the address.'

'You've written a letter?' That was a first. 'Are you all right?'

'Oh Alice, I haven't been, not right at all.'

'Mrs B says you must eat more. Look, I brought . . .'

He shook his head. 'I'll try. Now please, take this. I don't have an envelope or a stamp—you must find out an address for Arlen Winter, and send him this. It's important. Please?'

'All right. Should I go now?'

'If you wouldn't mind. Dear Alice. You're so kind and I've never thanked you.'

'Oh, it's nothing really.'

Alice walked back slowly. The letter was as heavy as the basket. Of course she'd never deliberately open anyone else's mail, but was this mail yet? He'd said it was important but he hadn't actually said not to read it. She held it to the light—it was just one line, on a piece of paper torn from an exercise book. She unfolded it. He'd used a blunt pencil and the handwriting was stiff and awkward.

I was wrong. You were right. Please come back.

What could he mean? Wrong about what? She pictured Daniel alone in his cabin with no one to talk to, except her, and how much could he talk to a child, after all? Hardly anyone else ever called on him. How lonely he must have been all this time.

Halfway up the meadow she came upon Paul,

sitting by himself. 'Hello,' she said, 'why have you got Sylvie's shoes?'

'Hello, Alice.' Now here, thought Paul, was a dose of ordinary, everyday reality of the sort he was going to have to get used to dealing with. 'They were lying about.'

'You don't happen to know an address for Arlen Winter, do you? Daniel has written him a letter.'

'I heard he has rooms at the Berkeley.'

'Just the Berkeley, London?'

'Put Piccadilly, London.'

'Thanks. I can take Sylvie's shoes up, if you like.'

Paul surrendered the shoes and looked at his watch. He had some typing to do, and Jarlath was expecting him later. That was going to be interesting. What would it feel like to be turned into an ass? If you didn't know, if you simply became an ass, it might not be so bad. You'd live an ass's life, and die an ass's death, and that would be that. But if you remembered you were really a man, it might be hell.

*   *   *

Alice put Daniel's letter in an envelope, stamped and addressed it, added it to the pile of outgoing mail on the hall table and went upstairs. From Sylvie's room came the sound of singing. *I won't dance with anyone else but . . .*

'Your shoes,' Alice said, at the door.

'Thanks, Alice, thanks so much. Listen, I'm sorry I've been such a bear. I, well, you wouldn't understand.' She was stuffing things into an overnight case.

Alice sat on the edge of the bed. 'Where are you

going?'

'Just up to town for a couple of days. I need, well, I need everything. I'm going in with Maggie, and she's leaving any minute, so I've got to hurry. Listen, could you tell, no, never mind. Don't say anything.'

'Don't say what? Not to whom? Don't worry, I wouldn't dream of it.' Alice picked up a silk slip. She tried to stroke it but it snagged on her rough skin. She noticed how dirty her hands were and put it down. 'Did you always like this stuff?'

'What stuff?'

'Oh, you know, silky lacy stuff.' She sniffed. 'Perfume. Jewellery.' She tried not to watch as Sylvie undressed, dropped her clothes on the floor and rummaged for a clean frock. 'You shouldn't use the secret passage as a wardrobe.'

'Why not?'

'Well, because then it's not secret, is it? And what if you need to escape in the middle of the night?'

'I suppose I'll manage.'

'When you go and live in London can I have this room?'

'No, don't be silly. I'll still be here lots. And besides, you can't pick your room till you're sixteen.'

'They could make an exception for me; I'm nearly thirteen and three-quarters and I'm obviously a lot more grown up than most children my age.'

'Have you had your period yet?'

'Well, no.'

'I'd started by the time I was your age, and I had to stay in the children's wing. Besides, it's ever so

194

convenient for the schoolroom, isn't it?'

'I'm glad you're not near me in age, Sylvie. Having lessons with you would have been awful.'

Sylvie laughed. 'Yes, it would have. I didn't have nearly as many as you, and I spent most of my time doodling in the margins.'

'When you live in town can I stay with you?'

'I don't think they're going to let me get my own place. Maggie says I can live at the London house, but she doesn't understand. I need a studio, and she hates the smell of turpentine. The last time I painted anything there I got some cadmium yellow on my shoe and tracked it all down the stairs and through the drawing room. A lot of my friends have their own places. Maybe if I find someone respectable to share with they'll let me. And then you can come, but it'll probably be very shabby and you'd have to sleep on the sofa, or maybe the floor.'

'That's all right, I'd like that.' It sounded terribly romantic and bohemian. 'Do you know anyone who has a tattoo?'

'No. Why do you ask?'

'I wondered how old you have to be to get one.'

'I'll ask around for you.'

'Thanks. And I'm glad you're not being so ghastly any more.'

Alice went up to the schoolroom; she had a Hebrew text to translate. She was looking forward to having the place to herself but Jarlath was there, poring over the bookshelves. 'Tell me,' he said, 'do you have a book of fairy tales anywhere around here?'

'It's there.' She pointed. 'Bottom shelf, far right. Green cover, that's it.'

'There's a story I was thinking about, something to do with a girl and a wolf and a grandmother.'

'Little Red Cap?' Alice said.

'Ah, yes.' He leafed through the book. 'Here it is.' He lit a cigarette, settled into a chair, put his glasses on. 'Have you such a thing as an ashtray in this place?'

Alice fetched him a saucer and sat at her desk, trying to pretend it was the most normal thing in the world for her father to visit the schoolroom. But she couldn't recall another occasion. He'd been away most of her life, travelling. He sent postcards with amusing drawings and brought exotic gifts: a talking drum from Africa, a ceremonial pipe from the Northwest Territories of Canada, an incense burner from Ceylon, a goaty-smelling leather bag from Tibet, ivory and mother-of-pearl chopsticks from Shanghai. What she liked best about his gifts was that they made no concession to her youth; they were just like the gifts that Percy got, or Maggie, or anyone else.

She studied him covertly. He made little hm's and ah's as he read, and seemed to find the text quite interesting. Why on earth was he reading old fairy tales? He rather over-filled the chair; indeed, he rather over-filled the room. One of his paintings hung on the wall behind him: an attic with overflowing boxes, odd bits of furniture, a stuffed fox, a gilt mirror, a marble bust of Plato adorned by a plumed hat, a dressmaker's dummy draped with a chasuble in a dusty shaft of light. It was called *The Memory Palace*, and she'd stared at it so often she knew it by heart. She knew all of his paintings by heart. Her favourite had always been the portrait of Odelia with Francis in Percy's

196

sitting room; she used to spend hours looking at it, wishing Francis would appear.

She hadn't seen Francis again. When she'd finally brought herself to ask, Theo told her she shouldn't expect to see him all that often while she was awake and in her earth-body. That was one of those occasions when her great-aunt's answer left her nearly jumping up and down with frustration. What did it matter if Francis came when she was dreaming, or sleeping, or in her moon-body, if she remembered nothing of it?

Did Francis visit her father? For all she knew, they met up every night. For all she knew, she was with them, but forgot. Did Jarlath remember? That was the question. How to ask? How to ask without saying she'd seen Francis herself, which she'd promised not to tell anyone. Did that apply to her father, a prior member of what she was coming to think of as a very private, secret club? How to find out . . . ?

'Alice my dear,' Jarlath said, 'why are you staring at me with such a ferocious scowl on your face?'

'What? Oh, sorry, I didn't mean to. I was . . . I was wondering . . . why you're interested in fairy tales.'

He removed his specs and studied her. 'You like ancient languages.'

Alice nodded.

'Why?'

'Well, because . . .' She'd never thought about why she loved the old tongues, no longer spoken, or only rarely, by the select few who had learned their secrets. There was Latin: hard-edged, determined and rational, chiselled into marble; and Greek, which she loved even better, cursive

197

and elusive and echoing like bronze, full of poetry and mystery; and her new adventure, Hebrew: bright, prophetic, precise, elegant, orderly.

'They're like people,' she said, 'like friends. They're very wise, and they each have their own way of seeing things. When I want to understand a word, the first thing I do is look up its roots. And sometimes it's something one wouldn't think of, from what it means now, in English, and I try to understand how the old meaning is still there inside the new one.' She pictured old words within new ones, emitting meaning like a candle emits light, or like a series of candles, receding in time. 'They're still there, behind all the other languages, back to the beginning, like signs that point to what things really mean.' Had that made any sense at all? She expected amusement or condescension, but he nodded.

'Yes,' he said, 'one meaning behind another, back and back to the beginning, whatever that was, or is. This is precisely why I'm interested in these old tales, because I think they mean something behind what they seem to.'

'I always thought they were just silly stories for children.'

'Hah. You have the intellectual's typical disdain for the power of symbolism—too rich for your blood, eh?'

And with that he got up, kissed the top of her head and left. He took the book of fairy tales, but left behind a cloud of cigarette smoke and perplexity.

*   *   *

198

Paul sat at his table in the library. From the courtyard came the sound of the Bentley being brought round; Maggie was going up to town. He heard Sylvie's voice and rose to look out of the window. She climbed in beside Maggie; the car disappeared down the drive. Why hadn't she said she was leaving? He shrugged and forced himself to sit down. Was it his concern if she went here or there? She hardly owed him explanations. Maybe she'd left word, or perhaps a note. He expected Tustian to appear any moment, but no one came. He allowed himself a glance at her portrait. Was everything going to be even more difficult now?

He concentrated on his typing and didn't pause until the stable clock sounded two. Oh hell, it was time to go to Jarlath's. He wasn't ready; he felt like he must smell of her, something any man would notice, and he reminded himself again that he'd come no closer than her fingertips.

He sorted through the shoebox containing the photographs he'd taken and selected a couple of dozen of the better ones—he would show them to Jarlath, see what he thought. It might help to keep the conversation away from Sylvie.

In the studio, *Don Giovanni*—of all things—was playing on the gramophone; Jarlath hummed tunelessly along. Paul reclined as directed, determined not to drift off into daydreams about Sylvie, but Jarlath refused to converse while working, and the absolute silence and stillness he required had a trance-like effect.

'Relax now,' Jarlath said, and as though commanded, the honey-thick light rose and he floated. Sylvie's there, just out of reach. She smiles and swims away and he follows, slow leaps through

199

the sweet golden air.

'That's it,' Jarlath said, some time later.

Paul blinked, stretched and yawned.

Jarlath made coffee; the smell helped bring Paul back to earth. 'My daughter's in a better temper all of a sudden,' Jarlath said.

'Oh, really?'

'Off for a bout of shopping, apparently. Took twelve quid off me.'

So that was why she'd left with Maggie. Paul put on his shirt, lit a cigarette and took out his photographs. 'I remembered what you said about words and images,' he said when Jarlath had settled himself opposite. 'May I show you what I'm working on? Percy's letting me use his Kodak Autographic, and I'm getting words from the *Pymander*.' Paul handed him the stack of pictures.

Jarlath put on his specs and studied them for a few minutes, then laid them out on the low table, studied them further, rearranged a few. 'You're making a tarot, starting with the elements,' he said.

'The elements?' Paul pictured the periodic table.

'Not those elements,' said Jarlath. 'The ancient elements that precede all those permutations.' He held up a photograph of a tree at the lakeside. 'The *Pymander* has already told you, see? "Nature works by the Elements of Fire, Water, Air and Earth,"' he read. 'The four fundamental principles which combine to make everything: the metaphorical elements, if you like. Look: here are pictures of earth; here of water; here of air. All you're lacking is fire.'

Paul saw that he was right; seeking patterns in nature he'd been drawn first to stones, rocks, pebbles; then to rain, the lake, puddles; then to the

200

sky, and birds in flight. The words from the *Pymander*, he noticed, did at times have an uncanny connection to the elements Jarlath had described. A pile of rocks by the side of the road: 'Carrying the body of Earth as a burden.' A glass of water on a windowsill: 'Nourish them with nectar of Immortality.' Birds crossing the sky: 'Air, as Light, follows Spirit to Heaven.' He looked at the photographs as though he'd never seen them before. He had the irrational suspicion that Jarlath had somehow, as he handled them, caused the words to rearrange themselves. 'I never noticed,' he said.

Jarlath waved his hand in front of his eyes and Paul saw imaginary cobwebs brushed aside. 'Percy said something . . . what was it? About the sense of meaning—without it, one was blind to what was right in front of one's face.' He also, for no reason he could think of, remembered planting the fennel seeds with Theo.

'Theo,' said Jarlath, 'is always saying that what one seeks is not, in fact cannot be elsewhere and elsewhen, but must be here right now. More coffee?' He lifted the brass pot and poured a thick, potent stream into Paul's cup.

Paul rubbed his face, lit another cigarette, drank his coffee, tried to assemble his thoughts. One question was inescapable. 'Can you read my mind?'

'Not exactly read, not like a book, but you have a remarkably strong imagination. When you're picturing something, the image is easy to pick up.'

Paul remembered the path through the mist. 'And can you put images in my mind?'

'If I did that without your knowledge or consent

201

it would be very black magic indeed, and you're not worth it, as far as I know.'

'I'm relieved to hear it,' said Paul.

'If, however, you happen to become aware of an image from my mind—which occurs quite naturally between everyone all the time—that is not my fault.'

Paul pictured Jarlath with a saintly expression, lowered eyes and praying hands, angel's wings and a halo. The halo gave a little twinkle.

'Don't, for God's sake, take things too seriously,' said Jarlath.

* * *

In the darkroom after dinner, Paul laid his photographs out on the desk. Was there really a meaning here to be grasped, hidden somewhere in these words and images? Like Alice's augury, a way to find significance in random events. Like the tarot, a symbol language. He remembered an old gypsy in Paris who'd read the cards for him; there had been lovers and death and a man full of swords—standard fare, he'd reckoned. It had all seemed like utter nonsense at the time. But now . . . well, perhaps his mind was more open, or perhaps it was just that the questions had deepened and become more urgent.

'So,' he said aloud, 'if there's anything real out there, if anything really means something, if anybody is listening . . . I'm asking now.'

He shuffled the pictures and laid out three face down—that was what the gypsy had done. Past, present, future, and one more, above, for . . . what had she said? Fate.

He touched the first one, the past, then hesitated. Did he truly want to know? He noticed that at least part of him had started to believe there really was a meaning to be found in his tarot. But if he hadn't thought so all along, why had he bothered? He laughed at himself, lit a cigarette, turned over the picture: an image of the island and its reflection in the lake—'First it must war against its own self.' Yes, that's exactly what the war had been—one stupid, lost, helpless man at war with his own reflection, tearing himself into pieces of dead raw meat, over and over again, year after year.

He turned over the second, the present: a shaft of light falling to the forest floor—'Within every moment, a Door to Immortality.' He remembered taking that picture; he'd been deep in the woods and had stumbled into a dense, brambly valley. It was a muggy, midgey day and he was so frustrated by the clawing thorns that he decided to charge through, no matter the cost to his skin and clothes. He'd taken two steps, fallen down a steep slope into a stream and had to work his way up, knee-deep in water, until he found a place where he could ascend the other side. He'd emerged, bloody and torn, into a glade just as the sun broke through.

The third, the future: a young tomato plant snaking up a stake in the kitchen garden—'The cause of Death is Desire.' Well, so what? Death was everyone's future. You're born from desire, live your life drawn by desire—a plant's desire to reach the sun, a man's desire to survive another day. Did freedom from desire mean life without death? Did freedom from death mean life without

203

desire? Who would want to live forever, desireless? What would one do with all that time? Contemplate the beauty of the good, he heard old Mr Pym say.

His hand paused above the last picture, then he gathered them all roughly together and dumped them back in their box. If he had a fate, there was no point in knowing it.

It was after midnight when he emerged. As he crossed the hall the piano began to play, very softly. The notes floated into the dark space like slow drops of light and he recognised Theo's delicate touch. He tiptoed to the door of the music room. A single candle on the mantel showed Theo, eyes closed, bent over the keys. Paul thought she was alone and was about to walk in when she raised her head, the candle flickered and Francis stepped out of the shadows. He glanced at Paul, nodded, and sat down beside Theo.

Paul slipped away because it was obviously a private moment; he was halfway up the stairs before he realised what he'd just seen. Something about Francis's presence there, with Theo, had been so normal, so unremarkable; it hadn't registered that he was seeing the ghost again. He almost went back to check, but no—whether or not Francis was really there, it was none of his business. He went to his room, sat in his armchair, smoked a final cigarette and got into bed.

Somewhat later he woke to the sound of his name. Francis stood by the window in a shaft of moonlight. Every moment, he said, is a door to immortality.

Paul sat up. He'd heard the words clearly although Francis hadn't spoken aloud and his lips hadn't moved. A strange tingling sensation filled Paul's body; wonder, tinged with fear, gripped his mind. When he tried to speak, no words came out.

Francis walked to the door, beckoned and vanished. Paul stood up to follow but took only a few steps before a wave of dizziness pulled at him; he turned, saw his body asleep in the bed and was sucked down, and down, and down through sleep to dream.

He's on his way to the temple of Hermes; Francis is expecting him. The track twists up the hill; small rivers run down the ruts and muddy puddles reflect the silver moonlight. He stumbles into holes, curses, pushes on. When he reaches the steps he's so tired he can't lift his feet. He looks down and sees that they're turning into stone. He tries to crawl up the steps, but his stone feet have melded to the earth. He touches them; they're cold and hard and numb. He moves his hand to his ankle—the stone is spreading upward. I'm dreaming, he tells himself. This is not real. But it doesn't work; the stone reaches his knees, his thighs. Help, he thinks, someone please help!

The owl hoots overhead; he hears footsteps coming up the track. He's seized with terror—never has he been more vulnerable. But it's only Alice. She takes the cup from the niche in the rock and pours the water over his feet. It feels like liquid sunshine; it melts the stone and in a moment he's free.

'Thank you very much,' he says.

'You're welcome,' she says, and he follows her up the steps.

13

Percy shifted in his chair and relit his pipe. He was no longer always certain he had spoken aloud; sometimes, when Paul read the previous day's dictation back to him, things he was sure he'd said were missing, and others that he couldn't recall speaking were present. Did it matter? The remembering was the important thing, the steady assimilation of each link in the chain, each turn of the path.

'After we abandoned Captain Pedro,' he said, 'Sinclair and I found our way to a village of the Caiyuna people. Although it was true that, as Pedro had said, they ate people, it was only after the people had died, and only the heart was eaten. It was an act of love, not war.

'Sinclair explored the jungle for orchids; I trapped moths and began to learn the language. The Caiyuna occupied a kind of middle ground between the assimilated tribes who had taken up Western ways and those of the deep jungle who had little or no contact with Europeans. Sinclair kept his distance, slept in his own tent, cooked his own food, but I slipped gradually into native ways.

'We had been there for several months at the time of the annual *meri-kherut* ceremony— literally, the love-war. I have to confess that around this time I started drinking *irip*, their very potent wine, rather more than before, as if to numb the clash of civilisations going on inside me. I could not go back; I had to go forward, and so with a sort of delirious surrender I . . . allowed

206

it all to happen.

'I'd always felt awkward in my pale, hairy skin. A head or more taller than anyone else, I'd acquired a stoop through not wanting to loom all the time. I was regarded as the clumsiest person in the village; women moved cooking pots aside when I approached, men discreetly put their spears behind them. When the time came to prepare for the ceremony I tried to argue that my clothing was part of me, but lacked the vocabulary to make a convincing case. They took my clothes, and in a procedure that lasted all day, they plucked the hair from my body and helped me to paint myself all over.

'The ceremony begins as a mock battle. Dancing follows, until one finds someone whose painted pattern fits with one's own. I didn't know what to hope for—that someone should choose me, or that I be left aside and remain safe as an observer.'

In the flicker and flash of firelight, bodies approach, touch, move on. The wine has gone to his head, his feet, his hands. The drumming slips under his skin. He closes his eyes, lifts his arms, lets the currents move him. Someone touches him, lingers. He opens his eyes; they meet another pair of eyes, bright in a painted face. It's Gulana—he recognises the scars beneath the paint and her lopsided smile.

'There was one girl who had always seemed less willing than most to make fun of me. We'd swapped language lessons a few times, and her brother sometimes brought me a cut of their meat. Gulana was kind, I expect, because she knew what it was like to be different. Some childhood accident had resulted in her face being badly burned; her mouth pulled down on one side. It helped, too, that she was skinny and taller than average, and a bit clumsy herself. When she joined me in the dance I could see that our patterns, if not exactly matching, were definitely complementary. And then, of course, there was the wine, which I later learned was spiked with a mild aphrodisiac. Many factors contributed, but the real truth was that for the first time I felt at home in my body. I was completely taken up in the moment, but the moment contained an entire imagined future in the jungle: a deeply contented life with no clothes, no position, no scholarly detachment, just Gulana and I, sharing a hut, having fat babies. I would finally learn to hunt; I would forget English; I would dream Caiyuna dreams and die a Caiyuna death, and my people would eat my heart before sending me away on the river.

'I followed Gulana into the jungle, and though we were still near enough to the village to hear the drumming and shouting and singing, she led me by so many twists and turns it seems we went very deep, the only illumination her little rush-light. The girls had each prepared their own bower: a low platform, thick matting, fruits for refreshment, flowers strewn. I think I was near happiness then, for the first time since Arthur died. I was also very drunk, though I didn't know it.'

Percy gave a short laugh. 'It went downhill from there. A gang of her friends was waiting and pounced as soon as I touched her, whooping and jeering, beating me with leaves and pelting me with rotten fruit. Gulana fled shrieking towards the village; I bolted into the jungle and hid, furious and humiliated, until morning, when I strolled back with as much dignity as I could muster. No one ever mentioned the incident, but Gulana never spoke to me again, and to this day I don't know whether she was in on the prank, or only a victim herself.'

*   *   *

Alice skipped tea and, shaking off Roger and Sophie, walked up the track towards the temple of Hermes. She had a feeling that Francis was waiting for her, though perhaps it was just a dream she couldn't quite remember. The more she recalled, the more she was beginning to realise had been forgotten. The book about dreams and augury said the ancients believed there were no blank spaces, that we were doing, thinking, living all the time, even when asleep. They viewed sleep as a sort of place, with different zones; in some you had dreams about the past, in others dreams about the future, and in between you went about in something she reckoned was very much like a moon-body.

Alice was disappointed to find the temple of Hermes still closed up. She opened all the doors, checked behind all the statues, but there was no one. She stood in the centre and closed her eyes. Francis, she thought, are you near? She caught an echo of music and a memory of dancing; Francis clicked his fingers and invisible musicians played a waltz . . . she could hear it now, and feel his arm guiding her. She let herself move, and imagined him so clearly that when she opened her eyes and saw he was really there she wasn't surprised. She

209

was about to ask a question but saw the look in his eye; just dance, it said.

*   *   *

Paul tucked camera and *Pymander* into his pockets and set off up the hill to the temple of Hermes. He'd avoided the place since his encounter with Francis, but today he couldn't shake off the strange feeling that Francis was expecting him. He walked through the green stillness of the woods, inhaling deep lungfuls of fragrant air. Sunlight spangled the path; he held out his hand and a sunbeam danced on his palm. He looked through the camera: light and shade, in constant motion. Click. 'Of change only are the things of Earth made,' said *Pymander*.

Branches met above his head; leaves fluttered like flames. He noticed again that tickling in the soles of his feet and when he reached the steps to the temple, sat down to take off his boots. The laces were knotted and as he struggled to untie them he had the absurd fear that he'd be trapped inside them forever. At last he loosened them and stepped free. The teacup in the stone niche was brimming with water; he drank some and poured the rest over his bare feet. It felt lovely.

He raised the camera: the teacup in its mossy frame, water dripping. 'This is both Nature and Art,' said *Pymander*.

All the doors of the temple stood open but there was no one in sight. Was Francis inside? He was curiously reluctant to approach and stood for several minutes stuck in indecision. He decided to turn back but there was a weird wrench when he

210

tried to lift his feet; at the same time he was drawn towards the temple as though by a strong magnet. When he relented and walked forward the sensation eased and by the time he reached the portico it had been replaced by a sense of calmness and peace, and a faint echo of music . . . a waltz?

As he stepped to the door the music grew louder, though he could see no source. The late sun laid golden oblongs on the floor and he caught a glimpse of movement; a couple was dancing among the statues, dipping and swaying. The man in his green velvet coat was unmistakably Francis, and as he twirled his partner Paul saw that it was Alice, eyes closed, smiling. The music ended; the dancers stopped. Alice opened her eyes and saw Paul. Francis bowed, kissed her hand and vanished.

'Oh damn,' Alice said. 'Where did he go?'

'I've no idea,' said Paul. 'Wherever ghosts go.'

Alice walked to the portico and looked around. There was no one in sight. 'He says he's not a ghost.'

'Then what is he?'

'I don't know. I don't think he likes to talk about himself.'

'Do you see him very often?'

'No, hardly ever. I'm supposed to keep it a secret, though I suppose not from you. I think I see him in dreams, but I forget. And also sometimes . . . between dreams.' Alice hesitated. 'Can I ask you something?'

'OK.'

'Have you ever been asleep but not completely— I don't know how to describe it. I call it my moon-body, and Theo understands about it, but she told me people forget it when they grow up. Do you have any idea what I'm talking about?'

'Maybe,' said Paul. Something stirred at the back of his mind, a sensation of rising and floating, swimming in air thick as water. A twist of vertigo passed through his body. 'How odd. I think I may. Is it like swimming in air?'

'Yes, that's it! It's just like that. Do you remember it?'

'Yes . . . no, not really.' A memory hovered out of reach. He tried to close in but it slipped away, leaving him with a nagging, dissatisfied feeling and the impression that the inside of his skull had tightened, then loosened again. He rubbed his head. 'Isn't it just a dream?'

'Maybe, but it feels different, somehow. More real, but not as real as being awake.'

'Well, if we don't remember, there's probably an excellent reason.'

'That's daft,' said Alice. 'Why wouldn't you want to remember?'

'Dozens of reasons, but don't be in any rush to find them. And don't listen to me; I don't know what I'm talking about.' He sat on a bench, lit a cigarette, took out the camera and framed the view of the valley and River Isis far below. Click. 'The forgotten Gateway to the Source,' said *Pymander*.

Alice sat on the grass and started a daisy chain. She was hoping that Francis would come back; it was all very well to dance, but she hadn't had the chance to ask a single question.

'May I take a picture of you?' Paul said.

'I suppose so. I always look awful in photographs. I won't smile.'

'You don't even have to look at me, and I

deplore smiles.'

Alice bent over the daisy chain; her hair fell over her face, but the sun was on her hands and the flowers shone like small suns on her lap. Click. 'I need a few words,' Paul said, and passed her the *Pymander*. 'Would you pick a line at random?'

'That's called bibliomancy—divination by book. People did it all the time, using Homer, or Virgil, or the Bible.' Alice took the book, opened it and put her finger on the page. "This only is the way to the Truth,"' she read. 'That's funny—it's what my name means. Alice means truth. May I try your cigarette?'

'Aren't you a bit young?'

'Oh, tosh. I only want to try. I'm not going to start smoking until I'm eighteen.'

'All right,' Paul said. 'One puff. And don't inhale, you'll get sick.'

She took the cigarette between her thumb and index finger, brought it to her lips, sucked, choked. 'Oh my, these are a lot stronger than Sylvie's.' She passed it back, dug out her handkerchief and blew her nose.

*   *   *

Sylvie returned on Monday night, laden with boxes. Paul glimpsed her in the hall and she sat nearly opposite him at dinner. When he caught her looking at him she turned away; she disappeared after the meal. Should he find her, confront her, demand to know her intentions, sit down for a long talk? Or not talk at all, just take her in his arms and—he'd worked out a variety of options, but fortunately he still didn't know which was her room.

She wasn't at breakfast on Tuesday, nor was she at lunch. Feeling very annoyed, and ridiculous for it, he settled grimly at his desk and pounded the typewriter. By late afternoon his fingers were sore, he'd smoked too many cigarettes and barely suppressed irritation gripped him in a dull ache. He put camera and *Pymander* into his pockets and headed up the hill. He had an experiment in mind. By accident he'd discovered that the film could be exposed twice, one image superimposed on another. Of course, the accident resulted in both being ruined, but it occurred to him that if he halved the exposure times and chose his images carefully, something interesting might result. He'd taken some pictures of himself, since he'd been at hand, rewound the film, and now wanted to add a second layer of birds crossing his favourite patch of sky behind the chapel.

Halfway up the hill his feet started tingling and his boots were suddenly unbearably hot and confining. He took them off, and his socks, and left them by the path. The pebbles were cold and smooth beneath his feet; he stopped to stand in the occasional puddle.

He began to hear odd snatches of music—was it rising from the house or stables? No, wrong direction. *'I won't dance with anyone else, anyone else but you-oo-oo,'* for God's sake. The door of the chapel was ajar; the gramophone evidently within. Now this really was annoying. Of all the places to pollute with silly songs. It was probably the children. He was going to walk round to the back without stopping, but as he passed the door he heard someone singing along. It wasn't the children. Christ, was it Sylvie? Was she alone? The record came to an end; the needle settled into the final groove and remained there. Paul stared at the door; trickles of oil darkened the wood below the hinges and the lock. He stepped forward, reached out, pushed. It swung open silently.

Sylvie stood on a ladder, swiping at a bit of elaborate stonework with a long-handled feather duster. She wore a jersey singlet and trousers held at her waist with a striped necktie; her hair was pinned on top of her head, though most of it had escaped. Paul was unwilling to interrupt because, he told himself, if he startled her she might fall. He had a brief and extremely enjoyable fantasy of catching her as she fell, saving her, being rewarded.

At the bottom of the ladder she looked around and saw him. For what seemed like a very long time they stared at each other as the needle rasped in its track.

'Hello,' she said.

'Hello,' he said.

She lifted the arm of the gramophone. 'What are you doing here?'

Paul swallowed. What was he doing here? 'I . . .' He coughed, choked, felt the camera in his pocket. 'I was on my way to the graveyard. To take photographs. What are you doing here?'

'I'm going to paint it,' she said.

'It?'

'The chapel—the walls. With pictures of . . . well, I haven't decided yet.'

'That's a lot of painting.' Could I possibly, he thought, say anything stupider?

'Yes, I suppose it is. But I've got all summer.'

All summer, alone up here. Christ. He forced himself to look around the room. Tables and boxes had appeared, jars of paint and brushes, sheets covered the floor and all the windows had been cleaned.

'Would you like a cup of tea?' she said. 'I was just going to have one.'

'I'd love a cup of tea.'

'I only have one cup. We'll have to share, is that all right?'

'Oh, quite all right.'

She poured from a flask and offered him the cup.

'You first,' Paul said. He noted where her lips touched the rim and when it was his turn, drank from the same spot with a hidden smile.

They passed the tea back and forth. Paul found himself grinning like an idiot and gave up on the idea of intelligent conversation. He just looked at her, and didn't conceal that he was looking. Her bare arms, slim and brown, her slender wrists, her beautiful hands. Her shoulders, her throat, her hair half fallen, half concealing her ear, the nape of her neck. Her collarbones, and their exquisite shadow, vanishing beneath the thin fabric of her singlet.

She talked about art and about Italy, about the relative merits of oil and egg tempera, about the limitations of perspective and the advantages of multiple points of view.

I want to kiss you, Paul thought. It's all I can think about. He took the camera from his pocket. 'May I take a picture of you?'

'All right. That's Percy's Autographic, isn't it? I used to make up silly things to write in the box.'

'Oh really? So do I—well, I don't make them up

216

but I get them from a book.' He took out the *Pymander*. 'Do you know this book?'

She shook her head.

As Paul framed her in the viewfinder, he remembered with a jolt of clandestine delight that images of himself already lay on the film, waiting for her. She held the empty cup between her hands, just about, he thought, where my heart is. Click. 'Would you choose me a phrase at random, please?' He passed her the *Pymander*.

She put down the cup, opened the book. What would old Mr Pym say?

' "Wash thyself, thou that art able, in this cup," ' she read. Paul blinked in wonder, wrote it in the box, advanced the film and framed her again.

She glanced to one side. Click. 'Could I have another few words?' he said.

She flicked through the pages. ' "I send unto God these reasonable sacrifices." '

Paul wrote, wound the film, waited. She looked down at his heart, open like the book in her hands. Click. Without being asked, she chose another phrase. ' "Look with the eyes of your Heart." ' She smiled. Each time he released the shutter was like a kiss.

Paul stepped closer. Now, he reckoned, his heart would be in her throat. She looked steadily at him through the lens. ' "Not with his hands, but with his word." '

He took one step closer, to place his heart on her lips. ' "For the Mind, being God, is male and female." '

And that, thought Paul, is about as much as I can take. He stepped back to a safer distance. Flimsy and ambiguous a shield the camera might be, but it was better than none. I should go now, he thought, before . . . Suddenly he couldn't bear to leave her. 'Thank you for the tea, for the pictures.' He turned towards the door.

'Wait, you've forgotten your book.' She held it out.

He caught hold of her wrist, plucked the book away, brought her hand to his lips, kissed it, turned it, pressed his lips to the palm. She looked up at him; let her hand cup his face. He kissed her fingertips, each in turn, and bit gently at the soft mound below her thumb. And fled.

Halfway down the hill it hit him. What was he doing? He was flinging himself into the seduction of this girl, of this astonishing, beautiful girl, as though she was the sort of girl . . . but she wasn't.

A pair of boots lay by the side of the path. How odd. Somebody must have taken them off, just here, and walked on barefoot. He glanced down at his feet, his bare feet on the wet, stony path, and it dawned on him that those were his boots, which he must have abandoned some time ago.

*   *   *

Sylvie appeared for drinks and dinner, lingered late but remained elusive. Every time Paul saw her she was wrapped in conversation with someone else, or just leaving the room by another door, and he never caught her eye. She wore a very revealing frock of olive green silk that barely covered her shoulders or her knees and she seemed to be enjoying the attention of every other man. Jarlath lounged on a sofa with his meerschaum pipe, his gaze hooded. Paul pictured all the men turned into

218

asses, braying and shuffling their hoofs and shitting on the carpet. Jarlath caught his eye, raised his glass.

Late at night, unable to sleep, Paul went down to the darkroom. He'd hesitated to print the roll of doubly exposed film because having the pictures on paper—if they came out, and he half hoped they wouldn't—brought that reality into this one, and he still had no idea how he'd handle that.

He mixed the chemicals, processed the film, prepared the frames, made the exposures, developed the prints. One by one the images swam into existence. Sylvie and Paul, Paul and Sylvie. He was like a ghost; she was too, except where they overlapped.

'Oh, Sylvie,' he said, 'what am I going to do?'

He left the prints to dry, locked the darkroom door and went up to his room. He took off his clothes and lay on his bed. Rain pattered the windowsill, the candle made shadows dance across the ceiling. Somewhere in this house she lay in her bed, too. He wished he could picture it, but it would have been agony to know where she was and not go to her. The night was warm; perhaps she'd pushed off her covers—did she sleep on her side, on her back, on her front? He imagined her in different positions; as she moved about, her nightgown rode up . . .

He's at the foot of her bed. She turns, stretches, settles on her back with one arm flung wide. Her sleeping face is perfection: the shadowed eyelids, the proud line of her nose, the almost unbearably beautiful dip that divides her upper lip and points the way to the mystery of her mouth. He extends his hand. She rises with him, twists and turns in the

219

shining air. Below, the meadow glimmers with tiny lights and the moon lays a silver path across the lake. 'Let's swim to the island,' she says, and dives in; Paul dives after her. She moves through the water like a seal, staying just out of reach.

14

The morning was warm and drizzly, with cloud over the far hills. Paul walked down to the lake before breakfast, a curiously hollow feeling in his bones as though some central pith had become open and transparent, airy and volatile. He remembered fragments of a dream: swimming to the island with Sylvie, naked, sliding through silver water. The sensation was so real he had to remind himself he stood fully clothed, wide awake, on solid ground. Wide awake? he asked. Are you sure? Solid ground? Fool. There is no solid ground.

Across the soft blurred expanse of water floated the dark mound of the island. Something moved among the trees at the top and he had the sudden thought that it was himself; he was really there, looking across to here, remembering a dream in which he'd stood on the shore. Which was real? How to know? As he walked up to the house the rain fell harder.

*　　　*　　　*

Percy reached for his pipe and began to dictate. 'The most dangerous beast is a man who believes

220

he is right; he's worse than a mad dog. The comfortable hypocrisy of Christians in England becomes in the tropics a disease of ignorance and arrogance so complete it relegates everyone else to the status of animals. The only man I ever wanted to kill was a Christian missionary, and although I did not kill him with my own hands I sentenced him to death. And yet what he did was common; in the settlements, few native girls made it out of puberty without being raped by someone. No, Father John's real crime was that he told them he was the Son of God, and would save them by that most ancient of means. I suppose he was insane; the heat, the isolation, the strangeness alone can send men mad quite easily. And people believed him; people always want to believe such things.

'Father John's *kharisma* was not salvation but syphilis, and it was not until the symptoms appeared among all the young girls that people began to wonder. It was lucky, in the end, that Gulana and I never consummated our romance; she'd been among his first victims.

'He had arrived among the Caiyuna about a year before, with three Brazilian nuns. Two had departed; the last one lingered, silent and shrouded in her habit. Father John conducted daily services and a Sunday school, where he taught Bible stories. No one understood a word; he bribed them with tobacco and sugar. And some received special lessons in the back room.

'He was eventually responsible for hundreds of cases, as his victims carried his message to the world. When I confronted him he didn't even try to deny it; he said he'd known he was infected before he left England.

'I dragged him from his church, stripped him, whipped him and drove him into the jungle at night. He never returned, but his poison remained. I wrote to his superiors in São Paolo; I wrote to the Archbishop of Canterbury. I asked them to send a doctor, or medicine, or an apology. I wrote for years. At first I was ignored, then politely deterred, then it was suggested that I was myself unhinged by my long sojourn in the tropics. In all my years I have yet to meet a Christian who makes the slightest attempt to live up to the most basic tenets of his religion. Damn them all to their own Hell.

'Sinclair and I left the Caiyuna and went further upriver to Lamarca, a verminous and dilapidated village perched above the steep bank of the Rio Jauaperi. The people were a vagrant mix of half-bloods, outcast Portuguese, dispossessed Indians. A rubber company boat stopped once a month or so and I sent a message down to the British outpost at Manaus requesting that some of the equipment I'd left in their care be sent up to me— cameras and plates, my microscope and, most important, a spare pipe, tins of tobacco and coffee and a supply of quinine. I'd realised that the bouts of weakness and delirium I was suffering were probably due to malaria. The storekeeper, who also served as barber, doctor and dentist, gave me a concoction of leaves and crushed roots to drink, but it made me violently ill and had no effect on the malaria.

'Sinclair went off every day on his own. He was warned that it was unwise, but he said he could hear the moon-flower calling. One evening he didn't return. I waited until nightfall, then went to the edge of the jungle and called in all directions; I

222

heard no response but the cackles of a perguna bird disturbed by my racket. I tried to get the villagers to mount a search; they refused. I walked a little way into the jungle by myself. In the silence between my shouts I heard soft noises I was sure were human footsteps; at first they seemed to come from behind me, then alongside, then ahead. No one answered my calls; I retreated and spent the night pacing by the fire.

'At daybreak we set out to search, led by Yano, the best tracker. He had no difficulty in finding and following Sinclair's path—we Europeans moved like elephants, leaving unmistakable trails of broken twigs, crushed leaves, churned ground. It soon became evident that Sinclair had walked in circles, now leaving the path, now returning to it. At last we found him only a couple of miles from the village. He was lying on his back in a clearing, one of those temporary gaps that occur when a giant of the forest has fallen and its children have yet to fill the space. *Bebit-akhu*, they call these places: spirit holes.

'He was very still. His eyes were wide open, staring up at the circle of open sky. I thought he was dead, but when I touched him his eyes swivelled to meet mine and it was I who nearly died of fright. Still he didn't move, and I thought he must have had a fit of some sort, or perhaps a stroke had paralysed him, but then he leapt to his feet and set off at a brisk pace. We followed; he went straight to the village, ate as much food as he could find, climbed into his hammock and fell asleep. I was furious, but he ignored me.

'The next morning he emerged for breakfast as usual. He claimed to have no memory of what had

223

happened; as far as he remembered, he'd been searching for orchids the entire time, and planned to do the same today. When I told him how I'd found him he didn't believe me. He admitted he couldn't explain how I came to be suffering such a delusion, but although he felt very sorry for me there was nothing he could do. He walked towards the jungle. I ran after him—he'd left his precious specimen pouch. He looked at it as though he didn't recognise it, waved it away with a bemused look—why was I offering him this useless and irrelevant object?—turned his back and disappeared. It was many weeks before I saw him again.'

He's here now, hovering at the edge of vision. 'Hello my friend,' he says. 'Still alive, I see. Poor old sod.' Every detail is clear—the dirty sweat-stained shirt, torn khakis, the unkempt beard.

'Did you find it?' Percy asks.

Sinclair smiles and opens his shirt, revealing a gaping, bleeding wound in his chest. He reaches into it and brings out a flower of such startling, perfect beauty it takes Percy's breath away. Its fragrance pierces him with a sweetness like pure sunshine; his bones melt, his head whirls and he falls down and down, into his aching, earth-bound body.

Henry knocked and entered. 'Miss Sylvie is here, sir.'

'Paul, thank you.' Percy dragged himself back to the present with difficulty as Paul got up to leave. 'We'll continue tomorrow. Come in, Sylvie dearest.'

'Hello Grandpapa,' she said. Her voice, slightly husky, always came from higher up than he

224

expected. She bent to kiss his cheek, the smell of her cigarettes mingling with a spicy scent as her hair brushed his face.

'Come and sit here by me,' Percy said.

Sylvie settled herself with a rustle of cloth; he heard the slip of silk stockings as she crossed her legs. She took his hand; her fingers were strong and long like her father's, soft-skinned as her mother's.

'It's your birthday next week,' Percy said, 'but as I very likely shan't stay up for your party I wanted to give you my present now.' He reached for the box on the table and put it in her hands. 'It's Odelia's wristwatch. I thought it would be useful, help you get to classes on time, and so forth. Go on, open it.'

'Oh Percy, it's . . .'

'I sent it up to London to be cleaned and whatnot; they said it runs perfectly.'

He heard her winding it. 'Yes, it ticks!' She held it to his ear. 'Thank you so much, Grandpapa. It's . . . beautiful, but far too nice for everyday. I daren't wear diamonds and emeralds to classes, I'll ruin it in no time. I'll save it for special occasions.' She kissed his cheek again. 'I'll treasure it, I really will.'

Percy sighed. His present hadn't been a success, but how was he to know what modern girls liked? He'd not seen Sylvie clearly since she was a small child. 'Maggie tells me you're beautiful,' he said, 'and Jarlath tells me you're very stubborn.'

She laughed. 'They both say I'm a great trial, and that I'm their penance for past sins.'

'They worry about you, that's all. They fretted quite a bit while you were in Italy, though they'll

225

never admit it to you. Now tell me more about Florence, paint me one of those word-pictures of yours. The view from the hills above the city—the Duomo, the river, the Ponte Vecchio . . .'

'And you come down the hill, through pine groves and vineyards, and along a wide avenue lined with poplars, and you look back and see the cypress trees silhouetted against the sky. And you pass farms and low, red-roofed barns and then you're in the city, in the dark, winding medieval streets; if you look up, the sky is a narrow blue river between tall houses, pink or ochre or umber, with green shutters and high, closed doors. There's an old Nonna in the archway, black dress, splayed slippers, her shopping basket over her arm: *pane*, *pomodori*, *basilico*, *finocchio*, *mozzarella*, *arancie*; outside the coffee bar men gather, unshaven, smoking, watching with their smoky eyes. And you step through a shadowed gate into a bright courtyard where a fountain splashes in a marble pool and then again into darkness through a cool antechamber and on into room after room of glorious treasures like dreams made real, frescoes on walls and ceiling, angels and gods and demons, patriarchs and holy whores in colours like jewels, vermilion and cobalt and viridian, clouds and mountains and horses . . .' she paused, out of breath. 'And then they make you come home; they jerk you back as though you were a dog on a lead. Oh Grandpapa, is it very awful of me to hate this place so much? I know you love it, everyone loves it and says I'm so lucky to have this for my home but ever since I can remember all I've wanted is to get away.'

'I love it now,' Percy said, 'but I used to feel

exactly like you, and I thought I was the only one ever to feel that way. I longed to get away, though I had to wait until after university.'

'But then you went really far, and stayed for years. I'm only going as far as London, and they want me to live at the London house. I don't think I can bear it. That's why I was thinking, well, that I'd ever so much rather have some money than a wristwatch and I wondered if I could possibly have a sort of advance on Granny Odelia's trust? Just a few hundred a year . . . dear Grandpapa . . .' She took his hand between hers and squeezed. 'It would make all the difference to me. I have to get out from under them. I have to be free. I have to.'

Percy could sense the urgency; her voice caught in her throat and her breathing was choppy. He remembered the feeling of wild desperation; he'd had it, too—like wings beating against an invisible barrier. Was there any point in warning her that freedom might cost more than money? No—such advice would have been meaningless to him, all those years ago; no one could have prevented his escape to the jungle—no argument, no reasoning, no objective assessment of the dangers. It was his choice, his fate; at the time it had seemed a bright and certain path into the future. Sylvie exuded the same certainty, she felt the same pull. There was no stopping her.

'I'll talk to your parents,' he said. 'If they agree, I'll arrange something.'

'Oh thank you!' Her joy burst over him like a shower of exclamation marks. There is nothing like money, he thought, to gladden the heart of the mercenary young. But it was the only useful gift he could give, and her delight was infectious.

227

'When I get my own place you must come and visit,' she said.

'Oh, no, I don't . . .'

'Yes, you absolutely must. Henry can be your chaperone, and I'll serve a very proper tea. Say you'll do it, please.'

'I'll think about it.'

*   *   *

After lunch (no Sylvie), Paul settled at the typewriter and tried to concentrate. In Percy's room, she'd brushed past him with barely a glance. She was probably up at the chapel. He pictured her there, on the ladder, her hair coming down, her clothes dishevelled. He pictured her on the ladder with no clothes at all. Several minutes passed while his hands rested unmoving on the keys, then he shook himself. Christ, Asher, get a grip. You're not some adolescent boy, drunk on your first infatuation. You've been in love before. Not like this, he thought, not like this.

He could walk to Exley, catch the next train. Disappear from her life and try to recover his own, such as it had been. She wouldn't miss him, and Percy could soon find another secretary. But the thought of leaving Farundell filled him with a strange new pain and he remembered that he'd loved this place before Sylvie ever appeared. The word 'home' floated into his mind; he pushed it away. It was a word to avoid, since the place he was from was the one he hated most of all places in the world. But it edged nearer.

No, he said, as though to an importunate dog who'd mistaken him for its master, you can't be my

228

home, I don't belong here. I'm just passing through. It nudged closer, certain in its doggy devotion that he was the right one. No! Please go away, it's impossible. He stood up, suddenly determined. He'd pack his rucksack, compose a note with apologies to all, and be gone.

He sat down again. Coward. How could I even think of leaving Percy like that? If I go, I'll have to give notice, and then it'll be awful. He groaned and put his face in his hands. It doesn't matter, carry on, it doesn't matter. Out of the darkness swam an image of Val, smiling ironically. 'Oh shut it, Val.'

'Val's not here,' Sylvie said.

'Christ! You've got to stop sneaking up on me.'

'I was not sneaking; I can't help it if you didn't hear me. You're not deaf or anything, are you?'

'Eh?' Paul cupped his hand around his ear and glared at her. 'What did you say, dearie?'

She grinned. 'It's time for your swimming lesson.'

'My what?'

'You really are deaf, aren't you?' She leaned closer. 'Swimming! Lesson!'

'But it's raining.'

She sat on the edge of the desk and clucked sympathetically. 'And blind as well. I had no idea, no idea at all. How very sad, how unfortunate.' She glanced out of the window.

Paul followed her eyes. The sky had cleared and the sun shone bright and hot. 'Oh. The rain seems to have stopped.'

'Yes.' She enunciated clearly. 'The rain has stopped.'

Paul watched her lips shape the words. I'm helpless, he thought. She can do anything she

229

wants with me, or not, as she chooses.

'I don't have a swimming costume,' he said: a last stand.

'Well, you know we don't really bother, not when there's just the family around.'

'Oh no, no. No, couldn't possibly, I'm very, er, shy.'

'Not really all that shy. But I brought this.' She lifted a flower-printed canvas sack on to the desk and pulled out a flimsy knitted object. 'And I'm wearing one too.'

'Oh,' said Paul.

'You do want to learn to swim, don't you?' she said. 'I mean, don't you?'

'Yes, of course, it's . . .'

'You don't think I can teach you, is that it? I can, you know.'

Could she really? He considered the possibility for the first time. To be able to swim, to dive and turn like a dolphin in the water . . .

'Come on,' she said. She led him to the bay where the stream from St Ælfhild's pool entered the lake and weeping willows crowded the shore. A heron, one-footed by the bank, regarded them with a doubtful eye and stalked away.

'Here we are,' Sylvie said. 'This is the best spot because the shore slopes very gently; there's no sudden drop to deep water.'

No sudden drop to deep water? She gazed up at him with what she no doubt imagined was a reassuring expression, but the dark pools of her eyes looked like very deep water indeed to him.

'I'll turn round while you change,' she said.

What the hell had he got himself into? He took the swimming costume and a towel from the bag,

230

retreated behind some bushes. Why, oh why, didn't I say I didn't want to swim? Why did I have to say I couldn't swim? And who would have thought she'd decide to teach me? Do I really want to swim, anyway? I've made it this far without it, after all. Afraid to succeed, he jeered at himself, or only afraid to fail?

He shed the last of his clothes and unstrapped his now incongruous wristwatch. Bees buzzed among flowers where he'd hung his shirt; he released one that had become trapped, followed as it dipped into a flower and drank; he tasted the sweetness on his own tongue. He forgot what he was doing and just stood, as much a bee as anything else, unless it was the flower or the sun or the warm golden air.

'Paul? Have you got lost?'

He blinked and remembered who he was. 'No. I'm coming.'

The swimming costume was a loathsome thing: striped, preposterous, with neither dignity nor elegance. He wished it were twenty years, fifty years earlier, and fashions not so utterly, utterly revealing. He wrapped the towel around his waist before emerging.

'You can't swim in that,' Sylvie said. 'It is a towel, for drying yourself, later.'

Her swimming costume was very fashionable; Paul gazed up into the trees. When he looked again she'd waded into the water. 'Come on,' she said.

Oh Christ, here I go. He dropped the towel on the bank and followed.

The slope was as easy as she'd said and as they passed the last lacy curtains of the willows the

231

water was only to his waist. Sylvie reached deeper water and began to swim, then turned and waited. When the water came up to his chest he stopped, heart pounding. Primordial fear of drowning, he told himself. It's a perfectly natural, a perfectly reasonable fear.

Sylvie swam back to him. 'Come on.'

'Come on? What do you mean, come on? How can you just tell me to come on? I don't know how, remember?'

'You do know how, remember?' She took his hand, tugged. 'I'll help you.'

'Wait, wait. Don't I need a demonstration first? Maybe I could watch for a bit while you swim, to give me an idea what to do. I gather swimming involves some very particular movements of the arms and legs . . .'

'Do you trust me?'

Oh God, what a question. 'Yes,' he said, gazing into her serious face.

'Then close your eyes and do what I tell you.'

Paul closed his eyes. And if I do drown, he thought, well, there are worse ways than this to die, being led out beyond my depth by my lady-love.

She swam at his side; the currents made by her movements pulsed over his skin. Bees hummed in the distance and beyond his closed lids the sun seethed like lava, red and black and gold. A cloud of honey-scented air wafted by, and for a moment he forgot where his skin was.

'You can float,' Sylvie said, and he realised his feet no longer touched the ground. There was that feeling, that strange feeling Alice had called moon-body; he remembered it now, it must be from a dream—no, from many dreams, in each of which he was remembering for the first time—this feeling that the air was liquid, buoyant; he could rise and float, leap and turn and swim in the air. In the dream he's always saying Oh yes, I remember, I can do this . . . how could I have forgotten?

'Breathe in,' Sylvie said, 'and now breathe out.'

She pushed his head gently underwater; the breath trickled from his nostrils. She released him and he bobbed up, arms and legs floating like waterweeds. He let himself submerge, listened to the soft rushing sounds, lifted his head just enough to breathe, dropped down. Sylvie hovered nearby; she gave him a push or a pull from time to time, and his limbs responded. When was she going to start teaching him how to swim?

He concentrated on the varied sensations of the water, the changes in temperature, the stroke of small currents. He stretched his toes down into a cool zone; a warmer stream wrapped his thighs. He floated with his nose above the surface, the rim of water circling his skull, the sun hot on his forehead. He slipped down; the water closed over his head.

'Aaaahhh . . .' The bubbles surged out of his mouth, his voice resonant yet muted. He rose again.

'You can open your eyes now,' Sylvie said.

Paul opened his eyes.

'Look around,' she said.

'Christ! How did I get out here?' The shore was a hundred yards away.

'You swam. And now let's swim back.'

She set off with a slow, steady breaststroke. Paul imitated her and soon found that the movements

233

came almost naturally, as though he was—she was right—just remembering. It would take some practice; she outstripped him effortlessly and his muscles began to complain. By the time his feet touched the bottom she was out and towelling herself off. He waded through the willows. I swam, he said to himself. I can swim? I can swim. 'How did you do that?'

'Do what?'

'Teach me to swim.'

'I didn't.'

'You sure as hell did.'

'I sure as hell didn't. I told you, you knew how. You only needed to remember.'

'You hypnotised me.'

She laughed.

'If it's as simple as you say,' he said, 'why are there still so many people who can't swim?'

'Now there's a mystery.'

Add it to the bloody list, Paul thought. He climbed out, picked up his towel, retreated behind his shrub. 'When I wake up,' he said, 'I hope I remember this one.'

He dressed in a daze. I swam. I can swim. His mind stuck like a needle in a groove and on the way back to the house he couldn't think of anything to say. Thank you? That sounded trite compared to the size of the gift. Nevertheless, it was the best the language offered.

'Thank you,' he said, 'for reminding me how to swim.'

'You're welcome,' she said.

'Do you do it often? Have you reminded many people?'

'No, you're the first.'

'Really? The first? So how did you know it would work?'

'I didn't, I suppose.'

'You were bluffing. Bluffing! Bloody hell, I might have drowned.'

'Yes, but you didn't, did you? You swam. You remembered how.'

*   *   *

That night he sat long at his window looking down on the lake. I swam, he told himself for the hundredth time, in that water. The memory of floating, of moving in three dimensions, was so vivid that for a moment the weightiness of his body seemed strange and unnatural, as though he had but to flick some switch in his head to enter that aquatic state of mind. He closed his eyes and imagined his room full of water instead of air; he could rise up and float, turn and somersault. Swimming in air . . . moon-body . . . with a twist of nausea the floor dropped out from under him. He wrenched his eyes open. Seasick in an armchair, whatever next?

He lit a cigarette and contemplated once again the complete shift, the utter transformation that Sylvie had wrought. And she had wrought it, he knew, despite her efforts to tell him it had all been his own doing. The difference between being the Paul who couldn't swim and the Paul who could was far greater than he ever would have expected, and he caught himself looking back on his old, unable self with some nostalgia. He might have preferred to relinquish that fellow gradually, to have learned to swim the usual way, in a series of lessons. Instead she'd opened a door, obviously within himself somewhere, and pulled him through while he was looking the other way.

But of course she could do what she wanted; having got inside him—which had happened in an instant—she could open any door she chose. Close your eyes, she'd said, and when he opened them, abracadabra, he could swim. The whole thing was, in fact, so much more like a dream than like reality as he usually encountered it that he'd hung the swimming costume over the back of a chair within sight to remind him, with its pathetic shrivelled stripes, that it had been real.

15

The next day, Sylvie left to visit friends—not that she deigned to tell him; Paul had learned from Mavis. He was angry with her; he knew it was childish and anyway, he couldn't help but notice what a pleasure it was to walk through the house with no hope of running into her on the stairs or in the corridors.

'Odelia,' Percy began, 'disdained spiritualism. Of the frauds she had nothing to say at all; of the others, the best she could say was that they prostituted their gifts. She described herself, if she had to, as a clairvoyant: a clear seer. At a very young age she had come into a vast fortune; she had an aesthetic distaste for money but accepted her circumstances and dedicated herself to philanthropy on a grand and anonymous scale. Why she married me I'll never know. Though she

236

loved me in her way, I know she loved Francis more. And Theo was like a daughter to her. Perhaps we were a family, ready made, and Farundell a safe haven. She never returned to America.'

Paul looked up at the portrait of Odelia, her crystal ball, Francis standing behind. She'd found her home, that was all.

'Odelia was a seer, and I am blind. Is that irony, tragedy, nature or fate? I was always viewing things through a dark tunnel of one sort or another—my camera, my microscope, my telescope. So my blindness grew, the tunnel narrowed. The last thing I saw was Jamie, my son James. He was dying. After that I closed my eyes; I had no desire to see anything.'

Percy moved tentatively through strands of memory. The war. He could not avoid it; it gaped like an abyss between then—beloved, cherished— and now—endured. How could the world bear to lose so much? He clenched his hands on the arms of his chair as though he could seize what had been lost and drag it back from wherever it had gone. Futile. He unclenched his fingers and let the words come.

'I thought the war would pass us by, leaving Farundell untouched, an island in a flood. The posturing of so-called statesmen was so preposterous, so obviously mendacious and self-serving that no one of sense or intelligence could believe in it. But it was like a plague of unreason, pumped-up fear and blind arrogance. And it came here.

'First Richard, my third son, joined up in a gesture whose sole purpose, I am convinced, was to spit in my eye. He spouted a lot of nonsense about patriotism and duty, king and country. He took everything I had ever said about the inanity of such notions, turned it on its head and served it to me with a sauce of sincerity that alternately turned my stomach and burned my blood. He taunted Jamie and Daniel and even, in a gesture whose grandiosity was matched only by its puerility, produced with a flourish a white feather for each of them. And went, because of his extreme short-sightedness, to serve nobly behind a desk in a nice safe bunker in London. But he had brought the pestilence to Farundell. Daniel went next. He didn't dare tell me to my face; he left a note. One line: *I'm sorry but I must*.

'When Jamie joined up he said it was for the horses. They commandeered his darlings; he had to follow. He'd always loved horses, and they loved him. When he was a child he'd slip out from his bed in the middle of the night and we'd find him curled on the straw in a stall, inches from the iron-shod hoofs of some great beast standing immobile and protective over him.

'We brought him home to Farundell in a box. I did not, could not, attend the funeral. I have never visited his grave.' Was he happy up there, in the earth, under the trees, with his grandparents, his uncles and aunts? Was he lonely, was he waiting? Suddenly, Percy had to know. 'Help me up, Paul. Pass me my stick, please.'

'Where are we going?'

'The graveyard.'

'Shouldn't I ring for Henry?'

'Bugger Henry. He'll only fuss about chills and damp.' And he's old, thought Percy, as feeble as I, and I need to feel a young man at my side. 'You survived, didn't you? You're alive . . .'

'I beg your pardon?'

'You survived. Thank God. Let's leave by the French door so the Old Hen doesn't see.'

He allowed Paul to guide him across the lawns to the track that wound up the hill. It had been a long time since he'd ventured much beyond the terrace; he was soon out of breath. 'Let's stop for a minute,' he said. 'I didn't remember it was so steep.'

They were just passing the bridge over Arcadia. 'We can sit here,' Paul said, and led Percy to the low stone wall.

Percy winced as he stretched his leg. Slow down, old man, he told himself, pace yourself or you'll never make it. He waited for his heart to stop pounding and listened to the day. The air was mild and verdant; no breeze here on the ground but an intermittent whisper stirred the treetops. He knew from the barely audible murmur of the stream that it was running low, and the faint smell of slime and black mud told him stagnant pools had formed under the bridge. 'Tell me, Paul, is all well in Arcadia?'

Paul surveyed the houses, wharves, small people and animals. 'All seems well enough. Do you remember which bits you made?'

'Of course,' Percy said. 'My great project was the castle overlooking the lake. It took years to build all those turrets, battlements and crenellations. Is it still there?'

'Yes.'

'And are there still horses in the meadow below?'

'Yes, a whole herd.'

239

'Jamie carved those horses.' A great howl rose to his throat and stuck there; he swallowed, coughed and reached for his handkerchief, put the handkerchief away, took out his tobacco, filled his pipe, then replaced it in his pocket unlit. 'Let's go on,' he said, and pulled himself to his feet.

'There's no rush,' Paul said. 'Here, take my arm.' Percy seemed terribly frail out here in the woods, under the open sky; a rough wind could push him over.

'Thank you,' Percy said. 'I'm sorry to be so much trouble.'

Paul looked down at the thin mottled hand that gripped his wrist and felt a rush of tenderness. Is this what it's like, he wondered, when one loves one's father? 'You're not any trouble at all. I, well . . . I'm glad I can help.'

The chapel was shut, grey and silent; no gramophone, no Sylvie, though Paul glimpsed flashes of colour through the windows where she'd begun to paint the walls. The path to the graveyard was crowded with shrubs and thick clumps of ferns, too narrow to walk abreast. Paul went first, holding the branches out of the way. He led Percy to James's plain headstone, put his hand upon it and stepped away.

Percy lowered himself carefully to his knees with the help of his stick. He touched the hard granite. There was no decoration; just the name. He stroked the letters: JAMES ARTHUR DAMORY. His fingers avoided the awful dates. He touched the ground. Damp grass, velvet moss, depth and depth of dark heavy earth, a rotted box, some bones.

'They shipped him, or what was left of him, back to England so he could die more slowly, in greater

240

pain, in the stink and horror of a hospital ward. His legs, right arm and eye remained at Neuve-Chapelle.'

'Oh,' said Paul. 'Neuve-Chapelle . . .'

'Were you there?'

'Yes.' An image came to Paul of a man whose legs had been crushed by a cannon. His horse stood over him, one leg shattered, bleeding from a great wound in its side. Half the man's face had been blown away, but he was alive. 'Please,' he'd said. 'My horse.' He tried to push his pistol into Paul's hand. 'Please,' he said again, as Paul tied tourniquets and shouted for the stretcher-bearers. 'It doesn't matter,' Paul had told him. 'Carry on.'

Percy forced himself to remember what he most wanted to forget: the look in Jamie's eye when the morphine wore off and he knew where he was, what he was. Had it lasted only three days? At the end the look said only, Let me die.

There was the unmistakable sound of a horse on the track, the click of iron shoes, the slither of shifting stones, then softer footfalls and the brushing of foliage as it moved through the trees.

'Do you hear that?' said Percy.

'Yes,' said Paul. 'Someone's coming.'

A horse stepped delicately into the clearing; a young man rode bareback.

'Jamie,' Percy said, and struggled to his feet. 'How . . .'

'Hello, Father,' Jamie said. 'I'm glad you've come to say goodbye.' He turned to Paul. 'Thank you. We both thank you.' He patted the horse's smooth neck. 'I know what it cost you.' He clucked and squeezed his knees; they walked into the forest.

'Wait,' said Percy, reaching out his hand, 'wait.

Please don't go.'

Jamie turned back. 'We'll meet again soon,' he said.

Horse and rider disappeared among the shadows and darkness closed over Percy's eyes. He felt a wave of vertigo and sank to his knees. 'Did you see him, Paul? That was Jamie.'

'Yes, I saw him.'

Percy was silent on the way down the hill; he held Paul's arm tightly and seemed unaware of the tears running down his cheeks. What was that? Paul wondered. What did I see? Was it an image I picked up from Percy's mind, as Jarlath said happens all the time? But he spoke to me; I heard his voice. And could he really have been that man at Neuve-Chapelle—there were so many; why would I suddenly remember that one so clearly? Was the simplest explanation the true one? He was a ghost—we were at his grave, after all. One could even say that Percy had called him up by remembering and thinking about him, by saying his name. But what, then, was a ghost?

In the courtyard they were met by a distraught Henry. Tsking through clenched teeth, he elbowed Paul aside, bundled Percy into a blanket and, giving Paul a look that blamed him for everything, shepherded Percy back to the house.

*   *   *

That afternoon Paul went to Jarlath's studio for his final sitting. He was looking forward to a cup of Jarlath's very strong coffee and the company of someone who was conversant with things like ghosts.

242

The portrait was nearly finished; Jarlath had depicted him surrounded by camera, *Pymander*, typewriter—the objects of his daily life and thought. The background was a lush jungle—La Selva; was it meant to represent Percy's memoirs or Sylvie? Best not to ask. He settled into the pose, accustomed, now, to the absolute silence and immobility Jarlath required, and drifted off into the dreamlike state induced by the warm sun, the distant birdsong, the soft, regular scratches of brush on canvas.

'I saw another ghost this morning,' he said later, as Jarlath prepared coffee.

'Jamie,' Jarlath said.

'You read my mind.'

Jarlath laughed. 'Not this time. I saw you and Percy from the window, noted your expressions, deduced where you'd been. Was he on a horse?'

'Yes.'

'He usually is.'

'I shot that horse nine years ago.' Paul dropped on to a settee. 'So you've seen him too?'

'Now and then. He's never spoken to me. I think he was waiting for Percy to visit his grave.' Jarlath brought the tray of coffee, poured two cups, reclined against a mound of cushions and dropped a ball of black hashish into the bowl of his hookah. He eyed Paul as he lit it and puffed slowly. 'Ah, that's better. It helps to put me in a question-answering frame of mind.' He offered it to Paul.

'No thanks,' said Paul. 'I'm sufficiently befuddled.'

'It would help you understand,' said Jarlath. 'And you need to start saying Yes a bit more. Now, you have questions?'

'Yes . . .'

'See how easy that was?'

The price for Jarlath's company, Paul observed, was this feeling that he was being played with. Or was it just that Jarlath refused to take seriously the things Paul wanted him to? An option was to relent, to laugh with him, to stop demanding answers as though they were objects he'd unfairly been denied. He reached for the pipe, inhaled the fragrant smoke. Ease soaked into his body and his mind—the questions were still there, but they floated in a clearer space, no longer fraught with anxiety and obscured by confusion. He tossed one lightly into play. 'What is a ghost?'

'An inhabitant of another dimension of reality.'

Reality? thought Paul. The hashish made the words luminous and alive. 'Reality' was a wide-open door, with nothing but light on the other side.

Another word floated by, rainbowed like a prism. 'Dimension,' he said. 'What is a dimension—or no, I mean—what is reality, that it has other dimensions?'

Jarlath laughed. 'Well, that didn't take you long. Straight to the unanswerable in under a minute. Stick to ghosts.'

'OK,' said Paul. 'Why am I seeing these inhabitants of other dimensions?'

'The question is, why weren't you seeing them before?' Jarlath held an imaginary telescope to his eyes.

'Ah. I shut them out. Well, I don't think I regret that. So what's changed?'

'Doors are opening.'

There was a sensation of cool wind and an image

244

of door after door blowing open, revealing room after empty white room, all full of reality. 'But why?'

'Because it's what you want. Once you make the choice to embark on this knowledge business, there's a certain inevitability about things.'

*   *   *

Percy took to his bed; Henry wouldn't allow Paul to see him. Sylvie returned but Paul saw her only occasionally, at meals. Had she decided to leave him in peace? Having reminded him how to swim, was she done with him? Had he perhaps failed in some inadvertent but merciful way? Or had she found someone else to torment? These thoughts caused, simultaneously, relief and despair; he countered with long walks at all hours, avoiding any place she might be.

The question of ghosts haunted him. Had they been there all along, unnoticed? He imagined he saw them out of the corner of his eye, flitting through the trees, gliding among the rushes by the lake, disappearing round corners. He dismissed his imaginings as ridiculous, and yet . . .

He sought out Stephen and found him in the kitchen garden, forking the ground beneath tall, twining peas. 'Theo says I need more Earth,' Stephen said, 'and d'you know, I find I quite like doing this.' He pulled out a strongly growing weed, shook the dirt from its roots, dropped it into a trug. 'Sorry,' he said to it, 'but there it is. You're compost now.'

Paul sat in the sun. 'Do you remember,' he said, 'when I first arrived I asked you about magic, and

245

you talked about inner worlds and Kathmandu?'

'Yes, I remember. Have you been there?'

'Well, maybe. A few days ago I saw another ghost.'

'Who?'

'Percy's son James. At his grave, with Percy. It was extraordinary; he was completely real. I talked to Jarlath afterwards; he was less cryptic than I'd expected, but all he really said was that ghosts inhabit another dimension, and I see into this other dimension because I want to, or because I'd stopped not wanting to.'

'He told me once it was like the wireless—the transmission was out there in the aether, but you had to have the proper device in perfect working order. Then you must want to tune it and know how, otherwise you heard only meaningless static if you heard anything at all.'

'A transmission comes from somewhere. Where is this other dimension?'

'Here, I suppose. Inside. Where else could it be?'

Paul pictured dimensions like Russian dolls, each one larger and stranger than the one that contained it. He had the feeling he was being turned gently inside out.

'So Kathmandu is here,' he said, 'and it's full of ghosts?'

Stephen leaned on his fork. 'Ghosts, yes, but there's a non-material aspect of everything and everyone. The ancients had whole sets of terms for different planes of manifestation, from pure spirit to densest earth. It was a science—it was *the* science. Now they call it magic, and most people think it's all either illusion or delusion.'

'I would have thought so too, but now I'm not

so sure. My wireless seems to have switched itself on. Can one turn it off?'

'That can be harder than you think,' said Stephen. 'It becomes addictive, like a drug. You see things, maybe they're real, maybe not. You get power, or the illusion of power—but it doesn't always work out as you plan. You think you want something, but by the time you've bent and twisted everything to get it, you've lost yourself. It's a bad bargain.'

'Is that what happened to you?'

Stephen made a wry face. 'Let's just say I burned out my wireless and now I couldn't go to Kathmandu even if I wanted.'

*   *   *

In the late-afternoon heat, Paul withdrew to the library and sat at his desk trying to read. This time he heard Sylvie coming and had time to prepare; still she came like a burst of electricity in a flower-sprigged frock.

'Hello,' she said.

'Hello,' he said.

'I'm going up to St Ælfhild's pool—to sketch. And I wondered if you'd like to come along.'

'I'd love to.' Paul pocketed cigarettes, camera and *Pymander* and they set off across the hill behind the house.

The spring that fed St Ælfhild's pool spilled over black rocks slick with moss. Sylvie studied the view from different angles, framing them with her hands. When she found a spot she liked she sat down cross-legged, opened a sketchbook on her knees, took pencils from her satchel and began to

247

draw.

Paul sat against a tree, lit a cigarette. The sun dappled everything with a leafy shadow pattern; if he narrowed his eyes, Sylvie merged into the changing light. He took out the camera. 'May I take a picture of you?'

'That reminds me,' she said. 'Did they come out all right, those pictures you took?'

At some point she'd have to see those doubly exposed pictures; he'd have to explain. But not right now. 'Yes, they came out. Very nicely. I'll show them to you later.' He framed her in the viewfinder. Click. 'Contemplate the image of God,' said *Pymander*. Gladly, he thought, if that's what she looks like.

'I thought you were painting the chapel,' he said.

'I am—with scenes from around Farundell. This is going on the north wall.'

He raised the camera, sought her again. Only her hand moved, and her eyes, as much a part of nature as the squirrels foraging on the forest floor, the calls of the birds, the trickle of water, the cinnamon tang of dead leaves, crushed where he sat, that mingled with the heady green scent of summer. She chewed her lips; it made them very red. A ray of sun fell in a golden puddle at her feet.

There was something about watching her through the artificial eye of the lens that made him feel he could see more of her—or perhaps it was his own sense of being hidden; but that was nonsense. He revealed himself by the very act of watching her from behind the camera; she revealed little, even when, as now, she looked up and stared straight at him. Click. 'Every path leads in the end to Knowledge,' said *Pymander*. Even the path of Sylvie? wondered Paul. Once you start on this knowledge business, he heard Jarlath saying, there's a certain inevitability.

He got up and wandered off among the trees, turning every once in a while to glimpse Sylvie framed in a new way. She grew smaller, yet there was always an arrangement of leaves and branches, light and shade, that drew the eye towards her. Click. 'The like also happeneth to them that go out of the body,' said *Pymander*.

Mr Pym whisked his meanings in and out of sight like a shell game. Paul had learned not to chase after them, but just to write the words. He wasn't sure what it was he didn't understand, but the sense that there was something to be understood grew with every enigmatic snippet. He was chasing shadows, shadows made of words, or shadows of words, that flickered in and out of the frame. He stood behind the lens and caught what he could with his alphabet net.

The ancient hazel leaned over the water, its boughs hung with ribbons and trinkets. Every time he came here some new charm had appeared. What did people wish for? Love and luck, health restored or danger averted, desires fulfilled. He glanced back at Sylvie. Oh, to wish for that was easy, but he didn't see how any tree could give him what he really wanted, even if he could catch the words for it. He framed her between a cluster of lace and a white rabbit's foot, a pale blur in the distance. Click. 'Divine acts and operations upon perfect bodies,' said *Pymander*.

She seemed hardly to have moved, but when she heard his step she looked up, closed her sketchbook, stretched her legs. 'Sorry, have I been long? I get so . . .' she made a spiralling gesture.

'Oh, I do too,' said Paul. 'Frequently.'

'I saw you at the offering tree,' she said. 'Did you make a wish?'

'Does it work, the tree? Do people get the things they ask for?'

'Oh yes, lots of people have things come true they wished for here. Provided, of course, they left something in return. Did you wish for anything?'

I wish for rather a lot, Paul thought. 'I don't have anything to offer,' he said.

'Yes you do. Could I have a cigarette? I forgot to fill my case.'

Paul lit her cigarette, and one for himself.

'The first time I came up here,' he said, 'soon after I'd arrived, I met your uncle Daniel. I thought he was the hermit of the woods.'

'He's not crazy or anything, you know,' Sylvie said. 'He just likes a quiet life.' She sounded defensive, and Paul supposed people were sometimes unkind about Daniel.

'I know he's not crazy. His life seems very appealing, in a way. And I always wanted an eccentric uncle.'

'Have you none of your own?' Her bantering tone returned.

'No, sadly. As far as I know all my relations are irredeemably conventional. According to my father I went mad a few years ago, so I suppose that makes me the eccentric relation.'

'Did you?'

'If I did, I'm not aware of it, though sometimes I do wonder. No, I just told him to bugger off.'

'I've told my father that lots of times but it

250

doesn't have the least effect. What about your mother?'

'She buggered off a long time ago. She died when my sister was born.'

'Oh, that's sad.'

Paul shrugged. 'Not if one doesn't remember it.'

'Val told me you lived in Paris. I've been to Paris twice, but only with a horrid chaperone. Would you take me to Paris?'

'What, now?'

'Yes, right now.'

'Not without a chaperone.'

She stuck out her tongue at him. 'You are an old nanny. That's not how Val described you at all. I saw him last Saturday and we had such a nice long chat.'

Paul cringed at the possible routes that conversation might have taken. 'So now you know all about me.'

'Hardly. There's lots he doesn't seem to know, though he did assure me that should I seek references they would be plentiful and glowing.'

'Oh for God's sake. Really, sometimes Val . . . Are you ready to go back? I have work to do.'

She gathered up her things and they made their way down the path along the stream. Sylvie stopped to pull off her shoes and Paul did the same. He was coming to dislike shoes more and more.

Sylvie paused to peer into pools and ferny crevices, greeting the flowers that crowded the banks like old friends. 'Sanicle,' she murmured. 'Oh, pennywort, and foxglove, ahh . . .'

'I sometimes wish,' Paul said, 'one could live like people in the jungles Percy talks about, barefoot

. . .'

'Eating fruits and nuts and berries . . .'

'Or living on sunlight . . .'

'And flowers.' She plucked one and bit off its base. 'Mmmm.'

'Did you really eat that flower?'

She ate another.

'I never saw anybody eat a flower before,' Paul said. 'I didn't know one could.'

'Of course one can. It's delicious. Why do you suppose it's called honeysuckle?'

'Well, I'd never thought—perhaps because bees like it.'

'They know what they're about. Have you really never tasted it?'

'I've really never tasted it.'

She picked a flower from the vine. 'You bite off the bottom and suck. You can eat the whole thing, of course, but this is the best part.' She demonstrated.

'Ah,' said Paul.

'See? Now you.' She selected a flower and held it towards his lips.

Paul gazed down into her smiling face. She knew, God help him, perfectly well what she was doing. He parted his lips; she inserted the flower.

'Bite off the end,' she said, and a drop of distilled sunlight spread over his tongue. 'See? Honeysuckle.' She leaned close. 'Kiss me.'

She left him there with a taste of honey, a sweet mad spinning in his head and an ache in his loins. When he was able to move he climbed down to the lake, took off his clothes behind the shrubs and plunged into the water, where he tried without success to wash away the memory of her kiss. He left the water reluctantly, put on his clothes and his damned shoes and returned to the house.

He was emptying his pockets on to the bureau in his room when he caught a glimpse of himself in the mirror. Several long strands of waterweed were caught in his hair, as though nature had attempted to reclaim him. He applied his comb but it snagged and broke a tooth. He took a deep breath and put his face in his hands, like when he was very small and he thought this made things go away. Ostrichism.

The dinner bell rang. He couldn't face a big dinner party, but neither could he hide in his room forever. He lowered his head over the basin, emptied the ewer, shook himself like a dog, combed his hair with more brute force than finesse, changed his shirt, put on a tie. As an afterthought he removed the exposed film from the camera, sealed it up and tucked it in his pocket. He could develop it after dinner—it would be an excuse to hide in the darkroom.

Several new house guests had arrived; the table was crowded. Miss Firth, the plain young lady on his right, was a student of Jarlath's; she discoursed at length about something called the aetheric plane. By the time they reached the fish the fellow on his left, Mr Dunne, had introduced himself and joined in. He was researching for a book about the nature of time; they seemed to have a lot to say to one another. Paul pulled his chair back so they could converse more freely and glanced at Sylvie. Her head tilted towards the man on her right and her eyes stared off into the distance. His eyes were on her breasts. It was evident that under her fashionably minimal silk frock there was little to

253

impede the imagination. He looked around for Jarlath, but he was sitting where he couldn't see her. Paul realised he was clenching his teeth.

While everyone gathered in the music room for coffee and entertainment he escaped to the darkroom. It was safe there, with the door closed, the curtains drawn, the soothing sound of flowing water, the red light glowing on its shelf like a living thing, silent and companionable. No one else came here; it was one of the most truly private places he'd ever known.

He laid out the doubly exposed pictures on the desk. What was a photograph? A secret talisman, a chemical transformation, pieces of shadow and pieces of light, those belonging to her now inseparable from his. He wished he didn't have to show them to her, as though that would somehow dissolve their effect. Or maybe, he thought, what I fear is that if she sees them it will work, and then what the hell do I do?

He prepared the processing bath, dipped the film. Amid the gurgling of the water as the trays filled and overflowed he almost missed the soft click of the door. 'Henry?' Perhaps Percy wanted him—only Henry would think to look here. He heard the swish of the first curtains. 'I have film exposed, Henry.'

'It's not Henry, it's me,' said Sylvie.

'Jesus Christ!' Paul dropped the film into the solution.

'You said you'd show me those pictures.'

Oh, for God's sake. 'I should have said I would get them and then show you.' He fished the film out with tongs.

'Why, am I not allowed in here? I know all about

254

this stuff. I know not to let light in.'

The timer pinged.

'The timer's pinged,' she said. 'Don't you have to do something?'

Paul took the film to the sinks, lowered it into the fix. He'd just been enjoying a bit of privacy—surely a man has a right to some privacy? Was nowhere safe? She had marched in, as though she . . . well, she had every right. It was her house, Christ, it was her darkroom a lot more than it was his. But she bloody well shouldn't have entered without knocking. 'Sorry,' he said. 'You startled me. No one comes here. Usually. Give me a minute, please.'

She waited until his hands were busy, then stood so close that he brushed the side of her breast every time he moved his arm.

'Sylvie,' he said.

'Yes?'

'Please. Please, please stop.'

'Stop what?'

'Stop standing there. If you must be here, please stand on the other side of the room.'

'What, stand in the corner, like a bad girl?' She pressed closer.

'Yes, like a bad girl.'

'I will if you kiss me.' She lifted her face.

He kissed the top of her head. 'There. Now go away.'

'No,' she said. 'More.' Her hand snaked up his arm.

He set the timer, turned to her, plucked her hand away, and the other that followed. 'Sylvie. Go away. Don't you know you must not visit a man alone in a dark place?'

She leaned against him, sighed. 'Not my rule.'

He sniffed. 'How many glasses of wine did you have?'

'Only three, and after dinner something delicious called a Monkey Gland . . .'

'You're tight, that's all.' He held her at arm's length. 'And very naughty. If someone caught you here I'd get the blame—you know that, don't you? I'm surprised your father hasn't turned me into an ass already.'

'Why are you treating me like a little girl? I'll be nineteen in a few days.'

The timer pinged again. Obviously, my darling, he thought at her, because you're all too obviously not a little girl, in your wisp of silk, your loops of beads, rouge on your red lips. Strangers ogle you throughout dinner, then you come here, to my darkroom . . . He slammed a dish into the sink; it shattered and a sliver of glass pierced his finger. 'Damn.'

'Don't be angry, please. I'm sorry.'

'It's not you. It's me.' He made himself smile. 'Of course I'm not angry at you.'

'You're bleeding. Hold it under the tap.' She pulled at his hand. 'Is there glass in it?'

'I don't think so. Now please let me go.' Paul wrapped his finger in his handkerchief and turned on the lamp over the desk. 'This is what you came to see.'

She looked once, then again. 'Oh, but it's you, too. How did you do that?'

Paul explained. 'I'm sorry, I should probably have told you at the time, but, well . . .'

'I think they're quite good,' she said. 'Maybe we should do some more.' She leaned over to consider each in turn; a lock of hair escaped from her chignon and pointed to the supple shadow where her spine disappeared under the low back of her frock.

Without thought, and as though with long familiarity, he stroked her smooth bare skin and before he'd had time to realise what he'd done she turned and pressed her body against his. It was very possible that there was nothing whatsoever under the frock. Oh, to push it up, slam her against the wall, and . . . 'Sylvie,' he said. 'Stop this. You don't mean it, you're drunk, and you're leaving now.'

He pulled her through the curtains, listened at the door, opened it. Sylvie wriggled in his grasp, suppressing giggles. A shaft of light from the hallway sconces fell across her bright dark eyes, her red mouth. He kissed her once, quite hard, pushed her out, closed and locked the door.

He sat at the desk, lit a cigarette. The photographs lay across the table like a line of certainty, when the only certainty was the impossibility of it. He should burn them. Too late; he should have burned them right away, said they hadn't come out. She had kissed him, that was all. Flirted, and kissed. And briefly, exquisitely, pressed the whole silken length of herself against him. He was still hard. Tie my bloody heart to the tree, shall I? Like a rabbit's foot. Would that be enough?

She tossed him on to the impossibilities like the sea on to rocks, over and over. He could see how it would be, like today, like tonight. She'd have a bit of fun, a flirt and a kiss now and then. Playing, testing the boundaries. He'd given himself away before they'd even spoken, with that letter to Val. From the very beginning she'd known her power. His only power was in resisting, in preventing something she was bound to regret and which would poison everything. He had to try to be her friend and if that meant not giving her what she seemed to think she wanted, well then, that was the price of staying friends, of staying here, of everything he liked in his life. After all, he only had to get through the rest of the summer—in September she'd go to London and the peaceful life of Farundell would return. He'd see her now and then, but she'd be with other men, men who belonged in her life. So savour the kisses while you can, he told himself. Painful, yes, but oh, so sweet. Sylvie's honeysuckle kiss.

16

Percy had refused to allow Dr Westlake to be summoned. He wasn't ill, only very weak; his body ached all over as though he'd been put through a wringer. His mind, too, felt wrung out and exhausted.

He slipped in and out of dreams; people came and went. Some were alive; others were dead and some weren't even people at all; his old dog, white-muzzled, lay at the foot of the bed. There was one state of mind—he called it the Henry-state because everyone else disappeared when Henry was there—in which he knew they were figments of his imagination, or dreams, or illusions, or ghosts.

'And what is a ghost?' Odelia asks.

Percy holds the word in his hands like a box; when he opens it, it's empty. 'Am I dying?' he asks.

'Yes, dear, but not today.'

After three days of rest, Percy overrode Henry's objections, summoned Paul and resumed dictation.

'I came to believe that the further into the interior I penetrated, the closer I would come to some sort of truth. I had the notion that beneath the pollutions and distortions of European influence, in the deepest heart of La Selva, the pure, real human still lived the pure, the real, the natural life. And so I set out again, upriver. I had heard of a tribe called the Isu, the "oldest people", whose village was hidden deep in the jungle. Binjao, the cleverest of my guides, believed it wasn't a real place at all, but a spirit-village that only appeared at certain times, to certain people, and then vanished. He told me that his wife's cousin's neighbour's son had come upon it once while hunting. He had been welcomed, given sweet cakes to eat; he'd been served by the prettiest girls he'd ever seen and entertained by the most delightful flute player. They sent him on his way with many blessings, good wishes, invitations to return and some cake wrapped in a leaf. Back in his village no one would believe him. He thought to prove his case by showing them the cake, which was unlike any they made, but when he unwrapped the parcel it contained only a round, polished red stone.

'Towards evening on the nineteenth day after we left Lamarca, as we rowed slowly against the current, I thought I saw Sinclair watching us from the jungle. That night I dreamed of him, and when

259

I woke he was standing next to my hammock. "Percy," he said, "it's waiting. Can't you hear it singing?" I understood he meant the moon-flower. "No," I said, "I can't."

'"Oh listen, just listen!" He raised his face to the moon, a raptured look in his eyes. I asked him where he'd been. "Here, here, here," he said. I understood him to be calling to his flower. He vanished into the night.

'Sinclair kept pace with us as we journeyed upriver. He appeared from time to time, always at night when I was sleeping. He would rhapsodise about his flower, ignore my questions, and disappear. Our whispered conversations, I later realised, were overheard by my guides and porters, and, since they couldn't understand what we said, it contributed to their belief that I was an *encantado*, an evil magician.

'The boat took us as far as the mouth of a small tributary; the intention was to follow it to its source deep in the interior, the reputed home of the Isu. We camped overnight and in the morning I discovered that half the porters had deserted; the rest were shifty and reluctant. Their suspicions had apparently begun back in Lamarca because I always wore a hat. Before I'd arrived the village had been plagued by an *encantado*, a shape-shifting incubus who appeared sometimes as a man and sometimes as a *boto*, a river dolphin. When in his human form he always wore a wide-brimmed straw hat—like mine—to hide the vestigial blowhole at the top of his head.

'The *encantado* was a romantic legend even in the cities, where he appeared as a suave white-suited man, irresistible to the girls. He would cut a dash at parties and festivals, dance devilishly well and lure his chosen victim to his underwater kingdom, the *Encante*. The next day people would find a dress and a pair of shoes by the riverbank, nothing more. Sometimes the girl was never heard from again; sometimes she'd return pregnant, but never quite right in her head. There were always a few "children of the *boto*".

'So it was with only five seriously overpaid porters that Binjao led us into the jungle. I had to send half the food and equipment back with the boat. In the confusion the box of medical supplies was put aboard, and with it my supply of quinine. By the time I wanted it we were already several days on our way.

'Once again I was at the mercy of the malaria. I tried to warn Binjao that I would be fevered and delirious, and would require special care, but I suppose it was too much to ask. I awakened at first light in a small clearing. The bouts of malaria usually lasted only a few hours, during which I knew nothing of what happened around me. Had they tired of waiting? Would they return? They had left no supplies. It occurred to me that I might have wandered off on my own while they slept. I waited through the morning, shouting until my voice failed, glimpsing nothing more than an occasional woolly monkey loping through the canopy and hearing nothing but the calls of unseen birds. Then I set out on my own.

'I would never have found the Isu if I had not fallen into a deep hole in the path. Fortunately it was not one of the ones with sharpened stakes and my leg was only broken in one place. It was a simple break and the skin was not torn—if it had been, I would surely have died from infection. But the pain was unbelievable, and I passed out. When I came to, my leg was hugely swollen and I could see that the bone was out of alignment. I realised that if I was to have any hope of walking ever again, I would have to set it myself. I needed some kind of a block to brace it against; I had nothing but my boots. Removing them was a massive undertaking in itself; I fainted several times from the pain that accompanied the slightest movement. I arranged the boots, summoned all my strength and willpower, and pushed as hard as I could. I felt the bone grate into place before I fainted again. I don't know how long I remained unconscious; when I woke it was dark, the kind of perfect and complete darkness you only get in the dense jungle, when there is no moon and the starlight cannot penetrate the canopy. I was trapped down there for three days, to the best of my reckoning, though it may have been four, and I was sure I'd die there.'

He lies on his back at the bottom of the hole. All struggle has ceased, all fear, all anger. He's done raging at God, at fate, at himself. The pain travels in waves, the incessant buzz of the cicadas crawls up and down the fibres of his nerves. The light changes constantly; never before has he done nothing but observe it, day after night after day.

'I had no chance of climbing out. I could not even stand. My only hope of being found was to wait for whoever had set the trap. The pain became my friend. I sucked on dirt for moisture, and for the illusion of eating. Sinclair appeared, as he always did, in the middle of the night. I tried to speak, to ask for help, but found myself curiously paralysed. He smiled sadly, shook his head and vanished. Perhaps I only dreamed him.

'Eventually I ceased to make any effort to distinguish between dreams and reality. I felt my death approaching; nothing else mattered. When the Isu appeared, tattooed faces peering down at me, I feared I was hallucinating. What they thought, I can't imagine. A strange catch, and a major disappointment, of course.'

*   *   *

After lunch, Alice made her way to Percy's rooms. She hated it when he was unwell; it was like a dark spot in her field of vision, a black cloud on a sunny day. An anxious feeling filled that part of the house; it seemed to come mostly from Henry, but it could just be that he felt it most. Usually she liked it when people were ill and she could read to them. She was sure it helped, but not in Percy's case. He was old and getting visibly older every day. She'd heard it said that time goes faster as you get older; she had found it impossible to imagine but now she could see it happening. Her grandfather was hurtling by like a boat caught in a very fast current.

Nevertheless, she'd brought a book and persuaded Henry to allow her to visit. She found Percy sitting by a roaring fire; as soon as Henry left he asked her to open the window and fetch his pipe. Henry had hidden it but she knew all of his places and soon found it behind the aspidistra.

'When Henry comes back he'll smell the smoke,' she said.

'The best thing about getting old,' Percy said, 'is

no longer caring what one's valet thinks.' He filled his pipe and reached out his hand; she passed him the box of matches. He lit the pipe and tossed the burnt match neatly into the fireplace. 'Now, you've brought something to read, haven't you? It always makes me feel better when you read to me.'

'I've brought *The Faerie Queene*—that's what I'm reading, but I can get something else if you'd rather.'

'Oh no, *The Faerie Queene* will do nicely.'

Alice pulled a chair close to Percy and began to read.

There did the warlike Maid her self repose,
Under the wings of Isis all that night,
And with sweet rest her heavy eyes did close,
After that long day's toil and weary plight.
Where whilst her earthly parts with soft delight
Of senseless sleep did deeply drowned lie,
There did appear unto her heavenly sprite
A wondrous vision, which did close imply
The course of all her fortune and posterity.

'Grandpapa,' she said, 'Spenser's talking about a temple of Isis where the heroine Britomart has a prophetic dream, but earlier there's a bit where I'm sure he's talking about the River Isis, our river.' She leafed back through the pages. 'Here it is. ". . . the ancient Thame, but much more aged was his wife than he, the Ouse, whom men do Isis rightly name." I've always wondered why the Thames is called the Isis around here. I asked Stephen, but he doesn't know.'

'When I was at Oxford,' Percy said, 'there was an Isis Society. It was very exclusive; I wasn't invited to join until my second year. We met for naked swims in the Isis at the full moon, regardless of the weather. The legend was that our founders in the sixteenth century—that would be around Spenser's time—had discovered a temple of Isis somewhere near the source of the river. In my day there was no temple of Isis but the initiation ritual involved having to spend the night alone in a mock Roman temple in a graveyard a few miles upriver. I took a bottle of whisky and a flask of tea—I didn't sleep a wink, so, unlike Britomart, I didn't have any dreams or visions.'

'I've read that in Egypt, in ancient Greece and Rome people went to temples for special sleep, to get messages from the gods in dreams. Why do you suppose it stopped?'

'Christianity put a stop to it, I imagine,' Percy said. 'If you allow people to contact God on their own you put the Church out of business.'

'So it could still work, right? Just because people don't do it any more . . .'

'Oh, people do it. Only us educated, civilised, highly progressive people don't. All over the world, Alice—the people I studied in Brazil and so-called primitive people everywhere—they all have techniques for inducing dreams and visions which they believe come from a truer, realer place.' Like ghosts, he thought, and for a moment ghosts and dreams were mixed up in his mind: ghosts were iridescent dream-bubbles; dreams were vaporous vortices of thought.

'Tell me, Alice, how is Daniel these days? I loved hearing him play again when that trumpeter was here, but since he left Daniel has been so silent. Is he all right, do you think?'

265

'He and Arlen have been corresponding, and Daniel's invited him to visit. He's coming out with Val for Sylvie's party, and he's going to stay for a while. I've had to make all the arrangements with Tustian.'

'That's very good of you, Alice. I'm glad Daniel has you to look after him. When I die, you know that things will change for him. He'll need your help more than ever.'

'But that won't be for a long time, will it?'

Percy laughed. 'It will be when it is. Next week feels like a long time to me. But don't worry about me—just remember I'll be counting on you to help Daniel.'

'I'll help him, Grandpapa. He'll be fine.'

Henry knocked at the door. 'Miss Sylvie is very insistent that she be allowed to see you, sir.'

'Just for one minute,' called Sylvie over his shoulder.

'Can't you see we're reading?' Alice said.

'That's all right,' Percy said. 'The reading has fortified me. Come on in, Sylvie.'

'I need a little word with you, Grandpapa. A private word. Will you please excuse us, Alice?'

Alice, who hadn't planned to leave, felt herself guided to the door and pushed gently out. Henry, eavesdropping, sprang back. The door closed behind her.

'Let me know if you hear anything interesting,' she said.

'Of course, Miss Alice.'

*   *   *

The matter of Sylvie's birthday had loomed over

the last few days with its awkward new problem of what to get for her. Paul heard here and there in the household of presents brought in and concealed; even Tustian, who did scrimshaw for a hobby, had made her a landscape of Farundell. A big party was planned for tonight; dozens of people were coming up from London.

He should have gone to London, he realised, looked around there, but it was too late; Exley was the only hope. He set off after lunch but got no further than the courtyard when Val drove up with Arlen Winter. Tustian took Arlen into the house; Val remained in the driving seat as though ready to flee.

'Val,' Paul said. 'My kind and helpful old friend Val.'

'Paul, good to see you, old chap.'

'You're a meddlesome bastard.'

'I?'

Paul raised an eyebrow.

'Yes, well.' Val slid down the seat. 'To tell you the truth, I don't know what got into me. Have I . . .'

'Made things immeasurably worse? Yes, you have.'

'Oh, dear, I am sorry. I just thought, you know, and then almost immediately had second, third, fourth thoughts, but it was too late, the post had gone, 'twas done.'

He looked so remorseful Paul almost took pity. Perhaps one more poke. 'You've made my position here extremely difficult.'

'Oh hell, I'm bloody sorry, I really am. I'm utterly thoughtless.' Val banged his head against his fists on the steering wheel. 'Mea culpa, mea maxima culpa.'

'All right, all right, don't overdo it.' Paul climbed into the car. 'Drive me to Exley. I have to find a present for her.'

'Oh, last minute, eh?' Val circled the courtyard and headed out of the drive. 'Well, you never know what will turn up in these provincial markets. I'm sure you'll find something. A book is always good.'

Paul didn't think she'd be very impressed with a book from him—it might even seem an insult. But he couldn't give her anything very personal either, it would seem presumptuous. What on earth was an appropriate present from someone in his position? Anything he could afford would never be much compared to what others gave, would be a token only. Was it therefore ridiculous to get a present at all? Was it better to get nothing or the wrong thing? What did he want to say with his present? What could he say? Oh, this was awful. He was vexed with her for having a birthday, vexed with society for the customs it imposed on people, vexed with himself for all this dithering. Well, he'd leave it to fate. He would browse around Exley and if something caught his eye, that he could afford, he'd get it. If—as was more likely—he saw nothing special, it would be a sign that he wasn't to bother.

It was market day; the square was filled with tables and stalls. Val helped him pick through piles of books, pictures, brass candlesticks and chipped porcelain. Loops of glass beads: pretty but tawdry. Antique ivory combs: tempting, but too personal. They abandoned the market to trawl the shops. At the bootmaker's, a pair of red Russian boots with a pointy toe and curvy heel. Well beyond his means, though he could picture her in them all too easily.

268

At the draper's, some embroidered India silk that shimmered like a mirage. Ditto. At the chemist's, perfumes from Paris: Mon Désir, L'Amoureuse, L'Inconnu, in elegant crystal flagons. Women, he'd learned, should choose their own perfumes. Anyway, too personal. And too expensive. He was losing hope; Val had already lost patience and disappeared into a pub.

Paul went into the stationer's, more to be soothed by its familiar smells, its decorum, its clear-cut square-edged order, than in the hope of finding a present. He rested his eyes on the calm stacks of paper: foolscap, demy, royal, imperial; buff, ivory, cream and snow-white; the tall shelves, the slowly turning fan. In the background the voices of the clerks, the opening and closing of the drawers of the plan chests, the soft bell at the door as a customer left.

Rows of beautiful pens gleamed beneath glass like insect specimens, patterned in tortoiseshell, agate and tiger's eye. If it weren't for the unfortunate but inescapable pun on penis, a pen would perhaps have done. His eyes were drawn to some leather-bound notebooks in the next case.

'Good afternoon, Mr Asher.' A clerk approached. 'What can we do for you today?'

'These books . . .'

'Oh yes, they're new.' The clerk laid them out on the counter. 'Suitable for writing or drawing. Could be a small sketchbook, or a diary or a journal.'

Paul picked up a green one with an embossed pattern of intertwined lilies and roses. He examined the paper—blank, creamy and smooth. It was edged with green, the endpapers marbled green and gold. There was a silver pen in a leather loop. Well, a pen might be all right if it wasn't the entire gift. An empty book, what could be better? Let it mean whatever she liked; let her use it for whatever she wanted. It was perfect.

'I'll take this,' he said.

'Very good, sir. Shall we deliver?'

'No, I need it for tonight, it's a present. Can you wrap it?'

'Certainly, sir. Shall I fill the pen first? It's always nice when the pen's ready to go.'

'Oh yes, it is.' Paul turned a snort of laughter into a cough.

The clerk's hand hovered above a row of bottles. 'Black or blue? Or blueblack. Or green? Or what about lilac? That's quite popular.'

No, thought Paul. 'Red.'

'Wine or rose, sir?'

'Whichever looks most like blood.'

'I believe that will be rose-red,' the clerk said. He filled the pen and wrapped the book in printed paper. 'On the account, sir?'

'No. I'll pay now.' The price made Paul wince.

*　　　*　　　*

Alice stopped by Maggie's room but the door was locked. Jarlath appeared at the end of the corridor, blew her a kiss and went into one of the guest rooms down the hall. It seemed like all one did when one was grown up was go shopping, have parties and sex.

She watched from a window as Arlen walked down the meadow with his trumpet case. She hesitated, then bolted for the path over the hill

270

and arrived at her position in the woods above Daniel's cabin out of breath but just in time. Daniel sat at the shore; he heard Arlen coming and rose to his feet. She wasn't close enough to see the expression on his face, but the sense of hopeful expectancy in his posture was unmistakable. Arlen stepped from under the trees; they looked at each other. Then Daniel made a small gesture; Arlen dropped his trumpet and in half a dozen steps had taken him in a passionate embrace.

Oh, I see! Alice thought. Now I see. Somehow it had never occurred to her they were that kind of friends. She hadn't thought Daniel did that sort of thing at all. He was so unlike other grown-ups in every other way, she'd never imagined . . . They were kissing deeply, their faces glued together, Arlen's hand in Daniel's hair, Daniel's fists clenched in Arlen's shirt. For what seemed like ages they stood like that, then untwined themselves with evident reluctance and walked towards the cabin. Arlen stopped to pick up his trumpet, said something to which Daniel responded with a full and open laugh. Alice had never heard that laugh before and it brought an involuntary smile to her lips.

They vanished inside. Part of her formulated a plan to creep down the hillside and look in at the back window; another part recalled her mother's instructions on etiquette: the correct thing to do, if you happen to come upon people making love, is to disappear before they notice. Maybe she could just peek in for a minute? Or perhaps she could come to the door as for an ordinary visit. No, it was all very well to be bad spontaneously—to do something before she could help herself—but once

271

she'd had that discussion in which she reminded herself of what would be right and what would be wrong—well, by then it was too late.

She traipsed back to the house, hot and sticky. It was Sylvie's party tonight; she'd have to bath, and comb the tangles from her hair, and wear a scratchy dress on which she was sure to spill something horribly staining, and chat to people about stupid things. Why was her family so bloody sociable?

She found Theo sitting on the bench outside the potting shed. She wore an old blue shirt, out at the elbows; she smelled of earth and thyme, a sprig of which she was rubbing between her fingers. Her hands were dirty, the skin brown and rough, the nails short. Theo was the only woman Alice knew who wasn't interested in how she looked, nor had she ever known Theo to enjoy a party, and she certainly never shopped. And she could no more imagine Theo having sex than, well, Daniel. But Daniel had surprised her there.

'Daniel and Arlen are lovers,' Alice said.

'Yes, I know,' said Theo. 'Daniel's been waiting for him for a long time.'

'How do you know?'

'He told me.'

Alice hadn't known Daniel spoke to Theo; but then, there was obviously lots she didn't know. The life of grown-ups suddenly looked like a very big ocean, into which she hesitated to dip her toe. What happened? Was there a divide that one crossed in an instant, forgetting everything one had left behind? Or was it a long slow journey, with steps so small one didn't notice until it was too late—one was having sex and going to parties,

272

and forgetting everything that seemed so important now?

'I've been thinking about what you told me,' she said, 'that people forget their moon-bodies when they grow up. And I was wondering if it had anything to do with sex, and if I could prevent it happening to me by not having any.'

'Not an infallible method,' said Theo.

'I could become a nun, or an anchorite like St Ælfhild.'

'Though it works in some cases. But then, for some people, sex is a way to remember.'

Alice had never considered that. From what she'd heard, it would be a messy and haphazard method. Surely there were better ways, other choices one could make. But one wouldn't know until after it was too late whether one had made the right choice or the wrong one. It hit her with surprising force that if one chose wrong, one couldn't go back and do it again—of course this was obvious to anyone who'd considered it, but she never had. The future seemed vast and uncertain, full of blind corners and impossible choices. 'How does one know what to do?'

'Oh, Alice. Dear heart. One doesn't.'

*   *   *

Paul returned to the library, took off his shoes and socks, which he now did at every opportunity, removed Madagascar from the chair and sat at his desk. He was retyping Percy's memoirs from the beginning; it gave him something to do and there was a certain satisfaction to be obtained from the rhythm of hitting the keys and whipping the

273

return.

Was Sylvie at the chapel? He'd hardly seen her since her visit to the darkroom, but it was always going to be like that. She could appear and disappear as she chose. Maybe later he'd walk up the hill, give her the notebook. He had avoided the chapel—a second visit could only be deliberate, and she'd not invited him. But with the excuse of the present . . .

It had clouded over; a few drops of rain splashed on to the sill, then a few more. Thunder rolled in the distance. There was a scurrying all through the house as people dashed to close windows.

'I'll close these,' he called as Tustian hurried through, but he'd keep them open as long as he could. He loved summer storms. The darkening sky, the premonitory rumbles, the first lightning, followed by silence and counting, the shivery anticipation of great events, the sudden change in air pressure that lifted the hairs on one's arms, the surreptitious patter of the rain, expected yet unfamiliar, as though one had forgotten what rain was.

It fell harder, battering the roses below the window; their fragrance blended with the smell of water on hot earth and stone. Puddles formed in the gravel of the courtyard; a wind shook the branches of the oak and swirled a scatter of leaves. Paul closed the window. The water fell in sheets; the gutters filled and overflowed. Sylvie, soaked to the skin, ran across the courtyard and disappeared into the boot room. He stood up to go to her, help her dry off, then stopped. Not his job.

He lit a cigarette and crossed to the far windows. The long wet green of the meadow drew him and he had such a strong image of himself and Sylvie tearing off their clothes and running, flying down to the lake, plunging in, swimming to the island, that he had to remind himself most forcefully it was not happening, and was not going to happen. He felt a twinge of vertigo and the floor shifted under his feet. There was that aquatic state again; it came and went frequently these days. He focused his eyes on a nearby object: the window frame, and studied its details until the sensation faded. He didn't know why that worked, but it seemed to. Only when things felt quite solid did he look up.

The sky to the south-west cleared and though thunder still rumbled, it was receding. The rain stopped, the sun came out. Paul returned to his desk and opened the window. The sounds of birds and insects swelled as the drip of the eaves faded. The atmosphere was thick with scents; it had rained just enough to intensify things, not enough to clear the air. Everything exuded a warm sigh, the gravel steamed and a cricket resumed its insistent creak under the roses.

Paul worked without pause until the stable clock struck five, then raised his head and stretched. A bee bumbled against the glass a few inches from the open window, unable to recognise futility even while flinging himself at it.

'I know exactly how you feel,' Paul said; he stood up and guided it to freedom. He'd always taken the trouble to help them, those poor deluded creatures, on the principle that he hoped someone would do the same for him should he be in a similar situation. Which perhaps he was. Which perhaps he always had been.

There was a soft click; out of the corner of his eye he saw the wall move. He froze. The panel on which Sylvie's portrait hung opened and her face appeared.

'Come on,' she said.

'What? Where?'

'With me.' She vanished.

Paul walked around his desk and peered up into the darkness. 'What is this?'

'Secret passage. Close the door behind you.'

Paul tucked the present under his arm and felt his way up the steep spiralled stairs. Fancy that, he'd been sitting in front of a secret passage all this time. He emerged into a dimly lit room with an elaborate ceiling, a massive stone fireplace and a high, ornate bed. 'The state bedroom?'

'My bedroom.'

'Oh no. No, Sylvie, it's not a good idea for me to be in your bedroom.'

'Well, can you think of a better place?'

'I can think of lots of better places.'

'For my first fuck?'

'Your . . . oh God, Sylvie.'

'It's my birthday, and I want a lover. I'm sick of being a virgin. Look, I have some champagne for us.'

Paul took in the champagne, the half-drawn curtains, the artfully rumpled bed and Sylvie's attire: a short silk slip and a flowered kimono falling off one shoulder. The stage was set for seduction in such a classic style that he had to laugh aloud.

'Don't you laugh at me!' She flew at him and he caught her hand just in time.

'I'm sorry, I wasn't laughing at you, Sylvie, please

276

. . .'

She wilted against him; was she crying? Oh, God. He led her to the bed and sat her down. 'Here, I brought you a present, see?' He put his package next to the champagne.

'You sound like you're talking to a small child.'

'Sorry. I'm extremely well aware you're not a small child.'

She sniffled; the kimono slid off the other shoulder. Her slip fastened down the front with a row of ribbons, the top two of which were undone. Christ, that was distracting. He pulled the kimono back over her shoulders. 'Look, let's have a glass of champagne to toast your birthday, and then I'll go.' He poured two glasses, handed her one. 'This is a beautiful room,' he said, and retreated to the other side of it. 'Is the ceiling Jacobean?'

'You said you were in love with me. You said I was beautiful.' A tear rolled down her cheek. 'You've loved lots of women. Why not me?'

'Oh, Sylvie.' She was, God help him, one of those women who could cry without becoming all red and blotchy.

'You kissed me.'

'A kiss is one thing.'

'You want me, I know you do.' She allowed one more tear to fall.

Paul looked away, fumbled for a cigarette. And did I not set out to seduce her, knowing I'd never have her? The photographs, the imagining—what kind of glass is that to fling myself against? No one's going to rescue me; there's no open window that I've somehow overlooked.

'Won't you even offer me a cigarette?' she said.

She touched his hand as he lit it.

'I have to go now,' he said.

She buried her face in the cushions and sobbed.

'Oh Christ, Sylvie, please . . .' He plucked the cigarette from her fingers, put it out and patted her shoulder. 'I cannot, you know it.' God, that sounded awful. 'How can you put me in this position? I'm an employee of your family, in case you hadn't noticed, not one of your rich friends. What would Percy say if he knew I'd seduced his granddaughter under his own roof? Or your mother, or for heaven's sake your father! How can you think everyone wouldn't find out within a day?'

'The secret passage?' Sylvie sat up; the kimono slid down.

'All right, I'll give it two days. And then? I'll get fired. I wonder if that will be before or after Jarlath turns me into an ass.'

'I made him promise he wouldn't.'

'You what?'

She seemed to be trying to keep a straight face. 'I had a word with him.' She sipped her champagne. 'And Maggie. And of course darling Grandpapa. So you see, it's all taken care of.'

Paul put his cigarette out and walked to the window. This is right above my desk, he thought. The courtyard looked very different from up here. All this time, when I wondered which was her room, when I imagined her in it but never let myself ask, or search for it, she's been here, a few feet away. And there's been a secret stair, behind the portrait at which I never let myself gaze. A cold sorrow crept into his heart. 'You planned this from the beginning, didn't you? It's all been a job interview.'

'Well . . .'

'How convenient I am, after all. In residence, as it were. And an employee already. I'd thought that was an impediment, how silly of me. It's after all only a small change in my duties. Secretary, factotum, gigolo. Percy's demands are light; there is free time in my day. The afternoons would be good, say between tea and drinks, unless you prefer late at night? Shall I ask for a raise, do you think?'

She crossed the room and tried to insinuate herself into his arms, but he kept them folded over his chest. 'Or is the enjoyment of your charms supposed to be recompense enough?'

'Oh, don't be like that. Kiss me.'

She was so beautiful; what a stupid insect he was not to take her at once, never mind what it meant or didn't mean to her. Why should he hang his bloody heart on the tree, when all that was wanted was his body?

She stood on tiptoe and pressed her mouth to his; the tip of her tongue slipped between his lips. Honeysuckle. 'Don't you want me?' she said, and he couldn't deny it; she knew his cock was hard for she was rubbing against it.

Why shouldn't he, after all? Her first fuck, what an honour. She'd interviewed him, checked his references, arranged the time and place, laid on the champagne and expensive lingerie; who was he to refuse?

She let the kimono fall to the floor, tugged at his hands, placed one on her waist, one on her breast. Why not? He could do what he knew he was very good at; he could do it just as well with a cold heart, perhaps better. Across the room his present lay on the table. Not a pretty leather notebook, then, not a pen. No metaphors. A fuck for my lady it shall be. He picked her up—a classic touch, that she no doubt would expect—took her to the bed she'd so carefully disarranged, laid her against the cushions, untied the ribbons one by one. 'Sylvie.'

'Mm?'

'Are you sure this is what you want?'

'Yes.' She raised her face, closed her eyes.

'No. Look at me.' He sat back to survey her, his unreachable love, and the ache of wanting her flooded him with something not far from madness. Ecstatic possibilities unfolded in every direction; he wanted to have her in a hundred ways at once, with his hands, his cock, his mouth. He kissed her face, her lips, her throat. She arched her back, offered her breasts; he pulled away, then returned and sucked at her nipples until she moaned and his finger in her cunt felt the response.

Now, at last, he had a power, some power of his own to set against hers. This was a game he could play; perhaps even one he could win. He was like a scientist conducting an experiment: he could touch her here, or there, and note the effect. He stroked the fluted shadows of her ribs, her belly, the arcing bones of her hips, her long thighs; he observed the changes he had wrought. He wanted to make her want him, he wanted to make her die from wanting him as he'd died for her, every minute of every day. Down her thighs, and back up; when he bent his head to lick her cunt she struggled simultaneously to close her legs and raise her hips for more. 'You are,' he said, 'absolutely delicious.'

'Am I? I never tasted . . .'

He kissed her open mouth, sweet honeysuckle

mingling with her sharp ambrosial tang.

He stood up, unbuckled his wristwatch, unbuttoned his shirt, stepped out of his clothes. What a strange way to go into battle, he thought, removing one's armour piece by piece. Sylvie's eyes followed him; he loved the starving look on her face. She squeezed her thighs together but at the briefest shake of his head let them fall open with a sigh. A surge of power flowed through his body in a hot golden tide. He kissed her mouth again and she bit his lip.

'Hungry, are we?' he said. 'I know the feeling.'

'Please, Paul. Please. I think I may scream if you . . . if you don't . . .' A beautiful derangement was flowering in her eyes.

'Oh, I'm sure you're far too well bred to scream.' But I'll try to make you, he thought.

He guided the tip of his cock to stroke her, then pressed in and waited until she pulled him deeper. Her mouth opened wide and Paul knew she was screaming, though only a long sobbing cry emerged. He watched her dissolution from far away, from high above, moving just enough to take her further, step by step; his eyes held hers so she couldn't escape. At the right moment, he took her nipple between his fingers and dipped his tongue into her mouth. He held her there for so long he thought she might never return, but at last her shudders ceased; she lay panting and dazed in his arms as he withdrew his blood-streaked cock.

'But you're still, I thought, I heard—doesn't it get soft after?'

'Only if I come.'

'And you didn't. Oh. I suppose I'm not very good, I'm sorry. Maybe if you teach me what to do . . .'

She looked so contrite Paul almost laughed, but kissed her instead, and lay down at her side. Her thighs remained open, as though that had become her natural state. He stroked the swollen flesh. 'Did it hurt?'

'Yes,' she said, 'no, yes, no. Oh. Oh. Oh? Again?'

'Oh yes. Again.'

17

Paul left by way of the secret passage and the library, where he collected his shoes. Although he'd fucked her twice more, he'd not let himself come; he was steaming with heat and reeked of sex. He alternately tiptoed and raced up the stairs, shut himself in the bathroom, drew a cold bath and sat in it.

How on earth was he to face Jarlath, and Maggie, and Percy? It was all very well for Sylvie—she'd made her arrangements—but he would still have to walk into the room tonight and meet people's eyes. He submerged, looked up at the world from underwater, exhaled a sigh of bubbles and pulled himself out. His face in the mirror was almost unrecognisable. There was a wild look in his eyes that the cold water hadn't reached and a number of red patches on his neck and shoulders where she'd bitten him. Christ, what had he started?

He returned to his room to dress. Clean shirt, jacket and tie made him feel re-armoured, and he was giving his hair a last going-over with the comb when there was a knock at his door.

'Come on in,' he called, thinking it was Stephen wanting to borrow something, but Sylvie slipped in. She wore a dress he'd not seen before, red, short and very low. Immediately his erection returned; the cold bath, the re-armouring, all undone in an instant. She closed the door and stood demurely with her hands behind her. She'd put her hair up with jewelled sticks; there was a dark red mark on her neck. He pulled her head back and bit her there again.

'I opened your present,' she said. 'The notebook. It's lovely. Thank you.'

Her nipples lifted the fabric of her dress; he stroked them with his thumbs. 'I'm glad you like it.'

'The pen,' she put her hand on his cock, 'is especially nice.'

'Well then, I'm especially glad you like the pen.'

She rubbed it. 'It's an excellent pen, a wonderful pen, a magical pen. At last, a pen of my own.'

He pushed her dress up. 'Nice girls,' he said, 'wear knickers.'

'Maybe I'm not a nice girl.'

He fucked her roughly against the wall. Her hands tangled in his hair, her teeth fastened into his neck, and when she came she bit him so hard he gasped. He pulled out fast, buttoned his aching cock away and went to sit in his armchair, which was as far as he could get. 'Now don't you have a party to go to?'

She pushed her frock down, went to his bureau and studied herself in the mirror. She took the sticks from her hair, combed it with her fingers, twisted it up. Her intention, Paul saw, was to be sure the bite mark showed. 'I wanted to ask you to

283

go downstairs with me,' she said.

Paul lit a cigarette. The problem, he thought, is that right now being in the same room with you is enough to keep me so hard I can barely walk. 'Sylvie, it's your birthday, your party.'

She perched on the arm of his chair. 'I want us to go in together.'

Ah, he thought, I see. You want to show everyone your latest accessory, the proof that you're not a child any more. 'I'll be down later,' he said, and though she made some very enjoyable attempts at persuasion, he resisted. After a while she gave up, quite prettily flushed with annoyance but not so distraught that she neglected to give herself an admiring glance in his mirror before she left, and tug her neckline lower.

Something lingered that was not just the scent of sex and her perfume. Paul smoked two more cigarettes, stared at the wall. His mind was so crowded with memories of her that they spilled out and expanded like foam. His hands still tingled with the touch of her. The Sylvie he'd been so hopelessly in love with receded as the Sylvie he'd fucked into oblivion surged forward to fill his mind. Everything was Sylvie. Everything except a cold, quiet warrior enthroned in his heart. There is Sylvie, everywhere, and me, here, and battle has been joined. I feel strong, but—he took a last drag of the cigarette, tossed it into the fireplace—am I strong enough to go downstairs?

A buffet had been laid out in the hall, the gramophone played at top volume. Paul took a glass of champagne from Tustian, drained it in two long swallows and took another. Sylvie, shining like a beacon, danced a very vigorous Black

284

Bottom with someone. Everyone was watching her; she had that indefinable but unmistakable air of a woman who has spent the afternoon in gratifying carnal pursuits.

You entertained fantasies of winning her, Paul mocked himself, like some idiot knight, though you didn't dare woo her. You took the scraps she threw and now you're not happy when she lays herself out naked for you. Are you holding out for the unobtainable Sylvie, who is clearly a figment of your imagination? Would you rather buzz at the glass until you die of exhaustion and starvation? There is not a different Sylvie beyond that impenetrable pane, beyond that pointless pain. There is one Sylvie, and she wants to be fucked, and she's chosen you for the job. Are you suddenly the delicate virgin, who'll only surrender his virtue for true love? A bit out of character, don't you think? Christ, how much of an idiot are you?

'Encore un coup à foudre,' said Val, at his elbow.

'Oh my, yes.'

'Happy now?'

'You must be joking.'

Val shook his head. '"Comme elle est une maladie précieuse qui me donne cette belle douleur . . ."'

'Oh bugger off, Val.'

'Quite, quite.'

A new record came on, a slow song; Sylvie was drawn into the arms of a man Paul instantly loathed. A man whose hand, hairy as an ape's, rested on her hip, a man who was learning that under the silk she was naked. My God, now he was actually stroking her with his little finger. She allowed herself to be pulled closer; her hips gave a

285

squirm. If I don't want the job there are others who do.

'Why don't you dance with her, then?' Jarlath appeared at his side.

Oh God, this was it. 'I . . . I . . .' He turned to face the other man squarely, but couldn't think of anything to say. He wished he'd not had the champagne, or perhaps had a lot more.

Jarlath studied him with narrowed eyes and a pitying smile. 'You're in love with her. You've been in love with her since the night she came home; it's been perfectly obvious.'

'Oh?'

'Her image has been emblazoned on your aura, my dear fellow, clear as day. And then of course there's the way you avoid her. Maggie spotted it right away. She's an old hand at these games, you know. Doesn't miss much.'

'No, I don't imagine she does.' This was definitely in the running for the most awkward conversation of his life. 'I've no idea what to say.'

'I haven't either. It's a new one for me; I don't know about you. I suggest we carry on as before and try to ignore the fact that you're fucking my daughter.'

'OK. And thanks for not turning me into an ass—unless you have, and I've not noticed?'

'No, old chap, decided not to. You're more use as a man, I think.' Jarlath slapped him on the back, rather harder than necessary, and wandered off.

Another glass of champagne came Paul's way, and another, before he dared dance with Sylvie.

'Why haven't you asked me to dance before now?' she said.

'Your card's been full.'

'We don't have cards, silly.'

'It's a metaphor.'

She pressed against him. 'Is that a metaphor too?'

'No. Yes. No.'

'Whatever it is, it's growing.'

She glowed like a furnace; the smell of her cunt wafted up to him. Everyone she'd danced with had smelled that.

Through the open windows came the sound of a motor car. 'I wonder who's arrived so late?' she said.

'Come this way, everyone, please,' said Jarlath.

Lamps had been lit in the courtyard and a silver Alvis two-seater waited, engine running. 'Happy birthday, sweetheart,' Jarlath said.

'Oh! A Super Sport!' Sylvie flung her arms around her father's neck. 'Thank you!'

Paul thought the car looked absurdly small and exposed, with its canvas top folded down and a pointed tail-end that gave it the appearance of a bullet going the wrong way. Sylvie climbed in, flashing a great deal of thigh; everyone stood back as she set off on a circuit of the courtyard. Does she even know how to drive? It appeared she did; she was going faster and faster, whipping the steering wheel around, skidding in the gravel at the corners.

'She kept you waiting long enough,' Maggie said.

'Er . . .'

'Have fun, dear.' She patted his arm.

Sylvie pulled up with a spray of gravel amid cheers and applause. Someone handed her a glass of champagne and she drank it down. 'It's the most beautiful car ever. The speedometer goes up to a hundred! I'm going to take it out.'

'Sylvie, it's nearly midnight,' Jarlath said.

'Good, then there won't be much traffic.'

'Well you're not going alone.' He looked around, caught Paul's eye. 'Go with her, for heaven's sake. We can't stop her.'

Paul climbed in; she revved the engine, spun the wheels. She'd reached forty before she had to slow to turn on to the road. 'By the river,' she said, 'there are some long straight parts.'

'How did you learn to drive so well?' Paul said.

'When I was in Italy a friend taught me. He has a house on the coast near Amalfi and the roads are lots of fun there, a narrow strip with a great drop on one side to the sea, the mountain on the other. All winding like flat ribbons, and you have to come at the turns as fast as you can and keep the revs up because the engine works best that way.' She changed gear and the exhaust made a throaty growl. As they hurtled through sleeping Farundell hamlet a dark shape leapt into their path. The car slewed around and stopped sideways in the road.

'Christ,' Paul said. 'It's that black dog.'

'What excellent brakes,' Sylvie said. 'Did I hit it?'

The dog jumped up at Paul, barking hysterically. 'Apparently not.' He fended it off with his elbow. It seemed to be trying to get into the car or perhaps pull him out. 'For God's sake, get us out of here. It's slavering all over me.'

He thought Sylvie was laughing too hard to drive, but she managed to turn and accelerate so fast they bounced over the bridge.

She took the car neatly down the hill, using the brakes sparingly, shifting gears smoothly. In the dim light of the dashboard her eyes shone with excitement. Paul relaxed his grip on the seat and sat back to enjoy the ride. The night was warm and overcast; the white beams of their headlamps swung past stone walls and pierced the woods. Sylvie held so tight to the turns that the hedgerows brushed Paul's shoulder, torn leaves fell into his lap and he caught a whiff of honeysuckle. When they reached the Oxford road she set her face in concentration and let the car out on the straight run.

The tarmac was a long grey blur, bordered by green on either side as the flat fields rushed by. Paul glanced at the speedometer as it touched seventy. The engine was a roar scarcely louder than the wild tearing of the wind. Sylvie's mouth opened in a maniac grin; she held the steering wheel with both hands and stared straight down the tunnel of the headlamps. The noise of the engine rose, and she began to scream along with it. 'Aieeee! Aieeeeeeeeee!'

Paul guessed she'd been holding that in for some time. It was a moment before he realized that the engine noise had changed; they'd left the road and were airborne. A ditch flashed beneath, branches scored the bonnet, then they landed with a bump in a muddy lettuce field. When they came to a stop, mired in the soft earth, Sylvie was laughing so hard she was crying. 'Oh, my. I forgot that bend was there. Are we stuck?' She tried to drive forward, then back; the wheels spun. 'Is the car all right, do you think? It would be too much, wouldn't it, if I wrecked it on its maiden voyage?'

Paul looked over the side. 'We're in up to the axles; it's not going to move without a tow but I didn't hear anything break or explode. We can say you thought it was a short cut.'

'It is, it absolutely is. This is obviously where I was going, and I really do believe I took the shortest possible route. And if we're stuck for a long time we can always eat lettuce. Did you know the ancient Egyptians thought lettuce was an aphrodisiac?'

'Is that why you brought me here?'

'Yes.'

When she shut off the engine the darkness closed around them, silent but for the faint tick of cooling metal. She fumbled around the dash. 'Let's see what's in the glove box. Oh, a flask of something. My father thinks of everything.'

Does he indeed? Paul wondered.

She opened it and sipped. 'Brandy. Sovereign for emergencies—I think this qualifies.' She passed it to Paul and he took a long pull.

Her hand crept up his thigh. A long, brandy-breathed kiss was like kissing the night itself, for though his eyes were wide open he could see nothing at all. Her mouth pulled away; she squirmed and wriggled. Paul recoiled as an elbow dug into his ribs. 'What are you doing?' he said.

'Ouch, damn!' Movement ceased. 'I was trying to take my frock off and climb on to you, if you must know, though I hoped to make it a surprise.'

'This is not the best car for sex.'

She guided his hand to her breast. 'Try,' she said. 'For England.'

She leaned back and sighed as he tugged her frock down. Somewhere a dog barked and Paul pictured a farmer and his wife asleep in their beds while in their lettuce field . . . he sucked at her nipples.

'I love it when you do that,' she said.

'I love it when I do that, too.' In the darkness he was seeing with his mouth and his hands.

'Oh, and that, and that. I had no idea there were so many different ways.'

He stroked her thighs; she parted them, lifted her hips. She came as soon as he touched her, riding his hand with soft muffled moans. Her breathing gradually calmed; he drew his hand away.

'Oh,' she said. 'Oh my.'

He licked his fingers, fumbled for his handkerchief, mopped her tenderly and pulled her dress into place. She'd come out without even a wrap; he put his jacket around her shoulders. He found the flask, drank, passed it to her, lit a cigarette and passed her that as well. He was trying to fend off the paroxysm of love that had seized his heart but it was like trying to fend off the night.

They passed the cigarette back and forth: taste of smoke, of brandy, of Sylvie. In the boundless dark there was nothing to measure the passage of time but the increasing circle of her face illuminated by a red glow as the burning end of the cigarette approached. When it was finished, complete inky blackness returned.

'Charming as this place is,' Paul said, 'I'm afraid I can't stay. I have to find some way of contacting the house. They'll start worrying soon. In fact they probably already have. They'll be picturing you bleeding in a ditch.' He got out of the car. 'The cigarettes are in the pocket of my jacket. Don't, for heaven's sake, eat any lettuce.'

'No, wait. I don't want to sit out here alone waiting to be rescued like some damsel in distress.

291

We'll both go.' She slid over and climbed out. 'Go where?'

Paul groped his way to the back of the car. 'This way. Follow me.'

'Wait, ouch. My shoes, high heels . . .'

He scooped her up. 'Is this what you want?'

He heard her contented smile. 'Yes.'

Clouds of honeysuckle hung in the dense night air. Her weight was as nothing; he carried a warm breathing fragrance through warm, breathing, fragrant space. An image of the field and the path he had to take formed in his mind and he moved as surely as though he could see.

From far away came the roar of a motor car; it drew near and headlamps swept across the field as the driver negotiated the bend. 'I think that was my father,' said Sylvie in a small voice. 'It sounds like his Bugatti.'

There was squeal of brakes, the car reversed, stopped and someone with a torch got out.

'She's here,' Paul called, putting Sylvie down on her feet. 'She's fine.'

The torch wavered and turned their way, bobbed up and down, drew near. 'Jesus Christ.' Jarlath scanned them with the beam. 'You're all right? Yes, I can see that. How on earth did you end up here?'

'I thought it was a short cut,' Sylvie said, then burst into giggles. 'I'm sorry, Papa darling, I really am. It was so wonderful, so fast, I forgot about that bend.'

'You tore a great bloody hole in the hedgerow in your haste to get here.' Jarlath shone the torch around. 'Hm. Did you know that lettuce was considered—never mind. Have you wrecked the

292

car?'

'I don't think so,' said Sylvie. 'It's over there.'

Jarlath stamped off and Sylvie huddled close to Paul. 'I hope he's not too angry,' she whispered.

Jarlath reappeared. 'Well, we won't know until we get it to the garage. We'll have to pay for all the salad you've made. Ah well, could have been worse. I'm surprised you didn't flatten someone's prize cow. Come on, I'll take you home, though really I should make you walk.'

Back at the Bugatti he gave three blasts of the horn. 'The signal you've been found safe. People have gone off in all directions looking for you.' Another horn sounded in the distance, and another.

'I'm really sorry for all the trouble,' said Sylvie as they climbed in.

'You're my daughter,' Jarlath said. 'Trouble is your middle name.'

At the house, Sylvie was swallowed up by the crowd of her friends. Paul went to his room and sat in his chair, mind burning, body burning. After a time he got up and had another cold bath. At last, exhausted, he climbed into bed.

He imagined Sylvie in her room; now that he could, he couldn't stop. She'd take off her dress, toss it on the floor—would she have a bath? There was an enormous tub in the adjoining bathroom; he saw her in it. She dried herself in front of the mirror, admiring the marks on her neck and breasts. She put on her nightgown, turned out the lights, got into bed, fell asleep.

Paul drifted on, too awake to sleep, too tired to think. Thunder rumbled, and the curtains lifted in a humid breeze.

He carries her through warm darkness like a fog. All around is the murmur of the jungle, the lapping of water. As day breaks he climbs to the shore and lays her on the grassy bank. 'Again,' she reaches for his cock. 'Again.'

'Wait, wait a minute. There's something I forgot.'

The path through the forest twists and turns, thick with the scent of flowers. Paul walks on and on, but can't find any of the landmarks he remembered. The shelling is faint in the distance, like thunder on a summer night. Somewhere a woman is crying in pain and fear.

'It doesn't matter, carry on,' he says, but she cries louder, and he hears his name. It's Sylvie. He turns to run back but he's lost the path and flails through the jungle, tripping on roots, entangled in vines. When he reaches the shore a huge black ape is crouching over her. It paws her breasts with long hairy hands, yellow nails sunk into her flesh; it snarls and bites her throat, its cock rips into her. The creature lopes off, grinning. Sylvie lies in a pool of blood, grey-lipped and blank-eyed.

'No, stop!' Paul says aloud. 'This is a dream, and I want to wake up now.'

'Paul.' She stands at the edge of the jungle; he looks at the corpse, and again at her, wonder crackling through his mind. Somewhere a bird calls. She turns and disappears into the green.

'Paul.' Sylvie stood next to his bed. 'Paul.'

He looked up at her, urging himself to wake, but he couldn't move. At last, with a desperate wrench, he dragged his eyes open and sat up. A flash of lightning lit the room; she wasn't there. Thunder cracked. Was that what had woken him? He'd been sure he heard his name. He leaned back and reached for a cigarette. Just another sign of incipient insanity, no doubt.

His door opened and Sylvie crept in, ghostly in a long nightgown. 'Oh, you're up.'

If I said I was expecting you, you'd not believe me, Paul thought. Thunder sounded again, quite near; she jumped. 'Ah, you're scared of the thunder.' He lifted the sheet; she slipped in beside him.

'Always have been, but since I got too old to get into bed with Nanny there hasn't been anyone. You're not wearing anything.'

'Well spotted.'

Thunder boomed overhead. She buried her face in his chest and he pulled the covers over her shoulders, smoked his cigarette and held her close. He remembered bits of a dream. A jungle like Percy's, bird calls, a horrible ape. He'd lost her, somehow, and when he tried to get back, it was too late.

The storm rolled away into the night, replaced by the sound of steady rain. Sylvie slept. It rained until first light and Paul sat unmoving, his eyes open but full of her, his mind empty. By dawn the sky was clear and the sun laid a warm golden blanket on the bed. He got up, pulled on his dressing gown and went for a piss, brushed his teeth, splashed his face with water. He was looking for an anchor in the ordinary things, the things he'd done yesterday and the day before that. He was light-headed, and reminded himself that human bodies need more nourishment than champagne and sex. He tried to remember the last time he'd eaten anything other than Sylvie, and couldn't. He didn't want to eat anything else, ever.

Nectar and ambrosia, he thought; sweet cunt and honeysuckle kisses. All one needs.

You're raving, Asher. He glanced at the mirror, but the fellow in there didn't seem to have any more coherent thoughts than he did. Sylvie is sleeping in my bed, he told it, but he didn't believe it and the more he thought about it, the more certain he became that not only would she not be there when he returned, but all yesterday's events, from that improbable secret passage onward, would turn out to have been an exceptionally long and interesting dream. There was an ape, a wild car ride, a field of lettuce, a lot of sex. Had to be a dream. He saw the relief in the eyes of his reflection.

Nevertheless, there she was, still asleep. He stood for long minutes watching her until the sun touched her face and she woke, smiled, stretched.

'Good morning,' she said. She tugged at the belt of his dressing gown. 'You're coming back to bed, aren't you?'

'What an insatiable little minx you are. Do you expect my services twenty-four hours a day?' He sat in his armchair, lit a cigarette, looked out of the window.

'Can I have a cigarette?' she said.

'There's a box by the bed. Help yourself.' Inside him a madman beat against the walls; at all costs he must be contained. 'You should go to your room before the maids get up.'

'Why?' She yawned. 'I like it here.'

'You can't stay here.'

'Why not?'

'You should be in your room when morning trays are brought.'

'Should, should, should. What are you, the etiquette master? Does Mavis bring your coffee? Well, she can bring mine here this morning.'

'No, she can't. One has to have some discretion. Mavis would be terribly embarrassed to discover Miss Sylvie in bed with a servant.'

'You're not a servant.'

'Of course I am.'

'Of course you're not!' Sylvie sprang from the bed.

She was too beautiful; Paul looked away. 'My dear Sylvie,' he said, 'I am your most humble and devoted servant.'

'Stand up.'

'Why?'

'I can't hit you properly when you're sitting down.'

He laughed. 'Then perhaps I should stay where I am.'

'If you're my servant you have to do what I say, and I say stand up!' Sylvie was pink with fury and her voice was rising.

'OK, shh, shh.' Paul put out his cigarette and stood; she slapped his face so hard his eyes watered. 'Ouch.'

'Oh, I'm sorry, I'm sorry.' She kissed his burning cheek, opened his dressing gown, moved her hips against him.

His cock rose and prodded her belly. She would get what she wanted; that was inevitable. He could delay, distract, interpose any number of games, wring from them whatever small triumphs were to be had, but in the end she would penetrate everything and she would have him. Because, of course, she already did. 'We have to talk, Sylvie.'

297

He held her at arm's length.

'What about?'

'Do you know where babies come from?'

'You're joking, right? Of course you are. I've taken care of all that.'

'Really?'

'Oh yes. One only has to worry for part of the month, you know. Oh, of course you do. Well, I just finished my, you know, so it's OK for a while. And for the dangerous time, I have a Dutch cap.'

'I see.'

'Yes, I got it when I was in town. One has to wear a ring and say one is married, but they don't check.'

'You're very well prepared.'

'Is that a compliment? I didn't want you to think I was a child who didn't know what she was doing.'

Paul looked at the clock; there were, after all, nearly two hours before Mavis would appear. Sylvie caught his glance, smiled, pulled her nightgown over her head and stretched out on the bed like a cat in the sun. 'Touch me,' she said, 'kiss me, do those things you did yesterday, or other things, and teach me what to do to please you, too, because it's not fair that you make me come so much but you don't.'

The honey-gold light stole into his blood like a drug. Her body glowed and every detail was magnified; there were prisms in her skin, in her hair, in each tiny bead of sweat swelling from her pores. He floated, forgot everything. Hands and tongues silver and gold, arms and legs swimming in a soft-flowing river. Divine acts and operations, he heard Mr Pym say. Perfect bodies. An abyss was opening. All right, he said, all right. He closed his eyes and saw the coiling ribbons of light and music that flowed beneath her skin. The air was thick as water, the sun poured down like rain. The abyss is everywhere, said Mr Pym, and the falling is forever.

*   *   *

Paul woke to the sound of Sylvie's voice, asking for her tray. He feigned sleep until Mavis left, then opened his eyes. The blankets were in a tangle on the floor with Sylvie's nightgown; she'd wrapped herself in his dressing gown and pulled a sheet over him. He could only hope she'd done that before Mavis entered. Better not to ask. He pictured Mavis's path downstairs, along which the word would spread through the house.

Sylvie lit a cigarette and passed it to him, turned and sat against the foot of the bed. She sipped her coffee, a satisfied smile on her face. He remembered falling asleep in her arms, telling himself it was only for a few minutes. He smoked in silence, dragging himself back from a sleep of such dreamless density it had obliterated time. He passed her the cigarette and received in exchange the cup, as though they shared their coffee and cigarettes like this every morning. Her bare foot lay alongside his thigh; he rested his hand on it, cradled the high arch. This was a heaven so simple, so ordinary, he wanted it to last forever, and since that seemed a humble enough wish, he allowed himself to wish it, for a moment, anyway. He imagined they were in their own flat in London, or maybe Paris—a small flat, perhaps just this one room on the top floor of a house in a quiet district, with a bed, and a window that let the sun pour in,

299

and they woke every morning in each other's arms, shared a cup of coffee and a cigarette.

That, however, was not the world in which he lived. In this one, Mavis knocked and entered with Sylvie's tray. He pulled the sheet up to his chin. 'Good morning, Mavis,' he said, as he did every morning.

'Morning, Mr Asher,' she said, as usual. She put the tray beside the bed, picked up the blankets and deposited them on a chair, hung the nightgown on the hook behind the door and left.

'Well done us,' Sylvie said. She put the cigarette out, shrugged off his dressing gown and tugged the sheet away. She kissed his neck, moved down to his chest. 'Does this feel as amazing to you as it does to me?' She flicked his nipples with her tongue.

'An unanswerable question.'

'And then, I was wondering if you'd like this.' Her mouth moved lower.

'Oh, God.'

'I'll take that as a yes.'

*   *   *

Paul sent Sylvie back to her room, took a bath and drank the rest of the coffee cold, bitter and black. He smoked three cigarettes but avoided his face in the mirror. Happy now? he heard Val say, and he knew that some part of him, at least, should be. He went down to breakfast in order to assert some normality rather than to eat; the sight of the food on the sideboard turned his stomach and he took a cup of coffee out to the terrace. He sat on a step and closed his eyes.

18

Long after the gramophone had fallen silent and Sylvie's guests had gone to bed, Percy listened from his window as, at last, Daniel played again. He could tell from the way the trumpet and violin intertwined that Daniel had found a way to return from wherever he'd gone. Percy went back to bed and slept better than he had in ages, and when Henry brought his morning tray he told him to summon Paul right away.

'They have a saying,' he began, when Paul had settled himself with pad and pencils, 'that La Selva is irresistible. And it's true, you know. She is. You don't need to write that down.'

Paul realised what Percy was telling him. 'Ah,' he said. 'I see.'

'I hope you know how fond I am of you,' Percy said. 'I don't think I could do this with . . . just anybody. And now shall we start?'

Paul reached out and gave Percy's hand a gentle squeeze; it was returned. He read out the previous day's dictation, checked a few references in Percy's *Encyclopaedia of Lepidoptera*, sorted through some correspondence. Percy dictated little, and dozed fitfully until Henry arrived with his lunch tray.

Paul couldn't face lunch. He had to find a place to reassemble himself in peace—a place to hide. He dropped the morning's dictation on his desk and put camera and *Pymander* in his pockets. Where could he go? Neither his room nor the darkroom was safe any more. Swimming would only remind him of her, though of course, now,

301

everything did. Not to the chapel, not to St Ælfhild's pool, or the stream that flowed from it. Certainly not the island.

So just walk, he told himself, and started up the hill behind the house. He paused often, ensnared in a twirl of birdsong that tasted like champagne, a drift of scent like the sound of Arlen's trumpet, a play of light and shadow among the green leaves like the touch of Sylvie's fingers. There was no path, so he went where the forest let him. He couldn't get really lost, but he enjoyed not knowing exactly where he was or what he'd see next. And yet the thought of wandering on and on was exhausting. He needed a place to stop.

High above a bird cawed and a parting in the shrubs revealed a little glade, sheltered all around and carpeted in moss and soft grass. It looked so inviting, so perfectly suited to his needs, that he was obliged to regard it with some suspicion. This sort of place invariably turned out to be infested with ants, or nettles, or whatever unpleasant counterpart the apparent perfection required. But inspection revealed neither ants nor nettles, nor brambles nor bogs; it was as perfect as it seemed.

He found a comfortable spot under a tree, gathered handfuls of dry leaves for a pillow and lay down. He ought to try to collect all the bits of himself that had gone adrift. But he was adrift, too, on a sea of Sylvie. Impossible to look away; eyes open or closed, he saw her. She was becoming infinite, as memory and sense, imagination, dream and reality overlaid one another, as she bloomed, branched, divided and multiplied, as details expanded to become universes in themselves, into which he was falling, slowly, slowly. He felt a wave

302

of vertigo but was too tired to make the effort to pull himself out and instead fell deeper until with a click in the back of his head he floated up and hovered in the air.

There was a buzzing in his skin and a humming in his ears and that strange falling sensation he remembered from his nightmares, except he wasn't falling; he was held in midair. He didn't dare breathe. He looked at his hands; they were silvery, luminous, almost transparent. Oh, he said, I see. This is my moon-body. I'm in Kathmandu! He felt something slot into place in his mind. All along, he thought. It's been right here all along. A curl of laughter trickled out to his fingers and toes.

A thrush's trill rippled the air, scarlet and violet, a whirling pool of song that sucked him in and stretched him out. A butterfly swam by in a cascade of orange. He tried to follow but was soon lost among the prisms that danced between the leaves. A warm breeze kept everything in constant motion and carried a melody of fragrances, green and white, pink and gold. It lifted him over the trees and he floated in sun-thickened air streaked with ribbons of birdsong.

There was a tug, like gravity but stronger; it pulled him back to the clearing in the forest as though attached to an elastic. Francis was sitting on a fallen log. 'So,' he said, 'you and my great-great-great-great-granddaughter.'

'Yes. Do you mind?' Paul noticed that Francis had greeted him as though they were friends who saw each other often, and didn't bother with Hello.

Francis shrugged. 'It's what they call fate. It's what happens while we wait for our plans to ripen.'

'What on earth does that mean?'

'Nothing you could understand.'

'Oh sod off, Francis.'

'Would that I could, my friend, would that I could.'

Paul's attention was drawn to a tribe of ants—Ah, he thought, I knew there would be ants—preparing to attack their neighbours on the other side of the clearing. His body lay in the path of the advance party now setting out.

'The hazards of nature,' Francis said.

'Should I wake up?'

'Just divert the ants.'

'How?'

'Look.' Francis moved his hand and a glowing line appeared around Paul's body; when the ants encountered it, they turned aside.

'Thanks.'

'It was nothing. You can do it perfectly well yourself.'

'Really?'

'Focus your intention; draw a line with your mind.'

Paul went to the head of the column of ants, concentrated on the idea of stopping them, gestured as Francis had done and imagined a line in their path. He watched to see what would happen. The first ones reached his barrier and paused briefly, then pushed through. The succeeding ants hesitated less and less until soon they crossed the line with no notice at all. Evidently he hadn't concentrated hard enough. 'How does that work?' he asked.

'Magic.'

Ah, thought Paul, as another piece of

understanding dropped into place. 'Is this a dream?'

'No, but that's probably how you'll remember a few little bits of it, if you remember any at all.'

I really want to remember, Paul thought. 'I want to remember what's real,' he said.

'That's a start,' Francis said.

Paul gazed down at his body. How tired it looked. The cheeks were hollow and shadows lay under his eyes. A wave of irresistible sleepiness washed over him; he fell into it, dropped deeper, and deeper, and slept.

The sun on his face woke him about an hour later. He sat up, lit a cigarette and in a single, sudden rush remembered everything that had happened since he lay down. The music, the colours, the light. Francis. The ants. The lesson in magic.

What on earth had that been? Not a dream, something else. Moon-body. He understood Alice's term exactly now. Near his feet, the ant army was on the march. About a yard from his body the column executed a sharp turn and continued as though along a wall before resuming its path across the clearing. When Francis had shown him how to draw a line with his mind it had felt like something he'd always known how to do—like remembering how to swim.

He gazed at a leaf. Now it was just green, but before, it had been made of millions of tiny spinning particles of solid, living light, each of which contained all the colours of the rainbow; it only looked green if you stepped back and considered it in its entirety, and called it a leaf. The air had been thick, buoyant and

305

impressionable. And I could just float up, he thought, and for a moment the memory of the experience was so vivid he was sure he could do it again. He closed his eyes and willed himself up, just to see if it would work. The world seemed to shift and a wave of vertigo passed through his body. It was like that swimmy feeling he'd been getting lately, that aquatic state of mind. He couldn't hold on; it faded into a pale buzz and vanished. He opened his eyes. Perhaps he'd thought about it too much.

But he'd remembered the beginning—the vertigo that for once he hadn't fought. Was this what had always been on the other side of that queer, awful feeling? Always there at the edge of sleep, like an antechamber he passed through without noticing. And the vertigo was the door.

There was pain somewhere . . . a hand, the left one. He glared at it as though it was a rude stranger; the cigarette had burned down to his fingers.

'Damn!' He put it out, stood up and stretched; something weighted his pocket. He removed it, examined it, and couldn't remember what it was. Oh, a camera. A little room. I wonder what's in it. He opened it, extended the bellows, looked through the viewfinder at a complex, abstract arrangement of light and shadow, released the shutter. Click: it became tree, branch, leaf.

And what does *Pymander* have to say about all this? His fingers were already riffling the pages. 'Going out of the body, he shall be guided,' said the book, which was so disconcertingly apt that he abandoned his usual stricture never to read on either side of the words chosen, and scanned up a few lines.

God has given Man two powers: Knowledge
and Will, and he who Dares to use them shall
differ nothing from the Immortals; rather,
going out of the body, he shall be guided and
led by them into the planes of higher existence.

Oh, blimey, Paul thought. I always think it's
going to help but it never does. He closed the
book.

On the way down the hill he couldn't feel his feet
on the ground and had to look at them often to
make sure. His body felt unfamiliar, like an ill-
fitting suit. As he crossed the stable yard the clock
struck five. I heard the clock strike five yesterday,
he remembered, then I got up to let the bee out,
and then I think I must have fallen down the
bloody rabbit hole. He realised he'd come to a
stop and may very well have been muttering aloud;
Mavis watched with interest from a doorway.

'Hello,' he called, gave a cheery wave and strode
into the kitchen garden.

The peace of the place floated over him at once.
There was no one about; the clatter and chatter
from the kitchen receded as he walked further in,
past sweet peas, lettuce and towering, pungent
tomatoes. Several beds were dedicated to flowers
for cutting and the madly coloured mass was
thronged with butterflies. Next came the
strawberry beds, mulched with pine needles, the
fruits red and perfect. Paul's mouth watered and
he bent to pick one. The redness sang like a
saxophone and exploded in his mouth with such
intensity he nearly fell over.

307

'Come and sit down,' said Theo from the bench in front of the potting shed, so still he hadn't noticed her.

He sat down gratefully. The sun shone golden and warm; bees hummed in the fragrant air. Theo said nothing, but he became aware of her presence as a vast kindness that reached out and touched his mind as a wave of longing rose within him.

He was kneeling, his face buried in her lap. Sobs racked his body until he thought he would break. Her hands rested on his head; she received him, and bathed him, and in time washed him on to the shore, drained and mysteriously content.

He sat back, found his handkerchief, blew his nose. He looked into her eyes and knew that she saw everything. He didn't mind at all.

After a while he stood, kissed her hand, and followed the path out of the garden. He didn't know how, but being with Theo had dissolved a layer or a crust of something hard, brittle and confining. He felt lighter for having shed it, but also restored to his solidity, smoothly reconnected to it instead of jolting along uncomfortably next to it. What had she done? Whatever it was, he felt better than he had in ages.

Tea was being served on the terrace. Paul was ravenous; he put extra sugar in his cup and heaped a plate with sandwiches. He spotted Alice sitting by herself at the far end, staring intently at the ground.

'Don't step on the ants,' she said as he approached; she'd been watching, he saw, a procession of ants emerge from a mound between two stones and carry hundreds of pale, seed-like eggs into another crevice a few feet away.

308

Paul sat down carefully. I wonder, he thought, if I focus my intention . . . he pointed his finger and drew an imaginary line across the ants' path. For good measure, he imagined that it was very hot, a bright, burning line, a line of fire. The ants stopped instantly; the procession backed up and, feelers waving, spread out across the barrier. It was only a few inches long; they found their way around it and resumed their progress.

'What did you just do?' Alice demanded.

'That's what I wanted to talk to you about,' Paul said. 'Francis taught me when I was in my moon-body and when I woke up I remembered the whole thing.' He told her what had happened; she listened, nodding sagely.

'I knew it,' she said. 'I knew one didn't have to forget. Show me again how you stopped the ants.'

Paul demonstrated. 'Francis said to focus your intention and draw a line with your mind.'

'"Imagine what you want, and you will make it out of liquid air!" I just remembered he said that, in a dream, or . . .' She struggled to remember more but it slipped away. 'Doesn't it feel strange,' she said, 'when you remember something that you don't remember having happened in the first place?'

'Yes, it does,' Paul said. 'I know what you mean.'

'Sometimes I remember a bit of something, like a piece of a jigsaw puzzle . . .'

'But you don't know what the whole puzzle is supposed to look like . . .'

'So you don't know where to put it. Are you going to eat all those sandwiches?'

'No, help yourself.'

Alice took a ham sandwich. 'So what did you do?

How did you make it happen?'

'I wasn't trying to make it happen at all; I was just trying to get some rest.'

'But why did it happen today? If we know what the conditions were, we can repeat the experiment. That's called the scientific method.'

The conditions, Paul thought, were sex and exhaustion. 'I was a bit tired,' he said, 'and I hadn't eaten for a while.'

'There must be more to it than that,' Alice said. 'I've missed dinner and stayed up all night lots of times.'

'Well, I expect there's a number of variables.'

'Are you going to try to do it again?'

'Do you think one can do it deliberately?' Paul recalled that he'd tried right away, and failed.

'Of course. I'm pretty sure Theo can, and what's Francis, after all? One just has to remember how. And practise, I expect.'

'You've obviously thought about this quite a bit.'

'Oh yes. I'm sure it's the most important thing there is. What I don't understand is why everyone takes it for granted that they forget everything that happens when they're sleeping.'

She was right, Paul thought. He'd never questioned it. How very odd—there was a great, gaping, blank unknown right in the middle of everyone's life and no one thought it strange, or tried to find out what was in there. Why does no one wonder? 'You're the only person I've ever met who thinks about things like that,' Paul said.

'It's actually very difficult,' said Alice. 'You don't know anyone who does tattoos, do you?' She showed him her wrist where REMEMBER twined in bright green letters.

'Tattoos hurt, you know. A lot.' Paul pushed up his sleeve and showed her the tiny green snake on his left bicep.

'A green snake? I have a green snake too, but he's imaginary. Why do you have one?'

'I had a girlfriend in Paris who was known as La Serpente, for . . . various reasons. We happened upon a tattoo parlour one night, while . . . not fully in our right minds.'

'Did she get one too?'

'Yes, a small red lion, never mind where.'

'Is Sylvie your girlfriend now?'

Paul raised his eyebrows.

'Mavis,' Alice said. 'I'm always the first person she tells things to. So is she?'

'Is she what?'

'Your girlfriend?'

'Not exactly, no, I don't think she is.' Sylvie had come out to the terrace a little while ago, taken a cup of tea and gone back in.

The shadows lengthened, the tea things were being cleared. The ants completed their transport operation; a few stragglers zigzagged across the stones. Alice stood up to go. 'We could have a pact,' she said, 'to tell each other if it happens again, if we remember.'

'OK,' said Paul.

'And try to find out what the conditions are.'

'OK . . .'

'And if you see Francis, could you tell him I'd like to see him too?'

'Yes, I will.'

*   *   *

311

At drinks Sylvie avoided him and he avoided her but after dinner she passed him a note: *Come to my room at eleven.*

Paul lingered in the music room, had a second coffee and a brandy, entered enthusiastically into a discussion with Stephen and Miss Firth about . . . about what he forgot even as he spoke. At eleven-thirty he went upstairs, bathed and shaved.

Shall I, he wondered, slope about in my dressing gown like some backstairs lothario? No, damn it. Shirt and trousers. Belt. Wristwatch? Of course. Tie? Don't be ridiculous. And I'll be damned if I wear shoes.

He stood for a long time on the stairs, as though once he set foot in the first-floor corridor something would be done that couldn't be undone; he would have agreed a set of terms, settled a contract. He wanted to go to her. He did not want to be summoned. But isn't it always a woman's right to summon, to dismiss? Is it wrong to obey when it's what I want too?

And what do you want? he heard Mr Pym say.

He pictured Sylvie naked beneath him, speared, transfixed, melting. I want to make her love me. No, to hell with love. This is war. I want to make her die of desire.

He stepped down. Now he knew which door it was.

*   *   *

He'd propped his wristwatch on the nightstand—there appeared to be no clocks in the room—and at half past three, when Sylvie had succumbed to sleep, he got up to leave.

'No, stay.' Sylvie woke up. 'So we can fuck in the morning.'

Paul pulled on his trousers. 'Think how it would confuse poor Mavis.'

'I told her to bring your tray here.'

'Did you? Well, I prefer to make my own arrangements for my morning tray.'

He walked up to his room, closed the door behind him and stood with his back against it. He'd left the window open; a sliver of moonlight lay across the floor. A moth danced in, fluttered around and out. From across the lake came the sound of trumpet and violin.

What do you want? Mr Pym asked again.

I want to know, he said as he lay on his bed. I want to know what's real. He felt around for that aquatic state, that floating feeling, that strange tingle under the skin. He closed his eyes, breathed steadily, tried to remember the exact sensation. Several times he felt the edge of vertigo approaching, but each time the very act of noticing it made it retreat, until at last he fell asleep.

The jungle crowds all around, the path narrows. Mr Pym walks alongside. They've left Sylvie behind on the shore; Sylvie is far ahead, a faint glimmer. Mr. Pym points; the path opens out to a glade; in the centre is a tiny house, so small that Paul can barely see it, but when he looks closely he recognises Farundell, many roomed, expanding as he falls towards it.

Paul stands in the hall for hours, but no one comes. Odd snatches of music come from behind closed doors, but they're all locked.

'Pssst.' A section of wall swings open and Sylvie appears. 'Follow me.'

313

'Every moment a door to immortality,' says Mr Pym.

Paul follows Sylvie down the steeply spiralled steps, further and further. 'Wait,' he says, 'wait, is this the right stair?' but his feet run faster and faster. 'No, stop, not this way, please.' Far below, the crater waits, full of death and he's sliding down, hands grasping only mud, falling, falling.

'No!' He wrenched himself awake and sat up, sick and trembling. His clothes were soaked in sweat. He dropped them in a pile, put on his dressing gown, which smelled of Sylvie, and sat smoking in his chair until Mavis appeared with his tray and a neutral face.

He bathed, and dressed so absent-mindedly that he twice buttoned his shirt the wrong way. When it came to putting on his shoes he couldn't remember which was right and which left; he had to experiment. He went down to breakfast and although the smell of food was very unpleasant, he forced himself to sit with a cup of coffee for half an hour before he went to the library, where Sylvie looked down at him from her portrait. Behind her face was a door, a secret passage, a stair that led down . . . no, up, of course, up to her room. Though he knew it went up, he couldn't erase the image of a downward spiralling stair behind the wall. He examined the panelling. Could he open it from this side? In thrillers there was always a piece of woodwork to twist, or a book to pull from a shelf. He tried every bit of wood and every book within reach, to no avail.

'Open sesame,' he said finally. He knew he was talking aloud to an inanimate object but what the hell. It was a mad world, madder, even, than he'd

314

thought, and perhaps he'd been trying to be sane for too long.

He sat at his desk and removed the cover from the typewriter. A flamboyant scrawl of blood-red ink had been rolled into the machine. *Come to the chapel at five*, it said, *for tea and whatever.* He tried to picture her there. What was she doing right now? It was none of his damn business; he shook himself and turned away.

The sun was falling on the glass cabinet by the far window; Odelia's crystal glowed. He'd crossed the room, unlocked the cabinet and reached for the crystal before he had time for second thoughts, but as soon as it was in his hand he was assailed by doubt. It was, after all, in a locked cabinet, even if the key was right there. It didn't belong to him. No one had given him permission. He felt like he was stealing it, though he knew he wasn't. He only wanted to look at it. No, he wanted more; he wanted to use it. A force drew him towards it; another was trying to repulse him. It was as though he was having a battle of wills with it, but that was ridiculous; it was just a piece of stone. He almost growled at it; he tightened his fingers, squeezed. Something yielded. He didn't know what he was doing; somehow, he knew exactly what he was doing.

He sat in a chair and held the crystal in his hands. He relaxed his grip; it grew warm and seemed content to rest in his palm. It was beautiful, light-full, spacious. Show me Sylvie, he said. He let his eyes enter the sphere; he floated, drifted, then was pulled deeper. An image appeared, expanding as he fell towards it. He knew what was coming—the slide of vertigo. Don't fight it, he told himself; everything twisted briefly as he fell through the stone. He remembered to breathe.

Sylvie was at a table, mixing colours, measuring out blue powders and white, adding black, ochre. Behind her, on the wall, a partly completed painting of St Ælfhild's pool, jungle-dark, with strange birds in the trees and serpents in the grass. Paul hovered above, observing. He couldn't alter his perspective; he couldn't move, or touch her, or make her notice him; he could only watch.

The image dwindled to a speck and vanished. The stone turned cold and opaque in his hands. He felt queasy, his head hurt; he was chilled and shivering. He replaced the crystal in the cabinet, ran from the room and barely made it to the WC before vomiting.

It took over an hour for the weakness and nausea to fade; he decided to leave the crystal alone. He had no doubt that what he'd seen was real, and when he went up to the chapel—not at five, as requested, but at a quarter to six—he recognised the painting, the table, the jars of coloured powders.

He could tell that Sylvie was waiting for him, though she made a show of saying, 'Oh, is it five already?'

He didn't say anything; he undressed her and fucked her on the sagging, musty sofa under the high round window.

Afterwards, she gave him tea from a flask and they shared a cigarette.

'You're so ithyphallic,' she said, wrapping her hand around his cock.

'Ithyphallic?'

'I read it on a card in the British Museum—the

316

same one that said about lettuces. It described a scene of offering to . . . can't remember. Some Egyptian god with a huge, erect thing. Except it was chiselled out. A lady was offering lettuces.'

'So you've offered your lettuces . . .'

'And this is what I got.'

Paul folded his arms behind his head, gazed up at the ceiling and applied all his attention to breathing.

'Can I ask you a personal question?' she said.

'OK.'

'Why don't you come really fast like everybody else?'

'Like everybody else? What do you know of everybody else?'

'Well, boys, you know, cousins and so forth, have been kissing me, or touching me, or trying to, since, well, since a while. And some men that I've met lately. And if I let them touch my breasts, say, or press really hard against me, well, they usually come right away. I can always tell—their breathing changes, they stop suddenly and leave in a hurry, or fumble for their handkerchiefs, and then they know I know, and it's all very embarrassing.'

'Yes, I can see that it would be,' Paul said. 'You can't blame them, though.'

'Can't I? Then why don't you?'

'My dear girl, I'd never keep up with you. The very first thing a man must learn to do,' he removed her hand from his cock, 'is not come every time.'

'Am I as good as other girls?'

'You appear to have considerable natural talent, and you do seem to be a fast learner.'

'I know I need a lot of practice.' She climbed on

317

to him. 'Oh, ah. That feels so . . . so . . . Gosh. Do you have any idea how that feels?'

Paul shook his head.

'Fucking is such a wonderful word,' Sylvie said. 'So apt. I wonder why people get so upset when one says it.'

'Because it's so apt.'

'Well, there aren't any other good words. People say "having sex" but that's stupid; it isn't something you have, it's something you do.' She shifted her hips back and forth. 'Let's fuck everywhere.'

Paul gritted his teeth. 'Everywhere?'

'Yes, everywhere—all the rooms in the house, at least once in every room.'

'That might present certain difficulties.'

'We'll conquer all obstacles.' She tried a side-to-side movement. 'And in the gardens. On the terraces. In the stables and in the temple of Hermes, and Arcadia, and on the island, and in the boathouse, and in each boat. Why does it . . . When you do that, I feel it down there. Yes, there. Oh.'

It was almost dark when they got up. They retrieved their scattered clothes and dressed each other, interrupted and delayed by the need to kiss every part goodbye as it was hidden away. They combed each other's hair with their fingers.

'I'll go first,' Sylvie said. 'Wait a bit before you follow.'

*   *   *

Late that night, after he'd left Sylvie sleeping, Paul lay on his bed. He imagined that he stood at the

318

border of a strange country, stranger even than Kathmandu, an ephemeral, liquid state between waking, when his mind was full of words and thoughts, and the blankness of sleep. How to get in? Scientific method, he heard Alice say. What are the conditions? Tiredness, not much food, sex. Sleepy but not asleep; awake but not too awake. The knowledge that I have done it; therefore I can do it, and I can remember. Not fearing the vertigo; allowing it, riding it, letting it carry me deeper. Falling, falling into myself, letting it happen, not fighting . . . With a brief squeeze as though every cell of his body had undergone a momentary compression, he was afloat in the dense silvery air. His surge of excitement nearly broke the spell; he steadied his breathing.

The air teemed with particles of light, or thought; or thought that was light. Waves of sense impressions washed over him from all sides—images of people, shadows of past events that had occurred in this room, ghosts, scraps of old dreams. He had just enough time to notice that being in a house was very different from being outside in nature when the tide of sensation spun him around and sucked him down, and down and down into his inert body and deeper, into sleep.

If he dreamed he didn't remember, but in the morning, when Mavis appeared with his tray, something clicked in his mind and he suddenly recalled the brief, tumultuous excursion in his moon-body. He'd hovered in the air, assaulted by a thousand images and sensations; he couldn't maintain his concentration for very long but he'd done it, he'd made it happen again. He couldn't wait to tell Alice.

319

The next night Paul skipped dinner and had only one whisky. He tore himself away from Sylvie by two-thirty and slipped up to his room, undressed and opened the window. Slow-drifting clouds occluded the moon; a pale glow waxed and waned over the meadow and the lake.

He lay on his bed and waited. When the vertigo came he breathed it in, let himself go, fell and rose with the wave until he floated in the shimmering air. To withstand the surge of images that threatened to drown him, he gazed steadily at his own hands. He imagined a clear area around himself and immediately the chaos calmed. He saw his body asleep on the bed but quickly looked away lest it draw him back too soon. Up, he thought, up! and up he went, through the ceiling and roof— weird grating sensation of plaster, wood, slate, almost too brief to notice—then he was high in the fluid, subtle air. He could feel the moonlight, taste it, smell it. Beneath him the house pulsed with the iridescent, multicoloured thoughts of all the people in it, coiling and mingling like ribbons, like smoke. Among them, one beautiful, strong, green-gold. Sylvie. As he thought, so he travelled; in an instant he was by her bed, watching her sleep. But he couldn't hold on; the act of realising what he was doing broke his balance and with a steep slide of vertigo he was pulled back into his body.

He checked that he was really awake and sat up, cautiously so as not to dislodge any part of the memory. Only after he'd run through what he'd done several times did he allow himself to fall asleep.

In the morning he told Alice, though he left out the part about Sylvie.

*   *   *

The next few nights, Paul couldn't make it happen at all. Alice, consulted, shrugged her shoulders.

'I told you it was difficult,' she said. 'Maybe it happened, but you've forgotten.'

'How can one know?'

'Well, exactly. One has to remember to remember.'

Remember, Paul thought that night, as he lay on his bed. He remembered how he'd floated over the house; he knew the exact sensation of the dark, luminous air, alive with thought and motion. That's what I want, he said. I want to swim in that air, sweeter and more real than earthly air. Please, he said, and when the vertigo came he reached for it like a lover and rode it up into the dense, buoyant night above the house, and higher, above the hills, the wooded valleys, the flowing, lambent river.

The darkness was bright; the night was full of colour. Strands of music floated across the land: the trumpet and the violin were dancing. The music penetrated his body; it was felt, tasted, seen. The air swirled with many fragrances which were people, thoughts, images. It's infinite, Paul thought; the word was a white crystal unfolding inwardly forever.

The night was molten with soft currents; he was wafted higher; he swam and turned in the air. I can swim, he remembered. I've always known how, and

321

Sylvie taught me to remember . . . As soon as he thought of her he saw her; she was asleep in her bed, naked as he'd left her. Desire flared through his senses; it dragged him down and he fell through the night, through the sleeping house until he hovered over her body.

I wonder, he thought, if I focus my intention . . . He imagined that his hand was solid and warm, he stroked her face, her shoulder, her breast; she stirred in her sleep. He felt his concentration slipping; he tried to hold on but was pulled back to his own bed, his own body. The sensation of falling that accompanied his return no longer frightened him; he waited for the vertigo to subside, then sat up.

I touched her, he remembered, with my moon-body, and she felt it, I'm sure she did. I could affect her, I could make her feel me.

In the morning he told Alice he'd again had no luck.

19

Overnight storms had cleared, and by early morning on the day of the picnic the sun was already strong. Guests started arriving right after breakfast and Alice helped Tustian show people to their rooms. He was in a dreadful flap—Uncle Richard had appeared unexpectedly with Aunt Cecily and their children, throwing all the room assignments into chaos.

Alice reminded herself not to omit the title with them—one time she'd called her aunt just plain

Cecily and was treated to a kindly lecture on form, with much gentle tsking, sad shakes of the head and references to careless upbringing and the unfortunate influence of unsuitable persons. Alice reported the conversation to Maggie, who'd snorted with laughter, tsked and shaken her head in turn.

They had a boy about her age named Michael and a girl a bit older, called Georgina. They were dull and snobbish and boasted endlessly about their enormous house in Singapore, their hundreds of native servants. They'd last been to Farundell a year and a half ago—a strained fortnight at Christmas that had culminated in Percy screaming with rage and becoming so ill that Dr Westlake was summoned in the middle of the night. Alice, despite her very best efforts, had never been able to discover what the row was about.

The children's wing was crammed with noisy cousins and the progeny of her parents' friends, their nannies and maids. Roger had laid out his train set across the floor of the schoolroom and attracted a large crowd, including some grown-ups, so there was no refuge there. She retreated to her room, but Sophie, with whom she'd been forced to share (it was either her or Enid, a smelly third cousin), had strewn her frocks everywhere, was in agonies over which to wear today for the picnic, which tonight for the party, and which tomorrow for the regatta. She insisted on discussing in detail the positive and negative attributes of each until Alice fled.

She found Theo weeding the herb garden, sat on the grass and watched her work. 'Are you coming to the picnic?'

'Maybe,' Theo said. 'Or maybe I'll go for a walk.'

Alice gazed across the meadow. The contents of the boathouse were lined up at the dock: rowing boats, canoes and sailing boats. A housemaid moved among them, arranging cushions on the seats and tying bouquets of flowers and ribbons to their prows. Arlen was walking up to the house. He'd been here nearly three weeks and Daniel was happier than Alice had ever seen him. He was becoming almost sociable; when she visited, she sometimes found other guests, usually Stephen or Paul, having tea on the porch. And Arlen was kind; he'd asked about her flute, made her bring it, and played with her, laying the trumpet so softly under her tremulous Mozart that it lifted her up and she'd played better than ever before.

'I think I'll go and see Daniel,' she said, 'and then take my coracle to the island—so I can get away if I want to.'

She walked along the edge of the lake, watching for thistles. Insect buzz filled the air and a heron hunted frogs in the reedy shallows. She sat on a rock and burrowed her feet into the soft earth, pressed it up around her ankles, sculpted giant feet around her own. She added six toes to each foot and painted her legs in wavy, muddy streaks. The marks dried in the sun and left a grey, cracking crust.

The boats plied back and forth, ferrying their bright, laughing cargo to the picnic place on the far side of the island. The mud hardened and reminded her of the cast she'd had to wear for what seemed an eternity when she'd broken her leg falling out of a tree. The wonderful thing about this, she thought, is that I know I can get free any time I want. She stood up and wiggled her toes; cracks appeared, widened. She lifted out her feet and walked on, leaving the mud forms empty on the shore.

The door to the cabin was ajar; Daniel was sleeping. His hand lay open on the sheet, his lips were parted; he wasn't grinding his teeth. She studied his face; he looked so young, despite the white hairs that threaded his beard and the fine web of lines around his eyes.

Something moved; she caught a glimpse of a face at the window and hurried out. 'Michael! What are you doing here?'

'Just wanted to have a look at the loony.'

'Leave him alone. He's not a loony.'

'Oh yeah? He was pretty loony last time I saw him. He was starkers in the middle of winter.' He tried to step past her to the door, but she closed it and planted herself in front of it. He went back to the window. 'Has he still got all that hair?'

Alice wished there were curtains she could draw, a lock on the door, but the cabin had neither. 'His hair isn't any of your business.' She had to get Michael away from here, or stand guard all day. 'Do you want to see my coracle?'

'Your what? I never heard it called that before. Has yours got hair on it yet? Georgie's does. Do you want to see my willy? Let's go into the woods.'

'What? Why on earth would I want to do that? I can hardly think of anything more boring and infantile. Even Roger and Sophie outgrew that sort of thing years ago.' She turned and walked towards the shore. 'A coracle is a boat,' she called over her shoulder. 'We can go to the island in it.'

As she pulled the boat to the water's edge it

325

occurred to her that there was a way to make this less boring. 'Do you want to paddle?' she said. 'You're probably a lot stronger than I am, and it's quite a long way to the island.'

He picked up the paddle with a manly, capable air. 'All right,' he said, climbing in. 'It's not really hard, if you're strong enough.'

Alice pushed off and knelt behind him. Michael dipped the paddle and gave a powerful stroke; the coracle spun in place and washed back up on to the shore. Alice pushed off again and Michael switched to the other side for an even more powerful stroke. The coracle obligingly revolved in the opposite direction. Alice wrapped her hands over her mouth and squeezed her eyes shut.

'Huh,' said Michael, and tried again. And again. Eventually he managed to achieve a small forward momentum, though still mainly spinning.

'You *are* awfully strong,' said Alice, when she'd regained a measure of control.

'Huh,' panted Michael, redoubling his efforts and halving his progress.

'So tell me,' she said, 'what it's like in Santiago or Surinam or wherever it is you've been.'

'Sing–' Michael said, '–apore.'

'Oh yes, of course, Singapore. Is it nice there? Do you still have all those slaves?'

'Uh,' said Michael.

'Sorry?'

'Mm.'

'And that enormous house? How many rooms did you say it had?'

'Hoo.'

'Sorry? I didn't catch that.'

'Uh.'

They were still less than a quarter of the way to the island. 'Oh look,' Alice said, 'we're nearly there already.'

'Uh.'

'So what brings you here?'

'Ffff.'

'I beg your pardon?'

'Fath.'

'Your father? Your father what?'

'Pahm,' Michael said.

'What?'

'Pahmen.'

'Parliament? What on earth are you talking about?'

'Stan–' Michael said, '–ding.'

'Uncle Richard's standing for Parliament?'

'Uh.'

Michael's shirt was soaked and he paddled slowly now, alternating between right and left, gasping with every stroke. At last he stopped and sat, head bowed, chest heaving. Alice considered whether to take pity on him; she was disinclined, but in truth the constant spinning back and forth was making her a little queasy.

'Are you tired, Michael?' she said. 'Gosh, look how far we've come. We're very nearly halfway there.'

'Uh,' said Michael.

'You have a little rest,' she said. 'Maybe I'll do a bit, until you catch your breath.' She plucked the paddle from his slack hands, turned the coracle and in a few minutes had brought them in among the boats clustered at the shore. Michael climbed out stiffly, his face set in fury. He stalked off without saying a word.

Percy sat under a tree, blanket over his knees. It was a perfect summer day; he'd known it would be. He'd invited everyone this year, even the ones he didn't like, and everyone had come: nieces and nephews, cousins of all degrees, old friends with their children and grandchildren. They floated up out of the blur; they spoke of this and that, of what they had and what they wanted; he listened more to the tone than to the words, and he wanted to say Stop, don't bother, it doesn't matter, you'll have to lose it in the end . . . but of course he didn't. No one liked to hear that; no one could.

He touched the papery hand of his cousin Millicent but the picture that arose was of a ten-year-old, holding his hand as he helped her into a boat on another summer day. Her dry old voice rustled among the memories of her laughter. 'Millie,' he said, 'do you remember . . .' and she did, and they sat together and remembered until it seemed to him that the child, moist as a green bud, would burst through his sere and ancient skin and he would run again, naked, light as a leaf, down to the water to swim and splash and play. Goodbye, Millie.

People came and went, leaned close, kissed his cheek, took his hands, enclosed him in their fragrant auras. Perfumes and colognes and hair tonics, cigarettes and cigars and pipes, food recently eaten, sweat stale and fresh.

'Hello, Father, it's Richard.'

'How kind of you to say hello, Richard. Tustian told me you had turned up. I must say it is very

328

inconsiderate to arrive at such a time with no notice to the staff.'

'I'm very sorry, Father . . .'

'Did you think I'd forbid you to come if you did me the courtesy of asking first?'

'Well . . .'

'I hear you're going into politics. Whatever possessed you to consider such a thing?'

'I don't see why I shouldn't.'

'Besides the inherent idiocy?'

'Really, Father, I don't know why you should care. What's it to you? I'm the dispensable third son—oh, I forgot. Number one is dead, number two is mad.'

'Don't you dare . . .'

'Dare what? Go into politics? Have my own life? Make my own choices? Survive the war?'

'If that's how you feel, why have you come? And why now? You think I won't make a fuss with so many people around.'

'It's my home, Father. Nothing you can do about that.'

Percy suppressed an urge to reach out his hand. What did Richard look like now? How did he wear his hair? 'Do you have a beard?'

'What? No, Father, a moustache.'

'Is that wife of yours with you?'

'Her name is Cecily, Father, and she's not right here at the moment, if that's what you mean.'

'I have decided you may stay, as long as you keep her and her religion away from me.'

'Oh really, Father! Why are you so rude?'

'You know perfectly well.'

'You can hardly blame her for the crimes of all Christians.'

'Indeed I can, since she refuses to apologise for them.'

'Why should she?'

'And if she tries to corrupt my grandchildren . . .'

'Michael and Georgina are your grandchildren too.'

'Oh, so that's what this is about. What am I leaving them in my Will?'

'That has nothing . . .'

'Quite right. I'm leaving you lot nothing, since you have God, or Jesus, or the Holy bloody Ghost to take care of you.'

'Oh for God's sake, Father!'

Richard stomped off, but the anger lingered like a bad smell. Percy sank back in his chair. He was breathing hard and his heart was beating unpleasantly fast. He pulled up the blanket, suddenly chilled. Henry was at his side in a moment, clucking under his breath. 'Tea, sir?'

'Yes, Henry, I think that would be nice. With a shot of brandy.'

*　　　*　　　*

Paul sat with Val near the edge of the woods and remembered how it had been when he and Sylvie were alone on the island. She'd shown him her kingdom, and only the birds and the wind in the trees accompanied her voice. Now, the meadow was filled with the sound of conversation and laughter, the clink and rattle of silver and china and glass. Rugs and cloths and cushions spread across the mown grass; canvas chairs stood in groups. Changing pavilions had been erected for those who wished to swim, though the children

330

ignored them, tore off their clothes and splashed about naked. Tustian presided over tables piled with poached salmon and jellied trout, lobster and pigeon, ham and lamb and tongue in aspic, cold roasted chicken and terrine of duck, three kinds of cheese, cucumber salad, tomato salad, cabbage salad; Mavis circulated with champagne. Paul put on his sunglasses and watched Sylvie move among the groups of people, stopping now with this one, now with that.

For two weeks they'd fucked in so many ways and places Paul had lost count: in the chapel, in the woods, in several, though not yet all the rooms of the house, in the afternoons and late at night. And later still, while everyone slept, he returned to her in his moon-body. Now that he knew how to do it, he couldn't resist; the vertigo was delicious as wine. Night by night he'd learned to extend his concentration, to intensify his effect on her. She felt him, he knew, though some part of her remained oblivious, unreachable. He'd asked if she remembered anything—perhaps a dream?—but she said she didn't and teased him for becoming like Alice, obsessed with dreams.

He lied to Alice every day now.

Then Sylvie disappeared for five days. She'd returned last night with a gang of her London friends. He hadn't spoken to her.

She was on the far side of the meadow, her back to him. As she bent to speak to an old lady in a deckchair, her dress tightened over her hips; he imagined his thought touching her like a hand, reaching under, stroking her thighs. She turned and looked around. Was it possible she'd felt something? Her eyes, like his own, were hidden

331

behind sunglasses.

An odd fellow in unseasonable tweeds wandered to and fro with a pair of metal sticks in his hands, attended by a woman with a notebook and pencil. Every so often, he would stop and say something and she would write it down.

'What on earth are those people doing?' Paul said.

'Well obviously, they're tracking the intrageometric psychomagnetism,' said Val. 'Can't you tell?'

'The what?'

'Or is it geomagnetic psychometry? Something like that. I had the pleasure of sharing a boat with the charming Mr and Mrs Macgregor, and learned all about it as we were rowed over. You see before you yet another genius unaccountably unrecognised in his time. But all that's due to change—he's writing a book, the frothily titled *History, Theory and Practice of Intrametric Psychomagnetic Geokinesiology*.'

'What?' said Paul. Sylvie walked by with a young man.

'She does it on purpose,' Val said. 'That's twelfth cousin Herbert; he's unbelievably dim, has spots and buck teeth, likes shooting. She couldn't possibly fancy him.'

Mavis appeared with a bottle; Paul held out his glass, had it filled, downed it and held it out again. Val laughed.

'What is so bloody amusing?' Paul said.

'You,' Val said, 'you.' He shook his head. 'I've never seen you like this. You look like hell, old chum.'

'Thank you very much.'

'Being in love usually puts a bloom on your cheek, a merry glitter in your eye. You have the air of a man who has sold his soul.'

'Don't be so melodramatic. It's only pawned, not sold.' I have become, Paul thought, an *encantado*, a demon succubus, a shape-shifting, night-swimming, virgin-seducing river dolphin. He laughed out loud. 'And I'm not in love any more. Besides, it'll all be over soon; she'll go and live in London in September.'

He lit a cigarette and stared at the nearest tree, studying the crevices and convolutions of its bark until they resolved into limbs and faces, intertwined as though the tree was writhing with lovers. He took out the camera. Would it show on film? Click. 'Those who understand, see,' said *Pymander*.

A small boy approached Val. 'Are you Mr Asher?'

'No, that's Mr Asher,' Val said.

The boy offered a note. 'I'm supposed to deliver this.'

'Thank you,' Paul said. 'Who sent you?'

'A lady.'

'Which lady?'

The lad shrugged, ran off.

Paul unfolded the paper. *Wait ten minutes*, it said, *then meet me at the temple of Aphrodite. S.* He realised he'd been holding his breath and released it with a hiss.

'Is it, O tell me, can it be . . . from *Her*?' said Val.

'Oh, shut it,' said Paul, rereading the note.

It was the 'Wait ten minutes' that was the killer. Ten minutes was a long time, long enough to become aware that while part of him raged to race up the hill, another part was urging him to run away. Too late for that, far too late. He waited twenty minutes then set off with, Val said, 'rather more the air of a man going to his execution than to his beloved'.

A couple strolled hand in hand among the columns of the temple; Sylvie was nowhere to be seen. Paul tried to look as though he wasn't on a secret assignation. He caught a glimpse of another couple among the trees; probably everyone was on a secret assignation.

'Pssst!' Sylvie appeared from behind the oak at the end of the clearing, beckoned. 'Quick, this way, before someone else comes along. Never thought it would be so busy around here.' She vanished down a steep path; branches swung in her wake.

She was waiting for him on a ledge. A fern curled over her shoulder, a bit of ivy tangled in her hair. 'Look.' She pointed to the near-vertical drop. 'There's steps. Follow me.'

Steps, Paul thought, was something of an exaggeration for the narrow stones, overgrown with moss and tilted by roots. Glimpses of water glimmered between the trees and a small sunlit pool appeared at their feet.

'This is a secret place,' Sylvie said. She stepped on to a slab of rock, took off her clothes and jumped in.

Paul sat on the warm stone, opened the camera and framed her as she floated on her back, pale in the dark water. Click. He reached for the book. 'Thou must forsake the body before thy end,' said *Pymander*.

She climbed out and lay beside him. She was strewn with rainbow droplets and rivers trickled down her sides. He lifted the camera again; it made him feel a bit more in control.

Click. 'Not ruling, but ruled,' said *Pymander*. Did he detect a note of disapproval?

He put camera and book aside. She placed his hand between her legs and pulled his mouth to her breast. There was a bite mark on her neck, not his.

Why do you leave me? he thought, when she lay smiling and drowsy, licking his fingers like a kitten. He clenched his teeth to keep the words in. 'Why . . .'

'Why what?'

'Why didn't you tell me you were going away?'

'Oh, don't be like that. Give me a cigarette.'

He lit one and passed it to her, took up the camera again: part of her face, her hand, the cigarette. 'Hold still.' Click. 'Every living body consisteth of Matter and Soul,' said *Pymander*.

Breast and arm, shadow and light. Click. 'Passions follow generation, as rust doth iron.'

Sylvie opened her eyes. Click. 'I have not learned the Truth.'

Her hand, palm upward. Click. 'No man can choose both.' He closed the camera and gathered pebbles: white and grey, yellow and black, and one deep red. He dropped them one by one into her open hand until it was full; then one by one she threw them into the water. When the stones were finished she stood and pulled on her clothes.

'Wait a bit before you follow,' she said, and disappeared up the cliff.

When Paul reached the top Sylvie was sitting on a fallen column at the far end of the temple, watching the methodical zigzagging approach of Macgregor and his wife. 'Are you dowsing for water?' she said. 'There's quite a bit just over there.' She pointed to the lake.

Macgregor laughed. 'Not for water, young lady, but for the psychomagnetic energy of the earth, which is extremely strong near here. There is a clear line coming along from there,' he indicated the temple of Hermes on the hill above the house. 'That is the obvious one; anyone could spot it. But I have discovered another, coming from thereabouts,' he gazed off through the trees, 'that crosses the first very near this spot where we are standing now. Narrower, deeper, but very strong. See?' He held the metal sticks in front of him; they swung about, then settled pointing towards each other. Paul wondered if the man was mad, but Sylvie nodded.

'I've seen people dowse for water with hazel sticks,' she said.

'Yes, hazel will find water. These are a special alloy that after many years of experimentation I have found to be the most sensitive to terrestrial psychomagnetism.' He held them up. They were a dull, silvery bronze, bent at a right angle near one end, forming a handle. 'Would you like to try? Not everyone feels it, but you'll know if you do.'

Sylvie took the sticks and walked as directed. When she came to a certain spot she stopped as they wobbled. 'I'm not doing that! And I do feel a bit of tingling in my hands.' She handed them back. 'What an odd sensation.'

'How about you, young man?' Macgregor said, and Paul stepped up with reluctance—it looked like party tricks to him. 'Come over here, that's it. I haven't done this patch yet, so I don't know exactly where the line is. All you have to do is go along slowly, don't think of anything.'

Paul walked forward, confident he'd feel nothing, but within a few steps a shock like an electric current shot into his hands. The sticks swung wildly and then hovered, facing inward, emitting a tense high-pitched hum. Paul would have dropped them, but couldn't open his fingers.

'Follow the line,' he heard someone say. He turned into the force and felt himself being tugged along. The ground wavered beneath his feet, the humming increased and a harmony appeared. The soles of his feet tingled, almost burning, and there was a pulling sensation everywhere in his body; it was holding him in this track. He felt resistance when he lifted his foot to step forward, yet he had to follow. The tingling-burning flowed up from his feet and met the electric sensation spreading from his hands.

Breathe, he reminded himself. Every blade of grass, every leaf was edged with light, glimmering and humming. Sylvie was swathed in colours, bright greens and golds. He knew this state well, but—he checked—he was still in his physical body. The corporeal sensations remained, overlaid and interwoven with currents of light.

He looked at his hands, fingers clasping the metal sticks. Open, he said to them, and they opened; the sticks fell. The golden world shattered; the humming sensation faded slowly, lingering in his hands and feet. He turned up his palms, expecting to see that they'd been burned, but except for a small red spot in the centre they were unmarked. He wondered why no one had spoken to him—he was sure he'd been standing immobile for several minutes at least.

Macgregor picked up the sticks. 'Did you notice it?' he asked.

'Er, yes, I suppose I did.' Paul rubbed his face. 'Tell me, how long was I holding those sticks?'

'A few seconds, I suppose. You took two or three steps and dropped them.'

'Huh,' said Paul. He looked down at the ground, now solid and opaque. 'Well, there certainly seems to be something right around here.' He was a little surprised to be able to lift his feet so easily. Sylvie was chatting with Macgregor's wife. Temple of Aphrodite, he heard her say. She didn't look at him, and when Macgregor resumed his survey Paul slipped away.

He was a bit dizzy, the ground felt unusually springy and there was a humming that wasn't bees. He shook his head, lit a cigarette, which helped somehow, and walked down to the meadow.

The shadows had shifted, the picnic had rearranged itself; Tustian and the maids were serving tea. He was so hungry he felt hollow.

*   *   *

Alice had wrapped some food in a napkin and climbed to the tree house high in the chestnut. She could see nothing of the ground below, though the noise from the picnic rose and mingled with the birdsong and the rustling leaves. She ate her lunch, opened the big tin box (Percy's old specimen chest), and rummaged through the books. She kept a small library up here in the summer, so as never to be caught without something to read. *Robinson Crusoe*—that suited her mood today. She'd read it several times before; he and Friday

338

were like old friends. She opened the book with a sigh of pleasure and didn't come down until she heard tea being served. It was surprising how hungry one got reading outdoors.

After tea, people trickled down to the shore and into the waiting boats as the servants packed up dishes and cloths, chairs and tables and tents. She wanted them to disappear with all their noise and clutter. She decided to wait until everyone had left; she'd have the island to herself for a while. She could take her coracle back any time. The sounds of the lakeside bustle faded as she walked up through the woods. The temple was deserted; she lay down among the roots of the old oak. The sun slanted through the trees, bees buzzed, she grew drowsy and had almost fallen asleep when she sat up with a start. Someone was climbing the steps from the grotto, humming a waltz. Suddenly she knew who it was.

Francis wore a rumpled linen suit and a blue shirt open at the neck. She drank in the details: the rings on his fingers, a pair of sunglasses in his breast pocket, his hair curling over his collar. He looked almost ordinary, which made him seem even stranger.

'*Thesaurum non aurum intra celatum,*' he said, put his finger to his lips and winked.

'What?' said Alice, but he'd vanished. *Thesaurum non aurum* . . . the treasure not gold, she translated . . . is hidden within. What was that supposed to mean? This habit he had of disappearing without answering questions was extremely annoying.

The sun was low in the sky as she walked down the hill. She could tell right away that she was alone on the island; a sort of peace had been restored. The meadow was trampled and sorry-looking, though meticulously tidied of all remnants of the picnic. All the boats were gone, except for her coracle on the shingle where she'd left it. She pulled it to the water and climbed in, but immediately began sinking. She scrambled out and dragged it back.

There was a large tear in the bottom, quite neat, V-shaped. She fingered the edges: no fraying, no roughness. She looked at the place where she'd left it, but there were no sharp stones. A stone couldn't have sliced through the thick, tar-coated canvas so cleanly in any case. Only a sharp knife, a penknife perhaps, such as boys carry in their pockets. She remembered Michael's tight-lipped stare, full of hate. All right, fair enough, she'd played a trick on him, but he could have admitted he didn't know how to paddle a coracle; he could have asked her to teach him. Instead he said nothing, waited, and took revenge. The sneaky little weasel.

Alice was so angry that it was several minutes before she realised she was stranded on the island. Robinson Crusoe indeed! A curious sensation ran through her, a mixture of pleasure and trepidation. It was a good thing I had so many sandwiches for tea, she thought, as I'm missing dinner. Feeling brave and intrepid, she strode up the hill and over to the other side of the island, in case a boat had been left there; if not, she could try to call across the water. There was no boat, and when she raised her voice a freshening breeze blew it back in her face. Could she swim it? She'd never tried to swim that far.

I will not, she thought, surrender to despair. Robinson Crusoe didn't, and I shan't. She rather wished her trial was a little more severe—it was hard to be too concerned when one's house was in sight. Nevertheless, as adventures went, it was quite good. It would have been better if Roger and Sophie had been with her—she could have had them doing useful things like building shelters and gathering firewood and . . . well, she didn't have matches in any case, and had no idea how to rub two sticks together. Fortunately it was summer.

She returned to the meadow. Her last option was to call to Daniel; the shore was further, though the wind might carry her voice. But he'd have to be there to hear, and he'd have to understand where she was calling from, and decide to come. If he didn't, she'd spend the night in her tree house.

As the sun dropped behind the hills she shouted until she was hoarse. When it was nearly dark she gave up and was walking to her tree when she heard Daniel's voice.

'Thank God you've come,' she said, though part of her was sorry that the adventure was over. She showed him the cut in the coracle.

'Poor little boat.' He stroked it tenderly. 'Don't worry, we can fix you. I'll patch it for you tomorrow,' he said to Alice.

He paddled back, Alice kneeling behind, towing her coracle. 'Watch out for Michael,' she said as they pulled the boats up on to the shore by Daniel's cabin. She was going to say, he thinks you're a loony, but stopped herself. 'He's not very nice.'

Daniel only smiled.

'Goodnight,' she said, and set off for the house.

At the edge of the clearing she looked back. Light spilled from the open door of the cabin; Arlen said something in a questioning tone, Daniel answered quietly and the door closed behind him.

Alice had an urge to stay and stand guard over her uncle; she imagined Michael sneaking back in the middle of the night, sharp little knife in hand. She hesitated, then turned towards the house. As she walked, she made her plans. She'd grab some food, make her bed look slept in, and return. Her main advantage was that she was familiar with the terrain. She could set a trap, perhaps a wire to trip him. She'd read about that, and it seemed perfectly straightforward. Here, she decided, would be the perfect place, where the path came around a blind corner and crossed the stream that flowed down from St Ælfhild's pool. She'd take a torch, to shine in his eyes when she caught him, and something to tie him up with. And a flask of tea, if she could manage. And a sweater, in case it got cold later.

With the house so crowded and the servants so busy, it was easy to obtain what she needed. She returned to the site of her ambush, tied a fishing line just below knee-height across the path and retired to a nook beneath a hazel bush. She had seen Michael at the house, though she'd made sure he hadn't seen her. She rearranged a few branches to give her a view of the path and settled down to wait.

The moon rose from behind the hill at her back and striped the world black and silver. Suddenly she knew he was coming. She crouched by the path; a flare of fear and excitement tingled her fingers and toes. He appeared around the bend,

342

pale against the night sky. She held her breath as he neared the line, but he managed to negotiate it with only a slight stumble.

Damn! She stepped out. 'Michael . . .'

He rushed straight at her, a malevolent glare in his eyes and a sharp little knife in his hand. A great calmness came over her and she had plenty of time to observe how the blade flashed in the moonlight. She leaned out of the way; the tip of the knife scored the skin of her belly, then she tripped him as he passed. He fell face down into the stream and she jumped on his back. He twisted and turned like an eel, but she kept her hold, seized a stone and hit him as hard as she could on the head. He subsided with a gasp and she held his head underwater until he stopped breathing, and quite a bit longer to be sure, then dragged him out to the lake, gave him a good, hard push, and watched him float away.

$$*\qquad*\qquad*$$

That night Paul, though summoned, didn't go to Sylvie's room. Instead he went down to the lake, took off his clothes, climbed from the dock and swam in the moonlight. He wanted the water to rinse him clean, wash away his desire, make him free of it. He saw the path he'd taken with Sylvie, from the moment he'd acceded to her birthday wish. He wanted to start over, do it again, make a different choice. But the water stopped at his skin and never reached the heat inside.

Later, in bed, the vertigo came like an old friend; he let it carry him up and out into the night. Not to Sylvie, he thought, but the hot metal hook of

343

desire drew him down to her side and the need to touch her kept him there.

Sylvie, he said, and she turned in her sleep. Push down the covers, and she did. He slid his silver form into her body and deeper, harder, into her mind. Let me in, he said. Damn you, let me in. Something yielded and he was in. Her mind opened like a book; a dream was unfolding and Paul flowed into it.

They're in a taxi in London; a man with hairy hands is touching her breasts. Paul pushes him aside and as they drive through the night he fucks her in all the ways she likes best. At last the taxi stops; they straighten their clothes and she gets out. 'Wait ten minutes before you follow,' she says. Paul sits back to wait, but the taxi starts moving. When he tells the driver to stop, the fellow ignores him and accelerates. Paul tries to open the door, but it's locked. Panic rises as they travel faster and faster through darkness so complete he has no idea where they are. At last they stop; the door opens and he climbs out. In the faint, pre-dawn light he recognises the craters of no-man's-land, the howling, heavy sky, the smell of cordite, gas, rotting flesh. The taxi drives off and he's alone but for a solitary figure atop a mound of mud and corpses in the distance. As Paul approaches, the figure turns and he recognises his father, white breeches, dress uniform, sabre drawn. Paul tries to run but his feet sink into the earth, a paralysis spreads up his body, an abyss opens below.

The awful falling sensation came as a relief; Paul let himself drop and drop down the sickening gap until with a shudder he awoke in his body, in his bed.

The nausea faded as he sat up, lit a cigarette and

remembered what he'd done. He'd finally penetrated her mind, he'd got into her dreams. He imagined the possibilities—the things he could do to her, the crazy desire he could make her feel, the images he could instil in her mind, in her memory. A new front had opened in the war, a new power had been granted him, if he dared to use it. So why, he wondered, don't I feel more satisfaction? This is what I've been trying to achieve. But the triumph was mingled with a strange sense of dread, as though he'd crossed some line, broken some barrier. Wasn't it black magic to violate her dreams, manipulate her, put images in her mind? He dismissed the thought. All's fair in love and war, he told himself, and in his battles with Sylvie he needed all the help he could get. But at what cost? As much as he'd affected her, so he too had been affected. Every detail of the dream was as vivid and real as an experience he'd lived when awake and fully conscious. He wished he hadn't learned how to remember, but it was too late. He couldn't shut the door.

20

Alice woke to the feeling of something digging into her side. She pushed it away, but it rolled back. It took her a while to identify the object as a flask. She opened her eyes, sat up and recognised the hazel bush where she had been lying in wait for Michael; in a rush all the night's events flooded into consciousness. Michael, the knife, the struggle in the mud. She'd hit him, hit him with a stone, and then . . .

She stumbled to the shore. It had been here—no, there. That was the stone, she was sure. She gazed at it in horror, surprised that it wasn't stained with blood, but it was half underwater and had evidently washed clean. Dread dragging her limbs, she waded among the willows that overhung the banks, expecting at any moment to come upon his ghastly corpse.

She searched for what seemed like hours, but found no sign of him. The sun was climbing in the sky—it was Sunday, she remembered, the day of the regatta, and the children would be drawing lots to see who was teamed with whom, in which boat. Soon, someone would notice she was missing, and Michael, too, and start looking. Maybe she should run away. The gypsies were in the fields by the river at this time of year; she could join them, hide among them, leave behind an unsolved crime. But no, someone else would get the blame—probably, due to his oddness and proximity, Daniel. And then all her efforts to protect him would have been in vain; she'd have murdered her own cousin for nothing. No, she thought, straightening her shoulders, I have to go back, and if the body is found, and if they figure out it was murder, I'll have to step forward and confess. It was, after all, self-defence, though there was only her word for that and it was possible no one would believe her. She felt quite calm about it, now that she'd thought it through. It was fate, that was all. She'd done something terrible, and if she got caught she would pay the price. She could, nevertheless, hope she didn't get caught. She hoped her weaselly little cousin had sunk to the bottom of the lake and was being eaten by the fishes.

She gathered her things and made her way to the house by a circuitous route that took her past Arcadia, where she washed in the stream. She hid her satchel under a bramble bush behind the coal shed and entered the courtyard from the stable yard, where the clock showed, astonishingly, that it was only seven. She crossed quickly to the boot room. From there it was a short, brisk stroll to the back stairs, encountering only an unknown lady's maid. In her room the curtains were still drawn and Sophie was asleep. Alice changed into her nightdress and had just climbed into bed when Roger burst in and flung the curtains wide.

'Wake up, wake up! It's the regatta today! Come on, let's go downstairs and find out our teams. I hope I get on a sailing boat, don't you? Though a canoe wouldn't be too bad. Come on!' He hurtled out of the door as fast as he'd come in.

'Where were you?' Sophie said. 'I stayed up really late, almost until midnight.'

'You were asleep when I came to bed.' Alice pretended to yawn, then it turned into a real one that nearly cracked her jaw.

Sophie peered into the corridor. 'Not much of a queue at the WC,' she said, and disappeared.

Alice got up and dressed more carefully than usual. If she was going to be arrested, and taken off in handcuffs, she wanted to look her best. Refusing to drag her feet or dawdle or in any way attempt to postpone the inevitable reckoning . . . Why on earth, she wondered, have I begun to think like a character in a thriller? Well, it wasn't every day one murders one's cousin.

In the first-floor corridor she paused. Should she

go to her parents? Or Theo? Confess everything, and let a grown-up decide what to do? She wished she could consult Francis. He had killed people in duels; he'd know how she should handle herself. She looked around, sure she'd caught a glimpse of him out of the corner of her eye, but there was no one. What would he do? *Scire, Velle, Audere . . . Tacere.* Know, will, dare . . . keep silent, she remembered, and resumed her walk downstairs. To my doom, she thought. Oh shut it, she snapped back.

The morning room was crowded with children clamouring for their turn at the draw; Alice came forward when her name was called.

'The yellow sailing boat,' Stephen announced, 'with . . .'

It would be just too ironic, Alice thought, if I draw with Michael.

'With Michael,' Stephen said. 'Now where's Michael?'

The blood drained from Alice's face. She'd always thought that was merely a gaudy phrase of the thriller writer, but that was exactly how it felt. Stephen's voice floated in from a great distance. 'Has anyone seen Michael today?'

The enquiry rustled around the room. Alice had a dreadful urge to blurt it all out, but she couldn't move.

'Where's Roger?' Stephen asked. 'Michael was sharing his room.'

'He was here a minute ago,' someone said.

'Here he comes,' said another.

'Roger, where's Michael?' asked Stephen. 'We have his draw for the regatta.'

Alice held her breath. Roger would say Michael

348

hadn't slept in his bed, and the search would begin.

'Michael can't come,' Roger said. 'He got really sick in the middle of the night, flapping about and yelling. Now he's got an awful streaming cold and he says his head hurts so badly he can hardly breathe. He has to stay in bed. With poultices.'

Alice listened, stunned. Had he somehow revived, swum to shore? Impossible. He'd been dead, quite dead, she'd made sure of it and anyway, Roger was saying he'd been in bed the whole time. But then, with whom—with what— had she fought?

She heard her name. Stephen was about to assign her another teammate. 'I think I may not feel so well either.' She backed towards the door. 'I'll just . . . er . . .'

She returned to the lake, sat on a rock overlooking the scene of what she still thought of as a murder and tried to remember every detail: the feel of his body as he writhed beneath her, the weight of the stone with which she'd struck him, the stillness that came over him. She knew what a dead body was; she'd seen and handled dead animals plenty of times, and he'd been dead.

But if he had been asleep, was I asleep too? It must be. I fell asleep, and woke up in my moon-body, and Michael was in his moon-body too. That was the obvious explanation, but it had been so real, from the first sight of him on the path to his death in the water—and, what was most extraordinary, she remembered it perfectly. She had a sudden urge to find Paul and tell him . . . but no, then she'd have to tell him what she'd done.

Why was Michael ill? Was it a coincidence—had he perhaps eaten something that disagreed with

349

him? But the symptoms—the watery cold and the headache—seemed like they could be, somehow, effects of being hit on the head and held underwater. What would have happened to her if he'd killed her moon-body? He'd aimed for her heart but the blade had only scratched her skin. She peered down her dress; a thin red line crossed her abdomen, neither a cut nor a weal—just a red line. Michael might have intended to murder me, she thought, but I beat him easily, and when I could have spared him, I held him under. Should I be feeling terrible remorse? Would I, if I actually had killed him? She wished they could talk about it; she'd say she was sorry if he did. Maybe they could even be friends, and meet in their moon-bodies, and help each other to remember.

Her musings were interrupted by the sound of approaching voices. A couple appeared on the path and Alice recognised Mr and Mrs Macgregor —she'd met them yesterday. They were so intent on the ground in front of them that they didn't notice Alice until they were almost upon her.

'Oh, hello,' Mr Macgregor said. 'You're Alice, aren't you?'

Alice nodded. 'I was wondering, what are those sticks?'

'Ah,' he said, 'these are my divining rods. I use them to find the lines of psychomagnetic force in the earth.'

'Psychomagnetic?'

'A term I invented. Imagine, if you will, that around and within the earth is a vast web, or network of channels, like rivers or roads, through which a sort of energy moves.' He made a wavy motion with his hand. 'It flows from one place to another, and in some places crosses other lines.'

He opened a small notebook and showed Alice a map with a line marked from the temple of Hermes on the hill to the island. 'Just here,' he tapped the island, 'I found another line that crosses the first, and it seemed to come from this direction. Now watch this.'

As he walked forward the rods swung about, then settled facing inwards with an almost audible twang. 'Would you like to try? It doesn't hurt. You may not feel anything at all.'

Alice took up the rods, which were heavier than she'd expected. 'What are these made of?'

'Silver, copper, tin, nickel, lead, iron and gold. And there is a diamond in the middle of each handle, and one at each tip, but in the metal; you can't see them.'

'Gosh,' said Alice. 'How do they work?'

'Ah, complex, very complex, that. Or perhaps very simple. Depends how you look at it.'

'Douglas . . .' his wife said.

'Yes, yes.' He winked at Alice. 'The rods serve to detect and amplify the psychomagnetic energy. Just as antennae pick up wireless transmissions.'

'I see,' said Alice, who didn't, entirely.

'Go on, try,' Mrs Macgregor said. 'It may make more sense after you've tried it.'

The rods were very heavy; Alice could barely hold them up . . . then it was as though she pushed through a curtain and they became quite light. The world had gone all swimmy and strange. The air was thick, like water, her body weightless and blurry, surrounded by a tingling silvery haze as though she were in her moon-body. She stepped forward; the air parted and swirled. An image

351

flickered at the edge of her vision: Michael ran at her, knife flashing. She leapt back and saw herself trip him, strike him, hold him down . . . then he reappeared, rushing forward, was tripped, drowned . . . It was like a movie, playing again and again within a sort of bubble. She realised she stood at the spot where the struggle had occurred. Instinctively she gestured the bubble away; it shattered and dissolved.

How long had she been standing like this? It felt like many minutes had passed. She took another step, and came to the edge of the . . . whatever it was.

'Did you feel it?' said Mrs Macgregor.

Alice nodded, staring at the now entirely ordinary air. Mr Macgregor took the rods from her hands.

'What was it like?' Mrs Macgregor looked wistful. 'I've never felt it myself.'

'It was like the air was all liquid and tingly,' said Alice. Liquid air? she wondered.

'Yes, that's what people tell me,' Mrs Macgregor said.

'It seems to go that way.' Mr Macgregor looked up the hill.

'St Ælfhild's pool is up there,' Alice said.

'Ah, a sacred site! Yes, we often find that the lines of psychomagnetic force pass through places that are considered holy. The question, of course, is were they holy before, and that made, or generated, or perhaps induced or stimulated the psychomagnetism, or was the psychomagnetism the *a priori* factor and its presence caused people to consider the places special, or perhaps the interaction with human consciousness affects . . .'

'Douglas . . .' said Mrs Macgregor.

'Ah yes, yes, sorry. Up there, then.' He set off, holding his rods out in front.

'Bye-bye, dear,' Mrs Macgregor said, and followed.

Alice returned to the spot where she'd seen the bubble containing her fight with Michael, but now all she got was a memory of the hate-filled look in his eyes. She had assumed that she was the hunter, and he the hunted, but perhaps she'd got that wrong.

'You've made an enemy,' a voice said.

Alice spun around. Francis sat on a rock, smoking a cigarette. He was barefoot, his trousers rolled up; one foot rested in the stream.

'Interesting place, this,' he said.

'Last night, right here, I thought I'd killed my cousin.' There, she'd said it.

'I know.' He pointed at the spot where the bubble had been. 'You've erased it now, but I read it earlier.'

'What?'

'The psychomagnetic force,' Francis said in an uncannily exact imitation of Mr Macgregor, 'is vairy strong around here.'

'What,' Alice tried to steady her voice, 'what is psychomagnetic force?'

'That which is below or within, beyond or behind the material world.'

'Ah.' Alice found something to latch on to. 'Like Plato?'

'More like his older brother.'

'I didn't know he had . . . oh.' She saw that he was teasing her. 'So, does it, is it—how can it hold a picture of something that happened?'

'It's sculpted by mind.'

Sculpted by mind, she repeated to herself, sculpted by mind. She didn't understand what it meant, but she wanted to remember. 'So when I, when Michael—did I . . . and then how . . .'

'Serious-faced Alice of the Many Questions,' Francis said. 'Slow down. Cheer up. Remember to breathe.'

Alice gulped, choked, coughed, stumbled to a rock and sat down. She didn't want to take her eyes off him in case he vanished. She sorted quickly through her questions, assigning priorities. 'Is your veritable simulacrum made out of the same thing as my moon-body?'

'You could put it like that.'

'And is it, is it like . . . is that why you're here? Where the psychomagnetic force is strong?'

'It's easy here but—and I hope you will not think me immodest—I can do it anywhere. That is, as it were, my fate. Now, enough questions. How do you know I haven't answered these questions a hundred times already?'

'I'm sorry,' Alice said.

'You're watching me like a mongoose watches a snake,' Francis said.

'Oh. Sorry. It's so nice to see you, and, well, I'm afraid you're going to disappear any minute.'

'I am, but it's nothing to be afraid of. I stopped by to say hello, and to remind you that you can call on me, if you need help, any time.' He started to fade.

'Wait! What do I do about Michael?'

'Use him,' Francis said, and with a brief shimmer, he was gone.

'Damn.' Alice extended her hands to the spot

354

where he'd been sitting, tried to sense if the air felt any different, but all traces of tingling had vanished and she couldn't recapture them.

A klaxon sounded; the regatta had begun. Strange to think that last year she'd enjoyed the regatta, had almost won. Now she was concerned with greater things—fighting, and murder, and how to remember, and what had really happened, and what to do about it.

Her stomach growled; with everyone at the regatta, she could return to the house, get some food. On the way she passed the pair of giant feet she'd made—had it been only yesterday? The ankle and heel of one had fallen like a rampart; a beetle scurried out.

She snatched a handful of scones from the kitchen and went to sit by the potting shed. She half hoped Theo would have found out about her fight with Michael, or somehow know as she often seemed to. But her great-aunt was nowhere to be seen. Perhaps she'd gone on one of her long walks. They often lasted for days. Alice looked into the shed; it was very tidy, and in the centre of the table under the window was a single upturned clay pot— Theo's signal that she'd gone.

Tired of being asked why she wasn't running silly circles round the lake in the regatta, Alice retreated to Arcadia, but there was a couple kissing on the path so she headed back to the house. The schoolroom was blessedly quiet and empty; she sat at her desk. She didn't want to think about Michael but unfortunately his presence was . . . very present. He was like a black cloud. She wanted to shove it under the carpet, push it out of her mind. The whole thing might so easily

355

not have happened at all, might have been a dream. Perhaps she was going mad. Maybe it ran in the family, and she'd never known—maybe there had been other mad relations, maintained in attics or cabins, and she could join them, be looked after and left alone. She rather fancied the idea.

She heard a door open and close and peeked out into the hall. Mavis was leaving Roger's room; Alice intercepted her. 'Is Michael still in bed?'

'Yes, Miss Alice, I've been sitting with him, the poor lad, but he's sleeping now so I'm popping out for a cup of tea.'

Alice crossed to the door, listened, heard nothing, opened it and tiptoed in. Michael lay flat on his back with a poultice on his forehead and one on his chest. She crept closer. His breathing was shallow and uneven and he looked rather grey. Gosh, she thought, he's really not well.

He woke with a start and stared at her, then clawed himself upright. Her twinge of sympathy evaporated at the sight of the malevolent look in his eyes. 'What's the matter, Michael?' she said. 'I only came by to see how you're feeling.'

He scrabbled in the bedclothes, getting as far away from her as he could.

'Poor Michael. Did you have a bad dream, or was it something else?'

He tried to squeeze himself into the corner; his eyes darted from side to side.

'Sit still. I'm not going to hurt you.'

He pulled his knees to his chest.

'Just this minute,' Alice said, for the pleasure of seeing him twitch. 'You. Leave. Me. Alone. Say Yes, Alice.'

He swallowed. 'Yes, Alice.'

356

'And leave Daniel alone.' She stabbed her finger at him and he flinched.

'Yes, Alice.'

The look in his eyes, though fearful, was still full of hate, and a chill ran down her spine. With a final glare, and a shake of her finger, she backed out of the room.

She started downstairs, starving again. The sound of cheering rose from the shore; the regatta had ended and Tustian was supervising the laying out of a lunch buffet on the terrace. Alice grabbed a few sandwiches and sat on the steps as the guests trooped up to the house. Uncle Richard and Aunt Cecily, she saw, kept to themselves. She could only hope they weren't planning to live at Farundell. Maggie was the best person to ask, but also the hardest to catch on her own, and it wasn't until coffee was being served that Alice managed to slip on to the end of her mother's chaise longue.

'Ah, there you are, darling,' Maggie said. 'Where have you been? Stephen thought you'd said you weren't well, and you missed the regatta, and you weren't in your room. I thought you liked the regatta. We worried you were coming down with whatever poor Michael seems to have.' Maggie reached out and lifted Alice's chin. 'Are you all right, sweetheart?'

'I'm fine. I didn't feel like the regatta this year.' On her mother's arm was a bracelet in the form of a green snake coiled three times around. 'That is a really nice bracelet,' she said.

'Alice interested in jewellery? Perhaps you *are* unwell. Or perhaps a sign that you are my daughter after all. If you like it, it's yours.' Maggie twisted it off her wrist and put it on Alice's; it

357

wrapped itself around with a series of little metallic snicks.

Alice moved it up and down her arm. It was made of enamelled scales linked by a complex, hidden arrangement of metal parts that kept it coiled and springy. 'This,' she said, 'is really wizard. Thank you. Now I don't need a tattoo.'

'Thank heaven for that,' Maggie said. 'Are there any other impending disasters I should know about, fend off with other bits and bobs?'

'Just one, actually, but I don't think a bracelet will help. I heard Uncle Richard was standing for Parliament . . .'

'And you think that would be a disaster—for the Empire? Well, you're probably right, but any nation stupid enough to ask Richard to govern it deserves whatever it gets.'

'Oh Maggie. Stop teasing. But they're not going to live here, are they?'

'Don't you like them?'

'I'm not that keen on Michael.' Alice decided to be forthright where she could. 'He's . . .' She pondered the possible adjectives. Sneaky. Vicious. Vengeful. Murderous. 'He's not very nice. He called Daniel a loony.'

'Ah. No, you're right, that's not very nice. But I expect he doesn't know any better. People can easily be misled by appearances. Perhaps if he got to know Daniel. Why don't you take Michael with you sometime when you visit?'

Not bloody likely, Alice thought. 'So they're staying here?'

'And that would be so terrible?'

Alice rolled her eyes.

Maggie relented. 'No, they will not be coming to

358

live at Farundell, but they'll stay for a few weeks while they look for a house. Richard will stand for Parliament, a safe seat in Devon somewhere, God help those poor pig farmers or whatever they are. I can't think of anyone in this family who has ever shown the slightest inclination towards politics, but there's always a first. Michael will go to boarding school. Poor Georgie will be married off as soon as possible, before that puppy fat turns to lard. There. Now you know as much as I do. Are you satisfied?'

'Yes, thank you very much. So it's over now, the quarrel with Percy?'

'Fishing, eh? I'd have thought that with all your sources of information and powers of persuasion you'd know more than anyone else.'

'No one seems to know, or if they do they're not talking. I think I'm old enough to be told these things—I mean, if I don't know what subjects to avoid, how can I have a conversation with them?'

'What a clever argument, darling. Very well. You should avoid the subject of religion.'

'The entire subject of religion?'

'To be on the safe side, yes, but in particular do not mention Christianity, or quote your grandfather's words on the subject, or anyone else's for that matter, and better not mention Jarlath at all, ever, or remark upon it if they attend church, or answer if they ask why you do not attend . . .'

'Not answer if I'm asked? Isn't that a bit rude?'

'Better to be a bit rude than a lot rude, which you might well become if drawn into a conversation. Just excuse yourself, say you remembered an urgent appointment, or a lesson,

359

or something. As a last resort say you have to pee. That always works.'

21

By Sunday night, half the guests had left, and—what a relief!—Sophie had returned to her own room. Michael remained, like a bad smell, though he'd been moved into the nursery. Alice was reluctant to sleep—she didn't know what might happen. She sat up late reading *The Faerie Queene*. She'd grown rather irritated with Britomart, whom she supposed she ought to like and admire, but whose name sounded so much like a scouring powder that Alice always pictured her in an apron with a bucket and mop, smiling and blonde like the happy ladies in advertisements. Unable to concentrate on Spenser, she picked up a book that Sophie had left behind, but it was all about voodoo and zombies lurking in dark alleys, and she put it down again with a sigh. Artemis went to the door and miaowed, but she was in season. 'You know perfectly well you can't go out,' Alice told her.

She played with the snake bracelet. She'd never had anything she liked so much, other than books, of course. But this was unique; she felt it had come in answer to her need, to help her remember. She would wear it always, never take it off. It looked at her with golden eyes and seemed to smile as she fell asleep.

About an hour later Alice woke from a dream in which she'd been trapped under a landslide and found herself still unable to move. She couldn't even open her eyes, though from behind her closed lids she saw everything. A huge black animal-like form crouched on her chest, holding her down. Artemis, tail bushy and fur erect, glared at it from the top of the wardrobe. The little green snake uncoiled from her wrist and slid up her arm, brought its head near her ear. 'This is serious,' it hissed.

Help me, Alice tried to say, but couldn't make a sound.

'Oh, I can't help, not much, not against one of those horrid black things. It wouldn't even notice if I bit it.'

The thing grew heavier, thicker, darker. Francis! she thought as hard as she could, shouting with all the power of her mind. Francis, help!

And there he was, solid and real, in a brocade dressing gown, reclining on the bed beside her. 'You've got yourself a nasty wee beastie,' he said, and pushed the thing aside with his elegantly slippered foot. 'Or perhaps we should say, it has you.'

'Thank you!' Alice leapt out of bed. The creature emanated hostility; it was struggling in a peculiarly horrid, mechanical way to get at her, but Francis wouldn't let it. Artemis was making a soft, continuous growling sound. 'What on earth is it?'

'Oh, it's a nasty wee beastie, as I said. And it's not on earth at all. Who sent it, is the question you should ask.'

Alice knew at once who had sent it—the thing somehow smelled of Michael, and its cloudy black form, now bear-like, now panther-like, exuded the same concentrated malevolence. 'This is Michael, isn't it?'

'Well, not Michael himself, but the best—or worst—he can do at the moment. He's a bit, shall we say, enfeebled, thanks to you.'

'I ordered him to leave me alone, and he said he would.'

'Well, guess what? This is the real world. People don't always do what they say they will. Why should you think he would obey you unless you have some means to coerce his will? Besides, he may not even know it's out and about. He's not all that much better at this than you are.'

'Why couldn't I move?'

'You were scared, so you tried to wake up too fast, got stuck between your moon-body and your earth-body. If you'd gone straight into your earth-body, you wouldn't see the beastie, so you wouldn't be able to deal with it. You'd think it was a bad dream, and forget as fast as you could. But it would still be here.'

Alice noticed her earth-body lying in bed. 'Oh,' she said. 'I see.'

'Come on,' Francis said, 'let's send it back, shall we? You, beastie!' He pointed at it. The thing ceased its relentless scrabbling and lifted what might be its head. 'Return whence you came.'

It turned away, shambled through the wall and along the corridor; Francis and Alice followed it into the nursery, where it oozed up Michael's bed and vanished into his sleeping form.

'And stay there,' Francis said.

Alice yawned, and an irresistible, comfortable heaviness pulled her back to her room. 'Why am I so tired?'

'This is hard work,' Francis said.

'Will I remember this?'

'I don't know.'

Alice hovered for a moment over her earth-body. 'I really want to remember.'

'That's the first step,' Francis said, and Alice tumbled through a brief twist of vertigo to settle in with a click. She could sense a dream world hovering near and was floating towards it when a sharp pain in her wrist brought her fully awake.

'Did you bite me?' she asked the bracelet. Of course it didn't answer. She rubbed her eyes and looked around the room. She'd fallen asleep with the bedside lamp still on. Why was Artemis on top of the wardrobe? In a flash, like a gate flung wide, it all came rushing back. She stared through the intervening walls towards the nursery. If she narrowed her eyes and concentrated very hard, she imagined that she could see right through to Michael, asleep in his bed with his horrid beastie. Would it be like this every night, having to fight him off? How to make him stop? What had Francis said? A means to coerce his will.

Sophie's book lay on the bedside table; in it, she remembered, a witch-doctor made a doll, named it and stuck pins in it to make someone ill. Might that work? One way to find out. She got up, pulled on her dressing gown and opened the top drawer of her dresser. Six Arcadians lay in a row. She selected one. 'Sorry about this,' she said. 'After Michael goes away, I'll make sure you have a really nice life.'

She undressed it and prepared the candle and basin. When all the appropriate ceremonies had been completed, she wrote 'Michael Damory' on a ribbon and tied it around his neck. 'You are Michael Damory,' she whispered into its ear three

363

times. She found a pin and with the doll in her hand crept along the hall to the nursery. Very cautiously she touched the pin to the doll's foot; Michael's leg twitched. Her heart was pounding. She stuck the pin in quite hard and he woke up with a yelp.

'I told you to leave me alone,' she said, and pricked him again.

'Ow! What . . . I . . .'

'I really mean it,' Alice said. 'I'm sorry I killed you, but you attacked me first, and if you don't leave me alone I'll kill you again.' She held up the doll. 'This is you, see?' She touched the pin to his head; he cried out and flapped his hands as though bees were stinging him.

'I can do whatever I want to you.' Alice closed her hand around the doll and squeezed; Michael gasped and clawed at his throat. 'OK,' she said, 'that's good. You should get some sleep now.'

She had neglected to close the door of her room; Artemis was gone. Damn!

*   *   *

Farundell drained of its guests slowly through the morning. Percy didn't participate in the leave-taking; he'd said goodbye to everyone yesterday while speaking of other things. He listened to the dim clatter on the stairs, the crunch of gravel as cars swept out of the drive, the muted chatter of unfamiliar voices as servants brought valises down. He wished that Richard and Cecily were leaving as well. He'd had a word with Tustian, and mentioned a particular room, at the opposite end of the house . . . of course Tustian had already installed them there. Percy didn't know why he'd decided to let them stay. Perhaps because tolerating their presence was marginally less awful than a fight with Richard. He hadn't the strength for a battle.

There was a soft knock at the door and Henry entered. 'Mr Winter is here, sir.'

Percy pushed the blanket from his knees. 'Please sit down, Mr Winter. Thank you for coming to see me. May I call you Arlen? I'd not dared hope to hear my son play again. I don't know what you've done, or how, or why, but I'm so glad you've come, and I want you to know you're always welcome.'

'Thank you,' Arlen said. 'You're very kind, you're all very kind. Daniel has asked me to give you a message. He was going to write a note and seemed surprised when I reminded him you wouldn't be able to read it yourself. So he told me to say that he knows he has been a trial to you, and is sorry for the distress he has caused, and grateful for the indulgence—he was particular about that word—of everyone, including the servants. Sometimes, you know, he's not aware how much time has passed; he speaks as though the war was just a year or two ago. But if I correct him he never takes it amiss.'

Percy listened hungrily. Arlen carried a fresh, immediate sense of Daniel's reality like his scent of clean linen and lavender toilet water. 'Never takes it amiss,' he repeated softly. 'No, he wouldn't.'

'He asked me to give you this,' Arlen said. He took Percy's hands and, turning them palm upward, placed in them a hard, heavy, smooth ball. 'It's his favourite stone, he told me, because it's

365

nearly a perfect sphere, shaped just by nature. It's red in colour, by the way, a deep red.'

Percy turned it in his hands. It was very warm, or perhaps it was that his hands were always cold now. 'Thank you,' he said, and couldn't say any more. After Arlen left he held it to his heart, and when Henry brought his lunch tray he turned his face away.

*   *   *

Paul lay back against Sylvie's silk pillows and sipped his whisky. The candlelight flickered, the curtains moved in a warm breeze, an owl called from the woods.

In the week since the picnic they'd returned to their routine of afternoon fucks in various awkward places and these late-night, more leisured sessions. What Paul did afterwards, he told no one, even when Sylvie, prodded, began to remember some of the dreams which he'd entered and altered.

She stood naked at the bathroom door and walked across the room, slowly so he could admire her. He reached for the camera. 'Don't move,' he said, opened the shutter and held his breath as he counted out the seconds. These candlelit pictures were always blurred, but he liked that. A flash would ruin everything. Click. His hand moved to the *Pymander*.

'You love that book more than me,' Sylvie said.

Paul laughed.

She took the book from his hand, opened it and read, ' "The soul in the body is straightaway misled by pleasure and sorrow, grief and delight." Fuck

366

me again.' She stretched out on the bed.

'In a minute,' Paul said. 'I want to try something.' He retrieved the book and sat in a chair across the room, holding the camera steady on his knees. 'Now lie very still and when I tell you, get up and walk away from the bed.' He opened the shutter, counted to fifty. 'Now,' he said, and released the shutter when she'd left the frame.

'Every thing that is, is moved by a Soul,' said *Pymander*.

'Do it again,' said Paul, 'but move more slowly.'

'No,' said Sylvie. She lay down and put her hand between her legs. Click. 'Time is manifest as Desire.'

Paul put the camera and book aside and replaced her hand with his cock. He looked into her eyes. Was she there? He pressed in. Are you there, are you there? She opened her mouth, closed her eyes. Desire, said Mr Pym, ever chases itself and finds itself not.

*   *   *

He left Sylvie sleeping and went downstairs, poured himself a drink at the sideboard in the music room and stepped out to the terrace. Later he would maraud her dreams, but now he wanted . . . He didn't know.

What do you want? said Mr Pym.

I don't remember.

He went to his room, lay on his bed, stared at the familiar ceiling. He'd thought he sallied forth an adventurer, a conqueror, but now? Could he choose not to do this? He craved it like a drug, the power it gave him to mould her dreams, to obsess

367

her, to possess her. But though he always found her, he always lost her, too, and was abandoned in his own nightmares, searching through cities, jungles and deserts, in crowds and among dancing throngs. The dreams all ended in the same place: the mud, the crater, the bodies. And he remembered it all.

The tug of vertigo slipped through his skin and he rose into the night. Sylvie, he thought. He swam to her through the dense, liquid light, hovered over her bed and slid into her mind.

He rows with long, slow strokes across the moon-metalled surface of the lake. He's naked, his skin red with heat, his cock erect. Sylvie sits in the stern and opens her blouse, shows him her breasts.

'Let's go to the island,' she says.

Paul pulls at the oars; every stroke is like fucking her. She stretches one leg so their calves touch, lifts her skirt and shows him her cunt.

The boat grates on to the shingle; he catches her at the shore, presses her into the stones, fucks her among the lapping waves. The moon shines in her face, she dissolves in the light and slips through his hands. He's holding only mud, mud between his fingers and mud in his mouth. He's alone and lost in no-man's-land. The shelling has stopped and in the silence that fills the night a voice calls his name. He struggles to the edge of the crater.

'It's Time,' says Mr Pym.

His father stands above: gold braid gleaming, sabre drawn. Not a speck of dirt mars the white breeches, the polished boots. He smiles, lifts the sabre, slices off Paul's hands, then his arms. There's no pain, not even surprise. Paul waits; the next blow severs his legs and he drops to the ground. His father looks at him, the question in his eyes.

'*Surrender,*' *says Mr Pym.*

Yes. The cool metal slides through his throat. His head falls; he gazes up, wide eyed. In the middle of the night, the sun blazes in the black sky. Oh I see, he thinks. Now I see. The light stabs him like a blade and he's falling . . .

When he opened his eyes his father was standing at the foot of his bed. A toxic cloud of fear numbed his limbs; he couldn't move. Wake up, he shouted at himself, wake up now! With a sickening twist he slammed awake, panting and sweating. The figure was still there. He flung himself at it and wrestled it to the ground; he felt as though he was grappling with some great force, but it slid away.

'Paul? You all right?' Stephen knocked at the door.

There was nothing under his hands; he was alone in the room. 'I'm fine, Stephen, sorry, just tripped over something.'

He sat in his chair and smoked, and didn't dare go back to sleep.

*   *   *

The letter from his sister, dated eight days earlier, arrived the next afternoon.

Dear Paul,
Father is dying. He suffered another stroke last week; the next will finish him. He has settled all his affairs; I am to have the house and an income, the rest is going to charity. There is nothing for you, but I'm sure you expected

that.

    Your loving sister, Muriel

  No, thought Paul, not dying. Dead. He died last night. He'd crushed the letter into his fist so tightly his fingers hurt; he released them, smoothed it out and reread it.

  He didn't need the letter; he knew. My father is dead. Father is dead. Dead. The words hit him like stones. Dead. My father is dead. Rage washed over him. How dare he die before I killed him myself? The bastard, the fucking bastard. A sudden exultation seized him; he leapt up and wanted to shout. My father is dead, dead, at last he's dead and I survived! He's dead and I'm free. He thought he would float off his feet, so light did he feel. He's dead, he wanted to scream. He'd dead, dead, dead, and I'm alive, I'm fucking alive! He ran out of the house and up the hill to the chapel. Sylvie was on the ladder, brush in hand. He remembered nothing of crossing the floor, of her descent to his arms, of the rapid dispersal of their clothing; with one long gasp he was inside her.

*   *   *

Paul floated in a sea of light. The last thing he remembered was . . . Sylvie, framed by the sun, moon and stars. He opened his eyes; the sun, moon and stars still wheeled above him. Were they moving or was he? A sense of motion pervaded his mind, though he knew, with another part of himself, that he was lying on the sofa in the chapel, Sylvie at his side. He blinked; sun, moon and stars halted and he recognised the painted apex of the ceiling. Golden light filled the air, not stopping at his skin. Sylvie was . . . there. No, here. She was. Where? He tried to feel the skin between them but couldn't find it. He looked down the length of their bodies. There were limbs, entangled, a shimmer in a haze of heat. Some, he knew, must be his, some hers. He couldn't recall how many one was supposed to have.

He felt as though he was falling, impossibly, upward. He tried to focus on a detail but he fell right through the woven pattern of cloth on a cushion as though it had no more solidity than the air. How is it, he wondered, that I'm not falling through everything all the time? You are, said Mr Pym, and the amusement in his voice was so contagious that laughter rose within Paul and spilled over.

'What's so funny?' Sylvie said.

Paul couldn't answer; he moved his fingers, stroked her with a bright effervescence. See? It's funny because . . . The words slipped away like fish in the currents.

Time moved; sun slanted through the tall windows. Outside the light was flickering green-gold; inside, three birds flew through a forest beneath the waving rays of a gilded sun. Sylvie stood at her table, wearing his shirt and nothing else, cracking eggs. She separated the whites and then, holding the yolks with delicate fingertips, pierced their transparent skin-sacs with a scalpel and let them drip into a bowl.

'What colour are you making?' Paul said.

'I want a nice dark red.' She pointed to the sketched figure of a man among the trees near St. Ælfhild's pool and searched through the jars of

371

pigments. Paul loved the names: Caput Mortuum, Burnt Sienna, Terre Vert, Red Ochre, Mars Black, Indian Red, Titanium White, Ultramarine Blue— made from lapis lazuli, she'd told him. She spooned and mixed, added a few drops of oil.

Take off the shirt, he thought; she looked at him, took it off, dipped a paintbrush in her red paint and drew swirls around her breasts, a wandering trail down her belly.

'Christ! Who's that?' She dropped the brush and pointed to the window; a face ducked out of sight and there were sounds of someone crashing through the bushes. 'I think it was Michael,' she said.

Paul pulled on his trousers and went to the door; running footsteps receded down the hill. When he returned Sylvie had dressed. 'He's a bit creepy, that boy,' she said. 'I wonder how long he was there.'

22

Very early one morning Theo found herself at the gates of Farundell; her feet had brought her home. As she walked up the long drive she felt herself congealing. Where am I? She recognised that view down to the lake. Farundell. Who am I? Theodora Damory. The words fixed amorphous aether into solid form. This one, not that one. Here, not there. From infinite possibilities, a line, a direction, momentum, a pattern that was home and self, theatre and alembic, prison and manifestation.

It would be some hours before she'd be able to

go indoors, so she sat in the herb garden and watched the light moving on the lake. Madagascar came to rub against her legs. The sun rose, grew warm. She raised her hands, cupped the golden juice, drank it in.

Sounds began to emerge from the house behind her: the familiar voices and clatter of breakfast. Percy appeared on Henry's arm.

'There she is, sir,' Henry said, and guided Percy to sit beside her.

Percy waved Henry away. 'You were gone for more than a week. Richard and Cecily are here.'

'I saw them before I left.'

'Hah. Don't suppose that was why? Wish I could wander off whenever I felt like it.' He coughed. 'I think I will die soon.'

Theo didn't reply.

'You make no demur,' he said.

'It is unknowable; how can I demur or concur?'

'Well, I believe it is so. What I want to know is about Daniel. What will happen to Daniel?'

'Oh Percy, I'm not some fortune-teller.'

'You know. Or if you don't you can find out. Don't tell me that's not true.'

'I do tell you it's not true. The possibilities are nearly always infinite. You speak as if the book is written and ask me to skip ahead a few chapters. It's not written, it's being written, and there's not one book, but an infinity of books. You choose the line of your own experience. I don't know what it will be.'

'Oh God, you sound like Odelia. What use is your bloodless metaphysics? It's this book I care about. Will Daniel be all right? That's all I want to know. Surely you can tell if things will go well for

373

him, or if he'll have to suffer any more. Please, Theo. I know you can look, I know you can see.'

'No, I'm sorry, I really cannot. Where family is concerned, and dear friends—I cannot see. I locked those doors long ago, for very good reasons, and threw away the key.' She took Percy's hand and held it between her own. 'Surely you understand. If one saw something bad happen to someone, how could one not try to avert it? And even without trying, just knowing, or suspecting or fearing would alter everything. Might even be exactly what brings it about. If I allowed myself this knowledge, how could I ever let myself care about anyone?'

'Fat lot of good you are, Dora,' Percy said. 'What about Arlen, then? He came to see me. He and Daniel—aren't they? I heard it in his voice. He's all right, you think?'

'He seems like a good person to me.'

'Well, then. As long as they keep quiet about it.' After a time he called to Henry and was helped back into the house.

Theo played with a sprig of thyme and listened to the strengthening rays of the sun. She let herself slip down among the roots and earth, into the soothing slow pulse of the stones. She noticed Alice, at first, only as a blur.

'I brought you some tea.' Alice held out a steaming mug.

'Thank you.' Theo took it and tried to remember what one was meant to do with it.

'You were gone a long time,' Alice said. 'Lots of stuff happened.' Theo didn't say anything and Alice wondered if she'd heard. She tried a direct question. 'Where did you go?'

'I don't know. Here and there.'

'Did you stay with friends?'

'With people, you mean? No.'

'But you must have stayed somewhere. Where did you sleep? Where did you eat?'

Theo made an effort. 'Sleeping and eating are not as necessary as they seem.'

'Don't you get tired and hungry?'

'No.'

'But what if you get lost?'

'How can you be lost if you have no destination?'

'But then how do you get back?'

'I really don't know, Alice. It just happens.'

'You mean it might not? You might wander on and on? But you wouldn't, would you?'

'It's possible, but I don't think likely.'

'Please don't go without telling me.'

'Don't worry, I'll never be where you can't reach me. And thank you for the tea, it's delicious.'

Alice made her way to the kitchen garden where she picked some plums and cherries. She was going to spend the day on the island. Michael had been avoiding her, which was good, though she carried his doll in her pocket just in case. Roger had taken to following him everywhere, while Sophie had attached herself to Georgie like a limpet, because Georgie let her try on all her frocks.

She heard a familiar miaow. Artemis strolled from among the tomatoes and rolled in the grass. 'Where have you been, naughty girl?' She hadn't been seen for a week. The cat writhed with pleasure as Alice rubbed her stomach. 'Oh Artemis, you're pregnant, aren't you?'

Madagascar reclined in the shade of a rhubarb

leaf, looking smug. Alice broke off the leaf to carry the fruit and went into the house for more supplies—an old rug and some cushions, a dozen books and enough food to last the whole day. It took two trips to get everything down to the dock where her coracle waited, neatly patched by Daniel. Alice paddled slowly across the lake and around the island to the picnic meadow. She unloaded everything and carried it up to the tree house, then took *The Faerie Queene* and a sandwich and made her way to the hidden pool below the temple of Aphrodite.

*   *   *

'Almost finished, I think,' Percy said.

Paul smiled; he'd said that before.

Death leaned against the mantel, waiting. Percy liked the fellow, his silence, his close observation of Percy's tick-by-tock dissolution.

Percy coughed and laid aside his pipe. The cough had worsened lately, but it didn't matter. A certain amount of time remained and though he didn't know its length, it was without doubt finite. And a certain amount left to tell, also finite. *Finito ergo sum*, he thought. I end therefore I am.

Death smiled.

What about everybody else? Percy asked. What happens to all the other dying people while you're here with me?

I'm there too.

Percy tried to picture that. Is it because you are so large or because you are so many? He felt like a child, with his simple questions.

You *are* a child, Death said. Look. He tapped

376

Percy's forehead and space abruptly unfolded, and kept on unfolding, faster and faster until Percy, head tingling, hovered within his expanded self, and further, until he floated in the space between atoms. He peered into them as they drifted by, slow as amoebae on the current. Within each one was a tiny Death, tick-tocking away.

With a wave of his hand Death plucked him back; space collapsed and Percy fell into his tedious old body. Death resumed his patient contemplation, bony fingers tapping, tick-tock; Percy found his way back to the story.

'When I first came to live among them, the Isu treated me as a child and taught me all the things that children learn, about nature, the ways of animals and, most importantly, the ways of spirits, which were far more dangerous to an ignorant simpleton such as myself. I was put in the charge of the *heka-wy*—that is their term for someone who deals with the spirit-world. She was a very old woman who had, most unusually, left the jungle in her youth and gone to live in a town, where she'd learned Portuguese and a smattering of English, and acquired a gloomy, cynical view of the influence of Europeans in her land. She had returned to her people with a poignant fatalism— she knew they were doomed. And in her lifetime— which I judged to be about fifty years, though she looked a hundred at least—she had indeed seen the decimations of alcohol, Christianity, wage labour and disease brought by the rubber-tappers and missionaries.

'She told me I was the sort of person who walked around carrying his house so that he would never have to go out, so thick-headed and stumbling did

377

I seem to her, so ignorant. She regarded me as we might a deaf, dumb and blind person. And feeble-minded, too. She thought I was very amusing in my witless way.'

Percy hears her cackling laugh as she summons him for his daily lesson; she's waiting in her little canoe made of the trunk of a tree, hollowed out and stained red. 'Percy-person!' she shouts. 'Come out of your how-ouse!' He climbs in, nearly upsetting the delicate craft; she clucks in irritation and hisses at him, 'Still! Why can you not ever be still?'

The water has risen to the treetops, all the birds have gone and it's unnaturally silent. She raises her hand to her mouth and calls, Caw, caw, cawcaw; a bird appears, circling above. Caw, it answers, circles lower and departs. A vivid red feather descends slowly to her hand. She gives it to Percy. 'For good luck,' she says. 'Because one day you will leave.'

'My memory of what happened is still incomplete. I know how it began, I know how it ended, but I don't know why. All I remember is that I awoke at first light in a small clearing. I had no idea where I was or how I'd got there. What was more frightening, I had no idea who I was. I remembered nothing, nothing at all.

'I stood up and discovered that I was naked and bleeding; beneath hundreds of scratches my body was scored with a pattern of deeper cuts. It meant nothing to me, only pain. The smell of distant cooking fires made me retch, but it drew me. My mind was functioning at a very primitive level; I had discerned that I was a wounded animal who needed food and shelter. And I had some dim

378

notion that I should seek others of my kind.

'When I staggered out of the jungle—a naked white man, covered in blood—I must have seemed like an evil apparition. I was greeted with screams of terror and would very likely have been speared on the spot if old Yano, the tracker, had not recognised me. I'd returned, somehow, miraculously, to Lamarca. I realised later I must have covered more than sixty miles.

'They treated me as if I'd been resurrected from the dead; the last they'd seen of me, more than a year previously, I'd been heading off in search of the mythical Isu village. The guides I'd hired had come back to Lamarca with the story that I'd simply disappeared into the night without leaving any trail. It had confirmed their suspicion that I was an *encantado*.

'About half the village, I later learned, now even more convinced that I was an evil magician, wanted to drive me back into the jungle forthwith, but Yano, pointing out the absence of blowhole and straw hat, argued in my favour. Of course at the time I understood nothing of this; I would not have understood even if they'd spoken English. I recognised that I was the object of dispute; I was terrified. I sensed Yano was my only hope and I'm afraid I clung to his ankles throughout the debate. I know all this because the whole drama was re-enacted many times; it became a legend.

'Yano and his family took me in. They tended my cuts, they fed and washed me and every day they told me who I was. After a few weeks, when the cuts had healed and I had come to understand that I was a poor crazy white man named Percy, I went to live on my own in a small hut at the edge of the

379

village. Yano's sister continued to cook for me. I believed that was my whole life.

'But I suffered alarming lapses; I'd come to myself suddenly in a strange place, go through all manner of panic and fear, then realise I was in my own hut. A strange man would appear at my door and we would argue, I would become angry, then I'd recognise Yano. Worst of all were the hallucinations: an ordinary object—a pot, a stone, an axe—would be transformed before my eyes into a severed head, or foot, or arm. I began to realise there was a very great deal I couldn't remember. My mind was full of holes. Insomnia further eroded my sanity. Whenever I fell asleep I'd be overcome almost immediately by a dreadful sensation of falling; my screams would wake the entire village.

'Finally even Yano had enough of me. When the next rubber company boat stopped on its way downriver to Manaus he gave me into the care of its captain, who kindly provided a tattered cast-off shirt and trousers to replace my loincloth and delivered me, like a filthy package, to the British outpost. I'd long since been presumed perished in the jungle but tropical inefficiency had insured that the boxes I'd left in their care remained.

'I was taken in hand by the junior clerk, a mousy bespectacled youth called Ferris. He brought me to a room whose right angles I found very disquieting. It was full of unfamiliar objects, sharp-cornered and possibly dangerous: chair, table, bed. It was strange and unpleasant to feel trees lying flat beneath my feet: the wooden floor. I missed the jungle, the green, the bird calls, the smells. I missed the uneven earth, I missed my loincloth, I

380

missed my hammock and my friends.

'That first night I tried to return. I got as far as the edge of the British compound when I tripped over Ferris, dead drunk in the path. He appointed himself my guardian, took me back to my room and locked me in.

'The next morning began my re-indoctrination. Ferris arrived with coffee in a china cup, food on a plate, a fork and a knife. He made me eat, then took me to the bathhouse and the barber, where he pointed out my reflection in a mirror—I didn't recognise myself at all.

'My boxes had been brought to my room and Ferris helped me to open them. "This is a tweed suit," he said, holding it up. "It has a jacket and trousers. It's made of wool, touch it. It comes from . . ." he read the label, ". . . Henry Poole, Savile Row. That is in London. Do you remember London? Do you remember buying this suit? How old were you? How old are you now? This is a necktie, made of striped silk. Feel it, it's very fine. The colours mean it is an Eton tie. Did you attend Eton? You were a small boy once; do you remember that? What is your first memory? What is your last memory?"

'It took me weeks to realise that Ferris was blind drunk all the time; his manner was precise and controlled; he was orderly and considerate. He was, perhaps, madder than I, but he was effective. I began to remember; fragment by fragment, I pieced myself together, though one piece was missing—whatever it was that had happened on the night of high water, under the full moon. I remembered the *heka-wy*; I remembered the months alone in the initiation hut. I studied the

381

faint remains of the pattern cut into my skin but I had no recollection of how it got there.

'Gradually I realised that I'd left behind a disaster, though I couldn't remember what it was. All I knew was that I'd made a terribly wrong choice and I had to return.

'I arranged an expedition, only to watch as one after another every aspect of my plans fell apart. I hired a guide; he left to tend his sick mother. The next one died. I hired porters; they disappeared one night and I never found out why. My supplies were eaten by rats or ruined by rain. I developed an abscess in my foot that would not heal. Every boat I tried to hire or buy developed engine problems; one even sank. Soon everyone was avoiding me; they said I was cursed. Even the Catholic missionary, a little cockroach of a Portuguese, made the sign against the evil eye when he thought I wasn't looking. I was becoming more deranged every day; the more my plans failed, the more determined I became. I no longer knew why I had to return to the Isu, only that I must.

'A profound malaise afflicted me, worsening steadily; it was as if the thing I couldn't remember was a great black hole into which I was falling. The darkness, the sense of oppression and futility, a creeping numbness of all my senses. Since I never slept, I dreamed while awake. And all the dreams ended in the same place: the river, the moonlight, terror. The *heka-wy* said . . .' He reached for the memory that had always eluded him. 'She said . . . something about a door. And then she showed me . . . I can't remember.

'Ferris at last persuaded me to return to Europe.

He booked my passage, paid my bills and escorted me to my cabin on a steamer bound for the coast. He made me drink a toast to a safe journey, and another to the Queen, one more to the Empire, and a last one to friends parted but never forgotten. When I woke up and decided to jump ship and escape to the jungle he'd disappeared; I was locked in and we were under way. By the time I got to Belem I was resigned to my fate.

'At Belem I got a passage north to Georgetown, and from there the clipper to Le Havre. On the way I acquired the final patina of English manners; I knew what to say and what not to say, when and how to eat, how to shave and dress, but I felt as though I was acting a role. There was a gap between me and my body, my language, my fellow humans. Only Odelia would be able to heal it, but I had yet to meet her; instead I took myself desultorily to clinics in France, Switzerland, Germany. I endured examinations and procedures, endless questions and the latest experimental treatments, but no one could find out what was wrong with me or relieve any of my symptoms. Finally, having nowhere else to go, I came home to Farundell.

'Although I had never met her, Odelia was waiting for me. I arrived on a weekend in July that I'd failed to remember was the annual picnic and regatta. Old Akers rowed me across to the island. My illness caused me to see everything as though through a dark lens, and not just physically dark, although the permanent twilight was a foreshadowing of the blindness that would take more than thirty years to complete. There was a sense of obstruction, uncertainty, and dread like an insidious and pervasive fog. And beneath it all a nagging feeling, like the memory of an old wound, that I'd failed at something desperately important. All in all, I was in a very strange state of mind and more than once, as I watched that old man rowing, I thought he was indeed a Charon, and death my destination. When a woman I didn't know greeted me as I stepped from the boat, I was already halfway to another world and nothing surprised me.

'All the others were at the picnic meadow on the far side of the island. She led me straight up the cliff path to the top where rugs and cushions lay on the grass. She told me to go to sleep and, to my utter surprise, I did straight away.'

There was a knock and Henry opened the door. 'Mr and Mrs Richard Damory would like to see you, sir.'

'Oh bloody hell,' Percy said.

'Good morning, Father.' Richard gave Paul a stony look and Cecily didn't look at him at all. Paul remembered the face at the chapel window. They'd never been particularly friendly, but now there was a distinct chill in the air. What had Michael seen, and had he told his parents?

'Don't go, Paul,' Percy said. 'I'm sure this won't take long.' He sniffed. A floral scent filled the room. 'Is that your cologne, Richard?'

'It is mine,' said Cecily.

'You overdo it,' Percy said. 'What are you trying to hide? And what is it you want with me now?'

'We would prefer to speak in private,' Richard said.

'Oh for God's sake. Will you excuse us, please, Paul?' Percy thought he should make an effort to be less rude, but he couldn't help it; something about Cecily set his teeth on edge. It wasn't just her bovine Christianity; he was able to maintain civil relations with any number of Christians. It wasn't just the fussy mother hen in her—plenty of women managed that with charm. It had a lot to do with her voice, which at first seemed sweet and kind but which soon rang thin and false. She had been speaking for some time before an increasingly strained tone brought his attention to her words.

'And so we feel steps must be taken at once to remove him.'

'Remove whom?' Percy said.

'Haven't you been listening, Father?' Richard said. 'Have you no idea of what's going on under your own nose? That fellow is . . . is . . . having relations with your granddaughter.'

'Oh,' Percy said, 'you're talking about Paul and Sylvie. I know about it.'

'Father, how can you! The man is obviously a fortune hunter, probably a degenerate. We have learned that he lived in Paris.'

'Oh my. I see. Dear, dear. In that case he can be none other than Beelzebub incarnate, in which case merely removing him will do no good; he must be exorcised.'

'How can you joke about something like this? We're only speaking out of concern for poor Sylvie. She is behaving with a complete lack of discretion and could very easily do irreparable damage to her reputation.'

Percy sighed. 'Let me understand you, Richard. You believe they should be more discreet, is that right?'

'No, that's not . . .'

'And how do you know, anyway? Do you go around spying on people?'

'No, certainly not, but they've been seen . . .'

'You should consider becoming missionaries, both of you. You have all the necessary qualities: stupidity, insensitivity, and a complete inability to mind your own business.'

*   *   *

There was a satisfying slam from the door as they left, but Percy's flush of invigorating fury died fast, leaving him chilled and exhausted, and he decided not to summon Paul back. He could finish tomorrow. One more day, just one more day.

Paul rowed slowly across the placid green water. Sylvie sat in the stern; the house receded behind her shoulder. Open your blouse, he thought at her.

'It's so warm, isn't it?' She unbuttoned and parted the fabric.

Rays of cloudy sun penetrated the lake. The oars dipped beneath the surface, bent, straightened. He'd been rowing forever. Sylvie moved her leg so that it touched his. Lift your skirt, he thought, and she did, showed him her cunt, smiled.

The boat scraped on to the shingle; he chased her up the steep path and caught her at the top. She slid through his hands, danced away, posed against a column. Take off your blouse, he thought; she smiled and slipped it from her shoulders. Leaf shadows patterned her skin. I remember this, Paul thought, we've done this before. She took off her skirt and lay down in the sun. 'Fuck me,' she said.

386

Alice drowsed by the hidden pool. High above, trees swayed in a breeze; their branches touched, then waved apart. Birdsong intertwined with a drift of Daniel's violin, faint and far away. Someone was singing along. No, it wasn't singing—it sounded like an animal in pain. Alice sat up, wide awake now. She remembered the fawn; had it hurt itself? Was it trapped? The sounds were coming from above; she crept up the cliff, silent so as not to frighten it, but even before she reached the top she knew it wasn't an animal. Soft cries mingled with gasps and grunts and through the screen of shrubs there was a flash of naked limbs. She caught a glimpse of Sylvie's face as she leaned over the man; then he flung her on to her back and pinned her to the ground. Her whole body jolted as though she was being beaten.

Alice had of course studied diagrams in books, but she'd never seen anyone actually doing it. Was this love? It looked more like a battle. Sylvie's moans grew louder and the man pressed his hand over her mouth; she must have bitten it, for he pulled it sharply away and laughed, then bent to kiss her and Alice saw that it was Paul. She couldn't have looked aside if she'd wanted to, and as Sylvie's body arched and shuddered, there was a stabbing in her own belly that was both pleasure and pain.

In the silence when the cries and moans stopped, Alice's breathing sounded very loud and she began backing away. She hadn't meant to spy; she could hardly bear to imagine the embarrassment if she was caught. She'd made it halfway down the steps when there was a loud rustling from the shrubs above, the sound of Sylvie's voice, and Alice realised with horror that they were coming down to the pool. She slid the rest of the way as fast as she could, but she was trapped; in a moment they'd see her. She grabbed her book and ducked through the ivy into the grotto; she'd be safe unless they actually looked in, in which case, well, too awful to contemplate. She hoped they'd at least be quick, but they started doing it again, and she had to turn her back and cover her ears.

She stared at the wall; as her eyes grew accustomed to the darkness she could make out the different kinds of shells and to pass the time counted how many of each. When she got tired of that, she tried to follow the pattern; there were waves, and a face, and what looked like a foot among a design of flowers. What she'd never noticed before was that the shells all stopped in a vertical line; the more she stared, the more certain she became that there was a bricked-up opening. How long had it been like this? It was as covered with moss and roots as the rest of the grotto. Although she told herself it was probably nothing, or even if it was a doorway, would lead to something utterly prosaic like a clogged-up old cistern, she imagined secret chambers, undiscovered tombs, hidden treasure.

When Sylvie and Paul finally left, Alice found a flat stone and scraped away the moss, but it was less effective on the ivy, which clung with thousands of brown hairy roots like millipedes. She managed to clear a small area and tried to dig out the mortar, but the stone was useless and it was getting dark. She'd have to return in the morning, with proper tools, and with Roger and Sophie to help. It was just manual labour; they could manage that, if she supervised. On the way back she made a mental list of what they'd need: a hammer and a chisel, a torch, a candle to test for bad air (she'd read about that in a book, and it seemed like a good idea), and of course lots of food and flasks of tea to sustain them as they worked.

* * *

Sophie turned up at the dock on time the next day after lessons and helped Alice load a rowing boat—the coracle wouldn't carry the three of them. Roger came late and he brought Michael, though Alice hadn't invited him.

'Truce?' Michael smiled tentatively.

'All right,' Alice said. 'Truce.' He didn't look quite so evil when he smiled. It didn't mean the war was over, and she'd keep the doll handy.

Sophie and Roger scrambled into the stern; Alice and Michael took an oar each. They synchronised their strokes and moved out on to the lake.

After a long deliberation Alice said, 'I'm sorry I made you paddle the coracle all that way.'

'I guess it was pretty funny,' Michael said.

'Well it was, actually. But I'm still sorry. I could have showed you how.'

'Would you, some time?'

'OK.' He hadn't, Alice noticed, apologised for cutting it or even acknowledged that he had. And neither of them mentioned the murder.

389

They landed on the island and secured the boat; Alice led the way up to the temple and down the steps behind the oak.

'Gosh,' said Roger, 'I didn't even know these steps were here.'

'One just has to look closely,' said Alice, 'and one notices lots of things. Mind your feet, it's quite steep.'

'Where does this go?' Michael said.

'A secret place—you'll see.'

When they reached the bottom Alice unpacked the baskets as the others ran about, making so much noise the birds left the trees. Michael and Roger picked up Sophie and threatened to throw her in the pool; Sophie squealed and kicked and Roger nearly fell in. Alice let them horse around; they thought they were here for a picnic. She took the hammer, chisel, candle and torch into the grotto, propped the torch so it shone on the bricked-up door and began to chip away. They appeared a few seconds later.

'Wow,' Sophie said. 'What is this place?'

'It's the grotto,' Alice said. 'Shells, see?' She resumed her work.

'But what are you doing?' Roger said.

'Oh, I'm just opening this secret door I found yesterday.' As expected, they fought to take turns and Alice sat back to supervise. The first brick came loose and fell behind the wall with a clunk; at least now she was sure there was an opening of some sort. Alice held on to the torch so she'd be first to look. When the hole was big enough for her head and shoulders she peered in. All she could see were narrow steps cut into the rock, smooth and worn, descending into utter blackness. She let the others look, then they set to work pulling down the rest of the wall and sooner than she'd expected they stood before the dark stairway.

'Well,' said Michael. 'I wonder where this goes?'

'Probably only an old drain,' said Roger.

'I don't think so,' said Alice. 'Why would they have a stairway to a drain, and why would they brick it up?'

'Who is "they"?' Michael said.

'That's the question,' Alice said. 'It was bricked up for a long time.' She had an image of Francis, smiling. 'Since Francis's time, I'll bet. I'll go first, with the candle to test the air.'

'Wait, shouldn't we get someone?' said Sophie.

'Someone?' Alice said. 'I'm someone, aren't I?'

'I mean a grown-up. How do we know what's down there?'

'We don't know, that's the point,' said Roger. 'It's like a thriller. Remember that one with the tunnel under the house, and the rising water?'

'Oh for heaven's sake,' said Alice. 'So far as I can see, it's just a flight of stairs. Follow if you want.'

The air smelled stale but not dank; there was no sign of water anywhere, nor any slimy bits. Whatever this was, it wasn't a drain. Alice descended to a small landing; her torch revealed a niche with a stone lamp. The steps turned right, narrowed, and turned right again, descending to another landing. She stopped on the bottom step as the others crowded close behind. The landing was lined with empty alcoves and seemed at first to lead nowhere, but as Alice shone the torch around she saw that one shadowy alcove was deeper than the others.

'Is there anything there?' Michael peered over

her shoulder.

Alice stepped down and shone her torch directly into the alcove.

'Is that a door?' Michael said.

'Yes, I do believe that is a door.'

'Should we open it?'

Alice snorted. 'As opposed to going away? Well, I suppose we might.' She gave him the candle and the torch to hold and tried the door. It stuck at first and she had to lean on it, but it grated and yielded. The hinges made ungodly creaks.

'Pass me the candle,' Alice said. It wavered wildly, but that was only her hand shaking. She blew it out as Michael shone the torch around. The narrow beam revealed a small rectangular room with a mosaic floor and two square stone pillars supporting the low ceiling.

Michael gasped and dropped the torch; it went out. Sophie shrieked and fled; Roger and Michael fell over each other as they followed.

Alice froze, heart pounding. The light had fallen on a pale figure against the far wall, strange and monstrous, not human. She fumbled for the torch, found the switch, turned it on, willed herself to breathe.

'Bleeding Jesus, Mary and Joseph,' she whispered.

Michael reappeared at her side. 'Sorry I bolted. What is that?'

'A statue.' She steadied the torch. It showed a figure carved in stone, a man, taller than life-size, with the head of a dog, or perhaps a wolf, or a fox. Or was it a jackal? He was draped in a toga and held a staff entwined with snakes and ivy.

'Oh cripes,' said Michael. 'What is this place?'

He stood so close she felt the warmth of his body, which was all right. It's always good, she thought, to have someone to cover your back.

'Maybe it's part of the temple Francis brought from Cyprus, and somehow everybody forgot about this bit.' There were wall paintings, flaked and faded, carvings in relief, other statues in niches. The torch was failing; she gave it a shake and it went out altogether. 'Bugger.'

'Alice? Michael?' Roger called. 'Are you there?'

'Do you mean has the monster eaten us?' Alice returned to the foot of the stairs. 'Not yet, apparently. Though it's a good thing you were so brave; it might have gone very badly otherwise. Where's Sophie?'

'She's here but she won't come down.'

Alice and Michael climbed up to the grotto where Alice convened a meeting and distributed the sandwiches. 'We have to conduct a proper archaeological excavation,' she said.

'Excavation? We just walked down some steps,' said Roger.

'Well, we have to make a scientific record of the find.'

'The find?'

'You know, that's what archaeologists call what they dig up. We must take measurements, make photographs, draw plans. Like Howard Carter at the tomb of Tut-ankh-amon. I know how; I read all about it.'

'We can give guided tours,' said Michael. 'We'll call it the Lair of the Dog-Headed Demon.'

'No,' said Alice, 'it has to be open to serious scholars only.'

'Which is only you,' said Roger.

'And Stephen,' said Alice. She couldn't wait to tell him—she'd glimpsed inscriptions in both Latin and Greek.

It was later than she'd realised; as they rowed back across the lake they heard the dinner bell. A new batch of house guests had arrived and in the rushing to and fro no one asked them where they'd been. Dinner was so crowded and noisy that Alice had no chance to make the dramatic announcement she'd planned, so she spent the evening gathering torches and lanterns, measuring stick and string, notebook and pencils.

*   *   *

In the morning, before breakfast, she got Stephen to accompany her down to the dock, telling him only that she'd found something interesting, though he was clearly mystified by the baskets full of food and equipment he helped to carry. At the lakeshore they came upon Paul with his camera; Alice decided he could come too, perhaps as expedition photographer.

As they rowed across the lake Stephen tried to guess what she'd discovered. 'Human, animal, vegetable or mineral?'

Alice smiled mysteriously. 'Some of each, as a matter of fact. You'll see. Follow me,' she said, as they landed on the island and climbed the path.

She relished their exclamations of surprise at the sight of the secret pool and the grotto, their amazement at the steps cut into the rock, but most of all their stunned silence when she led them into the underground chamber and suddenly turned her torch on to the dog-headed statue. They were speechless for quite some time. It was very gratifying.

'Hermanubis,' Stephen said at last. 'Roman. Second or third century. Or a bloody good copy.'

'Who was Hermanubis?' Alice asked.

'A cross between Hermes and Anubis, the Egyptian jackal-headed deity who, like Hermes, was a psychopomp, a guide of souls.'

'Is it from Francis's temple of Aphrodite, do you think?' Alice said.

'If so, it's a juxtaposition I've never heard of. Syncretism is all very well, but . . . Ah, just as I thought.' He directed his torch to the opposite wall: in a niche was a statue of a seated woman with a baby in her arms.

'The Virgin Mary?' Alice was disappointed. 'Is this to do with St Ælfhild?'

'Not Mary.' Stephen pointed to the horns and disc on her head. 'This is a temple of Isis, and I think it might really be . . . quite old. I mean not something Francis collected and put here. Good God, do you suppose it could be the Isis after whom they named the river . . .'

'Like in *The Faerie Queene*,' Alice said.

'The Romans were all around this area and Isis was the most popular goddess of the time; there's no reason why there shouldn't be a real Roman temple here, but . . . gosh.' He moved his torch over the walls. 'Look, another Isis. One of her most common epithets is Myrionymos, because she has so many names and forms.' This one was standing on a crocodile, with a cup in one hand and a cobra twined around the other arm. Alice fingered the bracelet on her wrist.

Paul had gone along on a whim but as Alice led

them up to the temple and down to the hidden pool he felt as though he was being pulled by something other than curiosity. He had pretended surprise—evidently the secret place was not as secret as Sylvie had thought, but the surprise he expected to feel at the sight of the grotto, the steep winding stair, the underground room was strangely not there. I've always known this was here, he'd started to say, but stopped himself.

'Those old Egyptian gods always worked in threes,' Stephen was saying. 'There's Hermanubis and Isis—or Aset to give her her proper Egyptian name—and so somewhere nearby must be Asar, also known as Osiris or Serapis. Ah yes.' The adjacent wall was crowded with figures in relief. 'Remember your Plutarch, Alice: Typhon, the evil brother, traps Osiris in the stone sarcophagus; he's cast into the sea and washes up on the shore of Byblos, where a tree grows around him. The King cuts down the tree, gilds it, and uses it to support his house.'

Paul blinked; the figures looked so alive. Traces of colour remained on the reliefs, ochre and red and blue. Out of the corner of his eye he was sure he saw them move.

'Look here,' Stephen pointed. 'Isis wanders everywhere in search of Osiris. She finds him trapped in the tree and persuades the King to let her take it home to Egypt, where she, er, awakens Osiris with her magic and they . . . make a baby. Well, it's all a metaphor, you know. Never mind. See here, in the next scene Typhon finds Osiris again, dismembers him, cuts him up and scatters the pieces.'

Images flicked at the edge of Paul's vision and

there was a strange sound, like a lot of people whispering. Cuts him up, dismembers him, scatters the pieces, the pieces . . .

'And so poor Isis has to search all over again until she finds and reassembles all the pieces. All except, er, one,' Stephen said. 'Osiris goes on to become the god of the underworld, the world of night and dreams.'

Paul shook his head, turned away and busied himself lighting the lanterns Alice had brought and positioning them around the room. He tried not to look at the statues or the images on the walls for fear he'd catch them moving. As he placed the final lantern beside Hermanubis he noticed that behind the statue was not a solid wall but a low doorway. Again, somehow, he'd known it would be here.

'Alice, Stephen, come and look.'

The beams of their torches revealed a shadowed opening guarded by a pair of carved snakes.

'Ah, I knew it,' said Stephen. 'There had to be an inner chamber—for secret ceremonies, initiations and so forth.'

Above the lintel were words Alice recognised: *Thesaurum non aurum intra celatum*. 'The treasure not gold is hidden within,' she whispered.

'My God,' said Stephen, 'do you suppose it means the Farundell treasure? But why "not gold"?'

'This has something to do with Francis,' she said. 'I'm sure of it. Remember that legend about how he found the treasure and hid it again? No one knows why. Or, for that matter, what it was.' As she spoke she caught a glimpse of him smiling his foxy smile. For an instant he even seemed to have a fox's head.

Paul started and caught his breath.

'You saw him?' Alice said.

'Yes.'

'Who?' said Stephen.

'Francis,' said Paul and Alice. They looked at each other, and at the doorway. Paul stepped forward and held up his lantern, revealing a short passageway and a further dark opening beyond. He had the irrational urge to let Alice go before him as though she was a great lady, a queen or a priestess, and he had to remind himself that she was a child and it was he who should precede her into danger. If there was any danger. He inched forward, but the feeling that he was on the verge of transgressing was so strong he could barely lift his feet.

'What are you two dithering about? I want to see what's in there.' Stephen slipped between them and disappeared into the darkness. A few seconds later his voice emerged, echoing weirdly. 'Come on, you two, it's another room.'

'Ladies first,' said Paul, and bowed.

Alice willed her hand to stop shaking and made herself step forward. Francis? she thought.

Don't be afraid, he said.

Paul followed; he had to stoop through the passageway. The inner chamber was smaller than the first; the walls were covered with paintings, less faded than those in the outer room. Paul caught a glimpse of the jackal-headed Hermanubis wielding a long knife, a crowned and winged serpent, the prostrate figure of a man with an enormous erection; Stephen's torch moved quickly on. There were other animal-headed figures, male and

398

female, gods or demons, guarding a series of gateways. Across the vaulted blue ceiling spangled with stars arced the long figure of a woman, barebreasted, smiling, her graceful fingertips touching the earth. In the centre of the room stood an ornately carved stone sarcophagus; its massive lid leaned against its side.

'Is this someone's tomb?' said Alice.

'Not any more, if it ever was,' said Stephen, shining his torch into the cavity. 'It's completely empty. It may never have been meant for a dead person; they used sarcophagi like this for the mock interments that were part of initiations into the mysteries. *Intra celatum* . . . d'you suppose it means the treasure was hidden within this?'

Non aurum, Alice thought. 'Or maybe it means the treasure never was a thing at all but this place itself.'

Or maybe, thought Paul, it means that the treasure is hidden within yourself. Somewhere inside, in another dimension.

Stephen crouched down and studied the carvings on the sarcophagus. 'Look, here's Isis coming out of the sea, and the priests on the shore. This is wonderful, wonderful. I was going to do the *Asinus Aureus* with you next year, but we'll start right away . . . oh look!'

Alice felt very peculiar, as though she'd gone a long time without food. The wild dance of shadows and light as Stephen moved about was making her dizzy.

'I feel quite peculiar,' said Paul. The air had thickened and seemed to be humming. 'My hands and feet are tingling. It's like when—did you see that fellow, what was his name?'

'That funny little man . . . Macgregor.'

'He let me try his metal sticks . . .'

'I did, too,' Alice said.

'He said the lines crossed . . .'

'On the island.'

'Right here.'

'Are we in our moon-bodies?'

Paul looked at his hands; they seemed oddly insubstantial. 'Yes and no, I think. It's this place, it has to be. It makes one see things that way.'

'Stephen,' Alice said, 'are you feeling unusual in any way?'

'Unusual? Well, I do feel somewhat unusually fascinated. There are inscriptions, come and look . . .'

'Excuse me,' said Paul. 'I think I have to get some air.'

He climbed the stairs and on up the cliff to the top of the island. He felt his body solidifying with every step. The last of the dizziness evaporated in the breeze, leaving him with only a slight headache between his eyes.

A boat was setting out from the dock below the house; in a few minutes Roger and Michael had arrived with a couple of curious house guests. The boys were charging, Paul learned, tuppence for the boat service and sixpence admission to the Lair of the Dog-Headed Demon. Paul smoked a cigarette while he waited, and got a lift back with them, for which he had to pay a penny.

23

Percy looked back; the river stretched behind him, millions of words long. He summoned his strength. Paul was waiting with paper and pencil; the last piece of the story was almost within reach. Let me remember now, he thought; let me remember and tell the story to the end, or the beginning.

'The floodwater was at its peak. I could see it through the trees, black and slow. The *heka-wy* arrived in her red boat. I fasted for three days, and each night she gave me the *tepi-saba* to drink, the first door. And each night, racked with strange pains, I vomited as though I was turning inside out. On the last night I vomited nothing but pale orange froth. Thunder rumbled down from the distant mountains, and every now and then came a great crash as the swollen river claimed another tree. She led me to stand at the shore, where the water swirled into a shallow pool. She took up her knife.

'"Don't move, don't speak," she said. "No matter what happens, no matter what you see." She closed her eyes and traced a pattern across my chest, down my arms and legs and up my back. The pain was sharp and cold, but nothing compared to the pain that followed. *Senu-saba*, the second door, was a pungent black ointment. She rubbed it into the cuts; it burned and stung a thousand times worse than fire ants. The pain dissolved my skin and cut into my flesh, even to the bone; it felt as though my very organs were dissolving in fire. I wanted to scream, I wanted to

401

run, but I forced myself to stand still, to stay silent as I'd been told, and the pain shifted gradually into something akin to pleasure, a bright, strong hum like an electric current. The moon was rising; the river was made of light, rainbowed and translucent. A procession of little rafts came downstream towards us; in each was a piece of a human body: a foot, an arm, a leg. The next one bore a hand, severed at the wrist. The fingers grasped a strange, exquisite flower and I knew it was Sinclair; he'd found the moon-flower at last. I was filled with a great sorrow that now, at my moment of initiation, he should have died, though I felt he'd have liked to die that way, his great quest achieved, his life's goal fulfilled.'

At last, Percy held the hidden memory in his hand; it waited only for him to look. He let the words come as the image unfolded. 'The last of the little rafts caught on a root and the current pulled it to my feet. It contained the head, face down. "This is *hemut-sabu*, the third door," the *heka-wy* said, as she turned the head. It opened its eyes.

'The sensation that washed over me was far worse than the burning pain; it was extreme vertigo, intense nausea—but those words don't begin to describe it. It was horror and chaos and death; it was endless falling, it was pure fear. The face . . . the face was my own.'

*   *   *

Percy sat late by the open doors of his sitting room. A feeling of peace had slipped over him like water. In the darkness behind his eyes he could see the moon rising, the gleaming black surface of the

402

lake, the island where Odelia waited. How easy it would be to slide across the small distance, slip out of time. He rose and stepped into the night, then turned and looked at his body in the chair. How terribly old it was.

'It's time for bed, sir,' said Henry, again.

Poor old body. Just a little longer. Percy slid back down with a sigh. 'You go to bed, Old Hen. I'll sit here for a while.'

Time moved very slowly now. A moth hovered near his face, soft wings beating. It flew away, returned, flew away again.

'Father.' A whisper like wings.

'Daniel?'

'Yes.'

Percy reached out his hand; it was taken and held. 'Oh Daniel, will you be all right?'

'I'll be fine. Don't worry about me.'

The hand slipped away and he was alone.

The moth returned, fluttered over his face, brushed his eyelids. The flurry of beating wings grew louder. It sounded like hundreds of moth-wings, all beating urgently at once. The sound was coming from the cases on the walls; they were trapped, trapped against the glass, they'd been trapped all this time and he'd never known. He felt his way to the nearest case; it was locked, they were all locked, and the keys were in a drawer. No time, no time. He broke the glass with the handle of his walking stick and they fluttered free; he found the next case, and the next; the moths flew off into the night.

Someone clutched at him, tried to pull the stick from his hands. He wrested it loose, turned and smashed open the last of the cases. When the

403

moths had all flown away things got a bit quieter and he could hear Henry's voice, soothing and cajoling. He allowed himself to be put to bed.

*   *   *

'Whisky, ice, cocaine, hatpin.' Sylvie arranged them on a tray, brought it to the bed and sat at Paul's side.

'Hatpin?'

'Let's pierce our ears. I'm told a hatpin is better than a needle.'

'Ouch,' said Paul.

'Only a little ouch.'

'I prefer to avoid pain, when it is avoidable.'

'Do mine, then.'

'Do you know, I'd rather not.'

'Oh come on, please?' She opened an enamelled box, dipped her fingernail in the white powder, extended it to Paul.

'I'll never get any sleep if I have any more.' The little box had come back with Sylvie from her last trip to London.

'Oh, sleep. What has night to do with sleep?' She touched the hatpin to his chest over his heart. He lay very still and watched her face; she drew it along his skin, across his ribs; she drew a spiral on his belly. His cock stirred and she laughed softly, pressed harder. Paul glanced down; drops of blood sprang up in a line. She bent and licked them.

'Now do my ears.' She held the hatpin in the candle, dipped it in the whisky and passed it to him. 'Please.' She lifted her hair out of the way, pressed the ice to her ear, tilted her head and closed her eyes.

404

It doesn't matter, carry on; it doesn't matter. Paul made the universe shrink to the size of Sylvie's ear, watched his hands move, the pin pierce her flesh, the red blood well and flow.

'Ow,' she said, and turned for the other. 'Ow.'

*   *   *

That night Paul couldn't sleep and he didn't want to dream. He sat in the chair, lay on his bed, got up, stood at the window. The night gave nothing back. He pictured Sylvie in her bed; the pain of wanting her pierced him like that awful hatpin. He opened his shirt, touched the dried blood, the raised weals. He imagined her pushing it into his heart—what would that feel like? Only a little ouch. How long would it take to die?

He lit a cigarette; the light of the ember swelled and faded, swelled and faded. Was she asleep? Sylvie, come here, get up, come to me. He closed his eyes, concentrated, sent his thought like a lance. Get up, come here, come to me. Sylvie. Sylvie. Sylvie.

He'd nearly given up when the door opened. 'Are you awake?' she said. 'I thought you'd be. You were right about the snow. Let's go and fuck in the Lair of the Dog-Headed Demon.' They tiptoed down the stairs, grabbed a torch from the boot room and slipped out of the house.

'We can swim to the island,' Sylvie said.

'I don't think I can swim that far.'

'OK, we'll take a boat. This time. But you could, you know.'

Paul rowed across the black water. The sound of Daniel's violin drifted through the air; Arlen

405

joined in.

'Oh, beautiful,' Sylvie said.

Beauty, whispered Mr Pym from somewhere in the night, is the death of time.

When they neared the island Sylvie turned on the torch; the thin beam probed the darkness.

Light, said Mr Pym, is the longing and the solace of your soul.

The columns of the temple were tall blurs among the shadowy trees; the earth felt hollow and springy beneath Paul's feet as Sylvie led the way down to the grotto. She shone the torch on the steps. 'Have you seen it yet?'

'Yes. Have you?'

'Oh yes, paid my sixpence, had the guided tour and all. It's not as creepy as I'd thought.'

There was a pressure in his head and a ringing in his ears; colours flared at the edge of his vision. Sylvie's voice came from far away, sounding like bells. It was all so familiar: the steps descending into darkness, Sylvie going on ahead. She lit a lantern; in the flickering shadows the images crowded from all sides: a procession by the shore, bright with horns and rattles, ribbons and garlands; a naked man crowned with roses walking into the sea.

Someone singing, or was it the violin? Sylvie with a child in her lap, with a snake on her arm. She led him to the inner chamber, drew him down, laid him out. Did she speak? He heard only a golden hum.

Everything was slow and heavy as though underwater; a pattern of waves, or was it snakes? A dog with a knife in its hand, a coffin bound in gold, Sylvie's skin cool as silk and everywhere else the heat. He blinked hard; what was real? The things that are real, said Mr Pym, are seen and not seen.

Sylvie arcs over him, lowers herself on to his cock. Behind her the images shift, seen and not seen.

Don't move, she says. Don't speak.

He can't tell if his eyes are open or closed; it's dark and burning bright, humming with soft voices, or bells, or violins. Sylvie's face changes, and changes again. Who are you?

The one and the many, she says: Isis of infinite names. Healer of men's souls, teacher of the heart, mistress of magic, queen of heaven and earth.

This is the door to immortality, says Mr Pym; this is the abyss at the end of desire.

Paul hears the words from far away, from deep within and he's falling, has always been falling. And will always be the falling, says Mr Pym, not unkindly, as the earth dissolves beneath him. He's back in no-man's-land, in the crater with only mud and death. The deadly sabre rises and falls . . .

Not this, no, please. This must be a dream, and I want it to stop now. Wake up. Wake up! But he can't; something is holding him down. The pressure grows, the darkness edges closer.

Just surrender, says Mr Pym.

No! He tore himself awake but the weight remained. He flailed at it, kicked out, fought free, stumbled away. There was a frantic pounding in his head and a cacophony in his ears; he ran blindly, crashed into things, scrambled on. He fought his way towards the surface and came to himself gasping and retching on the cool grass. Sylvie was calling his name.

'There you are.' She knelt at his side and shone the torch in his face. 'Jesus Christ, what came over you? You slugged me and ran off.'

He shielded his eyes. 'I what? Oh God, I'm sorry. I don't know what happened. I didn't know it was you.'

'Well who the hell else would it have been?'

'I don't know.'

'You knocked over the lantern and I cut myself on the glass, look.' She shone the torch on her foot. 'Oh Christ, you cut yourself too. You must have fallen in it.'

The torch revealed cuts on Paul's feet and knees, arms and hands. He couldn't feel them.

'You're shivering,' she said. 'I brought your clothes. Do you want to put them on?'

He felt sick and dizzy and he couldn't focus. He forgot the beginning of her sentence before she got to the end of it. 'What? Yes. No. Cigarette. Pocket. Please.'

'I think,' Sylvie said, 'you're asking for a cigarette.' She found them, lit one and passed it to him.

Thank God for cigarettes, he thought; sanity and order returned with the smoke. His cuts began to hurt. 'I'm sorry,' he said again. 'I can't remember what happened. Did you say I hit you?'

'Well yes, but just a glancing blow . . .'

'Oh Christ. I thought . . . well, I don't know what I thought. And your poor foot.'

'Well I suppose I'll survive, but I don't know about you. You're quite bloody. This is where the heroine tears her petticoat into strips and binds the hero's wounds, but I'm not wearing any undergarments. Sorry.'

Paul washed off the blood in the lake and pulled on his clothes. Sylvie sat silently as he rowed across the black water. As they tied up at the dock the stillness was broken by the sound of shattering glass. 'What on earth was that?' he said.

'No idea,' Sylvie said. 'Wait . . .'

'I know. Wait ten minutes.' Paul smoked a cigarette and then wandered up to the house by a roundabout route. He saw Dr Westlake arriving and lurked in the shadows until he'd disappeared inside before he slipped into the boot room and up the back stairs.

*   *   *

The next day Paul had nothing to do. Dr Westlake had mandated complete rest for Percy, which pleased Henry, and installed a professional nurse, which didn't. Paul went for a walk but got only as far as the terrace. There was nowhere he wanted to go. He returned to the library and checked the manuscript for typing errors, again. He browsed the shelves. What was he looking for in all these books? He opened one after another. Words blurred together, none made any sense. He couldn't focus on anything.

He didn't go to the chapel in the afternoon, nor did he go to Sylvie's room that night. He hid in the darkroom, door locked, and didn't answer when she knocked. All day, he realised, he'd been avoiding thinking about what had happened on the island. There was a gap in his memory he'd been trying to paper over. He steeled himself and let his mind edge closer . . . the last thing he remembered clearly was climbing into the sarcophagus, and

Sylvie leaning over him, or was it the goddess on the ceiling? And then there had been the falling, and the heavy weight that must have been just Sylvie but that had felt like a deadly force holding him down. Surrender, Mr Pym had said. But he hadn't surrendered; apparently he'd fought like a demon. Why? He couldn't remember.

The weather turned cloudy; Percy kept to his bed. Dr Westlake stopped by every morning. People tiptoed; Henry looked like a ghost and slept in a chair by Percy's door. Lawyers came and went, estate managers, accountants and stewards and consultants, yet everyone spoke as though Percy would soon recover and things return to normal.

Maybe it was the oppressive sky, or the general air of tension that filled the house; Paul was restless and uncomfortable. There was a constant, barely audible ringing in his ears and his skin felt itchy. Things seemed murky and uncertain, like the weather, only more so. He couldn't sleep, nor could he get out of his body and into Sylvie's dreams. Something bounced him back and he was held in a pallid no-man's-land where even his own dreams were closed to him. When he was with Sylvie in the flesh it was as if the polarities had shifted, and commingled with the irresistible attraction was an intangible strangeness that made him queasy and anxious. When he learned she'd gone off to London to look for a flat he was glad.

A week after Percy had fallen ill Paul received the expected letter from his sister.

Father died on Thursday. We thought he would go quietly, but at the very end he seemed to be

410

engaged in some great struggle and his death could not be called peaceful; he'd be glad of that, I expect.

Remember that locked drawer in his desk? This morning I forced it open. In the glimpses I'd caught it had always been full, but he burned a lot of papers last year and only one document remained. I can only assume he meant me to find it. As you see, it is addressed to you, dated two years ago, and comes from someone of whom I've never heard, a Mr Weissman, a solicitor in London. Jacob Benedict Asher was Father's father, wasn't he? He was never spoken of—I always had the impression he was a bit of an embarrassment for some reason. Wasn't he supposed to have died twenty-odd years ago?

Paul studied the enclosure. Beneath a modest letterhead with an address in Great Russell Street was one sentence.

Since you have not responded to our previous letters, I can only inform you that the bequest of Mr Jacob Benedict Asher is yours to claim should you wish to do so.
Yours sincerely,
Robert A. Weissman

Paul pictured an antique pocket watch, not working, or a mouldy box of bric-a-brac. Well, it was something to do. Percy hadn't called for him in days; he'd not been away from Farundell for weeks. Perhaps all he needed was a change of scene. He telephoned Mr Weissman's office; a

411

secretary gave him an appointment for mid-afternoon and told him to bring proof of his identity. He informed Tustian where he was going and got a lift to the station with Dr Westlake, just leaving.

As soon as he was on his own he felt better. The train was full of purposeful people going up to town; he stood in the corridor and read a newspaper someone had discarded. It was August already; he hadn't realised. There was, apparently, a world out there.

The river of bodies carried him through Paddington and into the din of London. At once his good mood evaporated. He couldn't see the sky, the air stank, it was unbelievably noisy; when he stopped to get his bearings he was jostled from all sides. For a panicked moment he forgot what he was doing here, then he dragged himself free of the crowd and made his way to Hyde Park; he had an hour to kill.

The trees were dusty and tired, but at least they were green. Grimy pastel boats for hire edged the Serpentine and a single rower plied the opaque water; a girl sat in the stern with her face in her hands. Was she crying? She looked up and Paul's heart gave a leap—it was Sylvie! No, it wasn't, of course not.

He sat on a bench and lit a cigarette with shaking hands. The girl didn't even look like her, so why did he now feel so bereft? He'd been trying not to think of her because it threw him into such a dark and tormented place, racked between desire and a desperate urge to flee. It was like the taste of metal; it was like a cat being stroked the wrong way; it was like never knowing if one was asleep or awake.

Francis sat down, crossed his legs and inserted a cigarette into a long jade holder. 'My friend,' he said, 'what you know about that would fill a postage stamp.'

Paul looked at him. 'Are you real?'

'It depends . . .'

'Yes, OK, I know. It depends what I mean by real.'

The things that are real are here and not here, said Mr Pym.

'And there and not there,' said Francis. 'Is that her?' He pointed to the bridge. Sylvie bicycled by, hair flying.

Paul's heart leapt again. He stood up to call to her, but then she looked right at him. It wasn't her.

'Oh look,' said Francis, 'surely that's her over there, see?'

It was; it wasn't; it was; it wasn't.

This is and is not what it seems, said Mr Pym.

'Just so,' said Francis. 'The lake, the bridge, the boat, the girl; the earth and heaven and hell.'

Paul saw a dozen more Sylvies before he reached Great Russell Street, and Mr Weissman's secretary could have been her sister. She brought him a cup of tea while he waited, then showed him to a cluttered office whose window, behind stacks of yellowing files, looked out over the street and the courtyard of the British Museum. Mr Weissman was surprisingly young; for some reason Paul had pictured an elderly gent.

'I'm Robert Weissman Junior,' he said. 'It was my father who wrote to you; he passed away last year. I have the file, however.' He patted a manila folder on his desk. 'The instructions were very

413

clear; the estate was to be maintained until claimed by you or your rightful descendants. So, to business. The bequest comprises . . .'

An omnibus stopped in traffic, the upper deck a few yards away. Was that Sylvie? Paul's heart, exhausted with lurching, only stared. Yes, that was her lilac straw hat, her white linen dress with the embroidered collar, her new gypsy hoop earrings.

'We will be glad to continue to manage things until you decide otherwise. All the accounts are up to date. Are you all right, Mr Asher? I gather it's something of a shock. Not inconsiderable, no indeed.'

'What?'

'Of course that's the income only; the capital is in trust for your children. Have you any children, Mr Asher?'

'Not that I know of.'

'For your future children, then. And the house in Red Lion Square has been well looked after; the caretaker, Mr Meredith, lives over the mews. Has a mechanic's workshop, does very well for himself. A good fellow. I look in myself every month or so, to make sure. Now, I expect you'll want to see it. I sent word when I learned you were coming, told him to give the place a good airing. I need you to sign this piece of paper that says you are who you are, and I'll take you there myself.'

Red Lion Square was lined with tall, narrow houses and mottled plane trees whose roots lifted the pavement. Their branches, rustling with pigeons, met overhead; the traffic was a muted hum. Mr Weissman jingled a ring of keys and led the way up the steps of Number Eleven. He unlocked and opened the door, removed the key from his ring and handed it to Paul. 'I trust you will find everything in order. You know where to reach me. Good day, Mr Asher.'

Paul stood on the step, key in hand, door open before him. He looked down the street. Sylvie pushed a pram, a spaniel frolicked alongside. No, not her.

The girl looked up as she passed. 'Hello,' she said. 'Do you live here? I thought the house was empty.' The dog tugged at its lead; the baby wailed. 'Well, hello, anyway . . .'

'Hello anyway,' Paul said.

When she'd vanished, he turned back to the door. Just walk in, he told himself, and made his feet move. Suddenly, he was certain that he was dreaming, which was a relief; it didn't matter so much whether things made sense. Stephen, he recalled, had said something about dreams like this. It seemed quite interesting; he should enjoy it while it lasted.

He set out to explore. Stairs ascended from the hall; to one side was a bare white sitting room, windows open a few inches at the top. He wandered in and out, up and down; his footsteps echoed. Sheets cloaked the furniture in some rooms; in others there was nothing but a strange sense of familiarity.

Francis reclined on his blue silk chaise longue.

'You look right at home,' Paul said.

Francis shrugged. 'It's your house.'

'It's my dream, you mean.'

'Ah, now you're learning.'

'Learning what?'

'What, yes, and also how. Though not yet why, of course.'

'You give me a headache,' Paul said.

'That's the least of my gifts.'

There was a crash from below. 'Ghosts, do you think?' Francis said.

Paul found his way down to the basement kitchen. Cool and dim, blue-tiled, the light from a window high in the wall filtered through green ivy. Sylvie stood at the sink, broken pieces of a vase in her hand.

'What are you doing here?' Paul said.

'I've always been here.'

'What?'

'You are Mr Asher, aren't you? I'm Imogen, Mr Meredith's daughter—he said you were coming, so I wanted to put out some flowers for you.' There was a bunch of roses and hollyhocks on the table. 'From the garden. Your garden. But I broke the vase. Your vase. I'm sorry. Father'll be here any minute. Would you mind not telling him?'

'I have a garden?' Paul said.

She pointed out of the window. Of course she didn't much resemble Sylvie; it was more the way she held her head, or perhaps her slim arms and long-fingered hands.

He sat at the table; the scent of flowers filled the room. He watched her collect the shards, drop them in the bin, find another vase, fill it with water. She arranged the flowers, her movements calm and deliberate. He imagined her skin beneath her clothes and a hot bolt of desire shot through him. 'I hope you don't mind my saying so, but this is such a fascinating dream.'

'Have you read Dr Freud on dreams?' she said. 'I think he's entirely wrong, myself, but he's so fashionable at the moment.'

'Imogen, for heaven's sake.' A smiling, grizzled man appeared at the door. 'Mr Asher doesn't want to hear that twaddle. Please forgive her. She reads too much. I'm Meredith, sir, welcome back.'

'Back? I've been here before?'

'Why yes, of course, though I suppose you won't remember; you were very young when you left, and your sister still a baby. Miss Muriel is well, I hope?'

'Yes, she's fine . . .'

'It's been many years,' Meredith said. 'Too many, if I may say. It does no good for a house to sit empty. We always hoped Mr Jacob would return to live in London, but he'd only stay for a week or two, passing through on his travels.'

'I thought he'd died many years ago,' said Paul.

'No, it was, let me see . . . it'll be two years next month. Since then, no one has come. An empty house is a sad house.'

Paul listened and nodded as Meredith and his daughter chatted and made him tea, and when they asked if he'd be returning to live in the house he could honestly say he had no idea.

On the journey back to Farundell, he took the key to 11 Red Lion Square from his pocket a dozen times in futile attempts to determine whether it was real. There was no proof; there could be no proof. Sense experience proved nothing but itself. Longevity, or apparent longevity and causality, or apparent causality, weighed on the side of being awake; he could not remember ever remembering such a long stretch of internally consistent and sequential events in a dream. By now he would have woken up and it would have faded into oblivion, but in this case he could remember an entire day. So it was real. Or a dream that was still going on. He took the key from his pocket again.

Time slowed as he walked over the hills. The air was soft and sweet; the clouds had cleared and beyond the western hills the sky was tinged with rose. A man was cutting a field of poppy-strewn wheat with a team of horses; their long-fringed fetlocks lifted and crossed in unison at the end of each row, the stalks rustled and fell, the reaper's wordless calls hung in the air.

It was nearly dark when he turned in at the gates of Farundell. Honeysuckle glowed pale in the dusk and clouds of scent drifted on small breezes, attracting moths just discernible as shadowy flutters. Bats flitted to and fro and took them in midair. Paul stopped and lit a cigarette. Was Sylvie back? He wanted to see her; he dreaded seeing her. He wanted to devour her; he could hardly bear to touch her. He turned away from the house and wandered down to the edge of the meadow, gazed out at the lake. How lovely it would be to melt into the night, dissolve like smoke.

'It's a beautiful night,' said Percy.

Paul turned. Percy stood at his side, erect, not stooped, and his eyes were bright with knowledge. 'My story is finished. You wrote it; have you understood?'

An owl flew low over the field and a shadow moved on the water; someone was rowing out to the island. When Paul turned back, Percy was gone.

*　　　*　　　*

The water rises, the river flows, and from far off

comes the sound of a violin. There is nothing left to do. The story is outside him now; all Percy has to do is wait and the river will carry him home. The moths hover, stroke his eyelids with their wings, flutter away.

Most faces are a blur, though some shine clear. Alice kisses his cheek, Jarlath's hand on her shoulder. Jarlath meets his eyes. Farewell, old friend, he says.

Everyone looks much older than the last time he saw them. Theo's hair is nearly all white, but around and behind and within her is something young and dazzling bright. Percy takes her hand; he steps free and she leads him past the crowding dull-bodied others and out, out at last, into the living air. Oh God, it's over, that awful weight, that incessant pain, that unbearable burden. He leaps and kicks and runs; he opens his mouth to scream in joy, but what comes out is laughter, laughter that bubbles like champagne, that flows like water, that soars like wild multicoloured birds from sky to sky.

24

'I heard from Muriel,' Paul said. 'My father died. What do they say? He hung up his spurs. As you can imagine, my only regret is that I'm unable at the moment to spit on his grave. I'll miss Percy far more.'

'So what will you do now?' Val stepped around a muddy patch. They were near the end of the long procession that wound up the hill to the chapel.

419

'I've been asked to prepare Percy's memoirs for the publisher, so I'll stay to see that through. And then, well, is there a place called Red Lion Square?'

'There's a Red Lion Square in Holborn.'

'That's the one. So it's real, is it?'

'Red Lion Square is, in my opinion, as real as any other location in London.'

Paul stood at the back of the crowded chapel. Sylvie's paintings, nearly finished, created multiple perspectives into other spaces, rooms, forests, vistas. Branches arced overhead, bare against the night at one end, full-leafed and green under a blue sky at the other. He was beginning to believe that Red Lion Square had been real, as had one of the Sylvies, the one on the bus. She'd been wearing the lilac straw hat and the dress with the embroidered collar when she'd returned the next day. They'd barely spoken, and with Percy's dead body in the house for the last few days it hadn't felt right to . . . whatever.

He wondered what kind of a funeral such a fervently anti-religious man would have; it turned out to be less different than he'd thought, and mercifully brief. In the absence of a priest, Jarlath presided; old friends got up to speak, there were readings, the children played some Bach, and everyone filed out to the graveyard.

At the graveside Sylvie held her hand to her face and as the earth thudded on to Percy's coffin she slipped away into the woods. Paul found her bent over in the bushes, racked not with grief but with vomiting. He patted her back and passed her his handkerchief.

'Thanks,' she said.

420

'You all right?'

'I suppose so. Must be something I ate, or a tummy bug I picked up in town. Give me a cigarette.' She inhaled deeply. 'Ah, that's better. I don't want to go back to the house; there's too many people.'

It was dark under the trees; layers of dead leaves softened their steps. The birdsong was in its late summer lull, the stillness broken only by wood doves' sad calls and the distant drum of a woodpecker.

'All those ghastly relatives,' Sylvie said. 'I hate wearing black; it makes me feel dowdy and fat. I hate it when people die. The smell gets everywhere, no matter what they do. And Henry whimpering all the time like a dog. It's so stupid. Why can't we just disappear in a puff of smoke?' She snapped her fingers. 'All this fuss doesn't do the dead person any good; I bet Percy is laughing his head off somewhere while we get all solemn about some awful bit of flesh that's already rotting.'

She rummaged in her purse, took out the enamelled box, offered her little fingernail, heaped high. It cleared Paul's head wonderfully. He fingered the key in his pocket. Yes, real.

'I thought I saw you in town,' she said. 'My bus was stuck in traffic and you walked by below; you were with a short fellow in a striped suit. I called, but you didn't hear, and then I decided it couldn't have been you.'

'He's a lawyer. I saw you too, from inside his office. At the time, I had every reason to believe I was dreaming.' He told her about the bequest. 'The caretaker said my sister and I lived there

421

when we were little. He has a beautiful daughter who reads Freud. I thought she was you. I wanted to fuck her on the spot. I would have if her father hadn't come in.'

'Fuck me now.'

'What, here?'

'Please. No one can see.' She leaned against a tree, pulled up her skirt.

'No knickers, even for a funeral?'

*   *   *

After lunch everyone gathered in the library for the reading of the Will. The family sat in a semicircle facing the solemn, bewhiskered lawyer; Paul leaned against the bookcase next to Jarlath's painting of Tobias. Did Tobias wink at him? Paul winked back and lit a cigarette.

Val came to stand at his side. 'I didn't think they did this sort of thing in real life. I'm going to put it in my script.'

'You are contributing,' Paul said, 'to a pervasive and not altogether pleasant sense of unreality.'

'Why thank you, dear boy. How kind of you to say. One does one's best.'

Alice sat between Roger and Sophie. Her side of the family, she noticed, had all seated themselves opposite Uncle Richard's side. Michael, between his parents, chewed his nails. He met her eyes and quickly looked away.

It was a long Will; Percy had provisions for everyone. All the staff and servants got nice sums of money; Tustian and Henry mementos as well. He'd left the cameras and darkroom paraphernalia to Paul; Jarlath got his collection of walking sticks;

Maggie, Sylvie and Sophie each got some of Odelia's jewels. He'd left Alice all his scientific equipment, his microscope and his telescope, which was so much better than trinkets. She could set up a laboratory in one of the spare bedrooms; she had always wanted to conduct experiments. Her attention wandered as the lawyer droned on, then was drawn back by the sound of raised voices.

'He's being kept like an animal,' Cecily said. 'Like a wild animal. He apparently goes about naked. It's a disgrace. No one seems to care.'

'The days are past,' Richard said, 'when one can keep these unfortunate souls locked away. This is the twentieth century; there are new treatments: surgery, electric therapy and so on. He can't be expected to manage the estate in his condition.'

'And so you should take over, Richard, is that the idea?' Maggie said.

'I have spoken to Mr Peebles,' he nodded at the lawyer, who nodded back. 'A temporary arrangement, and in the meantime poor Daniel can receive the care he needs. There is an excellent institution in Bristol; the director, Dr Hamilton, assures me he has had considerable success with cases like this.'

Alice couldn't contain herself any longer. 'Daniel is perfectly fine,' she said. 'He doesn't need any treatment; he just needs to be left alone.'

'I don't believe it is fruitful for children to participate in this discussion,' said Richard.

Maggie sighed. 'Daniel is perfectly fine. He doesn't need any treatment; he just needs to be left alone.'

'Neglected, you mean,' Cecily said. 'Neglected and abandoned to sinful living.'

'What on earth do you mean?' Maggie said.

'We mean he has fallen prey to evil influences,' Richard said. 'That Negro . . .'

'Are you referring to Arlen Winter?' Maggie's tone was icy. 'He is a friend of the family, a highly respected musician, a war hero. He was in the 369th; he received the Croix de Guerre while you were safe in London, Richard.'

'He's no friend,' Cecily said. 'We have reason to believe he has corrupted poor Daniel.'

'With jazz music?' Maggie said. 'I shouldn't think that would be any more corruptive than mindless slaughter, do you?'

'If you think jazz music is all that's going on down there you're more naïve than I thought,' Richard said.

'To stoop to that sort of innuendo, Richard, is beneath even you.'

'It's not innuendo,' Cecily said. 'They have been seen.'

'Seen?'

'Seen committing acts. Unspeakable acts. Illegal acts.'

'Seen by you, Cecily?' Maggie said. 'And you lived to tell the tale?'

Cecily was bright pink, and mute.

'Of course not by Cecily.' Richard looked at Michael.

Alice took the doll from her pocket and gave it a little squeeze. Michael coughed; she held it up and smiled.

'They apparently behave quite without discretion. Michael couldn't help but see,' Richard said. 'Could you, Michael?'

Alice pressed her thumb over the doll's mouth,

stared at Michael and concentrated hard. You cannot speak, you cannot speak, you cannot speak.

He choked and turned red.

'Michael makes things up,' Alice said. 'Don't you?'

He blinked hard and nodded.

Say it, Alice thought at him. Say it out loud. She lifted her thumb. Speak now. Say, I made it up.

'I made it up,' Michael said.

Cecily whispered urgently in his ear; he shrugged and shook his head.

'Dishonest children,' said Maggie, 'are a sign of careless upbringing.'

As soon as she could, Alice went to her room to change out of her good clothes. She transferred the Michael doll to her new pocket; she'd never thought the truce would last. She wished she'd made a doll for Uncle Richard too. And Cecily. Yes, definitely. A Cecily doll. It would be quite pleasant to stab it with pins.

She'd missed Percy badly; they wouldn't have dared to say any of that when he was alive. She sat on the edge of her bed and allowed herself a sniffle. Oh, why did things have to change?

She'd caught a glimpse of Daniel among the trees at Percy's burial, but he hadn't come near. Could he stay in his cabin, or would he have to live in the house from now on? Would that be horrible for him? Whatever it was he had to do, Percy was counting on her to help him.

She was halfway down the stairs when she heard Uncle Richard's voice. He was speaking on the hall telephone; she crept closer to listen.

'. . . why not come for lunch tomorrow, and then visit my poor brother to make your assessment?

Yes, in his den, ha ha. Mr Peebles has the papers ready for you to sign. One o'clock, then. Thank you, Dr Hamilton, very good of you.'

What a sneaky little weasel, Alice thought. Like son, like father. She had to warn Daniel. He was a grown-up, he was Lord Damory now—they couldn't make him have treatments if he didn't want to, could they?

Halfway down the meadow she came upon Arlen, gazing across the lake. 'I have to go,' he said. 'I'm a coward, Alice, I left without saying goodbye.' He turned, then looked back. 'Find him a wife. Then he'll be safe.'

Alice watched him walk away. A wife? She'd have thought that was the last thing Daniel would want.

Dragonflies patrolled the muddy fringe of the lake; the sky was hazy white. She stopped by the stream from St Ælfhild's pool, as she always did on her way to the cabin. The water was not much more than a trickle now, and nettles crowded the banks. She felt for the psychomagnetic force; it seemed a bit stronger every time, but if she tried too hard, it slipped out of reach. There was a fine balance, like a seesaw; she had to sense it without thinking of it, find it without looking for it. She walked back and forth for a while, then sat on a rock, the same one she'd sat on when Francis had appeared. Please, please appear now, she thought, but though a bee circled, oddly, round and round the place he'd been, nothing else happened. She noticed that she was dawdling, and that it was because she wanted to postpone bringing even the idea of Dr Hamilton and his treatments into Daniel's world, which was stupid. They were real;

he'd have to know about them, and best from her. She stood up and walked on.

Theo was sitting with Daniel on his porch; the air had the quality of a storm just passed. 'I came to warn you,' Alice said. 'Someone called Dr Hamilton is coming tomorrow. He'll want to give you treatments. You should go and hide in the woods until he's gone.'

Daniel was silent for a long time, then he glanced at Theo and shook his head. 'I've been hiding in the woods for years, Alice. I can't hide any more. I told Percy I'd be fine; I have to keep my word.'

'But he'll think you're crazy.'

'Then I have to convince him I'm not.'

'He won't understand you. He'll judge by appearances; Maggie says everyone does, they can't help it.'

'Then I'll have to improve my appearance.'

Alice looked at him doubtfully. He smiled. 'What, don't you think it's possible?'

'You need a valet,' she said. 'I could send Henry. He's awfully sad; he'll be glad to have something to do.'

'Tell Henry to come tomorrow,' said Theo. 'And you might ask Paul, as well.'

*   *   *

The next morning, Paul helped Henry sort through Percy's suits. Henry wept silently as he handled the soft tweeds, the linens and gabardines.

'Come on, Henry,' Paul said. 'Pick one. Or two, if you like; give him a choice.'

'These three,' said Henry, passing them to Paul.

427

'And this one as well. And shirts, and ties. Do you suppose he has underwear? No, perhaps not. And shoes, he's the same size if I recall. And socks, and a handkerchief for his pocket; a correctly placed handkerchief says so much about a gentleman.'

A light mist hung over the lake and the air had the faintest taste of autumn as they walked down to the cabin. Daniel was waiting on the porch; when he saw them he went in without a word and stood on the far side of the room. His collection of stones, Paul noticed, was laid out in an unusually regular pattern of squares and chevrons, precisely graduated in size and grouped by shape.

Henry laid out the clothes on the bed; Daniel looked at them as though they were dead animals of a species he'd never seen, and wouldn't choose. In the end, Paul and Henry settled on the light grey tweed, with a white shirt and a blue tie.

Paul found the kettle and heated water for shaving while Daniel paced between lines of stones.

'If you'd care to sit, sir,' Henry said.

Daniel perched on the edge of the chair and averted his eyes from the scissors and razor laid out on the table. Henry stood behind him and picked up the scissors, but at the sound of the blades parting in preparation for the first cut Daniel gagged and bolted.

'Give him a minute,' Paul said to Henry. He found Daniel at the lake, washing his face.

'I'm sorry,' Daniel said. 'You must think me a dreadful idiot.'

'No. Or if you are, I am too. With me it was the sight of blood.'

'There's nothing I can do,' Daniel said. 'I tried

for years, but something happens inside me and I can't bring myself to touch anything made of metal, or bear for it to touch me.'

'What really matters to you?' Paul said.

'What?'

'I mean why are you doing this?'

'I have to. For my father. I told him I'd be all right, and I can't let him down again.'

'Then concentrate on that. The rest doesn't matter, does it?'

Daniel shook his head.

'So shut it out and do what you have to do. That's what my colonel said, and it works. Find something to fix your mind on, like some words— he taught me to say "It doesn't matter, carry on" over and over. It blanks everything else out and you can do what you need to do.'

'It doesn't matter, carry on,' Daniel whispered, and followed Paul inside. He sat in the chair, closed his eyes, and though he winced when the scissors snicked and snapped, and shuddered when they touched his neck, he held himself still. When his hair lay on the floor in a pile, he took up the razor in his own hand and calmly shaved his face. He submitted in silence to be dressed; Henry laced up Percy's brogues, tied the tie and arranged the handkerchief in his breast pocket.

'Thank you,' Daniel said. 'I'll come up to the house in a little while.'

Paul turned at the door, took off his wristwatch and gave it to Daniel. 'You might need this. Your lunch is at one.'

*　　　*　　　*

429

Alice lurked in the doorway, trying to see into the dining room as the maids swung in and out. In one glimpse she saw Daniel holding a knife and fork; in another, he was eating a piece of roast chicken. It all seemed terribly civil. She wished she was a servant; no one minded what they overheard. At the end of the meal Dr Hamilton asked to speak with Daniel in private.

Alice watched them go into the library, then she raced up the stairs to Sylvie's room. She crept down the secret passage, pressed her ear against the panel and forced herself to breathe calmly; her heart was so loud she couldn't hear anything else. Daniel's voice was quiet and light, the doctor's a deeper rumble. A phrase had a questioning tone; Daniel responded with a small laugh, and words she couldn't hear. She bit her lip and crossed her fingers. The conversation went back and forth for some time, then ceased. A door opened and closed; they must have gone into the hall. She ran up the stairs, out of Sylvie's room and leaned over the banisters.

'Your car is waiting, sir,' Tustian said, handing the doctor his hat.

Dr Hamilton shook Daniel's hand. 'A pleasure to meet you, Lord Damory,' he said, 'and thank you for a very fine lunch.'

Richard and Cecily were watching from the gallery. Alice made the rudest of the gestures she'd learned from the butcher's boy.

25

'You're pregnant.' Paul held Sylvie's hair out of the way as she vomited in the toilet.

'What? No . . .'

'Yes, you are.' He put all the signs together. She'd been sick every day since the funeral a week ago. Her breasts were tender—she'd complained that he was hurting them. Her nipples were dark, the aureoles swollen. He moistened a cloth, mopped her sweating face. 'When was your last period?'

She didn't answer.

'How late is it?'

'Quite late.'

'Is it ever that late?'

She shook her head.

'You're pregnant.' He closed his eyes. A wave of love washed away all the doubt and strangeness of the last weeks.

'Shit,' she said. 'Shit, shit, shit. How can this have happened?'

'Sometimes it does, no matter how careful one is.'

'We have to do something.'

'Do something?'

'Oh Christ, you know what I mean, surely you know. Get rid of it.'

'Sylvie, that may not be wise . . .'

'Wise? I don't want to be wise! I want to be bloody free not bloody wise. There are people who can fix it, one hears. You must know someone. Has it never happened to you before?'

'It has.'

'Well, did you help her get it fixed?'

'Yes.'

'So you know someone.'

'In Paris, not here.'

'Then let's go to Paris.'

'I'd adore to take you to Paris, darling, but not for that. Come to bed; let's not talk any more tonight.'

Paul lay awake for a long time, curled against Sylvie's back. He rested his hand on her belly—a whole universe, tiny as a bean in its warmwet, safedark nest. A girl, he was suddenly sure. Hello, little one. Did she hear? A smile, a light, a mind that touched his like moth wings in the night.

*   *   *

The following day the argument began again.

'This is a wonderful place for children,' Paul said.

'Well maybe that's why I want to leave.' Sylvie burst into tears. 'I can't stand it any more. What's the point of growing up if I can't get away? I'll die if I have to stay. In September I'm starting at the Slade and I'm going to live in London and nothing will stop me.'

'Marry me.'

'Marry you! Christ, that's worse than having a baby. Talk about frying pans and fires. Bloody hell, you're part of all this, you even work for my family. Everyone wants to control me.'

'I don't want to control you. I seem to have a house; you could live in it. It's quite near the Slade. When the baby comes I'll hire a nursemaid,

432

a nanny, whatever. You won't have to do anything you don't want to do.'

'Except turn into a horrible fat slug. You won't want me. No one will want me.'

'Don't be silly. Look at your mother. How old was she when you were born? Not much older than you. She's had four children, and men still want her.'

'Grrrr.' Sylvie shuddered. 'I can't imagine wanting anyone wrinkled and saggy.' She looked down at her belly. 'And I hate babies, awful smelly squalling things.'

'You won't ever have to see her. Or smell her.' I'll take her to the park, he thought; we'll sit in the sun.

'Her?'

'Or him. Please just think about it. Come and see the house, and then, well, if you still want . . . I'll find someone to help.'

'Do you promise?'

'OK. I promise.'

'And you mustn't tell anyone. If you tell my parents I'll never speak to you again. I mean it. Promise you won't tell anyone.'

'I promise.'

*   *   *

On Thursday they drove into town. Paul was to deliver Percy's manuscript to the publishers in Albemarle Street; Sylvie had agreed to see the house. They'd skirted the argument off and on for days; he knew from the set of her jaw that further attempts at persuasion would have the opposite effect.

The London sky hung low, the air was humid and dense. 'I love the smell of the city,' Sylvie said. They left the car in Bayswater and took the bus. A couple with a small baby heaved themselves into seats across the aisle. Patches of yellowish, flaking skin crusted its red face; when it began crying the woman jogged it on her knee, but it only wailed louder. The man pulled up his shoulders and looked away; he spoke from the side of his mouth. 'Can't you make it shut up? I wish I never . . .'

'What?' the woman snapped.

'Nothing. Wish I never nothing.'

Sylvie nudged Paul. 'See?'

Red Lion Square was as Paul remembered; the key in his pocket fitted the lock. Imogen's flowers stood on the hall table in a chaplet of browning petals. He took Sylvie from room to room, opening windows, ascending from floor to floor. She liked the fireplaces but not the doorknobs; approved of the cornicing and the deep shutters but not the banisters. She lifted the white sheets and revealed the furniture; a sofa was quite sweet, the dining table ridiculous.

'I'll get rid of whatever you don't like,' Paul said.

'I don't like babies,' she said. 'Is there really only the one bathroom?'

'I'll put in more.'

She examined everything seriously, careful to give each its due. Was that a good sign? At least she was looking.

'These rooms would be perfect for the baby and her nanny,' Paul said on the third floor. 'And there's a little garden at the back. She could sit in it; she could play on the grass.'

A tree filled the window. 'I can't see it,' Sylvie

434

said. It had begun to rain; fat drops splashed on the leaves.

'It's there. Flowers, roses, things like that. Now come upstairs. You could have your studio at the top; there's lots of light.'

'You sound like one of those greasy estate agents.'

'You're right, I do. Shall I fuck you instead?'

'Does that come with the house?'

'If you want it to.'

There was a bed under one of the white sheets; clouds of dust puffed from the cushions and made them sneeze, which made them laugh. If this is a dream, Paul thought, it's the happiest dream I've ever had, and I hope I never wake up.

'It's nice,' she said, when they stood again by the front door. 'It's a very nice house. But . . .'

'But what?'

'But the baby may not be yours,' she said in a rush, not meeting his eyes.

'I know.'

'You know?'

He nodded. 'I figured. I can count.'

'And you don't care?'

Paul shrugged.

She glanced at her watch. 'Look, I have to go and see a friend, but I'll meet you at the car later, say around five?'

'OK. I guess.' He stood on the step as she walked away, opening her umbrella. Had she agreed, or had she in fact decided . . . He ran after her. 'Wait, stop!'

She turned.

'Sylvie, are you going to . . . I just had the thought that you'd found someone yourself.'

435

'No, don't be silly. I'm meeting a friend, that's all. Really.'

'Please don't . . .'

'For God's sake, I'm meeting a friend. Have you noticed you're telling me what to do already?'

He watched until she turned the corner. The wet pavement smelled of iron. Rain fell on his face and a wave of sadness washed through him. It might not be now, but she'd do what she wanted. In the end he had no power at all.

*   *   *

Paul drove out of London; Sylvie's style of driving was not compatible with other people's. The rain stopped, the sky cleared; they put the top down. The traffic thinned past Maidenhead and they only got one puncture. As Paul changed the tyre Sylvie slid into the driver's seat. 'We won't get back till midnight, at the rate you drive,' she said.

The roads were in good shape and she overtook everything in her path; they reached Exley before nightfall, and before Paul was ready.

If only, if only, if only, he thought, as they drove up the high street. But to what moment would I return, what would I change? Do I wish I'd not become her lover? I made my choice; it can't be undone.

'I'm leaving tomorrow,' he said. 'My job's finished. Please say you'll . . .'

'Oh Paul.'

'What?'

'I wish you wouldn't keep asking. I wish you'd see things from my point of view.'

'I'm trying to.'

436

'The house is very nice, and it's awfully sweet of you to offer, especially considering, but I don't want a house any more than I want a baby or a husband.'

'Shh. Just listen a minute. I know how you feel. I know you don't love me, but if we were married . . .'

'Stop pushing me! Can't you get it through your head that I don't ever want to marry?' The rear end fishtailed as she shifted gear with a jerk and swung on to the Farundell road.

Paul held on to his seat. 'If we were married things would be easier. No one would bother you; you could do what you want. Look out for that cart. You don't seem to understand. Married women can do what they like. Do you think Maggie could be so free if she weren't married?'

'That's absurd. It's just another stupid hypocritical game. You want to own me. It's parents all over again. You say that by some bizarre paradox it'll make me free, but once you've got me you'll start telling me what to do, you'll approve and disapprove, you'll want me to be like this and not like that or like that and not like this; you'll say one thing is suitable behaviour for your wife and another thing isn't; you'll want me to change, or stay the same, or both simultaneously.' She flung the car round the turns. 'And I might want to be different. I might be completely different from who you think I am. I might be completely different from who I think I am! How the hell do I know? And how can I ever find out if I get married and start having stupid horrid stinking babies?' She banged on the steering wheel.

437

'For Christ's sake slow down,' Paul said as they tore into Farundell hamlet. 'What's the hurry?'

'See? Already! Slow down, you say. You sound like . . .'

'Watch out for the dog!'

Sylvie twisted the wheel; there was a yelp and a thump; the car mounted the low wall of the bridge, teetered for a moment, tipped and fell into the stream. With a crack and a flash of pain the world went out; an instant later it came back. Shattered glass, blood running into his eyes, everything sideways. Paul pulled himself free. One headlight still skewed the dusk; Sylvie lay on the bank. Oh God oh God oh God. He crawled to her, felt for her pulse. She moaned, tried to sit up.

'Lie still,' he said. 'Let me check for broken bones. Can you move your fingers and toes?'

'Yes. Ow, my head hurts.'

He felt her skull. A bump was rising above one ear, but the skin wasn't broken.

'What happened?' she said.

'That fucking dog finally bought it and nearly took us with him.'

People were running from the cottages. 'That's Miss Sylvie's car,' someone said. 'Hello? Are you all right down there?'

'It depends what you mean by all right,' Paul said. 'If she'll marry me, I might be.'

There was laughter. 'Better marry him, Miss, before you kill him,' a woman's voice called.

Paul pulled the rug from the car, shook out the broken glass, wrapped Sylvie in it, picked her up and climbed to the road. 'I have to get her home,' he said to the crowd of staring faces. 'Sorry about the dog.'

'Put me down,' Sylvie said. 'I can walk perfectly well by myself.'

'Are you sure?'

'Yes of course I'm bloody sure. I really do know how to walk; I learned years ago and I believe I still remember how. Damn it, put me down!'

Their arrival during dinner caused something of a stir. Tustian ran to call Dr Westlake as Maggie and Alice put Sylvie to bed; Jarlath took Paul off to the drawing room and poured him a stiff whisky. 'That damn dog,' he said. 'Good riddance. I've nearly killed it every time I drove by. Is the car wrecked?'

Paul took a long drink and lit a cigarette. 'Quite possibly. Didn't look.'

'Bugger. I knew she'd wreck that car.'

'I asked her to marry me. It made her angry.'

Jarlath laughed. 'What an idiot you are.'

'I know.'

Dr Westlake stopped in to report that Sylvie had no concussion, but should rest and take aspirin. He poured half a bottle of surgical spirit over Paul's scalp and put in a couple of stitches.

*　　　*　　　*

'Shall I read to you?' Alice said. 'Being read to is the best thing when you're ill. What would you like to hear?'

'I don't know.' Sylvie reached for a cigarette. 'You choose. Whatever you're reading.'

'OK, I'll be right back.' Alice ran up to the schoolroom; there was the *Asinus Aureus*, which she could translate as she went along, or *The Faerie Queene*, which would probably put Sylvie straight to sleep. Jarlath had returned the book of fairy tales; she added that to the pile and carried it downstairs. Sylvie sent her out for some brandy, which she got from a dubious Tustian, and again for more aspirin. When she finally consented to be read to, Alice pulled up a chair and showed her the books she'd brought.

'If my head didn't hurt so much I'd laugh,' Sylvie said. 'You look perplexed. Never mind. What a choice. A fairy tale, then, please.'

'How about Little Red Cap? Jarlath thinks it means something behind what it seems to.'

'OK.'

'Ready?'

'Ready.'

' "Once upon a time there was a sweet little girl. Her grandmother loved her very much, and gave her a little cap made of red velvet, which she wore all the time. One day her mother said to her, 'Take this cake and bottle of wine to your grandmother. Behave yourself on the way, and do not leave the path.' Deep in the woods Little Red Cap met a wolf. She did not know what a wicked animal he was, and was not afraid . . ." '

'I remember this story,' Sylvie said. 'I like this one. It has a happy ending, doesn't it?'

'We don't know yet,' Alice said. She hated being interrupted when she was reading aloud.

'Keep reading.'

'I will if you let me.'

'Sorry.'

A few minutes later Sylvie interrupted again. 'Alice . . .'

'What?'

'Sorry. I have to go to the bathroom. I think I'm

440

getting my period. Ow, bad cramps. Hurrah!'

'Why hurrah?' said Alice when Sylvie returned.

'Because I'm not pregnant.'

'You thought you were pregnant?'

'Sh. Don't tell. It doesn't matter now. Pass me the aspirin, I'd better take some more.' She washed it down with brandy.

'Can I do anything?' Alice said.

'Just read to me. Finish the story.' Sylvie curled on her side. 'Ow, hurrah, ow.'

Alice picked up the book. ' "A huntsman was passing by. He thought it strange that the old woman was snoring so loudly, so he looked inside and there lay the wolf he had been hunting for such a long time. He has eaten the grandmother, thought the huntsman, but perhaps she still can be saved. I won't shoot him. He took out his knife and cut open the wolf's belly. He had cut only a few strokes when he saw the red cap shining through. He cut a little more, and the girl jumped out. 'Oh,' she said, 'I was so frightened! It was so dark inside the wolf.' The grandmother came out next, and they filled the wolf's body with heavy stones. When he woke up and tried to run away, the stones were so heavy that he fell down dead. The huntsman took the wolf's pelt, they ate the cake and drank the wine, and they all lived happily ever after." '

*   *   *

Paul had taken his whisky upstairs; Jarlath was more than he could handle. He listened at Sylvie's door, heard Alice's voice. If Sylvie wanted him she knew where to find him. He sat at his window. The night was still and mild; the moon cast a panel of silver light across the floor. He looked through his photographs. There were hundreds now, mostly of Sylvie's face or body, in motion or still, in shadow or light. He lay on his bed and closed his eyes. Sylvie, Sylvie, Sylvie.

He carries her home through the honey-scented night. She lies against his chest, her heart next to his. Be mine, be mine, be mine. Nothing else matters.

'Paul, I'm afraid.'

'Hush, don't be.' He holds her close. 'We'll soon be home, and then we'll live on flowers and kisses and sunshine.' Why had it seemed so difficult? It was simple, so simple.

'Paul? Paul, wake up.'

Her voice drifted into the dream; he dragged himself awake. She stood at the foot of his bed.

'Come swimming with me,' she said.

He pulled on a pair of shorts; they tiptoed through the silent house and ran down the meadow to the lake.

'Let's swim to the island,' Sylvie said, and without waiting for his reply she dived from the end of the dock.

Was this a dream? What did it matter? He climbed down the ladder and followed. She swam ahead of him and was soon out of sight; the rasp of his own breathing covered the small steady splash of her progress. Paul paced himself, stopped to tread water when he tired; by the time he reached the island she was nowhere to be seen. 'Sylvie?' he called, but she didn't answer. She must have gone up to the temple.

He glimpsed her among the moonlit columns; she flitted away. Oh Christ, she's gone to that awful underground place. He felt his way to the

442

grotto. 'Sylvie? I really don't want to go down there.' The ringing in his ears returned; when he set foot on the steps he was hit by a wave of nausea so strong it buckled his knees. He forced his way through, but the jackal-headed Hermanubis barred his path.

'What do you want?' he asked it.

'Everything.'

How easy it would be to surrender; he saw it now, that was the key. He should never have fought it—what did he want, after all, to keep that he wouldn't happily give for Sylvie? 'Take it, then,' he said. At once the ringing stopped and was replaced by the soft tinkle of a bell. 'Sylvie?'

She was waiting inside, a treasure not gold. Her skin pulsed with patterns of colour and light; she moved over him and sweetness filled the air.

*   *   *

When Alice woke she was stiff and cold; she'd fallen asleep in the chair. She sat up and the book of fairy tales fell to the floor. Sylvie had rolled and tangled in the bedclothes; Alice pulled them back to straighten them. A red stain spread over the mattress. 'Sylvie!' Alice shook her shoulder. 'Wake up. Are you all right?' Sylvie was pale and grey-lipped; she didn't answer.

Alice ran across the hall and pounded on her mother's door. By the time Maggie came, belting her dressing gown, Theo was there, and Jarlath from another room, and Tustian. Maggie sent Tustian to call Dr Westlake and they all disappeared into Sylvie's room. Alice crept in after them; Jarlath pushed her out and shut the door in her face. She ran down to the library, sprang the catch on the secret passage and tiptoed up to hide among Sylvie's frocks.

*   *   *

Paul woke shivering and alone in the dark. 'Sylvie?' His voice echoed in the empty chamber. The doorway was a paler shadow; he found his way out into the ghostly pre-dawn light.

'Sylvie?' No one answered. He washed his face and drank at the pool. His head hurt; his fingers found the stitches and for a moment he couldn't remember how they got there. He climbed to the temple; she wasn't there either. She must have swum back on her own.

A dense layer of mist obscured the surface of the lake; the far shore looked very distant. His teeth chattered as he walked into the water. When it rose to his chest he began to swim, but he couldn't see where he was going. He got a cramp in his leg and paused to tread water, then swam on. His chest was burning and he couldn't feel his feet at all. Surely he was nearly there? Or had he been swimming in circles? It was hard to keep his head up; he reached for air and swallowed water instead. Blood pounded, darkness crowded his vision. He was falling down a tunnel that narrowed and tightened; it stifled his breath and weakened his limbs. He flailed towards the surface, took another gulp of water and with a whoosh the tunnel expanded and he was floating in a sweet golden light. Oh of course, he thought, now I remember; it's easy, all I have to do is breathe.

Sylvie swims at his side. He reaches for her, she

flows into his arms, wraps her legs around him, pulls him deeper. Her face flickers and changes, her tongue speaks to his mind. You know me, she says, by my ten thousand names. Love me only and everything shall be yours.

Yes, oh yes, I see; he lets himself fall; nothing else matters. They swim down and down; how strange that it's growing brighter as they descend, not darker as he'd thought. The abyss opens, a crack in the world. He dares himself to look; the emptiness blossoms like a flower. But it's beautiful, beautiful . . .

'Sorry, my friend, not yet.' Francis hauled him up by the hair. The pain was excruciating; Paul fell gasping into the bottom of the boat.

'Thanks,' he said, when he'd finished spewing lake water.

'No, you won't thank me, not for a long time.' Francis looked at him with a sad smile and vanished as the boat slipped up to the dock.

26

It was raining again and a high wind dragged at the treetops. Everyone had finally returned to the house. Paul lay across the grave, pressed his face to the mud, sank his fingers into the earth. The world was a great gaping black hole; it stretched him to the very edge and pared him to a thin film of pain. Soon it would devour him; he had only to wait, wait and surrender.

'Well, my china.'

Paul opened his eyes as Val's pristine grey

trousers sank into the mud at his side. 'Jesus, Val, you'll ruin your suit.'

'See what I have to do to get your attention?'

Paul rolled on to his back, the rain washed his face. The roof of the chapel pointed to the void of sky. Three black birds flew across. 'What does it mean?'

'She's not here.' Val stood, helped him to his feet and led him down the hill.

*   *   *

Alice paddled to the island. The rain was keeping everyone inside, but she couldn't have survived another gloom-laden afternoon indoors. The atmosphere was thick with misery but no one except Paul showed it. He'd spent every day and night in the chapel with Sylvie's unfinished paintings, talking to Sylvie constantly, even when other people were there. He didn't eat the food Alice brought and he looked as though he hadn't slept either. Maggie and Jarlath told him it wasn't his fault; even Daniel had reasoned with him for hours, but he hadn't come out until the burial and now he wouldn't leave the grave.

There were two Sylvies in Alice's mind and she couldn't reconcile them. The alive Sylvie, the one she thought of as the real one, went along the same as ever, haughty and sarcastic, funny and bad, then she'd hit the image of the blood-soaked sheets, the grey lips, and the world would turn over again. She'd carry on through the sad dark gritty tunnel with that Sylvie, then find she'd somehow returned to the world of the real, living Sylvie, all bright and full of future. How could someone so

446

alive be dead? It was all right for Percy to die, he'd been old, and ready. And what about all those millions of the war? They'd gone like a harvest. She'd been too young, and now she couldn't even remember her uncle James. She'd never forget Sylvie. If being grown up meant knowing all this, feeling all this, having to remember all this, how did people bear it?

She made her way down to what even she had begun to think of as the Lair of the Dog-Headed Demon. The flood of tourists had abated, then ceased altogether when Percy died. Roger and Sophie had other interests; Michael and his parents had retreated to Devon. Stephen had cancelled lessons until further notice, but set her the task of transcribing and translating the stone tablets, called stelae, that they'd found in the inner chamber. She lit the lanterns, opened her notebook, unscrewed her pen and peered at the faint Greek letters.

Blessed is he who knows my real name. I am Isis, wife and sister of Osiris the king; I am Nature, firstborn child of Time, queen of the dead and of the immortals. Where was Sylvie now?

Great Hermes was my teacher, master of the language of the gods; I am the mistress of magic; I am mother of all and the eternal virgin; life is the speaking of my name. Sylvie was gone.

I compel men to give all for the love of women and women to be the redeemers of men. A spontaneous miscarriage, not uncommon, no one's fault.

I lay out the path of initiation; I reveal the mysteries; I teach knowledge of the gods through images and dreams. Sometimes the bleeding just doesn't stop.

I am the queen of rivers and winds and seas. I am the queen of love and of war. The thunder is mine, and the lightning, and the refuge from the storm. There was nothing anyone could have done.

How much time had passed? Alice's stomach clenched; was she hungry already? She'd left the basket with her sandwiches in the grotto. She stood on stiff legs, then doubled over as a sharp pain stabbed her belly. She felt something wet between her legs and when she climbed to the light she saw that her knickers were stained with blood. I'm not dying, she said firmly to herself; it's just my period at last, but she was shaking and freezing cold; was she about to faint? She pictured herself lying unconscious in the dark, bleeding slowly to death. No one knew where she was. She stuffed her handkerchief into her knickers and sat on a step. The pain faded, returned, faded.

After a while she ate a sandwich and felt better. There wasn't really all that much blood; she wasn't dying, but another fear crept over her. She could get pregnant. It sounded like a death knell. Something had broken open, some protection had been lost—now anything could happen. The world could do things to her that she couldn't control, could put a baby inside her that would make her bleed to death. Menses, from *menes*, the moon. Atop the stela she'd been translating was a carving of a woman with two moons, the early and the late. Was this what would control her now? Sylvie had to stay in bed for a day or two every month, with hot-water bottles, aspirin and, lately, whisky hidden in a glass of milk. She said it hurt to read, so she looked at pictures in magazines all day. I'll never be like that, thought Alice, but then how

448

could she know? Maybe everything had changed already, like a train shunted on to a new set of tracks, and there was nothing she could do about it.

She paddled back slowly, careful not to sit on her skirt. It had stopped raining and a hazy sun pushed through the clouds. Upstairs she found a towel and put it in place. She hated it. Why couldn't one choose? Why did this mindless animal thing have to happen to everyone? Why should she have to go through these grotesque manoeuvres, the smell and stain, the secret shame, unless she wanted babies, and she was pretty sure she didn't. She put on a clean frock and examined herself in the mirror. She did look different, somehow.

It was tea-time, but no one was in the music room or on the terraces. She made her way among Theo's herbs and into the kitchen garden; the murmur of voices drew her to the potting shed. Theo sat on the bench; Jarlath and Francis in lawn chairs.

'Hello, Alice,' said Francis.

'Hello, sweetheart,' said Jarlath.

Theo gestured Alice to her side. Mrs Beal appeared with four mugs of tea on a tray; Francis, Jarlath and Theo each took one. Alice had never realised that Mrs B could see Francis. 'How did you know to bring one for me?' she said as Mrs B offered her the last mug.

'Miss Theodora said you'd be joining them, dear.'

*　　　*　　　*

Paul packed the photographs into the rucksack

449

without looking at them. He slipped through the sleeping house, paused in the drive and gazed across the lake. The island was a dark, hollow stone floating under the distant moon. He couldn't rid himself of the notion that she was there, the real Sylvie, alive and beautiful, they'd gone there together; he'd missed her somehow, made some mistake, unwittingly refused some requirement or failed some test and the punishment was that in his ignorance he'd left her, swum off alone through a mist and landed in another world, an awful world. If only he could return, she'd be waiting.

Madagascar emerged from the shrubbery and rubbed against Paul's legs. 'Are you coming with me, old friend?' The cat ambled away, towards the house. 'No, thought not. You've found your home.' Paul turned and made his feet walk the long drive, through the slippery moon shadows under the trees.

Theo stood at the gate. 'You'll come back,' she said, and Paul had an image of years long as rivers. A tear slid down her cheek, a parting gift.

Paul waited on a bench at the station. The first train arrived at dawn, hissing and groaning and snorting. The sound of metal on metal was pretty near unbearable, but he sat in a corner and closed his eyes, and didn't open them until they'd arrived at Paddington. He found a taxi and directed the driver to Red Lion Square.

Time passed; it got dark, then light again, then dark. Imogen made soup and bread. Val stopped by most days; Paul liked to hear his voice but could never remember what he'd said.

Percy's photographic equipment arrived from Farundell; Meredith built him a darkroom. Paul

450

laid out his pictures on the floor of a room at the top of the house. Pieces of light, pieces of time. Words, bodies. Her mouth: God is. Her hand: Necessity. Her breast: Knowledge. Her eyes: Infinite. A gust of wind caused them all to lift and resettle. Her shoulder: Understanding. Her foot: incomprehensible Beauty.

He arranged and rearranged them, cut them into pieces word by word, then took pictures of the new configurations. Bodies dissolved into light and shadow.

He slept on the floor among them and dreamed that Sylvie stood over him. Let's swim to the moon, she'd say; he'd wrench himself awake, but she was never there. After that, sleep was impossible; he'd walk the streets until dawn.

*   *   *

It was autumn. Leaves were falling from the trees; when he opened the window they drifted in and settled on the pictures. He read the words on which they'd landed. Manifest, imperfect; unchangeable, real. Father, self, secret, sacrifice. Behold, voice, heaven. World, time. Light, death, truth.

On the night of the full moon he gathered up the pictures and dealt them out in a new pattern, spiralling in. Sylvie, Sylvie, Sylvie. Come to me. He lay at the centre and watched the moon through the open window. Sylvie, Sylvie, Sylvie. Come to me.

She came at last, when he'd almost given up, her bare feet stepping lightly. He was so afraid she'd vanish he didn't dare move. She sat beside him.

451

Very slowly, he reached out and took her hand; it was warm, solid, real.

'You're alive,' he said. 'I thought you'd died.'

'You're an idiot,' she said, and laughed. 'There is no death.'

Suddenly he knew it had all been a nightmare, another awful penalty for the black magic he'd wrought in her dreams. He'd lost her but now he'd found her again; they'd been together all along, here in their house, safe and well.

When he woke he held nothing but empty light, yet some living trace of her presence lingered as though she'd been and gone. He went to the window. Moonlight filled the square; leaves fell, rustling.

I'll just walk, he thought, until I can't walk any further. At the end I'll have to find her.

The night air streamed with subtle currents; they drew him through the familiar streets, deserted and silent. He walked down to the river, along the Embankment, then north through the parks, fragrant green islands in the dappled grey city. Hardly anyone was about, but now and then he caught glimpses of other sleepless wanderers. As he neared Hyde Park they all seemed to be converging. An owl hooted, soft and sad, as he crossed the bridge over the Serpentine and entered the maze of criss-crossing, tree-shadowed paths beyond.

Near the northern edge of the park was a dense stand of trees ringed by rhododendron so thick it was impenetrable. He'd passed this way often before, but now he noticed an opening where he was sure there had been none. In ones and twos people were filing in. He followed.

452

At the centre was a clearing, pooled with silver moonlight. Men and women stood in small groups, speaking in hushed tones. There was an atmosphere of waiting.

'Here he is at last,' said Francis. He took Paul's arm and led him in.

'We saved you a space,' said Mr Pym. 'Look, She's coming.'

There was a murmur among the assembly, a sudden intake of breath.

'It's Her,' someone whispered.

'She's here,' said another.

The words rose in a sibilant invocation. Lady Aset, mistress of magic. Queen of Heaven, beloved sister, wife, mother. Isis of a thousand names, Isis of a thousand faces.

She came near; Francis knelt and she touched his bowed head. She smiled at Mr Pym, who winked and kissed her hand.

'Sylvie?' said Paul. It was and wasn't her. 'Who are you?'

'You know who I am,' she said, as her face blurred and shifted into other faces, young and old, all the women he'd ever known and many more he had yet to meet. 'Now do you see?'

*   *   *

Paul lay on the floor in a panel of warm sunlight. The open window showed clear blue sky; a bird was singing in the tree outside, its song a long, winding ribbon of light, gold like the sun. Another melody appeared, strange yet familiar. Paul went to the window. Sara Paragon stood on the pavement below, playing her violin among the

453

swirling leaves. She looked up.

'Hello,' she said. 'Can I come in?'

Epilogue

Nothing was visible in the dense white mist. It clung to the ground and billowed through the air, heaving gently like a sea.

'Where are we?' Francis asked.

'How would I know?' said Mr Pym. 'It's you who makes it.'

The mist cleared, revealing a shoreline, an island across the water, a boat. 'Ah, Farundell,' said Francis.

'You are fated to inhabit your own metaphors,' said Mr Pym.

'Oh, fate. If it's all fate, tell me, why must we suffer so for our actions?'

'But that is why you act. To experience the effects of your actions.'

'Another of your cruel teleologies.'

'Cruel? How so? There is no power in the universe like a man. As he is, so he chooses; what he chooses makes him what he is. You know this well, I think.'

'I hate to be reminded.'

They walked on in silence. A bird called, and called again.

'So what, then, is fate?' Francis said.

'To you or to me? You might as well ask, what is time?'

'It's true, I've often wondered. What is time?'

Notes and Sources

The First World War and the 1920s

A brief list of some of my favourite sources: Wyndham Lewis, *Blasting and Bombardiering*; Viva King, *The Weeping and the Laughter*; Philip Gibbs, *Now It Can Be Told*; Robert Graves, *Goodbye to All That*; Naomi Mitchison, *You May Well Ask*; Sydney Giffard (ed.), *Guns, Kites and Horses: Three Diaries from the Western Front*; Grant Allen, *The Woman Who Did*; Denise Hooker, *Nina Hamnett, Queen of Bohemia*; Anne Chisholm, *Nancy Cunard*; Michael Holroyd, *Augustus John*; and in particular, Virginia Nicholson's fabulous *Among the Bohemians*.

The Amazon

Other than Percy's Jean de Léry, I found *Margaret Mee's Amazon: The Diaries of an Artist Explorer* and Peter Fleming's *A Brazilian Adventure* most delightful and informative. The latter is one of the funniest books I have ever read.

The out-of-body experience

Also known as aetheric or astral projection or travel, and similar, if not identical, to lucid dreaming. This phenomenon, well known in ancient times and in other cultures, has only recently begun to be systematically explored by western science. I can do no better than point interested readers to the Wikipedia article.

The Hermetica

The books of the *Corpus Hermeticum* date from the second or third century CE, but the material clearly derives from a far older tradition. They were written in northern Egypt at a time when that part of the world was a great melting pot of religions and philosophies from East and West. Most take the form, standard in that era, of dialogues between a teacher and a student. There are several English translations but my favourite is still the first, *The Divine Pymander* by Dr John Everard in 1650 (http://www.sacred-texts.com/eso/pym/index.htm); although Tobias Damory's version contains some lines of my own invention, I believe them to be entirely in the Hermetic spirit. I also recommend Garth Fowden, *The Egyptian Hermes*; Florian Ebeling, *The Secret History of Hermes Trismegistus*; Brian Copenhaver, *Hermetica*; Clement Salaman, Dorine van Oyen, William D. Wharton, *The Way of Hermes*; and, of course, the Wikipedia article.

Isis

You see me here, Lucius, in answer to your prayer. I am nature, the universal Mother, mistress of all the elements, primordial child of time, sovereign of all things spiritual, queen of the dead, queen of the ocean, queen also of the immortals, the single manifestation of all gods and goddesses that are, my nod governs the shining heights of Heavens, the wholesome sea breezes. Though I am worshipped in many aspects, known by countless names . . . some know me as Juno, some as Bellona . . . the Egyptians who excel in ancient learning and worship call me by my true name . . . Queen Isis.

Apuleius, The Golden Ass (Aureus Asinus)
c.170 CE

The presence of Isis worship in Roman Britain is undisputed, however no temple has been found. No one knows why the Thames above Oxford is called the Isis. Plutarch's *On Isis and Osiris*, source for much of the mythology, is available at http://thriceholy.net/Texts/Isis.html. The text on Alice's stela is a composite of various Isis aretalogies, in particular the *Kyme* and the *Thunder Perfect Mind*. Good secondary sources include: R. E. Witt, *Isis in the Ancient World*; Robert Turcan, *The Cults of the Roman Empire*; Ockert Meyer, *The Ancient Mysteries*; James B. Rives, *Religion in the Roman Empire*.

Acknowledgements

Thanks to Carlyle Clark, Nadine Gallo and Annie Simko for early comments; to Annie also for medical advice. Thanks to Ronald Hutton for confirming that a Roman temple of Isis in Oxfordshire is not unlikely, and that it could be quite well preserved; to Peter Gandy for confirming that the Isis/Osiris iconography of that period remained true to its Egyptian origin. Big thanks to Sally Child, Penny Billington and Stephanie and Philip Carr-Gomm for reading and invaluable comments; also and particularly to Philip for his steadfast support and encouragement, and for introducing me to Kate Parkin, editrix extraordinaire. My heartfelt thanks to Kate and to my mellifluous agent Judith Murray; *Farundell* would not be half as good without their comments, and any remaining imperfections are entirely due to my not having taken all of their advice.

'The further in you go, the bigger it gets' is a line I first encountered in *Little, Big* by John Crowley (to whom I bow), although now one hears it everywhere.